# Chapter One

**How true it is, yet how inconsistent...that while we all desire to live long, we have all a horror of being old!**
**—Fanny Burney, *Cecelia* (1784)**

When a young lady finds herself on the wrong side of thirty, she had better, perhaps, give over calling herself *young*. And Miss Rosemary DeWitt had done so. But she found it much more difficult for others to give up the habit. Her kindly father still referred to his children and their peers as "the young people" and still beamed upon his firstborn as if she were a dewy-eyed miss fresh from the schoolroom. In vain did Rosemary drop hints that she was content to live always at Marchmont, or that she looked forward to the day when she might be an aunt of her younger brothers' children. "Aunt?" echoed her father Sir Cosmo. "All well and good, my love, but I suspect you will have children enough of your own gathered at your knees." As for Lady DeWitt, Rosemary's mother, if she had fears about her daughter's dimming prospects, they were rarely raised, smothered at birth by her husband's optimism.

Rosemary herself shared this optimism for a time. She knew she resembled her father, with his long nose and plain features—a look that served a man better than a woman—but she also knew Sir Cosmo's elevation to the knighthood had obscured the humble origins of his sizeable fortune. And what might not a prospective son-in-law bear, if he could share in Sir Cosmo's abundance? Such a man might tolerate a plainer wife, she realized, if that wife brought five thousand pounds to the match, as she would. And indeed there had been an offer or two, which Rosemary very nearly steeled herself to accept, only, when the moment of truth was upon her, she found she could not do it. She might be not the prettiest; she might be growing older (as one of her would-be swains reminded her, most ungallantly); but she was also, to her suitors' dismay, too clever for her own good. She was no bluestocking, with her nose always buried in a book, but she had a way of seeing right to the heart of matters which could be disconcerting. It was not that Miss DeWitt would say unseemly things or even make a show of her understanding. But one *knew* that she knew, and that was enough.

"I could see her skepticism when I offered," grumbled the last of her rejected young men to his father. "She thought I had more of an eye for her fortune than her person. But what can such an ordinary-looking creature expect? Had I pretended to be carried away by her beauty, she would have deemed me a greater fool."

In that, at least, he understood her.

So the years passed, and Rosemary remained at Marchmont. She helped her mother run the household and kept peace between her brothers after their return from university. She visited the poor and mixed socially with other "young people" of the neighborhood, although she was older by many years than the daughters of the closest estates. And in her thirty-first year she accepted the vicar Mr. Arthur Benfield's suggestion to teach some of the village girls their letters and sums, although her brother Roscoe deemed it an "old-maidish" thing to do.

"We're rich enough, Ros—no need to go out for governessing."

"It's hardly governessing to spend four hours each week going over a primer, Roscoe. And Mr. Benfield already tutors some of the little Patterton boys. Why should not the girls have their turn?"

"Because they're going to be farmers' and bakers' and chandlers' wives, not gentlewomen, Rosemary. They would be better served learning how to make cheese and small beer."

"Well, they have other people to teach them those skills," she returned, "and I hardly see how writing their names and being able to make out a Bible verse or two will spoil them for the future."

"Might spoil your own future," Roscoe persisted. "Only resigned spinsters and old church matrons teach school, and they do it on a Sunday."

"And only trifling, idle young men would say so," was her retort. "If your beloved Miss Porterworth took time to spell letters with the village girls, she would not cause you a fraction the woe she does. Her capriciousness comes of frivolity."

This silenced her brother at once. He had, for some time, been quite enamored of Miss Constance Porterworth, a feeling that young lady seemed to return—at least when she had no better fish to hook.

But when a year of ABCs and simple sums had passed, Rosemary had to admit to herself that she was not, after all, satisfied. It was not the fault of her pupils—on the contrary, it never failed to delight her when one of them mastered the art of stringing letters into words, or another applied her primitive comprehension of mathematics to the world at large. Nor was it the fault of the less promising girls who only stared out the window during the lesson and made little progress, if any. No, the fault lay with Rosemary's own growing ambition. After all, why should such rudimentary achievements be considered enough? The average tenure of her pupils never exceeded a few months. It seemed the moment a girl could laboriously make out a parable in the gospel, she was gone. Back to work alongside her parents or to care for younger siblings. Rosemary was no revolutionary; she understood as well as Roscoe that her task was not to produce so many Catharine Macaulays or Mary Wollstonecrafts, but must so little learning suffice? Could not the more clever girls continue?

Of course not.

They were, after all, the daughters of farmers and bakers and chandlers. Rosemary understood and even accepted this, but her frustration remained.

One afternoon, her father asked her to return a book to the vicar, and, just as Mr. Benfield was replacing it upon his library shelf and sliding out another to recommend to his neighbor, the maid opened the door to admit a tall man with dark hair and a forthright jaw. Rosemary thought his presence commanding, but perhaps that was due to his height and the deep mourning he wore. He brought to mind a portrait she had once seen in the gallery of a forgotten great house: that of a Cavalier forbear, dark-haired and dark-eyed, mysterious in velvets and plumed hat.

She could not imagine who the stranger might be, but managing to tear her gaze from him to glance at the vicar, she noted Mr. Benfield's expression was one of pleased surprise.

"Mr. Hugh Hapgood," announced Betsy.

Rosemary's eyes widened at the name, it having been much bandied about in recent days. Everyone knew Mr. Hugh Hapgood was the heir to Bramleigh, an entailed estate some two miles from Marchmont. He was cousin to the present owner, Squire Richard Hapgood, who had the misfortune to bear only four daughters. The news had been all over the county in recent weeks: how Mr. Hugh Hapgood had suddenly lost his wife and come into Somerset to stay at Bramleigh, there to choose a new spouse, presumably. Everyone imagined he would propose to one of his cousin's daughters, and the recent ill health of the squire made it likely that this proposal would be well-received. For her part, Rosemary had thought it kind of Mr. Hapgood to provide in such a way for his cousin's children. It would be a great relief, she was certain, to the squire, his helpless wife, and their three remaining unmarried daughters, if their future could be made secure. The Hapgoods of Bramleigh had no five thousand pounds apiece to bestow on their girls, certainly, although at least one daughter, Alice, had been successfully married and sent out into the world.

And that was one daughter *more* than the DeWitts managed to launch into a matrimonial state, she told herself wryly, five thousand pounds notwithstanding! But then, of course, the Hapgood girls were pretty young things, whereas she—

"Ah, Mr. Hapgood." The silver-haired Mr. Benfield came forward to greet the guest, beaming his courtly smile. "I received your note. You are very welcome here. May I present my parishioner Miss DeWitt?"

"I need not intrude on your appointment," said Rosemary, as soon as she made her curtsy.

"There was no particular time mentioned in my note," replied Mr. Hapgood in a dry, somewhat rusty voice. Rosemary suspected he had not used the instrument much that day.

"But you must not go yet, Miss DeWitt!" cried the vicar, when she reached behind her for her bonnet. "Mr. Hapgood wrote that he wished to learn what education is to be had in Patterton. If you remain, he will receive a full picture of our efforts. Be seated, both of you, I beg. Betsy is surely already arranging a tray of little sweets."

Rosemary supposed the vicar must view Mr. Hapgood as a potential benefactor to their little schools, and her own curiosity made her willing enough to stay. Reading no open objection on the visitor's face, she perched obediently on the sofa and folded her hands in her lap, prepared to do her part.

After glancing about him, Mr. Hapgood took a seat opposite, placing his hat on the cushion beside him. She saw that his hair was more plentiful than she imagined it would be, from the gray at his temples, and she wondered if the gray, along with the deep lines flanking his mouth, were of recent acquirement. Had he loved his late wife so dearly?

Mr. Benfield made a gesture at his guest's attire. "I am sorry for your loss."

Clearing his throat, Mr. Hapgood nodded. Plainly he did not wish to discuss it, and as Mr. Benfield was of the same mind, never knowing, despite his years of experience, what ought to be said in such circumstances, the subject was allowed to drop.

"I was referred to you, Mr. Benfield," began his visitor, "by the curate over at Bramleigh, whom my relations call Father Thomas."

"Yes, yes. Good man, Mr. Thomas."

"He—Mr. Thomas—tells me you take pupils into your home." Here Mr. Hapgood frowned in puzzlement at Rosemary, she clearly not being a pupil of Mr. Benfield, nor, from her introduction, that clergyman's wife.

"I do," replied Mr. Benfield cheerfully, not noticing Mr. Hapgood's confusion. "Many, over the years. They've mostly become fellow clergymen, although I have yielded one solicitor, and one academic—now a professor of history at Wadham."

"And you tutor them in the usual subjects, I suppose. Greek, Latin—"

"—Yes, yes—and a little Hebrew, mathematics, geography, history, philosophy—" supplied Mr. Benfield. "A thorough preparation for university."

Mr. Hapgood frowned once more at Rosemary, and, knowing that Mr. Benfield rarely noticed the subtler social cues, she decided to answer the man's unspoken question. "Mr. Benfield also teaches the humbler boys of our village, Mr. Hapgood, in a parish school," she explained. "And I have taken on the same for some of the girls. There we promote letter-learning and a foundation of arithmetic."

"Indeed," said Mr. Hapgood. He considered this a moment, and then Rosemary could see him put it aside. "What a boon for the village children."

"So it is, so it is!" agreed the reverend happily. "You will find we are very eager about such things in our parish—and I'm sure Mr. Thomas would take on such work as well, if he were not already overspread with those two curacies." He added this last out of a fear that Mr. Hapgood would think him boastful. But it was certainly true that the parish of Patterton had village schools and the parish of Bramleigh had none.

Rosemary could have told the vicar that Mr. Hapgood cared not a fig for who had village schools and who had not, but there was no opportunity, as Mr. Benfield threw himself into an anecdote-filled speech about what progress he saw in the village boys, and what good that must do the community, and how he had dreams of making Patterton the most lettered parish in England. He scarcely drew breath until Betsy came in with the tray of sweets, and then he only hesitated long enough to press some upon his guests before taking up the thread again. He told of spelling contests and intricacies of arithmetic and recitations— "Why, Miss DeWitt," he turned to her after some minutes, with an encouraging nod, "do tell our visitor how your little Meggy Cropper has learnt by heart the Sermon on the Mount found in the Gospel of St. Matthew—"

"She has," Rosemary rejoined, almost too curtly. But she wished to rescue Mr. Hapgood from his mounting impatience, and she had long ago discovered that Mr. Benfield was never offended by terseness, oblivious as he was to people's fidgets, throat-clearings, or other signs of restlessness. A merciful blindness, she supposed, in a man who must give sermons for a living. "Clever little Meg," she resumed. "But we must not tire Mr. Hapgood with tales of our triumphs. Suffice to say we are pleased with our pupils' progress and hope hereafter to see more of the same. But I suspect it is not about the village schools that you have come, sir?"

"It is not." The man looked at her again, and an impulse of gratitude warmed his features. She almost thought she detected a trace of humor, and she was surprised by the glow that filled her—it was so rare that she felt those fleeting moments of connection with another person who was not part of her immediate family. Of course—Rosemary was irritated to feel she was not beyond the age of blushing—it was ridiculous, not to mention inappropriate, to claim a shared understanding with a strange man whom she had just met. What would he think of her, if he could read her mind? Probably that she was *angling* for him, as her brothers might put it. Horrible thought! Should not her advancing age excuse her from such suspicions? But—no—perhaps she was not so far out of danger. In many minds, one and thirty still straddled the fence between desperation and resigned spinsterhood.

Before Rosemary could do more than think again of gathering her bonnet and book, that she might take her leave, Mr. Hapgood began to speak. "Miss DeWitt has discovered me, I'm afraid, Mr. Benfield. I am not come on a mission of mercy toward the village children—though I applaud your efforts." (Here he bowed at the vicar and once more at Rosemary.) "I come rather to ask if you might consider taking my son Lionel on as one of your pupils. He is a likely, lively twelve-year-old boy. I had hoped there might be a place for my girls, as well, but I was mistaken in believing your wife also taught."

"My wife?" cried Mr. Benfield, his eyebrows flying halfway up his forehead. "Oh, dear, dear. I am unmarried, Mr. Hapgood. There is no Mrs. Benfield—apart from my dear mother, who keeps to her room. Quite frail now, you know. And then, there is a *Miss* Benfield, my sister, who is occupied with tending to our mother and keeping house for me. No teaching to be done by either of them, you understand."

"Of course not. Forgive me."

"No need for that," Mr. Benfield assured him, recovering somewhat. "Never mind, never mind. Suffice to say, I should be pleased to meet your son Lionel. I must meet him. And if he be as likely and lively as you say, I am certain I could take him under my wing."

Here Mr. Hapgood almost slumped with relief, and the harshness of his features softened still further. Rosemary forgot her momentary embarrassment in her sympathy for him, as she watched him fumble to arrange an interview for his son. Poor man. To lose his wife and have young children to care for! Well, this Lionel Hapgood would have little to complain of, if he were accepted by Mr. Benfield.

A kindlier, more learned instructor could hardly be found, and the Benfield parsonage was snug and kept well in hand by Miss Benfield. It was too bad no place could be found for the sisters as well, but separation was something that happened to most families of their class—Rosemary herself had boarded at school in Taunton while her brothers were tutored at home, when they were younger—but for the little Hapgoods the loss of each other might be doubly painful, so soon after the loss of their mother.

"Lionel will miss his sisters, naturally, and they him," said Mr. Hapgood, as if his thoughts had followed Rosemary's own, and he startled her yet again by flashing her a sudden look. "You do not, I suppose, take pupils into your own home, Miss DeWitt—?"

"I?" breathed Rosemary. The first thing that popped into her head was the scornful voice of her brother Roscoe. Were he present, he would have resented the implication that Miss DeWitt, daughter of Sir Cosmo DeWitt, should be thought to board and teach pupils, as if she were some sad curate's sister or daughter. *But Roscoe is not here*, Rosemary reminded herself. *And Mr. Hapgood meant no offense by it*. He meant it, she realized, rather as a compliment. He would trust his daughters to her.

"I am sorry to say I do not," she murmured. And she was indeed sorry to say it, she found. She would have liked to help this man. Rosemary's lips parted briefly, as she thought to mention Mrs. Goodrich's school in Taunton, where she herself had attended, but she could not recommend it, in all honesty. Mrs. Goodrich was an indifferent teacher in all subjects save needlework and etiquette, and after four years there, Rosemary could boast but a smattering of French, awkward watercolors, and halting piano concertos. Sir Cosmo and Lady DeWitt had been obliged to engage a governess after Rosemary's return, to give her the proper "finishing."

"Have you thought to engage a governess?" she blurted, the memory fresh in her mind.

"I considered it but thought it—not best—for one in my position," he said with a repressed sigh. "A widower in a small household..."

"Of course," rejoined Rosemary, vexed to feel her face warming again.

"Has the squire no governess engaged at present?" asked Mr. Benfield, unaware of their discomfiture. "I do believe his youngest daughter might still be of the age for instruction."

There was a pause and Rosemary saw Mr. Hapgood's face darken, as if shutters had been snapped closed. When he spoke, his voice was guarded. "There is none. Nor, I believe, any intention of hiring one in future. Miss Edith Hapgood is but ten or eleven, yes, but I think her older sisters—Miss Hapgood in particular—undertake to give her lessons."

"Oh, yes. Quite." Tardily, Mr. Benfield remembered Squire Hapgood's straitened financial circumstances, though the vicar could hardly mention them, when the squire's heir sat before him. "Well. Miss Edith Hapgood could not wish for a better example," he resumed with a smile. "Miss Hapgood is renowned in this corner of Somerset as a paragon of beauty and womanly charm. I have heard her needle praised to the skies by my sister, and one could go far without seeing a more graceful dancer."

"Just so." Mr. Hapgood rose abruptly, taking his hat. "Mr. Benfield, Miss DeWitt, I have been pleased to make your acquaintance and thank you for your time, and I will return with Lionel at the hour agreed upon."

He took his leave almost before Mr. Benfield could register his intention to go, and when the door had shut behind him, the vicar turned in amazement to Rosemary. "What a brusque man! He did not even touch his biscuit! But we must make allowances for his situation, my dear."

"Indeed, Mr. Benfield. He has much to trouble him."

"You are not going so soon!" Mr. Benfield cried, seeing her take up her bonnet and begin to tie its ribbon beneath her chin. "My visitors decamp so hastily I must have said something to cause offense."

"You have certainly caused me no offense, sir," she murmured. Without meaning to, she emphasized the *me*, and this time even the vicar made note of it.

"Ah—but you think I have annoyed Mr. Hapgood. No, no—do not demur. When I have done wrong, I must take my medicine like any man. I wish Charlotte were here. She is ever quick to tell me precisely when and how I have erred."

Rosemary smiled, thinking Miss Benfield an ideal companion for her brother. She kept not only her brother's house, but her brother himself on the straight and narrow. And, as those in the parish had learned, no one was permitted to criticize Mr. Benfield in her hearing, that being a prerogative she kept solely to herself.

"Well, sir, since you ask—I think Mr. Hapgood would not have made so hasty a departure, except that you touched on a tender subject."

"Do you mean the late Mrs. Hugh Hapgood? But Miss DeWitt, I hardly mentioned the woman!"

"Not her, Mr. Benfield. I mean, rather, *Miss* Hapgood. The squire's eldest."

"Miss Hapgood?" cried the vicar, bewildered. "I only praised the girl generally. What can be the harm in that?"

"No harm at all," Rosemary replied patiently. "But you remember—they say Mr. Hugh Hapgood is come into these parts to find a second wife and mother to his children. I suppose he has our own Miss Hapgood in mind. As no engagement is yet announced, I imagine he would rather her name not be discussed at present, even if done with all good intentions."

"Ah ha," breathed the parson, as comprehension dawned. "Indeed. Thank you, my dear, for enlightening me. Well. There can be no wonder if Mr. Hapgood marries his cousin's daughter. Lovely young woman, Miss Hapgood. Quite unexceptionable. Yes, indeed. No wonder at all."

And as Rosemary made her way home to Marchmont, pacing the dry, beaten road, she could not help but agree completely with Mr. Benfield, even if she sighed a little when she did. Of course Mr. Hapgood would offer for Miss Hapgood. Lovely, young Elfrida Hapgood, with her face and figure, her golden hair and violet eyes and quiet disposition. What man in his right mind would *not* prefer such a specimen of womanhood, five thousand pounds or no five thousand pounds?

# Chapter Two

**The hand of mariage once confirmed,
is inoughe to cover all faultes.**
—Barnabe Rich, *The Adventures of Brusanus* (1592)

Mr. Hugh Hapgood had met his late wife in the usual fashion, at an assembly, where she was presented to him by his university friend Wellington Sidney as "the charming Miss Harriet Morrow, sister to my own darling Miss Morrow." Sidney had, in fact, already proposed to the elder sister and been accepted, and he longed to see his friend equally happy.

And Miss Harriet Morrow *was* charming, in the ordinary sense. She danced lightly, boasted quantities of shining brown hair, asked him light-hearted questions and listened with attention to his answers, played, sang, spoke French and Italian. Hugh was *coup de foudre*—as she intended him to be.

They married within months. He had no parents to consult, and hers were pleased to have their younger daughter settled as promisingly as her sister, and with such little difficulty to themselves. This Mr. Hugh Hapgood had been the only son of a well-off gentleman and was heir to an estate in Somerset that might yet come his way, although the current possessor was married with daughters. Miss Harriet Morrow, as a girl who had never known want, weighed these virtues of her suitor more lightly. She cared, rather, that he was dark and dashing and made much of her. And he was so very eligible! She heard her father say to her mother, "Why, he's an even better match than Lavinia has found! How blessed we are." They knew nothing of Mr. Hapgood's reputation at Balliol College for being the resident prankster, or how, indeed, Mr. Wellington Sidney had often been the victim of his friend's jokes and more than once had turned the tables on him. There was no mention of midnight races through the Front Quad (unclothed) or of dressing the porter in a woman's court costume and hoisting him to the roof of the chapel. The young men were on their best behavior now, and it was not many years before this playful aspect of their characters was stifled in earnest by the trials of daily life. That is, by marriage to the Morrow sisters.

The Morrow sisters were as intimate as they were competitive. Harriet soon convinced her husband to take a house for them not a quarter mile from dear Lavinia—but a house just a touch larger and newer, naturally, because how Lavinia could bear such cramped conditions was a mystery to Harriet, although she supposed Mr. Sidney could not afford better—

"We are vastly pleased with our little nest," Harriet informed Lavinia, on one of her daily visits. "Hugh already begins to plan where we will place the nursery and schoolroom, when the time comes."

"Well," replied Lavinia, "if you are quite sure Fernwell Cottage will not overtax your income…Mr. Sidney says—"

"Overtax our income!" cried Harriet. "By no means. My Hugh is a wondrous manager of money. I had no fears placing my entire portion in his hands. And if his cousin's estate of Bramleigh passes to him eventually, Bramleigh will be the better for it."

"Why so? Is Mr. Hapgood's cousin such a spendthrift?"

"Mr. Richard Hapgood may not be, but Hugh says he allowed his wife Augusta for years to spend money as if it were water. Only the bearing of her daughters managed to curb her extravagant ways. Now she stays home and fancies herself an invalid, and one must always bear with an inventory of her aches and pains when one visits, but I daresay that is an improvement over driving them into the poorhouse."

"Have the Richard Hapgoods given up hope of having a son, then?" pursued Lavinia.

"I imagine not," Harriet shrugged. "The entail, you understand."

"Oh, yes," agreed her sister. "Inconvenient things." She made a disapproving sound. "Having already borne three daughters, however, and now suffering from ill health, it strikes me that the chances of Mrs. Richard Hapgood now bearing a son have diminished greatly. Shall you visit Bramleigh often, Harriet? I imagine the estate's management occupies your Mr. Hapgood little less than it does its current owner. Supposing it should fall to Mr. Hapgood? He would not want it all gone to waste beforehand."

Harriet gave another shrug. "We have done our duty, but I doubt we will go often. Our little home here in Crawley is all our concern. Besides which"—with a modest duck of her head—"when the happy event is upon us, Hugh does not want me exerting myself. Nay, I may never travel farther than Eastbourne again, he is so solicitous of me!"

And he was solicitous. Hugh soon discovered in his wife a tendency to overexcitement, to pressing herself beyond her strength. While this usually exhibited itself in high spirits, the arrival of the Hapgoods' first "happy event," their son Lionel, plunged Harriet into a morass of lowness from which no efforts of her husband could rescue her. Even the news that the Richard Hapgoods' fourth (and likely last) child was yet another daughter did little to cheer her. Life was weary, stale, flat, and unprofitable. She was scarce emerging from this depression when the coming of the second child Hetty pitched her back in headlong. Harriet soon lost her good humor, the pleasing roundness of her limbs, her quick laugh.

Hugh hired a succession of nursemaids, with whom Harriet would alternately find fault and then cling to, when he tried to dismiss them. She became querulous, short with her husband and children. Only with Lavinia did she rally and recover some of her former vivacity. Hugh was content to let her spend more and more time in her sister's company for the residual cheerfulness that benefited the rest of them. When Harriet discovered she was with child for a third time, she wept for a week. "It is not that I do not love them," she growled into her pillow, as Lavinia patted her shoulder, "but the whole process is so fearfully uncomfortable, and the noise and uproar they create—! You would not know because you have only Caroline, but Lionel does holler and run about, and he broke my china shepherd when he tried to wrestle poor Hetty to the carpet."

Lavinia bristled as her sister pressed this tender point of sonlessness, and she could not entirely swallow her annoyance, despite Harriet's distress. "Well, naturally, it is providential you have Lionel, however lively he may be. After all, with Bramleigh likely coming to your Mr. Hapgood, and he being the third generation in the entail, it is convenient he will not have to partition the estate."

"I do not think Hugh would do so even if we had no son," asserted Harriet, forgetting her woe enough to sit up. "Divide up Bramleigh! I assure you my husband appreciates the Saxon glory of the Hapgoods as much as his great-uncle did, who created the entail in the first place. No—if we had any need of money, which I assure you we do not, I imagine he would scrape together whatever he could, from his own property and my portion, to provide for a widow and children, rather than be the first Hapgood to break up the estate."

"There, there," soothed Lavinia. "I should not have mentioned it. To be certain, Mr. Hapgood has plenty of money and proper family pride and will do his best. But you mustn't take on so. I can see his concern for you growing."

Rather than mollify her, this reminder served to exasperate Harriet. "And well he should be concerned!" she cried. "My condition is entirely owing to him. I *told* Hugh I did not want any more children. If he truly cared for my constitution, he would have listened to me.

He *pretends* to coddle and indulge me, but his actions belie him. I should not be surprised if I go into a decline after this child, one every bit as genuine as Augusta Hapgood's is imaginary!"

Despite her firm intention of making good on this threat, Harriet Hapgood delivered her third and final child, little Rosalie, with unbecoming ease. She even found herself won over by the docile, quiet baby, and did not languish as long as she had with the previous two. Hugh allowed himself to hope that, at long last, there might be peace in their home and the family might flourish.

He was mistaken.

"There shall be no more children, Hugh," declared Harriet one evening, when the nurse had trotted her charges off to bed. "I have recovered my health at last and am feeling more the thing. Besides, much as we love Rosie, I suspect any further attempts on our part will only yield more daughters. Look at your cousin Richard, with his four! Your proud Hapgood line must be faltering at last, to produce only girls and more girls."

Hugh might have observed that Harriet's Morrow line was as daughter-prone as the Hapgood, but he knew such an insight would only provoke his wife and banish their fragile harmony. He did not misunderstand her: she meant to bar him verbally from her chamber. And while he minded such an injunction as much as any man, the years of marriage had taken their toll, and he found his own objections overpowered by indifference. There were other things to occupy him. Not other women, to be sure. He shuddered at the thought. Harriet had cured his youthful tendency to prize beauty above all else. She was, to her credit, as lovely as ever, her hair as rich, her eyes as bright, her figure still light. Even her complexion still boasted the color of her earlier years, though neither Harriet nor her husband realized at the time that her rosiness owed more now to insidious disease than to defiance of time.

No, Hugh Hapgood was now an older and wiser man. And those who had known him for any amount of time would also say he was grown serious. His smiles were rare, and the old reputation he had at Oxford, for wit and humor and mischief, was long forgotten—even by himself. With envy Hugh looked upon other men, who found companions and intellectual equals in their wives. (This envy did not include his brother-in-law Wellington Sidney, however—the only man of his acquaintance who seemed even more reduced by marriage than himself. How long ago were those carefree days at Oxford!)

But he had chosen his lot, and for everyone's sake, he must make the best of it.

He had found over the years, in his desire to be doing something (and something out of the house and away from Harriet), an interest in work and financial ventures. Beginning as an army agent, handling the payroll for several regiments in Sussex, he went on to become a partner in banks in Cuckfield, East Grinstead, and Ryegate. The Hapgoods' income increased, as did Hugh's busyness. The children did not see much of either parent and came to rely more upon one another.

However Harriet Hapgood's spirit might rally, the time came when her constitution could not boast the same. The consumption took hold, and the last years of her life were spent in whirlwind trips with Lavinia to spas and bathing establishments, from Ramsgate and Brighton to Bath and Barmouth. The treatments in those resorts had no lasting benefit on her health, but they satisfied her eagerness for stimulation and self-consequence. And it was on one of these jaunts that Harriet met her end. She and Lavinia were in Tunbridge Wells on that occasion, when, in crossing the Parade from the milliner's to the circulating library, Harriet was run down by a carriage! Only Lavinia's dawdling at the milliner's, to inspect yet again an insert of Mechlin lace, spared her her sister's fate, and Lavinia was ever after unable to abide Mechlin lace, or even Bucks Point, if it followed a Mechlin pattern.

Thus Hugh Hapgood found himself, in an instant, a widower with three motherless children.

He mourned Harriet, naturally. As much as any man would mourn a woman who had allured, teased, tormented, discouraged, and finally rejected him over the course of thirteen years. He mourned her, draped his family and household in black, took a leave of absence from his banking duties, had a serious and uncomfortable discussion of Death with his children, dismissed the current nursemaid (who was far too young and pretty for a widower to keep on without comment), and, when he had a moment to think, set himself to consider how Providence had afforded him another chance at life.

It was not long before he realized he must marry again. If the idea had not occurred to him for his children's sake, the interest of neighbors would not have kept it long a secret. Mrs. Carstairs, for instance, who lived across the way, took care to visit often with her unmarried daughter in tow, bearing food and condolences. Her Miss Carstairs, a sly, pretty, penniless thing, had little to say to Hugh, but she made much over the children while giving their father periodic glances, to make sure he witnessed these attentions. He did—as did Lionel, Hetty and Rosie, who were puzzled by the young lady accosting them with questions and pats on the head and offers to play at spillikins. Lionel was polite and Rosie willing enough, but Hetty rudely asked Miss Carstairs why the elbows of her sleeves were worn so thin, and hadn't she another frock to call upon them in, if she and her mother were going to come every day?

Something would have to be done.

Hugh decided he would take Mrs. Carstairs' broad hints. He would seek another wife. To his wonderment, he realized he had not lost one jot of eligibility in all the intervening years. Yes, he had three children now, but his wealth had increased beyond the promise of his youthful expectations, and he was now quite certain of inheriting Bramleigh. He was perhaps less "dark and dashing" than when he won Harriet Morrow, but it seemed a man could safely lose his looks if the loss were counterbalanced by increase in fortune. While he supposed Miss Carstairs would leap upon him, if he offered—or the mother and daughter would both leap upon him—he preferred to choose a second wife himself, and to choose according to different criteria than he used as a younger man. This time around, he would not let beauty blind him, nor feminine intrigues ensnare him. He would prefer his second wife not to be aggressively unattractive, of course, or altogether without charm, but far more important would be a cheerful, calm, rational nature and kindness toward the children.

He thought anew of his Hapgood cousins. If something were to befall him, he would be sorry to think his children would know only their Morrow and Sidney connections. Lionel, at least, should know much more of the Hapgoods, as he stood second in line to inherit Bramleigh. And as the Morrows in particular were overcome with grief and favored Hugh with what he felt were unjustly reproachful glares, it seemed better and better to leave Sussex for a time and renew the bonds with his cousin's family.

Only one more day passed before it came to Hugh that he might, in the same visit, solve his other problem as well. Had not his cousin Richard four daughters? And would not at least two of them be now of marriageable age? Hugh had not seen them for many, many years, but he was certain his memory did not betray him. What could be better for both families, but that they become more closely joined? The Richard Hapgoods would be rescued from any financial straits, and the Hugh Hapgoods would once more be whole and entire.

Well, there it was. He would travel to Somersetshire and, God willing, enable his diminished family to regain its footing in life.

Difficulties arose almost immediately.

"Going to visit your cousin's family?" cried Lavinia, clutching her nephew Lionel to her bosom and stroking his golden-red hair, much to his squirming discomfort. "If I recall aright, Harriet ever spoke of them as 'that pitiful, house-poor man, his silly wife, and their four burdensome daughters.' Whatever can you want with them?"

Hugh blinked. Harriet had never used those exact words in his own hearing, but she had come close, and he felt vexation stir. Fortunately, Lionel chose this moment to wrench himself free of his aunt's grasp and escape the room, drawing Hetty and Rosie flying after him, giving their father time to regain his composure. "They have been, indeed, in financial difficulties for some years," he admitted, "and my cousin's wife Augusta has not enjoyed the best of health—"

"She's been as sick as a healthy imagination could make her!" sniffed his sister-in-law, with the righteousness of a woman whose sister had absolutely suffered from an actual illness.

Hugh affected not to hear and went on. "—And I'm certain it has been cause for some worry to Richard that he cannot provide as he would like for four daughters. But, whatever their shortcomings, they are my children's only family on the Hapgood side, and I would like them to know each other. Their short lives have been spent all among the Morrows and Sidneys—"

"—Where they have been dearly loved!"

"Where they have been dearly loved," he bowed, "and I hope the same for them from the Hapgoods."

Lavinia frowned. She had always thought her brother-in-law a dry, straight-ahead sort of fellow, for all that her sister had boasted of him, but she suspected for the first time that the still waters may have been running deeper than she imagined. Glancing at her own husband (whom she still called Mr. Sidney after fourteen years of marriage), she saw that he was hiding intently behind his newspaper, the coward.

She tapped her foot on the carpet. "How old are these daughters of your cousin now, Mr. Hapgood?" Lavinia asked innocently. "They must be of an age to be playmates to Lionel and the girls."

Hugh cleared his throat. "The two youngest, perhaps. The two eldest are somewhat older than Lionel."

"Indeed? How much older?"

"I cannot say with precision. I suspect Miss Hapgood must be nearly of age and Miss Alice Hapgood not a great deal younger."

"Ah." For some minutes Lavinia breathed no more than this syllable, but Hugh felt himself on the edge of an unseen danger. Therefore he was not wholly surprised when, after slowly sipping her tea to the very bottom and replacing the cup with a *clink* upon its saucer, Lavinia turned hard eyes upon him. "My dear brother. You must excuse my candor. Or see it for what it is: the affection and concern of a sister to you. I am obliged to warn you that, if you go among those relations of yours in Somerset, among all these impoverished, unmarried female cousins and solicitous parents, there will undoubtedly be *designs upon you*."

Pressing his lips together, Hugh counted to ten.

Before he reached eight, Lavinia had begun to speak again. "Beside which, you are in a fragile emotional state. You will not be able to withstand their maneuverings."

"Thank you for your concern, Lavinia. Forgive me if I persist in thinking I am my own master." He paused, frowning. Really, it would not do. If he were, after all, to marry one of his cousin's girls after having been warned so baldly by Lavinia, she would ever after think him overmastered by his Richard Hapgood relations.

No.

Much as he disliked it, he must let her see some ways into his mind.

Sitting forward on his chair, he tented his fingers together. "Although this may come as a surprise to you, Lavinia, Wells"—with a nod to his brother-in-law, who peeped around the corner of the paper at the sound of his name—"to be encouraged to marry one of my cousin's daughters would not be wholly unwelcome to me. They—hear me out, please, Lavinia—they are some of my nearest connections and my gain will be their loss, should something happen to their father."

"Isn't that just like a man," she cried, "to think so soon of remarrying, when my sister lies hardly cold in the ground! To remarry and call it consideration and thoughtfulness! I suppose these daughters are all beautiful, as well as young!"

"I know nothing of their appearance, beautiful or otherwise," Hugh retorted, his temper rising, in spite of himself. "When last I saw the Miss Hapgoods, they were all rather small and spindly—verging on sickly—Miss Alice, in particular, was thought not long for the world. And you must not accuse me of forgetting Harriet. It is not out of forgetfulness that I consider this course, but rather out of mindfulness of my duty to her children."

Here Lavinia sighed and glanced once more (in vain) to her husband for support. Men! She supposed if she were to be struck down that very night, Mr. Sidney would be paying courting calls the next morning. Duty to the children, indeed! If Mr. Hapgood meant to do his duty by them, he would teach them to cherish their dear mother's memory—not replace her with some interloper before they were even out of mourning.

Getting to her feet and forcing her husband and brother-in-law to theirs, Lavinia Morrow Sidney pulled her gloves on with a snap. "I see my advice is unwelcome here," she said coolly. "You must take your chances, then, brother. But you will not have such freedom to choose as you imagine. When I was seeing to your correspondence after Harriet's passing, there was a letter from your cousin the squire (if two sentences might be called a letter) to say that the second eldest—the Miss Alice who was so sickly in your memory—has recently married. Therefore, unless you plan to give the children a stepmother no older than themselves, the eldest Miss Hapgood had better be to your liking. Whatever you may say of duty and consideration and your own inclinations, you must brace yourself. I suspect she will be the one aiming for you."

Wellington laid one hand on the arm of his old friend, as he passed out after his wife, a hand accompanied by a meek glance. And it was this silent sympathy, even more than Lavinia's interference, that determined Hugh fully on his course.

Was it not enough, that that woman would go through life with her triumphant foot on the neck of that formerly happy man? Certainly it was. It must be.

Because she would not be allowed to add Hugh Hapgood to the subjugated.

# Chapter Three

**If it were done when 'tis done, then 'twere well
It were done quickly.**
—Shakespeare, *Macbeth* (1606)

To his dismay, Hugh found his cousin's daughter Miss Hapgood every bit as youthful, and even more beautiful, than Lavinia Sidney foretold. Elfrida Hapgood was a mere twenty, with golden hair and violet eyes and an admirable figure. Hugh winced inwardly to think what his sister-in-law (or the neighbor Mrs. Carstairs, for that matter) would have to say, should he return to Crawley with this diamond of the first water beside him. He was no more afraid of gossip and insinuations than any true man, but neither was he one to relish notoriety. Which meant that, while he would not let fear of others turn him from his plan, he might regret making such a plan in the first place.

Bramleigh was in uproar when he arrived. His cousin, the squire Richard Hapgood, had met with some sort of accident and lay abed. Richard's wife Augusta was thus all a-flutter, her lesser, imaginary ailments having been laid aside for the moment, while her emotional tremors came to the fore.

"Cousin—you find us crushed beneath Fortune's wheel," she cried, giving Hugh her hand as she leaned heavily on the arm of her balding brother Mr. Alec Arbuthnot. "My dear husband was struck down in the same day by hail as large and hard as unripe quinces and by a fit of apoplexy. If not for the comfort of my brother's presence, we Hapgoods should have collapsed under our burden."

Hugh made appropriate sounds of commiseration as he bowed over Augusta's hand and made similar acknowledgement of Arbuthnot's presence. He was spared having to look too hard at the daughters by the efforts of making his own Lionel and Hetty and Rosie do what politeness required. Lionel was easy enough—the boy had a winning manner (if a little more awareness of it than Hugh approved)—as was little Rosie, who stared at her cousins with big eyes, but Hetty took one look at all the strangers and crossed her arms over her chest, refusing to speak even when spoken too. Hugh's lips compressed into a line. Hetty had ever been the most difficult of the three. She was passionate, excitable, willful—like her late mother and namesake, if the truth be told. Even when Hetty's beautiful cousin Miss Hapgood crouched beside her and murmured, "You are welcome here, Harriet," Hetty only roared, "Don't call me Harriet! No one is allowed to call me Harriet. I *loathe* Harriet. I am *Hetty*."

From such a beginning, things steadily worsened.

Hugh decided he would be best served by plain-speaking and getting to the point. If he were going to offer for Miss Hapgood, he had better do it while his intention was firm and before he let misgivings (or Hetty's conduct) make such an offer impossible. Therefore he quietly asked for an interview with his cousin's daughter not two days after his arrival at Bramleigh.

Her expression vague and unreadable, Miss Hapgood nodded and led the way to her father's study, seating herself at Richard Hapgood's desk and folding her hands across the blotter. She turned those violet eyes on him calmly and waited for him to begin.

In the weeks following, the mere thought of that afternoon's work made Hugh Hapgood grimace and rub his temples.

"Miss Hapgood, allow me to express my regret again, that we have descended on your family when your father is so unwell."

"There is no need for apologies," she said in that mild voice of hers which Hugh thought her best feature. Perhaps because it was the precise opposite of his first wife's excitability.

A little silence fell, as he waited for her to say more and she did not. Hugh cleared his throat. Very well, very well. Let it all be laid upon the table.

"You are very young, Miss Hapgood," he began. A statement which drew no response at all from her. He went on quickly. "And I do apologize for the hasty nature of what I have to say to you today, but I assure you I have given it much thought and believe it for the best. As you know, I have had the misfortune to lose my wife Harriet"—here Miss Hapgood made a small, sympathetic sound in her throat—"and my three children have been rendered motherless.

It has grieved me for some time that we have not seen your family for years. Family is too valuable a thing to be neglected and cast aside. In short, Miss Hapgood, I wish the Hapgoods of Bramleigh and the Hapgoods of Crawley, Sussex, to be more closely allied in the future. That is—I hope there might be a still more intimate connection. What I mean to say is, I hope that you will do me the honor of becoming my wife."

For all of a minute Miss Hapgood gave no more of a reply than the looking-glass had, when he rehearsed this speech in his chamber that morning. She sat utterly still, her hands gripping themselves perhaps a shade more tightly, but that was all.

He waited, trying his utmost not to pace or fidget with nervousness. He hardly knew if hope or dread filled him more, though he was inclined to think the latter. Did her silence bode well or ill for him? And if he dreaded her response, did that mean he truly wished to be refused?

*Nonsense.* Setting his jaw, he tried to will reason into himself. This would be for the best. He had observed enough in the past two days to see she was a practical, calm, orderly sort of young lady, with intelligence and an affectionate, if not demonstrative, nature. The children—apart from Hetty—seemed to have embraced her already, and he saw how Miss Hapgood's own sisters and mother and even uncle looked to her for guidance. If she seemed at times to be lacking in spirit, at least she would not be prone to Harriet's high flights, and a girl could be forgiven some lowness, when her father lay desperately ill.

Hugh wished again that Miss Hapgood were not so lavishly beautiful. Perhaps she dreamed of dukes and castles—he supposed all young women did—and an older banker cousin struck her as unbearably prosaic.

But would she never speak?

At last, she did.

"Cousin Hugh, I find I am not prepared to give you an answer."

And when Miss Elfrida Hapgood said she was not prepared to give an answer, she meant exactly that.

Hugh found himself, against his better judgment, peppering her with arguments in favor of the match—the fitness of it, how it would answer his needs and those of her own family, the peace of mind it would give her father—! When he thought it over later, his hands rubbing his temples, he could only shake his head to think that maybe he spoke with such vigor because he needed convincing himself.

Worse yet, besides trying to persuade Miss Hapgood of the rightness of it all, he had wasted breath apologizing for his unromantic manner and then tried to pressure her into naming a reason for her hesitations. The poor girl had been forced to mention Hetty—Hetty who had been nothing but vexation since coming into Somerset. Indeed, what young lady dreaming of dukes and castles ever imagined a willful, spiteful ward of the duke, who took singular delight in causing trouble?

But Hetty was a worry for another day.

Suffice to say, Miss Hapgood would give him no definitive answer that day and shortly after took herself into Buckinghamshire to visit her sister Alice. Hugh could not say who was more relieved by her departure—he or Miss Hapgood. As a gentleman, he could not rescind his offer, however many second thoughts might plague him. He could only wait for her verdict. But there had been whispers and hints caught after his proposal that made him suspect more lay behind his cousin's reluctance than mere missishness.

"...Why did you let them do it?" demanded Miss Margaret of her younger sister Edith one morning in the drawing room, unaware of the open window and Hugh's presence on the lawn outside. "They have quite ruined your masterpiece, after all the trouble we took to convince Elfie she should let you paint him!"

"I should never have been able to finish it in any case," answered Edith stoutly. "Not with Mr. Frederick Tierney gone."

"Supposing he were to return and ask after your progress?" persisted Margaret. "How should you explain that you let your cousins paint that ridiculous hat on his head?"

"I did ask Elfie if she thought Mr. Tierney might come back and why he left at all, and she nearly bit my nose off with her reply! She said, as far as she was concerned, Mr. Frederick Tierney might go where he pleased over the whole range of creation—it made no matter to her."

(Hugh Hapgood had taken a stride away from the window, to avoid eavesdropping, but he halted here, unable to help himself.)

"They've had a disagreement of some sort," said Margaret, adopting a knowing tone. "You remember when we saw them out the window—"

"And he got down on one knee!" cried Edith. "Elfie said he had merely dropped something in the grass."

"Dropped something!" Margaret scoffed. "If he dropped anything, it was his pride, I'll warrant. *I* think he was asking Elfie to marry him, and she refused."

Edith's gasp covered Hugh's own indrawn breath. "You think—you think *that*? Oh! Oh-h-h-h-h...But of course she refused him, Margaret. Remember? There was that actress who knew him at the Taunton Fair and Mr. Tierney's reputation to think of. And he was always teasing Elfie!"

Crossing her arms over her chest, Margaret shook her head maddeningly. "All that's as may be. But he's still rich and handsome. Elfie might have refused him, but you saw how she took to her bed right after he left Somerset."

There was a long silence in which Edith mulled this over, and Hugh tried to shift his weight in silence. "You think Elfie *loves* Mr. Tierney?" Edith breathed at last.

"Who can read Elfie's mind? She's not indifferent to him, at any rate. I say—let's trap her, Edith! We will show her your *Judgment of Paris* which Lionel and Rosie have defaced, and see how she responds."

"How will we know what her response means?"

"Isn't it obvious, Edie? If she is furious, we will have to ferret out why. Is she furious because the likeness of her beloved has been made ridiculous, or is she only furious because we went to all that cost and inconvenience, only to have your painting ruined?"

"And if she isn't furious?" prodded Edith, unable to picture her eldest sister in such a state.

"If she isn't furious, she will be...either disappointed or indifferent."

"And what will those mean?"

"Disappointed: that the likeness of her beloved has been made ridiculous, or that we went to all that cost and inconvenience only to have your painting ruined. Indifferent: that she has other things on her mind, such as father's illness, or that she never thought it was a good likeness in the first place."

"I'm afraid I don't see how we'll learn anything at all from Elfie's response," said Edith.

"Never mind. Only let us try the experiment. Come, Edie. And for goodness' sake, let's go around the house. I hear Hetty coming."

Hugh no sooner heard this than he was compelled to dash some distance away and turn back as if he were just approaching the house, not that this prevented his young cousins from starting with dismay when they saw him.

"Oh! Cousin Hugh. Good morning," blurted Margaret, eyes on his kneecaps. Edith could not manage even this much, having gone scarlet and taken hold of her sister's hand.

Hugh was not much more collected himself, and he only mustered a "good morning" of his own before passing on, hoping the girls had been too flustered to notice the trampled grass beside the window where he had stood.

So there was the secret.

He had no need of seeing his fair cousin's response to Miss Edith's picture to draw his own conclusions. This Frederick Tierney, whoever he was, had made an offer to Miss Hapgood, and she had refused with reluctance. Well, then.

Miss Hapgood was, as Hugh knew, a lovely young woman. Lovely enough that a "rich and handsome" gentleman might overlook her lack of fortune. He rather liked her better now, for the knowledge that she had rejected such an offer, even if it tore at her. If *he*, Hugh Hapgood, had been wise enough to choose with his head, rather than with his eyes and naïve heart, he would never have wed Miss Harriet Morrow all those years ago.

Frowning, he veered in the direction of the terrace steps, kicking at a tuft of weedy grass between the stones as he went. There was no point in entertaining such a possibility, of course. If he had not married Harriet, there would have been no Lionel. No Hetty. No Rosalie. And who knew, but that he might have chosen someone even more unsuitable? Heavens. If Wellington Sidney had not snatched up Miss Lavinia Morrow before Hugh came on the scene, such a fate might have been his!

So be it. He would give the rational Miss Hapgood time to mourn her handsome blackguard. He could not say he did not wish his own offer to her unspoken, but it *was* spoken and the point moot. At least Miss Hapgood promised to be a more sensible woman than Harriet had been, and he must be content with that.

But it did not prevent a barely audible sigh from escaping him.

Had he, at the advanced age of eight-and-thirty, made another foolish decision?

# Chapter Four

**All good Boys and Girls take Care to learn their Lessons, and read in a pretty Manner; which makes every Body admire them.**
—John Newbery, *A Little Pretty Pocket-Book* (1744)

"A—a. A-a-b. Ab." Nollie's head bent over the hornbook, and she pointed at each mysterious shape on the leaf of paper. Rosemary should have been feeling triumph—Nollie having been her most obtuse and stubbornly inattentive pupil—but her thoughts were too scattered that day. And not that day only. It seemed the vague restlessness which had begun to creep about the edges of her life now threatened to overwhelm it completely.

But why? Why should her brother Roscoe's disapproving comments only now begin to weigh with her? Why should it trouble her, if people thought teaching poor cottagers' daughters was work fit only for old ladies and spinsters? Was not Rosemary DeWitt well down that path toward confirmed spinsterhood, in everyone's eyes but her father's? Certainly. She had convinced herself of it before this, and yet—

And yet, ever since she had met Mr. Hugh Hapgood in Mr. Benfield's vicarage sitting room, and ever since Mr. Hapgood had made exactly that assumption—that Miss DeWitt must be a confirmed school-teaching spinster—all of Rosemary's hard-won self-acceptance had drained away.

The question was *Why?*

She was not a woman accustomed to excusing herself, when she turned her clear-seeing vision on human foibles. Humanity had flaws; Rosemary was human; ergo Rosemary had flaws. And the better she understood her own weaknesses, the better she might overcome them, had always been her philosophy.

"B-b-b-b. B-a. Ba," Nollie struggled onward.

Rosemary squeezed the girl's thin shoulder, her eyes wandering to the window. There was never much to be seen from that source which had not been seen many times before. The small back parlor at Marchmont which Rosemary used for her schoolroom faced a clump of gray-greeny woods, and only the smallest fraction of the winding gravel drive intruded on this monotonous scene. But it was enough of a fraction this late August morning for Rosemary to glimpse her brother's curvaceous would-be love Miss Constance Porterworth trotting up in a gig, accompanied by her bosom friend the Honorable Miss Birdlow, daughter to Viscount Marlton.

Birdie Watters, ever prone to distraction, let her battledore slide from her lap as she sprung to the window. "Look, Miss! It's fine ladies come to call. Have they come to look at us?"

"If they have," Rosemary returned mildly, "you must show them how diligent a pupil you are, Birdie." She nodded toward the girl's chair and waited for Birdie to sigh and sidle back, plumping down again with reluctance.

"What beautiful clothing they wear!" Birdie said, giving the battledore an absent twirl. "All the princesses can't look a bit finer, I'm of a mind. Not even the Princess Amelia."

It took Rosemary some time to return her four pupils to a semblance of studying, although she suspected they only pretended to concentrate. Everyone, including Rosemary, was too busy listening. There was the carriage pulling up before the house. The footman opening the door. The housemaid scurrying to announce the visitors to the lone DeWitt home and unoccupied—Rosemary's younger brother Norman. But as Norman was not much for conversation with anyone, much less pretty young ladies, it did not surprise her when, after the passage of a few minutes, footsteps were heard approaching the makeshift classroom.

Miss Porterworth and Miss Birdlow had visited Rosemary's little school but once before, on a similar occasion when there was nothing better to be done and no one better to be seen, and Rosemary supposed they must be very hard-pressed for amusement to seek them out again. She braced herself for the noise and disruption, casting her eye over Nollie and Birdie, Meg and Ruth. All four girls kept their heads bowed and their lips moving silently, but the tension in their little shoulders and the quick darting of their eyes gave them away.

A rap on the door. Rosemary smoothed her gown and marched over to open it.

"Oh! Rosemary! How do you do?" gasped Miss Porterworth, her gaze flitting unseeingly over the students.

"We see you are occupied," added Miss Birdlow, in her cool, calm voice. Her reserve seemed to apologize for her friend's intrusion.

The two young women were as unlike as possible, with Miss Porterworth round and soft and effusive, and Miss Birdlow tall and elegant and unapproachable, but perhaps their friendship arose from necessity. Rosemary was too old for them, and the only other young women of their class in the vicinity, the four Miss Hapgoods, kept largely to themselves.

"Your visits are always welcome," Rosemary replied. "My girls are honored."

The girls rose dutifully and scraped curtsies with varying degrees of grace. Birdie's mouth hung open as she admired the fine stuff of the visitors' gowns, but otherwise they did their teacher credit. Miss Birdlow stalked majestically past each pupil's seat, bestowing a nod here, a question or comment there, but Miss Porterworth could not bring herself to do as much. Rosemary could see she was almost a-tremble with suppressed excitement.

"I was sorry Roscoe was not at home," whispered Miss Porterworth.

With difficulty, Rosemary refrained from raising her eyebrows. Truly, Miss Porterworth lacked discretion. Did she not know that referring to Mr. DeWitt by his Christian name before these girls would arouse all manner of discussion and curiosity?

"He will regret missing your call," answered Rosemary. "With your permission, I will give him your and Miss Birdlow's compliments."

"Oh, never mind that!" cried Miss Porterworth. "When will you be done teaching school today? Should Agnes and I wait? But we cannot wait!"

"It is no matter," put in Miss Birdlow from beside Nollie. "Perhaps you might be so good as to call upon us at Pattergees, when you have done for the day. Constance and I will drive back directly."

The placidity of this suggestion almost provoked Miss Porterworth into stamping her foot with impatience, but Rosemary was growing too curious herself not to take Miss Birdlow's hint. She clapped her hands. "Very well, girls. We will end a little early today. Please remember to practice your memory verses. We will continue on Wednesday."

No sooner had they shuffled and trooped away, curtsying once more and hardly clearing the room, than they burst into chatter and giggles and glances thrown back. Rosemary did raise her eyebrows then, and she strode to the door to shut it behind them.

Turning, she crossed her arms over her middle. "To what do I really owe the honor of this visit? You had better tell me, Constance. You vibrate like a boiler about to explode."

Miss Porterworth needed no further invitation. She swooped upon her neighbor, unwinding Rosemary's arms to clutch at her hands. "You will never guess! It is not to be believed! We would not believe it ourselves, but that their maid told Agnes' housemaid who told Agnes' maid—"

"Constance! You made me dismiss my class early, that you might share servants' gossip with me?" Rosemary protested, pulling away. "Surely this could wait."

"It is not merely servants' gossip," interjected Miss Birdlow, her lips thinning.

"Not at all!" rejoined Miss Porterworth. "Because I ran into their uncle in town and I openly and roundly *asked him* if it were true, and he said it was absolutely so!"

Rosemary threw up her hands. "You asked him if *what* were true? Constance, if you were under my tutelage, I would be forced to shake sense into you. You had better begin at the beginning because I have not the least idea what you are trying to tell me."

"Oh!" Miss Porterworth fairly hopped with eagerness. "It is simply this: Miss Hapgood has eloped!"

Rosemary felt as if someone had struck her a blow, and for several moments she could not gather her breath.

A satisfied smile blossomed on Miss Porterworth's face. "You see? I knew you would be shocked. We are all *beside ourselves* with shock. The behavior of those Hapgood girls! First Miss Alice entraps that nice Mr. Joseph Tierney through her unnatural, shocking schemes, and now this! Now Miss Hapgood—whom we all thought so lovely and sedate and irreproachable, even if her younger sister was a hoyden—Miss Hapgood *elopes*! What will we hear of next from them? Perhaps Miss Margaret will run away to perform at Astley's, and

Miss Edith will become a highwayman! Is it not altogether too, too shocking to be credited?"

Sinking into Birdie's empty chair, Rosemary grasped the back of it to steady herself. "But what—what—" she stammered, "what need had they to elope, when they might merely have married from Bramleigh, with everyone's expectation and approval?"

Miss Birdlow sniffed, her face hardening. "Perhaps Miss Hapgood could no longer govern her passions."

Rosemary could only dismiss this remark as a young woman's unfairness to a rival because Miss Hapgood had never struck her as a passionate girl. She was ever quiet and modest. Rosemary had always thought she would have liked her well indeed, if she had been more often in her company. If anyone could not govern his passions, Rosemary suspected it would have to have been Mr. Hugh Hapgood—perhaps the constant nearness of his beautiful cousin had been too much for him. She had suspected dark currents running through him, currents held in check.

"But why should they elope?" Rosemary asked again, her brow knitting. "Surely they did not bring the children with them? But, then, how could they leave the children behind?"

"Children?" chirped Miss Porterworth. "*What* children?"

"If there are any children, I suspect we will not hear of them for some months," said Miss Birdlow dryly. "Say, nine more months."

"Agnes!" Miss Porterworth shrieked, collapsing with giggles. "Shocking, shocking."

"I mean," Rosemary began again, bewildered anew, "the Hapgood children already in existence."

It was Miss Porterworth's turn to frown. "Miss Margaret and Miss Edith? I'm sure Miss Margaret must be nearly fifteen now—hardly a child."

"Heaven help us!" cried Rosemary. "Why would I mean Miss Margaret and Miss Edith Hapgood? Of course I mean Mr. Hugh Hapgood's children: Lionel and the two girls—what were their names again?"

"What on earth have Mr. Hugh Hapgood's children to do with the matter?" Miss Porterworth demanded. "Did you mean they wanted to be bridal attendants?"

Rosemary groaned and covered her face with her hands, but here Miss Birdlow interceded. "Miss DeWitt—Rosemary, rather—I believe we are talking at cross-purposes. Constance's vagueness has led to a mistake on your part. You see, Miss Hapgood has not eloped with her cousin Mr. Hugh Hapgood. She has eloped with Mr. Joseph Tierney's brother. You remember meeting him at the Midsummer Ball and our Pattergees card party, among other places? Mr. *Frederick* Tierney. Miss Hapgood has eloped with Mr. Frederick Tierney."

"The handsome popinjay?" Rosemary was startled into rudeness. "The one with the bad reputation, who was forever teasing and wearing embroidered waistcoats?"

Miss Birdlow's mouth quirked ruefully. "The same."

"I see."

In truth, Rosemary could not see at all. She was conscious only of a mysteriously powerful sensation of relief. Miss Hapgood had not eloped with Mr. Hugh Hapgood! The girl had chosen instead a frippery, idle young man in dandified clothing, when she might have had a good, wise, steady one in sober blacks. Mr. Frederick Tierney was handsomer, of course, and charming and eligible and so on, but Rosemary had thought Miss Hapgood a more practical creature than one to choose a man for his appearance. On the other hand, her father's cousin might have daunted a girl as young as Miss Hapgood—he being so much older and widowed and burdened with three children. Nevertheless. The obvious superiority of Mr. Hapgood must have been apparent to all, she thought! But Rosemary supposed that even good sense in girls like Miss Hapgood occasionally yielded to a gentleman of dash, which only proved that good sense could not be confused with the wisdom gained by age.

Having drawn her conclusion, Rosemary dismissed Miss Hapgood's scandal from her mind. She found she cared not a snap for Miss Hapgood's elopement. Let the Hapgood girls be as wild as they pleased—it touched her not at all. How could it, when it meant that Mr. Hugh Hapgood was then still...free?

"...Did you never see it coming?" Miss Porterworth was saying. "I suspected Miss Hapgood of a *penchant* for Mr. Tierney, naturally—we having all conceived ones of our own, I imagine..." Neither of her companions seconded this, Rosemary because she had not conceived anything of the kind and Miss Birdlow because she could not be brought to admit it.

"Those Hapgood girls are wily indeed, where gentlemen are concerned," Miss Birdlow said simply. "And Mr. Hugh Hapgood had better beware the allures of Miss Margaret and Miss Edith, however young they might be."

In Rosemary's opinion, this smacked of sour grapes, and she had not much to say for the remainder of the visit, her mind eager to range over different fields. Miss Porterworth and Miss Birdlow did not stay much longer, in any case, finding Miss DeWitt a most unsatisfactory gossip, but hardly had they departed and Rosemary begun to straighten up her classroom, than another step was heard in the hall, and in came the vicar's sister Miss Benfield.

Miss Benfield was a small, rounded woman whose softness and youthful expression belied the steel running down her spine. Rosemary had never envied Miss Benfield's state, unmarried, with her life divided between care for her querulous mother and the duties of her brother's household, but Miss Benfield neither invited pity nor felt any for herself, and Rosemary was rather awed by her.

Matter-of-factly, Miss Benfield untied her bonnet and tossed it on Rosemary's table. "I passed Miss Porterworth and Miss Birdlow in the lane, so I expect the news is already told."

"Miss Hapgood has eloped with Mr. Frederick Tierney."

"Yes."

"Well, I wish them both very happy," said Rosemary.

"Indeed. I must say, I am surprised that a girl with Miss Hapgood's mild disposition and good sense should—"

"Yes." Rosemary straightened Nollie's chair and retrieved from the floor the slate Meg shared with Ruth. "Did you learn of it all from the servants, as the others did?"

Miss Benfield's brown eyes widened. "I should say not! I hope you know me better than to suppose I would trumpet servants' tittle-tattle through the parish." Dropping into Meggie's seat, she folded her hands in her lap. "I had the announcement from Mr. Hugh Hapgood. You remember Mr. Hapgood—the squire's cousin who was recently widowed."

"Certainly." Rosemary decided the classroom was neat enough, but it did not occur to her to ask Miss Benfield to retire to the drawing room—her mind was filled with a memory of the tall, severe-looking gentleman in his black weeds. The mourning Cavalier. "Did Mr. Hapgood call upon the vicar again?"

"He has called several times," declared Miss Benfield. "As you know, he engaged to bring the boy Lionel to see if Arthur would accept him as a pupil and boarder."

"And did Mr. Benfield approve of the boy?" asked Rosemary, more eagerly than she intended.

"He's a lively one, no doubt," Miss Benfield said, shaking her head. "An intelligent, winning child. He has, perhaps, that boyish tendency to think highly of himself, but I suspect we will all end in spoiling him. Arthur was quite happy to take Lionel on. We did not expect him nearly so soon, however."

"Indeed? How soon will Lionel join you at the vicarage?"

"My dear Miss DeWitt! He comes tomorrow. That is what I meant to say: that Mr. Hugh Hapgood called to announce he would be leaving Lionel with us sooner that he expected because he absolutely must get back to Sussex and settle his daughters in their little school. And while he told us this, he said as calmly as you please that, were we aware Miss Hapgood had married Mr. Frederick Tierney, the brother of her brother-in-law? Yes! Exactly like that. You will imagine our surprise. But we hid it as well as we could and wished the couple all happiness, of course."

"Of course. Did Mr. Hapgood appear very...grieved?" asked Rosemary.

"No more so than he always appears," Miss Benfield replied. "It can only be supposed that he must be disappointed to lose such a beauty and to be frustrated in his attempts to help his Hapgood relations. Why else would he flee the county thus? But I do not suspect his cousin's elopement broke his heart."

"No?" asked Rosemary, hoping the vicar's sister would elaborate.

"No," Miss Benfield cooperated. "—I think the loss of his wife accomplished that already."

"Oh," said Rosemary.

Miss Benfield retrieved her bonnet and smoothed its ribbons. "So, our little corner of Somerset is to lose both the beautiful Elfrida Hapgood and its most interesting visitor. Not to mention that Mr. Frederick Tierney, whom I suspect aroused interest in other quarters."

She raised questioning brows at Rosemary, who stared in return until she realized Miss Benfield was concerned for her!

"Miss—Miss Benfield, I cannot think whom you mean, but I assure you, there were no interests raised at Marchmont on Mr. Tierney's account."

The vicar's sister merely pursed her lips in an if-you-say-so fashion and tied her bonnet strings. This only served to irritate Rosemary further and to provoke her into bald speech. "For heaven's sake, Miss Benfield, I had hoped, at my age, to be past the age of suspicion.

Not only did I have no designs or hopes, where Mr. Tierney was concerned, but I think it uncharitable of you, or anyone else, to imagine I did."

To her surprise, Miss Benfield's skeptical look melted into a smile and laugh. She pressed a placating hand on Rosemary's arm. "Forgive me my impudence then, Miss DeWitt. But—if you would permit me another instance of it—how old *are* you?"

"One-and-thirty." To her vexation, she felt her face glow.

"One-and-thirty," repeated Miss Benfield. "Very well. When you are one-and-*fifty*, Miss DeWitt, as I am, I promise never to have such thoughts about you. But in the meantime, I cannot be so accommodating. You see, my brother and I think you a woman of sense with a cheerful manner, and we have not so entirely lost our faith in mankind that we think your charms will go unnoticed—"

"I have had two offers of marriage," Rosemary interrupted, her tone unwilling, though she felt a pleased twinge to be praised. "So you see, my 'charms' have not gone unnoticed. Particularly the charm of my portion."

"Ah." Miss Benfield's hand tightened on her arm, and she gave it a little shake. "There. One-and-thirty is too young to give up on marriage, and far too young to grow cynical. I won't hear of it. Mr. Frederick Tierney is gone—*not* that you cared for him in the least—but I do not doubt there will be another man at some point. One more to your taste, perhaps, and you to his. Mark my words."

Rosemary did not trust herself to reply to this well-meant but painful oracle, and her relief was great when Miss Benfield departed.

Picking up Birdie's battledore, she twirled the handle absently, the letters and figures blurring into streaks.

Alas.

Miss Benfield was kind but mistaken.

There would be no other man, Rosemary was certain. *Especially with Mr. Hapgood gone*—the thought flashed through her before she could catch or stop it. But she punished herself for it nonetheless.

"What *are* you about, Rosemary DeWitt?" she muttered aloud, with nothing but chairs and schoolroom implements to hear her. "You know nothing of the man, nor he of you. Don't build castles in the air from such flimsy material! You will likely never see him again. And, if you do, he will not notice you in the least. You will be no more to him than 'that parishioner of Mr. Benfield—the one with the long nose and spinsterish ways.' Take yourself in hand and hear this terrible truth: you probably did not register at all, nor will his thoughts ever, ever light on you with interest. There, at least, your purported charms will always go unnoticed."

But on that point—however sensible and intelligent she was—*there* she was wrong.

# Chapter Five

**"Ah, me!" exclaims the Prince with fond desire,**
**"Thou art not—no, thou canst not be my sire."**
**—Pope,** *The Odyssey of Homer* **(1726 trans.)**

It was not long before Rosemary met the vicar's new pupil.

For some time, she and Mr. Benfield had discussed having their village schoolchildren give a recital of their little learned speeches and verses for their parents and any interested parishioners, and, at Mr. Benfield's request, Rosemary made the walk to the vicarage one morning to plan the event.

"He's not here, Miss," breathed Betsy, wringing her hands on her apron. "Pasty the swineherd has met with a little accident of sorts, and Mr. Benfield was called out, and Miss Benfield went along with 'im. Won't you step in, though? They left near on an hour ago and should be back shortly. Did you have tea with your breakfast?"

In all her chattering, Betsy neglected to mention that Mr. Benfield's pupil was still at home, and when Rosemary was deposited in the library, she turned to find she was not alone. At a table by the window sat a boy of perhaps twelve years. Or, to be more accurate, he was not sitting by the table, but rather standing—teetering—on a chair beside it, a pounce pot in his hand, cupped against the window. The former contents of the pot were poured out in a heap on the table.

At the sound of the door, the boy called over his shoulder, "I've got him, Betsy!"

"You've got what, then?" asked Rosemary, unable to stifle a laugh.

With a gasp, the boy's head whipped around and he toppled from his position, the sander giving a hollow clang as it hit the floor, while the formerly imprisoned housefly was set free to buzz again.

"You're not Betsy!" declared the boy.

"I'm not, I'm afraid. Betsy quite forgot you were in here, I suspect, and there is no one to introduce us," said Rosemary. "You must be the vicar's new student, Lionel Hapgood. I am Miss DeWitt of Marchmont. I teach a little village school for the girls, as Mr. Benfield does for the boys, and have come to discuss it with him." She extended her gloved hand and helped him up from where he sprawled. "How quick you must be, to capture that fly."

The boy was not only quick, he was handsome, and mischief gleamed in his countenance. Rosemary could understand what Miss Benfield meant about spoiling him. She made a quick survey of his features but could find little of the father in the lad's reddish-gold hair and blue eyes. And certainly Hugh Hapgood did not pass on the easy playfulness which characterized his son. Perhaps there would be some resemblance in their frame—? The boy showed signs that he would inherit his father's height and lean figure.

Lionel did not appear the least embarrassed to be discovered thus, and he gave her hand a vigorous shake. "How do you do, Miss DeWitt? It's been the adventure of a morning to catch that fellow, and now I will have to do it again. Betsy complains that it's been plaguing her for days."

"My brother Roscoe catches flies with his hands," offered Rosemary. "He says you hold them just above the fly"—she pantomimed this—"because it always has to go straight up when it takes to the air. I've tried, of course, but I don't have the knack of it."

Naturally he could not resist this challenge and spent the next several minutes darting about, pursuing the fly from pillar to post while Rosemary pointed and directed and counseled, finally sharing his whoop of triumph when the pest was captured, bumping and buzzing within the confines of Lionel's hands. She got the casement open for him to toss it outside just as Betsy reappeared.

"Here's your tea, Miss—oh, Master Lionel! I forgot about you. What are you up to over there?" she scolded, shutting the window and frowning over the sand spilled on his paper. Setting the pounce pot upright on the table, she made a funnel of the paper and carefully poured the grains back in, murmuring all the while. "*You're* supposed to be writing your father a letter, you are. And here you are with no more than 'Dear Father' after twenty minutes!"

"There's gratitude for you," said Lionel, with a roguish wink at Rosemary. "You may ask Miss DeWitt, Betsy, what I've been doing with my time! Nothing short of delivering you from the buzzing menace which you said made your life a torture."

"He caught the fly," explained Rosemary.

Betsy softened instantly and she chucked Lionel on the chin. "Well, isn't that a good lad. It's a hero you are! But no more rescuing me. Mr. Benfield will be back any moment, and he expects that letter done, so you can get on with your studies."

With another bob at Rosemary, she whisked from the room, and Lionel returned to his seat with a heavy sigh. "There's no need to finish any letter because there's no need to get on with my studies," he grumbled.

"Whatever can you mean?" Rosemary asked lightly. "Do you not want an education?"

"I'm not going to be any clergyman or professor or lawyer," he answered.

"I see." She took a seat on the sofa. "What shall you be, then?"

Rosemary thought he struggled with himself. He was too old now to shout that he wanted to be a pirate or an admiral or a highwayman, but she rather thought those daring occupations still appealed. She was surprised, therefore, when at last he said, "I will be a country gentleman and marry my cousin Edith."

"Miss Edith Hapgood?"

"Yes. You are acquainted with her, Miss DeWitt?"

"Certainly," said Rosemary. "I have met her on several occasions. A modest, well-mannered girl."

Lionel's disgusted expression made her want to laugh. "If that were all, Miss DeWitt, I should not care a bit for her. How dull a creature she would be!"

Hiding a smile, Rosemary murmured, "Forgive me. I confess I am not as well acquainted with her as I should wish. Nor do I pretend to know what young gentlemen like yourself desire in their future wives. Prettiness?"

His scorn abated somewhat. "My cousin Edith *is* pretty, isn't she? Her hair is black and her eyes gray. But what I really like is, she's clever but doesn't make you know it, and she draws and paints better than anyone. Best of all, she isn't silly. So many girls are silly, you know."

Rosemary could not help but feel flattered, to be taken into his confidence.

"In any event," she rejoined, "Miss Edith seems an intelligent young lady. Do you think, then, she might accept an unlettered, untutored man for a husband?"

That made the boy pause. He frowned and turned slowly back to the table. Answer enough, Rosemary supposed. She wondered if his desire to be a country gentleman arose from his expectations of inheriting Bramleigh eventually, or if he would have chosen that lot in life whatever the circumstances. She left the question unasked, however, that he might write in peace.

Another few minutes passed, but nothing was gained, beyond studious mending of the quill with his pen knife and the whisking of a few stray grains of sand to the floor. Quietly, Rosemary closed the volume she had selected from a side table and ventured, "Is it so hard to write, then?"

Lionel tossed both pen knife and quill down and scraped his chair back to look at her. "Do you like writing *your* father, Miss DeWitt?"

"I rarely have occasion to," she replied. "I am so little from home. But when I was a schoolgirl in Taunton I wrote him a letter once a week."

"And what did you say in those letters?"

"Why, I suppose I wrote what little lessons I'd had and my greetings to my younger brothers." She made a little face, remembering. "But I think more often I wrote to say that I missed him, and when could my next visit home be?"

A cloud crossed Lionel's brow. "You must be fond of your father, Miss DeWitt."

"Indeed. Very fond," she said warmly. "My father is a good man. He may seem stern to those who do not know him—and my brothers would say he is often thus with them—but I have only known him to be cheerful and encouraging."

The boy's shoulders sagged and he turned back to his blank page. She was relieved to hear him begin to scratch away, and she resumed reading her book. But the words meant little to her because she found herself wondering about Lionel's attitude. It was difficult for many boys to put their feelings into words, she knew. She had never had more than ten hasty lines dashed off by Roscoe, and if Norman wrote more than a paragraph, all the DeWitts would gather round and marvel over it as if he had penned the Magna Carta. But why had Lionel made that strange comment: that she must be fond of her father, as if *he* were not? Perhaps boys' relationships with their fathers were always more complicated. Roscoe would say so. He insisted that Rosemary might do and say whatever she pleased, but such freedoms were not allowed him. "Sometimes he fixes me with the old evil eye, Ros, and I swear he is thinking, *why has Providence charged me with this wayward, hopeless son?*"

"There." Lionel threw down the quill and poured a generous amount of sand over his letter to blot it. "I wrote almost exactly as you suggested: the lessons I've had and my greetings to Hetty and Rosie."

Before she could stop herself, Rosemary heard herself ask, "And did you also end by saying you missed him and hoped to see him again soon?"

Lionel grunted. He rattled the sand over the letter, back and forth, up and down. Then, as Betsy had, he made a funnel of the page to pour the grains back into the pot.

"I said I hoped he was in health," he replied at last. "But to say I missed him and hoped to see him again soon—why—it would be easier to write a sonnet to Pasty the Swineherd!"

"Would it? I cannot think what rhymes with 'Pasty' but 'nasty,'" teased Rosemary. "And, as for 'swineherd'—well, there's 'potsherd,' I suppose."

He favored her with a do-be-serious expression. "Have you met my father, Miss DeWitt?"

"Oh!" her eyes widened and she hoped her complexion did not change. "As a matter of fact, I have. Right here, when I happened to be visiting Mr. Benfield on another occasion. Your father seemed a...serious gentleman. A man with much on his mind. It was a relief to him, I know, to find so good a placement for you."

"Yes," agreed Lionel, without conviction. He slid the pounce pot to the far corner of the table and replaced the quill in the inkstand. "He is just as you say, Miss DeWitt—serious."

"To be serious is no bad thing." Rosemary could not keep the reprimand from her voice. "And I think you very fortunate to be here with my good friends." Catching herself, she relented. Had not the boy just lost his mother? That alone might excuse complaints. "I am sorry. I suppose you had a tutor before—before Mrs. Hapgood—your mother—"

"Before Mother died," he supplied.

"I am sorry," Rosemary said again.

The boy was silent a moment. He pressed the first crease into the letter. Then he said, "I did have a tutor. Not that I miss him either. Mr. Benfield is far preferable, in fact. But—shall I tell you something that might astonish you, Miss DeWitt? I wish—I wish Squire Hapgood were my father."

"Lionel!"

"I do! He's hearty and likes to be active and can do so many things."

*And he is loud and bluff and as unlike your father as it is possible to be*, Rosemary added in her head. Aloud she said only, "He is indeed."

The boy was warming to his subject. He popped to his feet and strode back and forth, hands clasped behind his back in unconscious imitation of his hero. "One knows exactly where one stands with him. And he says he likes boys with spirit, ones who would rather make a rumpus out of doors. And that, if Providence had not seen fit to saddle him with four daughters, he should have liked a son like me!"

The squire's opinion on the subject of daughters was hardly news within a fifty-mile radius of Bramleigh, and Rosemary was not going to argue that particular point.

"Lionel," she began again firmly, "your father cares very much for you—"

"—And the squire is such fun! He is always surrounded by dogs and yelling and hallooing and making such excitement. My cousin Edith says he is much quieter since his illness, so I can only think what a great, rumbustious, noisy, *wonder* he must have been, and will be again when he fully recovers."

"I would not be surprised if it was the squire's very rumbustiousness which first caused his apoplectic fit," was Rosemary's dry rejoinder.

The boy halted in his striding and cast her a reproachful look. "That is precisely what the doctor Mr. Lewis told him, according to my aunt Augusta. Would you all have him live on, if he cannot be himself?"

She had no answer to this one. Lionel returned to the table, carelessly completing the folds in his letter. "If the squire should live forever and Papa never inherit Bramleigh, I should not be a bit sorry."

"Oh, Lionel."

Even if Rosemary had known what reply to make, the return of Mr. Benfield and his sister would have prevented her making it.

There was much bustle and greeting and discussion of the swineherd's mishap and course of recovery. Lionel was prompted to take up his Latin volume while Miss Benfield sealed his letter, Betsy darted in and out with tasks and messages, and Mr. Benfield and Rosemary had all to plan for their pupils' recital.

It was another hour before Rosemary took her leave, and she had her hand upon the gate to shut it when she heard her name called and found Lionel rushing out to her.

"I say, Miss DeWitt," he urged, an impulsive hand clutching at her sleeve. "I was wrong to speak so freely and disrespectfully of my father to you—no, no, I was, I admit it—and I assure you I feel all a boy should toward his father—or I would, perhaps, if he invited it. I suppose what I meant about the squire was only that—"

He broke off to kick at the dirt at his feet, color rising in his face.

"That—?" she prompted gently.

Blue eyes flashed up to meet hers. "—That I wish Papa cared for me half as much."

"Oh, my dear boy—" Rosemary breathed.

She got no further because said dear boy released her suddenly and dashed away, leaving her alone and thoughtful at the vicarage gate.

# Chapter Six

**The Scarlet Fever...most commonly comes at the latter end of Summer; at which time it seized whole Families, but especially Children.**
—T. Sydenham, *Observationes Medicinae* (1696 trans.)

H ugh Hapgood had the headache.

There were four possible causes for it.

Firstly, he had left his cousin's Bramleigh estate in a rush, thrusting Lionel upon the Benfields and rebuffing the clumsy attempts of Squire Hapgood to apologize for his oldest daughter's elopement. The squire, still recovering from his recent ailments, had been stricken dumb by news of Elfrida's caper, and the younger Miss Hapgoods went about the house whispering to each other and avoiding Hugh's eyes. Only Mrs. Hapgood managed a response, in her fluttery way: "Well, Cousin Hugh, I had rather Elfie had chosen you, so we wouldn't be turned out when Richard's dead, but I've nothing against Frederick Tierney. Quite handsome and charming—enough to turn even a sober head like my eldest's—Margaret, help me nearer the fire. I declare summer's burnt itself out early and we will have a cold spell." Hugh, finding the blaze more than superfluous in late July, only nodded briefly and excused himself. Whether his chagrin at the turn of events was due more to disappointment or embarrassment he could not determine even for himself, but one thing was clear: he was longing to be gone and to put it all—and his relatives' solicitude—behind him.

Secondly, while Lionel had shed honest tears over being parted from his sisters, he did not seem to mind taking leave of his father one particle. Of course, the boy was twelve, Hugh reminded himself, and not given to introspection, but surely something was amiss, that his son viewed his only remaining parent with what could only be called indifference. Hugh sighed. He had been an absent father, he knew, but he wanted to remedy the matter. Was it too late? And, if it was not, how exactly did one go about it? Especially now that his son would be living several counties away?

Thirdly, his two daughters Hetty and Rosie had clung to him fearfully and tearfully before they walked from the inn to Mrs. Farthingale's School for Young Ladies in Broadwater. He could not blame them—they had only ever lived at home with nursemaids—and of a certainty they must all make adjustments to their new life, but it broke his heart just the same. And he could not say if it worried him more that Hetty cried (Hetty, who *never* cried) or that Rosalie cried so hard. He had patted them helplessly, floundering for the comforting word he should speak but unable to come up with more than, "There, there. Be brave, my dears." The girls had been brave. They had dried their eyes and taken each of his hands and accompanied him up the street, past the cobbled flint walls of St. Mary's churchyard to the neatly swept step of the brick-and-flint school, which, despite its lofty name, was little more than Mrs. Farthingale's house and the cottage adjoining it, connected by an avenue of spindly trees. And there, with the bustling and tight-mouthed Mrs. F, he left them.

They must all be brave. Very, very brave. And, if being so brave gave him the headache, there was no wonder in it.

And yet, he might have withstood these three blows and soldiered on with no wounds but those to his heart and conscience, had not his return to his empty home in Crawley been shortly followed by a visit from his sister-in-law Lavinia.

Therefore—*fourthly*—Lavinia's company.

"I wanted to be the first to congratulate you, brother," she announced, swishing past him and sinking onto the pink padded stool of the ridiculous *duchesse brisée* which had been one of Harriet's final purchases. "Have you settled it all, then, with your Hapgood relations? When will Miss Hapgood—the new Mrs. Hugh Hapgood, that is—come among us?"

Suppressing a sigh, Hugh drew back one chair of the *duchesse* and perched on the edge of it. "It so happens, Lavinia, that Miss Hapgood's affections were previously engaged."

Lavinia's rosebud mouth fell a half-inch open before she recovered and snapped it shut. "Indeed? Then she refused you? I cannot imagine a more eligible offer fell in the way of such a penniless girl!" After waxing indignant that her brother-in-law might marry again so soon, Lavinia now seemed in danger of waxing indignant that someone—and such a one!—had the effrontery to refuse him.

"I do not know about more eligible," returned Hugh, "and I am not acquainted with the gentleman who won my cousin's heart, but I have been told he is nearer her in age, possesses a good name and respectable fortune—"

"—And is handsome, I suppose," sniffed Lavinia, as if she herself had never been tempted by any man's looks. And, indeed, if one were to judge by her husband Mr. Sidney's present appearance, with its spreading paunch and few, straggling hairs punctuating a pink scalp, one would believe rather the reverse—that she cared not a jot for beauty.

"That, I cannot venture to say," said Hugh patiently, with the air of a man determined to take his medicine. "But the man's looks are neither here nor there. Miss Hapgood has chosen to marry him, and she is *not* to marry me."

Here Lavinia threw a quick look at him. Her brother-in-law was not a demonstrative man, but he did not appear to be nursing a broken heart. She allowed herself to relax somewhat. "I confess, brother, I am not sorry to hear it."

"Yes, Lavinia. You made yourself clear on the matter."

She had, and she was too wise a woman to parade her satisfaction at gaining her point. Changing the subject, she questioned him about the children's schools, lavishing approval on his decisions as a reward for his continuance in the single state. Then followed a discussion of the correspondence she had overseen for him in his absence, the scrutiny she had subjected his housekeeper to (and the faults thereby discovered and corrected), and a thorough canvassing of Mr. Sidney's digestive state. She wound up her call with the latest Crawley gossip, of which only the rumored movements of the troops interested Hugh. It was not until they had both risen, and she was drawing on her gloves again a half-hour later, that she let a hint of her triumph escape.

"The paragon Miss Hapgood aside, I suppose there were no women in Somerset to equal my departed sister," Lavinia sighed. "Alas. Such a one will come along eventually, I am certain, brother. All in good time. I *knew* your nature was too constant to contemplate so sudden a change. I *knew,* once the shock was past, it would be years before you could think of another woman in the way of our lost Harriet. Years and years...if ever!"

With this pronouncement she had gone, and Hugh shoved the three sections of the *duchesse brisée* together and threw himself across them, his boots scuffing the pink upholstery and his hands massaging his pounding temples.

The headache.

He had no reason to suppose his future would hold much beside headaches, with only his work, his empty house, his middling housekeeper, and visits from his oracular sister-in-law to look forward to, but he had the comfort of having attempted to do his duty. He had thought it proper to provide his children with another mother; he had tried and failed. He had thought it proper to join his fortunes with the other Hapgoods whom his own inheritance would rob; he had failed in the same degree. Ah, well. At least he had seen to his children's education, and his failure at matrimony would delight his neighbors the Carstairs, as well as his Morrow and Sidney relations. With this he must be satisfied.

Perhaps, in days to come, he might be sufficiently worn down and lonely as to marry Miss Carstairs, but that doom need not be contemplated now.

For now there was his work to take up again, and letters to write to the children, and perhaps, even, the occasional letter from them in return.

---

The first epistle he received from Mrs. Farthingale's School for Young Ladies, however, came nearly a month later, and it was not from Hetty or Rosie, but from the proprietress herself. It found Hugh in his study, where he readily laid aside the account books of the Cuckfield Bank over which he had been poring, stacking them alongside those of Ryegate. He had to catch a teacup which threatened to tumble off the desk and, finding no better place to put it, piled it upon another which the housekeeper had yet to take away.

The sheet contained but a few lines:

> *My dear Mr. Hapgood:*
> *It is with regret and trepidation that I inform you the school has been stricken with scarlet fever. Eight*

*of the twelve pupils have been taken ill, among them your Rosalie. We have quarantined the sufferers in the main house, where they receive attentive care from the doctor Mr. Turvin.*

*In her fever, Rosalie calls for her brother and sister, and Harriet has wrought some havoc here, in her attempts to escape the annex and steal into the main house. I respectfully request that you send for Harriet until the dangers have passed, as my staff and I have quite enough on our hands in caring for the sick.*

> *Yours in tribulation,*
> *Millicent Farthingale*

"Quite enough on their hands"?

Hugh nearly tore the letter in two as he sprung to his feet, knocking his thigh painfully on the desk. His heart was pounding. Scarlet fever? That dread disease with its blooming rash and spiking temperatures, which claimed so many young lives it touched? Gladly would he relieve Mrs. Farthingale of the burden of, not one, but both his daughters! Incompetent creature—how could she not write until fully two-thirds of her students were struck down? (It must be admitted that, in his panic, Hugh had little sympathy for the trials of a put-upon schoolmistress, whose establishment had never undergone the like of this epidemic before, and who now feared the loss of all her pupils to Death or Distraught Parents. A schoolmistress who, with such crosses to bear in this time, had been further plagued by Hetty's determined efforts to see Rosie. Hetty had been caught climbing trellises, hiding under beds, even dressing as one of the scullery maids. It was enough to reduce a stronger woman than Millicent Farthingale to storms of tears and fist-shaking at heaven.)

Within the hour, he was in the mail coach, jolting down what those of Crawley still called the New Road, bound for Worthing. The equilibrium of work and solitude he had so precariously re-established in the past month vanished as if it had never been, and he found himself fretting over the same questions as the miles crawled by. What if he were to lose Rosie? And Hetty, as well, if the troublesome girl had managed to expose herself to the fever? Lose them, before he had truly begun to know them?

It could not—it would not—be. Not if he could prevent it.

No—he would retrieve his girls as soon as ever he might move Rosie. As soon as she was out of danger (God willing!). He would take her and Hetty, and fetch Lionel too, and bring them all...home. They had lost their mother, but his children should gain a father. He would seize this chance and do his utmost to know them and to love them. He was even willing to marry the thrice-blasted Miss Carstairs, that they might have a second mother—Lavinia's opinions on the matter be damned!

So thought Hugh as he rode with gritted teeth. And, as is often the case, the curses and imprecations he uttered were very close to prayers.

A bolt of flame-colored hair flew to meet him, and Hugh found himself clutched about his waist by a pair of skinny arms. "Papa!"

"Well," grumbled a weary Mrs. Farthingale, eyeing her charge. "Did I not tell you I had summoned your father, Harriet? And lucky it is you haven't been stricken with your sister's fever, the many times you might have infected yourself."

"But I *haven't*," cried Hetty, still clinging to her surprised parent, whose own arms, after a hesitation, encircled her in return. "I haven't infected myself, and I *had* to see Rosie—she would surely have died if I hadn't. She would have been so lonely and scared, don't you see? Oh, Papa, how glad I am you've come!" Hetty burrowed into his waistcoat. "Won't you take us away from here? I am so sorry I drove away Cousin Elfrida, so that she ran away and wouldn't marry you! I was horrible at Bramleigh, but I will be so good now, if only you will let Rosie and me come home—and Lionel, too. You may even marry Miss Carstairs or whomever you please, and I shan't trouble her one bit! Please say you will."

Hugh colored, wishing in vain that the thickness of his waistcoat had prevented Mrs. Farthingale from understanding Hetty's speech. The good woman cleared her throat and made herself busy adjusting the pince-nez clipped to her bosom. "There is always some homesickness involved, when one goes to school," she murmured, "and I'm afraid the scarlet fever has only exacerbated matters."

Patting Hetty's disheveled hair, Hugh asked, "Is Rosie still in danger, Mrs. Farthingale?"

"She is weak, and the sight of her may shock you," replied the schoolmistress, "but her fever has broken and Mr. Turvin declares her out of danger." Seeing Hugh droop with relief, Mrs. Farthingale made so bold as to pat his forearm before she continued, "Her throat is still tender, and she has little appetite. It may be some weeks more before she is strong, but by the time Harriet returns—say, in a month?—I believe you will find Rosalie completely recovered."

Without releasing her father, Hetty turned pleading eyes upward and gave the tiniest shake of her head.

Hugh said firmly, "Mrs. Farthingale, Hetty will not be returning." (His daughter gave a squeal here, while Mrs. F straightened up in alarm.) "Nor will Rosie, as soon as she can be moved. You must forgive me—when I lost my wife, I acted hastily. I have since decided that I would rather have my children at home."

"Mr.—Mr. Hapgood!" protested Mrs. Farthingale, "the fever has been sweeping the town and quite driven away the visitors and bathers. My school is neither the source nor the sole victim of this disease. You must not imagine I do not run the very best of establishments, and you must not make a second hasty decision, on top of the first—Harriet, run and fetch your drawing of the Point—"

"I do not question the running of your school," Hugh interrupted, drawing Hetty closer (though, to be sure, she had shown no signs of obeying Mrs. F), "and I am certain Hetty's drawing has improved under your tutelage, but the fact remains that I would prefer my family gathered about me now. I have—I have missed them this past month."

Mrs. F's expression plainly indicated that she thought it neither here nor there that the father missed his children, so he hastened to add, "However, I realize you might have made financial decisions based on the girls' fees, and I assure you, I understand. Though I withdraw them prematurely, I will not be requesting any return of payment."

"Well, then!" A practical woman, Mrs. Farthingale found little to object to after that. She would be sorry to lose little Rosalie, but the removal of Harriet Hapgood would go nigh to make up for it. And, if she could keep the fees without keeping the children, why, she would not weep to see every last one of her pupils depart, and she doubted any schoolmistress would feel differently.

Not for the first time did Millicent Farthingale sigh inwardly and berate her late husband for his inconvenient and inconsiderate early death. It was all very well to work herself to the bone, trying to keep these children alive—if her Bertram had only done his duty and stayed alive himself, such slings and arrows would not have been hers to take!

"Come," she said. "I will take you to your little one."

Hugh was grieved by the sight of Rosie, diminished beneath the coverlet, and he felt his throat close when her pale face brightened and her hand crept out for his. Could it be his girls did love him, after all? Or was this no more than the homesickness Mrs. Farthingale suggested? Whatever it was, he must not waste it.

He made arrangements for Mrs. Farthingale to nurse Rosie another several weeks—enough time for him to fetch Lionel from distant Somerset—all the while holding Rosie's hand. Hetty continued to stay close as his shadow, and she whispered to Rosie that she must leave, but she promised she would send a few lines and a picture every day and give all her love to their cousins Margaret and Edith.

Rosie's eyes filled, and Hetty leaned in even closer to whisper, "Don't cry, poppet. I must go with Papa because I need to choose him a wife. I didn't want a new mother before, but that was before I knew The Alternative. And if he can't find another wife, we'll all be shipped off to school again eventually, don't you see? I must go, if we want to go home. You know Lionel can't be trusted with such a charge."

Her sister nodded, and Hetty turned solemnly to her father. "She'll do just fine now, Papa. Rosie is brave, and if we let her sleep, she'll soon be good as new."

Hugh felt a smile curving his mouth. "I believe you're right, Hetty. And in the meantime, we will go on a journey." He paused, uncertain what to say next, but unwilling to dispel that unfamiliar intimacy between them.

Hetty's pale blue gaze took this in, and, with an answering smile of her own, she put her hand in his. "Yes, Papa. My trunk has been packed for two days. I am ready."

# Chapter Seven

**Tis not good to have an oare in another mans boate.**
—Henry Porter, *The Pleasant History of the Two Angrie Women of Abington* (1599)

Rosemary held her bonnet on with both hands as Roscoe urged the horse to greater speed. While his gig was well-sprung, the roads were hard and ridged after the summer, and brother and sister bumped and jostled along through the cool morning.

"Must we go at such a pace?" she demanded, after one particularly deep rut threw her against him. "I am sure the squire's shooting party will wait for everyone to gather."

"Then you know the squire not at all, Rosemary," her brother replied. "He lives to hunt, and after being ill abed for so many weeks, I suspect he will be stamping with impatience. Those Hapgoods of Bramleigh aren't known for standing on ceremony—if I am not there by eight of the clock, I suspect I'll have to set off in pursuit of them."

"So odd," Rosemary said. "I do not recall the squire ever inviting so many to shoot partridge at Bramleigh. His recovery must put him in a celebratory mood."

Roscoe gave a short laugh. "That, and marrying off two daughters, be the circumstances of their marriages ever so irregular."

Nudging him with her elbow, she pulled a face at him. "Why, naturally he must rejoice! Unmarried daughters being *such* a burden!"

"They are, when you're as out at heels as the squire," he returned.

"I do not see why I should be asked to accompany you," Rosemary began again after they rattled through Patterton. "I don't care for shooting any more than Norman, but I had not his courage to refuse. The squire cannot possibly want me there to applaud your exploits, can he?"

Her brother only shrugged, but she saw the light of eagerness in his eye and knew well enough that Roscoe hoped Miss Porterworth would be present, to gasp and clap over every bird he bagged.

Roscoe was doomed to disappointment, however, as the party gathered on the steps included no other young women besides Miss Margaret and Miss Edith Hapgood. There was the squire, thinner and not so ruddy as he had been in July, but shouting and clapping his guests on the shoulders. About his feet capered a pair of hounds, while a third sat off to the side, scratching his ear. There was Viscount Marlton and his son, the Honorable Mr. Frank Birdlow, Mr. Lewis the doctor, and—to Rosemary's surprise—young Lionel

Hapgood, who appeared to have sprouted an inch since their time together, she having only caught Sunday glimpses of him in the pews since then. In this context she might not have recognized him but for his bright hair. She was amazed both that the squire had invited his cousin's young son, and that Mr. Benfield had permitted his charge to accept.

"Mr. DeWitt, Miss DeWitt, you are welcome at Bramleigh," boomed the squire as they alighted. "We are just setting out. I have been demonstrating to Lionel here how to hold his piece properly—you know Lionel Hapgood, of course."

The DeWitts murmured their acknowledgement, and Rosemary could not help but smile at the wink Lionel gave her. "We are old friends, are we not?" the boy said when she drew near enough, his rifle tucked under his arm in a presumably Squire-approved manner.

Miss Benfield had said he was a charmer, and here seemed to be proof. Rosemary found she was glad to see him again. Though Mr. Benfield was no hunting parson, Rosemary imagined Lionel did not encounter much difficulty convincing his tutor to let him join the shooting.

"Friends indeed," she answered Lionel, "though I own myself surprised to find you here. I suppose it is because Miss Benfield makes an excellent partridge pie?"

Lionel's grin widened. "You disapprove, then? Oh, they wrangled some over letting me come, Miss DeWitt. Miss Benfield thought Mr. Benfield should write for Father's permission first, or, the next thing you knew, I would be 'riding to hounds like a neck-or-nothing.'" His mimicry of Miss Benfield's high, stern voice made Rosemary's lips twitch in amusement.

"And how did Mr. Benfield answer, pray?"

Glancing toward the squire, who was debating with the viscount over which way lay the more coveys, Lionel said in a lower voice, "Mr. Benfield suggested the squire might no longer ride so hard as he was wont. And he promised Miss Benfield he would certainly have Father's permission before *I* rode, in any case. A letter was dispatched, and here am I."

"If the Benfields have approved, I cannot do otherwise," Rosemary conceded with a laugh. "They are the most honorable people."

"They are," he agreed. "For, as you and I know, Miss DeWitt, they had nothing to fear of Father hearing about it from my pen!"

"Miss DeWitt?"

Rosemary turned to find Miss Margaret Hapgood at her elbow, trailed by her younger sister. Miss Margaret was a tall, angular girl still in her coltish stage, with ash-blonde hair and a carrying voice, while Miss Edith stood in stark contrast: small, black-haired and timid. Remembering Lionel's declaration that he would marry his youngest cousin and become a country gentleman, Rosemary was amused to see him sweep his rifle from under his arm and polish it with elaborate ease. If he hoped for applause, however, it was not forthcoming, though little Miss Edith gazed upon her cousin pleasantly enough.

"Miss Margaret. Miss Edith."

"Miss DeWitt, I hope you have not set your heart on watching the gentlemen shoot this morning," Miss Margaret began.

When thus addressed, Rosemary could hardly admit it to be the case, even if it were so, but she only said, "By no means. I had hoped in fact otherwise—that I might be excused from serving as an admiring onlooker. Had you other plans for me? I might, perhaps, call upon your mother, if Mrs. Hapgood is well enough to receive me."

"Oh, Mama never rises so early," answered Margaret artlessly. "It would only fluster her if you tried to see her. But Edith and I hoped you might advise us. You see," she added, her chin coming up, "I have only served as lady of the house a little while, you know—since Elfie went away—and I have never been the hostess to a shooting party..."

Now Rosemary's smile revealed itself, and, with her usual quickness she understood the young girl's request. "Of course. And to think—the very first time you must play hostess, it must be to a viscount and an 'honorable'!"

Relief washed over Margaret's face. "That is exactly it. Button—that is, our cook—is preparing a collation for the guests, when they have finished their sport, but she is all in a pother about it and—"

"Say no more." Rosemary took each girl by the hand and set them toward the house. "We will see to it together."

More guests were driving up as they climbed the steps, but Rosemary guessed aright that the presence of a confirmed spinster and the squire's two underage daughters would not be missed, and so they proceeded inside.

Two hours later, Rosemary flung open the drawing room windows and sank into the armchair farthest from the small fire. The repast was prepared: a long board laden with cold meats, cake, sandwiches, and fruits, supplemented by mead and fruit cordials. Porter was also at the ready, and Rosemary had left the cook in the kitchen putting a kettle on for tea, should someone be chilled and desirous of a hot drink. Mrs. Button had been in as much a "pother" as Miss Margaret foretold, and there had been great, protesting clanging of pots and complaints under her breath and louder verbal thunderbolts hurled at the maid-of-all-work Dorcas. No one could find the key to the tea cupboard, moreover, which meant Miss Margaret added her own agitated, conflicting orders to the tumult, while Miss Edith wrung her hands and dashed to and fro, searching in all likely and unlikely places. Rosemary discovered the key quite by chance when the clumsy Dorcas kicked over Miss Margaret's workbasket, sending it rolling across the floor and unspooling a length of calico. (Spying a gleam of metal, Rosemary snatched it up and asked, "Could this be it, Miss Margaret?" "Oh!" cried the girl, clapping a hand to her mouth. "I quite forgot—I *knew* I had hid it in a safe place.")

"Gracious," Rosemary uttered, putting fingertips to her temples. It was all well and good to rejoice at marrying off one's daughters, but *someone* must remain to do the job of lady of the house. At Marchmont Lady DeWitt was a capable housewife, and she made certain her daughter proved equally competent. Rosemary could, if called upon, manage the servants, approve the menus, oversee the harvest of the kitchen garden and the output of Marchmont's small dairy, supervise household expenses—even brew passable beer and make wine. But poor Miss Margaret Hapgood—with a bed-ridden mother and two older sisters married and decamped—poor Miss Margaret must fend for herself.

The sound of the drawing room door opening roused Rosemary from her thoughts. "Am I wanted again?" she called, without raising her head. "What has spilled or caught on fire now?"

"Pardon me," an altogether unexpected but familiar voice replied.

Rosemary bolted upright in the chair, her hand flying to twist and pin up a lock of hair which had loosened during the kitchen campaign. "Mr. Hugh Hapgood!" she blurted.

It was none other. There he stood, tall and spare in his black mourning attire, his beaver hat in his hands, his normally solemn face startled into surprise. "Why—it is…Miss DeWitt, is it not? I beg your pardon for intruding—I could find no one to answer the door and I let myself in."

"It is no intrusion." Already on her feet, she felt her face coloring to be thus discovered, alone and lolling about on furniture that, if not yet his, was certainly not hers. "I am not surprised there was no one to answer the door. You see, the men are all out shooting, the servants are finishing preparations for the set-out, and the Miss Hapgoods have gone to—to make themselves tidy again."

His gaze fell to her own person, and Rosemary felt as awkward as a girl at her first ball. Dorcas had overturned the cordial and splashed her, leading Button to berate the maid so thoroughly that Rosemary felt her own annoyance give way to pity. That annoyance revived, however, to think that, when she should finally meet Mr. Hapgood again, she should have a crimson streak running the length of her gown.

Recalling himself, Mr. Hapgood hastily stalked to the open window. "The squire is shooting, you say?"

"Yes. For the first time this season, I believe. His neighbors rejoice that he has so far recovered his health." She bit her lip. Did saying so to Bramleigh's heir imply that she hoped he would not come into his inheritance for ages to come?

"I, too, am glad to hear it," murmured Mr. Hapgood. To his credit, inheriting Bramleigh was, at the moment, the furthest thing from his mind.

"You—you have not come to shoot, then?"

"I?" He almost smiled. "Certainly not. No. I have given my cousin Richard little warning, I'm afraid. But I am come into Somerset again to collect Lionel."

Rosemary blanched. "Collect Lionel?"

He must have received Mr. Benfield's letter about Lionel going shooting and descended like a Fury! *Was* Mr. Hapgood so opposed to the boy hunting, then? So violently opposed that he would snatch Lionel from Mr. Benfield's care and tuition? She thought of her friends—what a blow a pupil's removal in disgrace would be to the vicar, and how Miss Benfield would be torn between taking up arms on her brother's behalf and remonstrating with that same brother when they were alone.

These alarms drove her to speak where she had no business to speak.

"Mr. Hapgood," she began, forgetting the condition of her dress and striding over to join him at the window, "I must ask you not to draw overhasty conclusions or act rashly." In her anxiety, she forgot herself enough to lay a hand on his sleeve, as if she would physically forestall him.

At her touch, Hugh drew back, startled, his eyes flying to hers, and Rosemary's hand dropped back to her side. Mortifying! What had possessed her to clutch at him like that? She, who knew him hardly at all! He had clearly found it disturbing, and Rosemary could not defend or even explain herself. "Pardon me," she whispered.

"Of course," he replied too quickly to her bowed head. He could see her color rising, and he found himself wishing he had not jerked in surprise and so embarrassed her. And it had only been surprise—as if an exotic butterfly had landed on him before his sudden movement caused it to take flight again.

It was not that people touched him so rarely—though, come to think of it, such contact *was* rather rare for him now, apart from Hetty's newfound propensity to hug him. Had not good Mrs. Farthingale patted his arm only days ago? Why this Miss DeWitt's touch should be so very different from Mrs. Farthingale's he could not say, but it was. Entirely different. Chalk and cheese.

Giving his head a shake to clear it, Hugh tried to focus on what Miss DeWitt had said, rather than what she had done. For her words had been equally unsettling. In truth, Hugh wondered how she could possibly know what was in his mind. He would never have imagined she could, except that she voiced now the very doubts which had assailed him from Worthing to London to Taunton.

Perhaps he was being overhasty, flying back and forth across the countryside, determined to re-collect the children he had just distributed. He was acting rashly, compounding one bad decision with another.

Once Hetty was restored to him and he calmed enough to accept that Rosie would recover, he found himself bound by just the rash acts he had envisioned. He must fetch Lionel, and he must marry, that his children could remain with him. And if he must marry, that meant he must either take Miss Carstairs to his bosom or suffer his sister-in-law Lavinia to matchmake for him. When not viewed in the glow of desperation, however, Hugh found he could not resign himself to Miss Carstairs, after all. She struck him as rather like his lost wife Harriet—Harriet, but with sly blue eyes and a thin mouth. And, as for letting Lavinia choose him a wife, it did not bear thinking of.

But how could Miss DeWitt know of all this? Hugh wondered. Had he been the subject of gossip in his absence? Unlikely as it seemed, had Lionel spread stories? Or had Lavinia taken it upon herself to write to the Hapgoods, heaven forbid? Had she somehow enlisted this Miss DeWitt as a lieutenant in her campaign to run her brother-in-law's life?

Hugh's own fears drove him to be rough, where he had no business to be rough.

He straightened, his brows coming together. "Miss DeWitt, I must ask you in return not to interfere in private family matters."

"Of course I am ill-mannered to do it," she admitted, thankful he was politely going to ignore her grabbing at him. "But you understand I am driven by my loyalties. Will you not hear reason before you make a decision that might bring harm?"

"What 'harm' I may do, if any, concerns solely myself," he insisted through tightened lips, "and I refuse to discuss these things with someone—begging your pardon again—so wholly uninvolved."

The sight of his anger gave her a pang. Not of fear, but of regret, knowing this memory of him would replace the more pleasant one of their seeming rapport at the vicarage. The regret softened her reply. "I am not as uninvolved as you suppose, Mr. Hapgood, having long counted Mr. and Miss Benfield among my dearest friends."

Confusion overtook him then, and he sputtered, "Have no fear that my choices will injure the Benfields—I will remove Lionel, naturally, but I will leave them the tuition—" He shook his head again, as if to remind himself that these details were not Miss DeWitt's business.

"But do you not see that such a hurried removal of Lionel will speak for itself?" Rosemary pleaded. "People will think—people will *know* you thought something amiss, whatever Mr. Benfield might say of tuition. Fiddlestick to the tuition!"

In her earnestness, the lock of black hair which she had pinned up tumbled down again, and she pinioned him with the vehemence of her gaze. Some detached part of his brain noted that Miss DeWitt possessed rather arresting eyes, tawny brown with thick, dark lashes—eyes alive with intelligence. Had she turned the force of those eyes on him when she touched his sleeve, he might have responded rather differently, he thought. But she had not, of course. This realization dawned upon him, accompanied by a second: Miss

DeWitt's zeal for Mr. Benfield's reputation must spring from that tendency shared by many aging spinsters to idolize, if not adore, their vicars. (Suffice to say, it was fortunate Rosemary could not read this thought of Mr. Hapgood's, or he might have had more to fear than her interference.)

"Mr. Benfield may throw the money in the gutter, if he pleases," Hugh retorted, "and he may *say* what he pleases to the gossips. You may rest easy that my withdrawal of Lionel implies no criticism of the good vicar's tutelage."

"But how can it imply otherwise? Lionel—your son—has not yet been with the Benfields for two months! Of course people would know you were displeased."

"I am not displeased!" Hugh almost thundered. Remembering himself, he withdrew a step from the provoking woman and glared out the window at the overgrown garden until he could command his voice. "Whatever you or others may conclude, Miss DeWitt, my reasons to withdraw Lionel so soon are entirely my own, and nothing at all to do with the Benfields. Nothing. I assure you."

Rather than appearing mollified, Miss DeWitt seemed to struggle with bewilderment. She opened her mouth once—twice—and shut it again having managed little beyond "I—" and "But—" Then, to her companion's astonishment, she gave a whooping laugh and whirled away from him to hide her inexplicable change of mood.

Hugh frowned as he watched her collect herself, and it did not take her long. But when she turned back to him, a smile still tugged at the corners of her lips. "What you must think of me! To pry and accuse as I have done—Mr. Hapgood, I most humbly ask your forgiveness. I do believe I have made a muddle of things and indeed been guilty of 'sticking in my oar,' as my brothers would put it. You see—I thought you meant to remove Lionel because you disapproved of Mr. Benfield allowing him to shoot with your cousin."

"*Has* my son been shooting with the squire?" was all Hugh could muster at this unexpected turn of events.

"He has not. But today marks the first time. Mr. Benfield has written you, of course, but—"

"But I have not been at home to receive my letters," finished Hugh. He passed a hand over his forehead, imagining Lavinia receiving such a letter and having an Opinion on the matter. "And I did not forward my sister-in-law any addresses. I meant to write to her here, from Bramleigh."

"Yes," agreed Rosemary, as if this all made sense to her. "Please—Mr. Hapgood—I would not like us to be at odds. Please say you will pardon my unpardonable interference."

He was silent for a minute. Not because he begrudged her her outburst any longer, to be sure, but because he was reviewing their conversation with clearer understanding. His own touchiness about Lavinia's meddling had caused him to behave rather abominably himself, and to a woman he hardly knew!

Before he could begin to form his own apology, however, the door burst open, and in tumbled red-haired Hetty, grasping her cousins Miss Margaret and Miss Edith by the hands. "Papa!" she hollered, "you must see the little rabbit I have cornered in the garden! Edie says she will have Hal build a hutch for it!"

"If it hasn't already died of fright," Margaret added wryly, as she and her sister made their curtsiess to their father's cousin. "I am sorry there was no one to greet you, Cousin Hugh. We've been in shambles this morning because of the shooting party."

"Miss DeWitt greeted me," he rumbled, bowing. Hetty flew to him and clutched him about the waist, as she was wont to do now, and he laid a hand on her vibrant hair.

"Miss DeWitt has done *everything* this morning," Margaret sighed, throwing her guest a grateful look. "Button would have killed us in her rage and the shooting party all *starved* if Miss DeWitt had not come and set all to rights. Please do not deny it! I assure you, she has been little short of an angel sent from heaven today."

"Yes," whispered Edith. Her father's dark-browed cousin intimidated her, and she worried he might still be displeased with every last Hapgood of Bramleigh because of Elfrida's elopement. "We are so grateful for Miss DeWitt's kindness."

"I was happy to be of assistance," murmured Rosemary, her hand waving away their effusions.

"Miss DeWitt, I believe you have not met my second oldest child Harriet...?" asked Hugh, taking the girl by the shoulders to turn her outward.

Hetty obeyed his prompt and fixed Rosemary with a gaze that quickly sharpened into something more. The little rabbit cornered in the garden seemed all forgotten. Hetty glanced to her cousins and back at Rosemary, and then at her father. Then she stepped forward, smoothing the front of her dress and dropping a curtsy.

Rosemary felt herself blushing for some reason, and though she was usually so at ease with young girls, she found no easiness of manner available to her now. It had been no difficulty to chat with Lionel when no one observed them, but to show similar warmth at present to Harriet might be misconstrued. Especially when she had already been too warm with the father!

After her hesitation, Rosemary gave the girl a small nod.

To her astonishment, Harriet's face fell, and the girl glanced again from Rosemary back to her father. Then she said in a muted voice, "Miss. I'm not always so wild and clamorous. I can be quiet, too."

Rosemary had no idea what to make of this and only said, "Yes. I'm sure." Her own discomfiture prevented her from noticing the exchange of glances between Margaret and Edith. *Hetty—quiet?*

"I—I hope I might draw you a picture sometime," the girl persisted. "I'm not nearly so good as my cousin Edith, but I have learned better at school."

Over Edith's modest demurral Rosemary managed to reply, "That would be nice, Harriet."

Her father and cousins braced themselves, knowing Hetty disliked being called by her mother's name, but Hetty only turned anxious eyes on their guest. "But I didn't like school. I *hated* it. And please won't you call me Hetty? Papa says we shan't go back to school, and I have promised my sister Rosie—" She felt her father's hand on her shoulder now, and she hushed, but she continued to regard Rosemary with speaking eyes.

What on earth could the girl's behavior mean? Had it all something to do with the "private matters" Mr. Hapgood referred to, with which he declared Rosemary "wholly uninvolved"?

She was not left long to consider the question because a hubbub of voices and tramping feet announced the return of the shooting party. Among them Lionel was easily discerned, shouting and laughing about "bagging nine birds," as the hounds capered in circles at his feet. When he caught sight of his father, he went as ashen as his sister Hetty, but he came over to make his greeting, followed by Squire Hapgood. It occurred to Rosemary all at once that the Benfields would not be the only ones grieved by Lionel's possible departure from Somerset. She didn't imagine the boy himself would go willingly.

While the party broke into humming groups of conversation and milled about the long table set with food, and Dorcas and Button scurried to remove cloths and offer beverages, Rosemary found Roscoe's arm about her. Her brother had much to say of fog and missed shots and bunglings on the part of others, as well as his own triumphant run of four hits in a row.

"We will have partridge pie of our own, Ros!" he crowed, planting a kiss on her hair before releasing her to visit the sideboard.

Rosemary watched the men fill their plates and gave an occasional nod to Dorcas or a raise of the eyebrows to Miss Margaret to prompt them to their duties, and it was not until most had been served that she felt a tug on her skirt and looked down to find Hetty beside her again, now appearing quite woe-stricken.

"Good heavens!" cried Rosemary, not the least bit conscious, now that Mr. Hapgood's eyes were no longer upon her. She leaned down so that she would not tower over the girl. "Whatever can be the matter, Hetty? Did you find nothing you liked to eat?"

Glumly, Hetty shook her head. "I don't want to eat."

"Not want to eat? When your cousins and the servants and I have slaved away over this delightful feast?"

The girl ignored this. "Miss DeWitt," said Hetty, "was that young man who held you and kissed you your sweetheart?"

Rosemary blinked at her, before breaking into a laugh. "Roscoe? Not a bit of it. He's my younger brother. And what you saw was a rarity. Roscoe would ten times oftener rather tease me and trouble me to show his affection, as I'm sure Lionel must you."

Light broke over Hetty's brow, and she clapped her hands together. "Your brother? I don't mind that, then. I will not dislike him now. Lionel does treat me wretchedly sometimes, but I deserve it because I'm terribly naughty. But I'm trying so very hard to be good now. I promised Rosie."

"Promised Rosie that you would be good?" asked Rosemary, still puzzling over why Hetty should have disliked Roscoe in the first place, her brother being generally very popular with children.

"No, Miss," Hetty answered, dropping her voice to a whisper. "I promised Rosie I would pick a wife for Papa, that we might have a new mother and live all together and never again go away to school. That is why I am happy to hear that young man is your brother, and not your sweetheart, and why I hope you will like me."

Rosemary felt her cheeks flame, and she retreated a step. But Hetty only followed her and even reached for her hand, and it was only with effort that Rosemary resisted flinging it off. Instead she tried to give it a casual swing. Attempting a jesting tone, Rosemary said, "Have you already set your heart on me, and you are only this day arrived in Somerset? There's plenty metal more attractive, my dear."

Hetty shook her head with vehemence. "I don't know what you mean by metal, but I don't want any. There isn't much time. You understand, don't you Miss DeWitt? You are old like Papa and not silly, and my cousins said you are kind and helpful. I asked about you just now, and they said you like children and even teach them! And then when I asked about other young women nearby, Margaret said Miss Porterworth talks a lot and that everyone is in awe of Miss Birdlow. But I shouldn't like a stepmama who talks too much or one who is frightening, so it had better be you. And Lionel likes you—I can tell. Therefore, I have chosen you. If Papa marries you, we children need never go away to school or be separated again."

"Hetty," Rosemary hissed, at last interrupting this barrage and breaking free of the girl's grip. "This will not do at all. You had better let your father choose for himself and say no more of this to me."

"But if he asked you," Hetty pressed, "does this mean you would refuse? He is stern, Papa is, but not cruel. And he was very patient with Mama. Promise me you will try and like him."

"I promise nothing. This is not an appropriate matter for discussion. And I beg you, you must never speak of it again. Your father would not thank you for your efforts." Rosemary could not say why, but she did not answer Hetty's question, and this evasion was not lost on the girl.

Hetty's anguished face gave halfway to relief, "You like him then, Miss?"

Rosemary ignored this and made to walk away, but she could almost feel the girl behind her, now beaming with hope.

It appeared Rosemary was not the only one with a talent for seeing straight to the heart of things.

# Chapter Eight

**What are you, sir…,that deale thus with me by inter-
rogatories, as if I were some runne away?**
**—Robert Greene, *Menaphon* (1589)**

"I say, why the hurry, Ros? I hoped for another slice of the ham." Roscoe frowned at her as they drove away in the gig, the horse having been torn away from its contented munching of oats in the Bramleigh stables.

"We have ham enough at Marchmont," she replied shortly, turning her face that he might not see it color. What she wanted more than anything was to be alone in her chamber, that she might think over the uncomfortable events of the day.

"Not like you to be easily fagged," he persisted, oblivious to how Rosemary had spent her day. "And I wanted to hear the squire's opinion on Miss Hapgood's recent elopement."

"For pity's sake," snapped his sister, "she is *Mrs. Tierney* now, and has been for more than a month, and I cannot see what more can be said of the matter. Besides, if there were anything new to impart, had not the squire the entire morning to share it with the party?"

"You do not know the squire at all. When the man is shooting, he thinks of nothing else. I don't believe he even knows he has daughters when the hounds are about."

They rode some ways in silence, Rosemary's thoughts returning to that other branch of the Hapgood family. What could have possessed young Hetty, to light so quickly on Rosemary as a possible stepmother? And not only to think up such a preposterous idea, but to give it such emphatic voice? Rosemary prayed the girl would not be so forthright with her father. What would the man think, if his daughter told him she had found him another candidate, and—still worse—that she had canvassed the matter not unsuccessfully? His thoughts would surely return to that moment when she...*grabbed at him*. And he would think—he would think—oh, it was too embarrassing!

When the DeWitts had taken their leave, Rosemary had not been able to look anyone but Miss Margaret and Miss Edith in the face. She addressed her farewell to Hugh Hapgood to the mantelpiece and merely waved her fingers in the direction of that troublesome little girl. Horrors. She would consider herself fortunate if she never saw another Hapgood again.

Roscoe gave a slap to the reins, his brow knitting. "What a sluggish pace we set! Does not the carriage seem to drag? And yet Jambles had rest and feed enough, I warrant."

"Perhaps it is the birds you bagged," said Rosemary, not altogether attending.

Her brother grunted, and she returned to her thoughts, as a tongue will to a sore tooth, but after a few minutes Roscoe gave an oath and pulled Jambles to a halt.

"It's only the slope of the ground," Rosemary protested as he climbed down to check the wheels. But the next moment she gave a shriek of surprise when the gig gave a bounce and a head popped up over her shoulder. A red-gold head.

"Lionel!" she cried.

"Miss DeWitt. Mr. DeWitt," he answered, with a sheepish grin, nodding at each in turn. Stiffly he uncurled from the rear platform to step down.

"I knew we were heavy!" crowed Roscoe.

"Never mind that," said Rosemary. "Whatever can you be doing, Lionel, concealing yourself like this?"

"Running away from Papa, of course."

"Running *away*?" echoed Rosemary helplessly.

"Not so very far away," said Lionel. "I planned to roll off when you were nearest the Benfields', but, come to think of it, that will be the first place Papa seeks me."

"But—but—" Rosemary looked from the boy to her brother, but it was clear Roscoe expected her to deal with the matter, as he did most inconveniences. For his part, he went to pat Jambles and make his apologies for thinking her lazy.

She turned again to the boy. "Lionel, if you ran away because you thought your father would be angry about you joining the shooting,

I assure you he is not. I clarified that with him." To put it mildly, she thought. "He was indeed surprised, perhaps, but not angry. Not with you nor with Mr. Benfield for allowing it."

"Oh, I know. It isn't that, Miss DeWitt." Throwing a glance at Roscoe, he came around the gig and lowered his voice. "It's that I suspect Papa's come to fetch me back to Crawley, and I don't particularly care to go."

"Oh, Lionel," Rosemary sighed. "I know you like it here. And, in truth, the Benfields will be sorry to part with you so soon. But do you not miss home and your—your sisters?"

He kicked at a stone in the road and ran a smearing hand along the gig's glossy varnish, which action she was glad her brother didn't see.

"I'm twelve now, ma'am, and I must learn to do without family constantly about," he declared.

"I see. And is that the only reason you don't wish to go—your increasing maturity?"

He shot her a look, but she kept her face neutral. The gig received another handprint. "You, of all people, know my reasons," he said, lower still.

Smothering a smile at his earnestness, she said gently, "Has it to do with your feelings toward your father?"

A shrug was her only answer.

"Will not going home again give you both another opportunity to know each other better? Surely he would not want you back in Crawley if he did not care for you, Lionel."

Another shrug. "Papa believes in duty."

"Duty alone would be served by leaving you here to receive your education," she pointed out.

"He is stiff and unfeeling!" the boy burst out, causing Roscoe to look up from Jambles' side and raise his eyebrows. "Miss DeWitt, he wants to make me go home because he sees I love it here and that I love the squire and that the squire loves me and that I should be a thousand times happier here than in stupid old Crawley with him and my aunt forever at my shoulder!"

"Now that is nonsense, Lionel," she returned. "Since we both know you wrote him *nothing* of those opinions or of those feelings! Therefore, how could he have formed ideas about any of those things, until this very morning when he saw you again?"

"You take his side," he accused, scowling. He made a restless movement and Rosemary wondered if he were about to flee across the fields, finding her such an unsatisfactory accomplice.

"I take no side," she insisted. "Indeed, as little as I know you, I would rather you remained in Somerset with the Benfields. They are already fond of you, and Mr. Benfield will give you a proper education. But you have a duty as well, to your family, and there is such thing as moral education, as well as book learning." Seeing his scowl only deepen, Rosemary added, "Your father will get you a tutor, and imagine if you liked him as well as Mr. Benfield or the squire! Then you will have both a new friend, your family, and the satisfaction of doing your duty."

"I won't have Somerset and the squire."

She didn't quite succeed in suppressing her sigh. "No. That is true. But I'm hopeful that, in future, you and your family will visit here more often."

"Perhaps. Or perhaps Father might marry again, and we should never come at all."

A pang struck her at the thought and she fought it ruthlessly, though it silenced her for the moment.

"I don't see why we can't live here," the boy persisted, now scratching at the gig's varnish with a fingernail.

"For one thing, you haven't any place to live," she said reasonably, recovering herself. "It isn't the custom at all for the heir to take up residence in the same house as the incumbent, when that heir is not the incumbent's son. And haven't you a perfectly nice home in Crawley? Don't you miss it, even a little?"

"It's just a house," he dismissed it. "And in Crawley, Papa works, and my aunt Lavinia hovers about constantly."

"Hmm. Haven't you a cousin there, as well?"

Lionel gave a scornful toss of his head. "Caroline? She's afraid of her own shadow."

"She's no Edith, of course," smiled Rosemary.

"No."

Lionel's feelings for his cousin Edith were not a subject for levity, in his opinion. But Rosemary saw another avenue of persuasion there. "I spent a good part of the day with Miss Edith, Lionel, and I must say I like her very well. When she is grown, she will have her pick of young men, I imagine."

"Then I had better stay here to chase them away."

"Indeed? Are you so certain she would prefer you? A runaway, at odds with duty and his family? A runaway living, perhaps, under a haystack?"

"Mr. Benfield would have me," he argued. "Or the squire. I needn't live out in the fields."

"That is what you do not understand, Lionel. Grown people cannot behave that way. Neither Mr. Benfield nor the squire would shelter you, if it put them in direct opposition to your father. They would both, ultimately, believe in your duty to him. You must be brave and mature and do as your father asks. And that would be to return with him to Crawley and reunite with your family and continue your education with a tutor."

Now he thumped a fist against his thigh, and the mulish expression that accompanied this gesture put Rosemary in mind of his younger sister Hetty. For a moment she thought he might run off again in earnest. But then she saw him swallow, hard, several times. She saw his chin lift, as he stared down the fate that seemed so miserable to his twelve-year-old eyes, and her own mouth twisted in sympathy and amusement.

"Papa will choose a tutor as stiff and unfeeling as himself," grumbled Lionel.

Pleased to see he would at least consider this new vision of his life, she leaned down to him and even placed a hand on his shoulder. (At least the boy could not misconstrue her concerned touch.) "Oh, no, indeed, Lionel. It needn't be like that! You see, if you will only speak to him as openly as you have done to me, I feel sure Mr. Hapgood will take your wishes into consideration. He has no desire, I am certain, to see you wretched."

The boy gave a scoffing grunt rather like the squire. "Miss DeWitt, I have known my father a good deal longer than you."

"So you have. But you have been wont to deal with him as a child does a parent. I have seen your father in conversation with other adults and believe him to be a reasonable, well-meaning man who has your interests at heart. He chose Mr. Benfield, after all, whom you like very much. And don't you see, Lionel? When you get your education, you will go to university, and then you would be at liberty to visit where you please, no matter if your father remarries and stays at Crawley. I am sure the squire would welcome you to Bramleigh at any time."

"University? Why, I might be *sixteen* before I go to university!"

"You might be younger, if you studied very hard with your tutor," Rosemary pointed out.

"How can I study hard, when Father will get me a serious, stuffy tutor whom I will despise?"

Roscoe began to pace along his side of the gig, and Rosemary hastened to say, "I will speak to Mr. Benfield about a tutor for you," she floundered. "Perhaps he might have suggestions."

"But Mr. Benfield will not choose my tutor. Father will. Shouldn't you rather speak to my father, Miss DeWitt?"

Rosemary shut her eyes against this picture. Imagine what Mr. Hapgood should think of her if she proposed to choose his son's tutor! She took a deep breath. "Lionel Hapgood. I would not presume to interfere between you and your father." Or, she would not presume to interfere *again,* she added inwardly. "It is not my place. Not my place at all. I can only offer to speak to Mr. Benfield and perhaps persuade *him* to speak to Mr. Hapgood."

"But you're a teacher as well, Miss DeWitt," he urged.

"Perhaps. But I am not *your* teacher."

"Shouldn't be anyone's teacher," her brother interjected unhelpfully, dropping his pretense of not listening in. "Only see where it's got us." To the open air he added, "We must be on our way. Jambles cannot stand here all day."

Rosemary threw her brother a speaking look, in answer to which he merely grimaced and resumed pacing. Before she could gather her thoughts, she found her hand snatched up and clutched by Lionel's. "I know it's a lot to ask of you, Miss DeWitt. But only promise you will have one word with Father, and I will come with you now—straight to the Benfields or even back to Bramleigh! If you'll just have one word with Father...as a teacher...and make him agree not to pick a tutor like himself—"

"Lionel, honestly! I hardly know your father and cannot be asked or expected to influence him, much less *exact a promise* from him. You have taken leave of your senses."

"I haven't, Miss DeWitt—or, not entirely," wheedled the boy. "I see how everyone respects you – the Benfields, my cousins Margaret and Edith. Papa will too, I am certain of it. Please, only speak to him and persuade him! Then I will do all you ask, I assure you. *Please.*"

Blast the boy and his charm! Though there did truly appear to be tears standing in his eyes.

It was the very last thing in the world Rosemary wanted to do—to stick her oar in—again!—where it didn't belong, with the man whose good opinion she inexplicably craved. But, indeed, what did it matter? If the Hugh Hapgoods were to leave Somerset, rarely to be seen again, what did it matter if Mr. Hapgood thought her a meddlesome old spinster who possibly had her eye on him? Lionel was right: the man probably would marry again, and all her own flutterings and scruples would be for naught. The worst he could say was No, and please to mind her own business, and that was no more than could be expected. At least this time she would keep her hands to herself.

Feeling surrender inevitable, Rosemary withdrew her hand from Lionel's and patted the seat beside her once more.

"Come, then, Lionel. I will speak to your father at some point. I promise."

"Lord," muttered Roscoe, staring heavenward as if beseeching sympathy. But with a brother like Roscoe, Rosemary couldn't be certain if this chagrin was due to his sister being monstrously inconvenienced or, more likely, his horse.

# Chapter Nine

**Your fall and mine alike do they conspire.**
**—Robert Southey,** *Madoc* **(1805)**

Lionel's disappearance from Bramleigh did not go unnoticed by his father, though, until the note from the vicarage arrived, Hugh had just supposed the boy somewhere about. After his tumultuous conversation with the meddlesome Miss DeWitt, Hugh did not mind postponing his announcement to the Benfields to another day. He still intended to take Lionel back to Crawley, but he felt within himself an inexplicable desire to prove to Miss DeWitt that her counsel had been heard, if not obeyed. He remembered her vivid eyes, the persuasive hand she laid on his arm. Further than this, he did not choose to think.

Little Hetty Hapgood's mind, on the other hand, was all a-whirl. She was unusually silent the rest of the day. Silent and still, her eyes often fixed on her father. Silent through supper, through tea, through the squire's slapdash evening prayers. She didn't even notice that the squire's voice tailed off somewhat, and his pasty complexion gave evidence that the day had exhausted him. It was during those household prayers, as she knelt on a cushion between her cousins Margaret and Edith, that she turned over and over again the problem before her. Somehow, she must plant the thought of marrying Miss DeWitt in her father's mind, and that as soon as possible. Papa had promised Mrs. F he would return to fetch little Rosie shortly, and Hetty did not imagine he meant to prolong his stay in Somerset. No, they would collect Lionel and be gone. Back to Crawley and the dangers of Miss Carstairs and hoverings of Aunt Lavinia. If Papa broke down and married Miss Carstairs, would she pack them off to school again? Would not any stepmother? Any stepmother but Miss DeWitt, Hetty thought, as she scratched absently at the worn velvet of the cushion. Miss DeWitt, who was a teacher herself and so kind would keep them, would not she? But how to bring about a match between them, in the too-limited time available?

For a moment even Hetty's determination wavered, daunted by the prospect before her. If only she could talk to someone—even little Rosie! But she could not. She pictured her cousins Margaret and Edith recoiling at the thought of manipulating their older cousin's fate, even as Miss DeWitt had drawn back, horrified. What was wrong with everyone? Did they not see that a little arranging would make all well, and that such things as politeness and proprieties only got in the way? She thought with admiration of her brother: he knew Papa might or might not approve of him shooting, so Lionel went shooting without first telling Papa.

Lionel.

Hetty's eyes popped open, just one instant before the squire's "amen," and her cushion was already restored to its place before the other members of the family had even struggled to their feet. "Good-night," she called, hardly stopping to hug her Papa before she snatched up one of the little lamps and fled the room.

Not ten minutes later she was sneaking down the servants' staircase to the kitchen. Hetty didn't know what she'd do if the boy Hal wasn't there, or if the terrifying cook Button *was*, but, to her great relief she found only the Hapgoods' male servant, replacing the bin where Button threw kitchen scraps, after having emptied and cleaned it. The look he gave her could only be described as wary, Hetty's presence having too often led to mischief at Bramleigh, and she tried to make her expression reassuring.

"Hal, I need this note delivered to Lionel at the Benfields' *immediately*!" Hetty thrust it into the boy's grubby hand.

"This late, Miss?" Hal gawped. "That's a twenty-minute walk, and it'll be full dark before too long."

"It is a matter of great, great urgency," she insisted.

Hal hesitated, envisioning himself tangled up unwittingly in dreadful scrapes that would lead to Button boxing his ears and raining verbal abuse on him.

As if her own thoughts followed his, Hetty added, "Please. Much depends on it. And—I've got this for you." A coin flashed which both made his eyes widen and cheered him considerably.

"Do you need me to wait for a reply, Miss?"

"No, but I do need you to wake him up, if he's already gone to bed."

Hal gulped, his reluctance reviving. "That Miss Benfield is a right strict one. She won't like that."

"Then *don't let her know about it*. You're a clever one, Hal. Pretend you're a spy, and I'm sending you into the French camp. Now go!"

The next morning found a small figure, wrapped in a cloak, stealing out of Bramleigh before anyone but the servants were stirring. In the old days, the figure would have been Miss Alice, off to do some fishing, but today it was Hetty, her bright hair covered by her hood. She avoided the road, instead scaling the rise that led toward town. Once she reached the cover of the trees, she perched on a stump to wait beside the nearly-dry brook.

Before long she heard footsteps, coming at a run, and then her brother burst out, taking the brook bed in a leap and skidding to a halt.

"Halloa, Het! What's the big secret? Not that I minded sneaking out, but you know Miss Benfield will have words with me when I get back."

Hetty brushed this off, suspecting Lionel would not be in any terrible trouble. He never was. She wasted no time in beating about the bush. "You know Papa has come to fetch you, just like he came to fetch Rosie and me, after Rosie got the scarlet fever at school. Fetch us all back to Crawley."

Her brother's brow darkened. "I know it. I don't want to go. I like it here better."

"As do I," she agreed, "but I prefer Crawley to being sent away again to school, at any rate."

He grunted. "Well, then you'll be happy, Het. I guess you and Rosie will get a governess, and I'll get some miserable tutor. And I suppose Papa will leave it all to Aunt Lavinia, and only imagine what dry sticks she'll choose."

"Don't be thick, Lionel," his sister chided. "That isn't the worst of it. Don't you guess what will happen?"

"What will happen?"

"Why, Aunt Lavinia will choose her dry sticks, and we will have to bear them, but then Papa will see us unhappy and grow unhappy himself, and he will end in marrying Miss Carstairs, and we will be sent away again."

"Miss Carstairs!" Clearly her brother had followed her imaginings (and imagined them himself) up to a certain point and no further. What Miss Carstairs had to do with anything, dumbfounded him for the moment.

"Miss Carstairs. Of course you remember her, Lionel."

"Miss Carstairs the neighbor?" he repeated idiotically. "What has she to do with anything? Why should he marry Miss Carstairs?"

"Because he won't be able to help it, after a while."

He took another moment to consider this alarming prospect and then gave a huff of exasperation, dragging the toe of his boot in the dirt. "I had thought it bad enough when I imagined the dry-stick tutor," grumbled Lionel. But, then, just as quickly, he brightened.

"But—I suppose—if Papa sends us all away again, I will tell him I want to return to the Benfields'."

That made Hetty spring up and clutch at his sleeve. "You would not abandon us!"

"Why shouldn't I?" He shook her off. "Suppose it takes two years for Papa to yield to Miss Carstairs? I will be fourteen then, and nearly ready for university, if I study hard with the dry stick. And you might find you'd rather go to school again, than have Miss Carstairs for a mama."

"No. No, Lionel. I have formed a better plan. That is why I sent for you. But you must help me with it."

"Oh, Lord," he sighed, "this will be rich."

"I think, rather than let Papa fall prey *eventually* to Miss Carstairs, or possibly someone even worse, we had better marry him off now. To someone of our own choosing. Would that not be better? I promised Rosie I would arrange matters. She *depends* upon it."

Her brother rolled his eyes. "Rosie is a ninny, if she thinks you know anything about choosing wives for Papa. I'm certain I would rather choose *my* own, than anyone you suggested."

Hetty waited out this amount of brotherly disparagement. She expected as much, as anyone with a twelve-year-old brother would. And her patience was rewarded when Lionel had done and felt his curiosity overcome him: "And whom would you choose, Miss Know-All, if you could bring it about?"

She squeezed her hands together to hide her eagerness. "What would you say to…to Miss DeWitt?"

"Miss DeWitt?" he squeaked.

"I know she isn't pretty, and she's old—"

"Miss DeWitt?" demanded Lionel again, this time throttling his voice back to a manlier register. He dropped down on the stump Hetty had abandoned, thinking hard and drumming fingers on his knee.

"Do you not like Miss DeWitt? When you know her better, you will like her. It seems everyone does."

"I do know her," he asserted. "Better than you, I suppose, since you've been away at school, and I've been living in this neighborhood. And I didn't say I didn't like her. I was just surprised. No, no—I like her all right. In fact, Miss DeWitt is topping!"

"Yes!" Hetty was relieved to find he agreed. "So kind, and she likes children and can manage a house. I saw that yesterday. I only wish she were a little poorer, because then she would not be able to resist Papa's money. But at least she's so plain that she must certainly accept him and feel grateful to him."

"She isn't like Mama," he conceded, before adding, with what he considered chivalry, "but Miss DeWitt isn't *so* very plain. Not her hair and eyes, and I like her face when she laughs. I told you I've got to know her some, too. And, you're right that she's kind and friendly. And she doesn't talk to a chap like he's a baby. Nor flutter her eyes in that stupid way females do, neither." He favored his younger sister with approval. "You might just have hit on it, Hetty. And I'll tell you something: do you know, I even asked her yesterday if she might help Papa pick my tutor because she wouldn't pick any dry stick."

"Oh!" Hetty glowed and couldn't refrain from squeezing his arm again, to which he submitted briefly. "I'm so glad you agree, Lionel! See, don't you think it would be better to have her for a mama than the alternative?"

"Well, surely." This was just common sense. But the same common sense caused Lionel's good humor to fade presently. "But Het—you can't make grown people marry each other just by thinking it's a good idea."

"I know it." Her brow creased over this problem. "Do you think we had better just ask Papa if he would like to offer for her?"

Lionel whistled. "I don't think it works like that."

"I tried to tell *her* yesterday that I thought she should marry Papa, but she—don't look like that! I couldn't help myself because the idea just *hit me* like a pile of firewood, so I had to tell her. But she didn't seem to like the idea right off."

"Of course she didn't, you simpleton," groaned her brother. "How should you like it, if I told you you should marry someone you hardly knew? Not to mention, Miss DeWitt seems a contented person. Perhaps she doesn't want a husband."

Hetty could understand that. She wasn't sure she ever wanted one herself, if they were as forbidding as Papa or as smug as Lionel. But something about Miss DeWitt's panic when Hetty broached the matter told her Miss DeWitt might not be as contented as she seemed. If she were so happy to be unmarried, would she not then have laughed, to have a husband nominated for her?

"I think she might take him," Hetty returned stoutly. "But she can't ask *him*, you know. He must be made to ask her."

The two of them fell into frowning thought. A shiny beetle made its way up the side of the stump and across its surface, but when Lionel went to flick it, hurtling, into space, he paused, his thumb and middle finger poised to strike.

"I say, Het—did you hear how cousin Alice and her husband came to be married?"

"How?" Hetty had heard Margaret and Edith make sidewise references to the matter, but they always hushed up if they caught her listening.

"He *compromised* her. Somehow they spent all this time alone, collecting bugs and such, because he thought she was a boy. And then, when he found out she was a girl after all, he had to offer for her."

"He thought she was a boy?"

"Yes. Because she dressed like one."

"That may have worked for our cousin Alice, but Papa already knows Miss DeWitt is a girl, and I don't think either one of them wants to collect bugs."

"Don't be a noddle! Of course I don't mean Miss DeWitt should dress up like a boy. I only mean that it might be possible to get our father to compromise her. She could be...kidnapped by pirates, and he rescues her!"

It was Hetty's turn to roll her eyes. "Who's the noddle now?"

"I suppose you have a better idea?"

"I haven't," she admitted. A defeated silence fell for some minutes, as Lionel turned over in his mind other scenarios involving violence and hairsbreadth escapes, and Hetty wished she had not already alerted Miss DeWitt to any schemes.

"...You know, Lionel," she began at last, when he had begun to make restless movements and to recall the existence of Miss Benfield, who had surely noticed his absence by now, "if you say Miss DeWitt already likes you, you must be the means of throwing them together. My involvement will put her on her guard."

"Ah ha!" he cried, springing up. "You know I said I made Miss DeWitt promise she would intervene with Papa for me, in choosing me a new tutor. That will bring them together at least once."

She caught his excitement. "Yes! Good. And then, when Papa consults you about it, you must say all you can in her favor."

Lionel shook his head, his carriage sagging suddenly. "What makes you think Papa will consult me about it? He is more likely to dictate than consult."

"He can hardly remove you from the Benfields' without making some sort of explanation," she insisted, "and on that occasion, you must kick up a fuss and say how you prefer the Benfields,' and when he says you must have a tutor and Rosie and me a governess, you must ask why cannot we stay here, and Mr. Benfield teach you and Miss DeWitt teach Rosie and me? And when he asks why, you must sing her praises."

"And what will you do, while I am making Papa angry with me?"

"I will say I prefer to stay here too, and I will also ask why Miss DeWitt cannot teach Rosie and me."

"And then?"

"And then the idea will be planted in his mind," said Hetty firmly. "Perhaps he might call on her once or twice on his own, after that."

"What then? I don't suppose Papa will spend all autumn and winter dawdling about here."

"No, he cannot. We cannot. He promised Rosie he would return for her, and I suppose she will be all better in a fortnight."

"A fortnight!" echoed Lionel, throwing up his hands. "Impossible. Had you told me that at the outset, I should never have listened to this. I'm going."

"It's not impossible," she insisted, though she did not sound convincing even to her own ears. Her brother didn't even turn to acknowledge this.

"It only means we must contrive a supper or a party to bring them together," she urged, trotting after him. "Something that requires Miss DeWitt to wear evening dress. I have heard it said that older ladies prefer to be seen by candlelight. And then, on that occasion, we must lure them both somewhere to be locked in a closet or a shed or somewhere where they cannot escape or be found until it is *too late*."

At this, Lionel gave a bark of a laugh. But when met her pleading gaze, she saw he wasn't smiling. "I've asked Miss DeWitt to speak up for me, and if Father ever asks my opinion of her I will offer it, gladly. But you must give up the rest, Het. It's more likely after all they'll be kidnapped by pirates than that we'll have a chance and the nerve to lock them in a closet."

Taking her by the shoulders, he turned her back toward Bramleigh and gave her a little push. "Resign yourself to your fate, sister. To Crawley and to Miss Carstairs and to school."

She watched his retreating back through tears, but they were tears of annoyance, and her hands were clenched.

# Chapter Ten

**Then be not with your present lot depresst,
And meet the future with undaunted breast.
—Horace, *Satires* (35-34 B.C., Francis trans. 1742)**

It was with some reluctance that Hugh Hapgood found himself covering the ground to the Benfields' vicarage again. He had put his visit off yet one more day, but, when he neither saw nor heard from Lionel again, and when he found the squire eyeing him askance as he loitered around Bramleigh, he felt the unpleasant task of withdrawing his son could be no longer delayed.

"Mr. Hapgood, sir," Betsy greeted him with a bob and backed up a step to open the door wider to him. "Welcome—I believe Lionel is in the library."

In his imagined conversations, Hugh had not foreseen speaking with Lionel first, and he hesitated on the doorstep. "Is Mr. Benfield not also at home?"

"He's gone with Miss Benfield to the church, to see about the school recital, sir. And he's only just gone. It may be some time. Perhaps you'd like to follow him there?"

Well, he could hardly trouble Mr. Benfield about removing Lionel when the good vicar had his hands full of schoolchildren. Should he simply return to Bramleigh and put off the task still longer?

Betsy was watching him expectantly, and Hugh felt his feet begin to move. Not wanting to face Lionel was cowardice, he supposed. He must put his relationship with his son on a new footing, and perhaps this moment could be seen as providential.

He found the boy in the library much as Rosemary had weeks earlier, an open book on the table before him, but Lionel himself teetering atop his chair at the window, leaning over the sill.

"Good morning, Lionel."

The boy's red-gold head shot up, and he nearly overbalanced and tumbled out, only managing to catch himself by scrabbling at the edge of the casement. "Papa! Good morning, sir."

An awkward pause followed, in which Lionel righted himself and climbed down, pulling his book toward him, and Hugh tried to think how to begin.

"I came to speak with Mr. Benfield, but he is out," he said at last. Though perhaps this was too obvious a remark to make because

Lionel said nothing. He tried again. "So, then. What is your lesson today?"

"Horace, sir. I had only to put out a spider that I saw on the wall. Betsy has given me charge of insect and arachnid removal in the vicarage."

"Ah." Hugh suspected Lionel's authority might be self-appointed, but he chose to pass over this. Leaning over his son's shoulder, he pretended to study the words on the page, though honestly Greek was a distant memory at this point. "Well, then. Horace, you say. 'Of writing well, be sure, the secret lies in wisdom: therefore study to be wise,'" Hugh quoted.

"Yes, sir." Lionel swallowed.

Another silence fell.

Hugh debated how to approach the matter at hand, and Lionel how to avoid it. Then, collecting himself and thinking how he might aid his own cause, the boy blurted, "Mr. Benfield is a great fan of Horace. He says I shall attempt my own Horatian lyrics once I have learned to translate them well. Mr. Benfield is pleased with my progress."

His father's face clouded. "Yes, so he has written me." He thought how unjust it was: his first conversation alone with the boy in months, and the first thing he must do is disappoint him. "You have…adjusted well…during your time here in Somerset?"

"I love it here," declared Lionel, his hands gripping the corners of the *Satires*. He would take Miss DeWitt's advice, he decided abruptly. He would tell his father his thoughts. If his father didn't care to hear them—well—Lionel would know soon enough.

"Mr. Benfield is a trump," Lionel said roundly, "and so is Miss Benfield. And I love to see my cousins and—and—and the squire."

With difficulty Hugh stifled a sigh. Was it not what he had originally intended? That his children should grow closer to their Hapgood family, in the loss of their mother? The boy was happy here—that was plain enough. But leaving Lionel in Somerset and taking the girls home to Sussex would be a compromise that resolved nothing. The family would still be separated, and Hugh would still have the problem of the girls' education. And he certainly could not have a governess living alone with him and the girls at Fern Cottage, if no son and tutor were there for propriety's sake.

"I plan to withdraw your sisters from the school in Worthing," said Hugh. "Do you not miss them and...and Crawley?" He had not quite the courage to ask whether Lionel missed him, his father.

Lionel squirmed. For all his callous dismissal of Hetty's fears and the silliness and futility of her plans, he *did* care what happened to his sisters, and he *had* missed them. But not enough to be dragged back to Crawley without protest. "Not Crawley in particular, no, sir," was all Lionel could manage.

"Ah," said Hugh again. He had taken a seat in a chair beside the table, but now he rose to his feet again to pace before the bookshelves. Would it serve any purpose to tell his son that he, too, little missed Crawley when absent from it? He missed his work, to be certain, but Crawley now meant to him the rattling, empty house and the too-nearness of his sister-in-law and neighbors. To have his children back would remedy the empty house (especially if a governess and tutor were added to their numbers), but the unpleasant figures of Lavinia and the Carstairs' hovered nevertheless in the wings.

In the meantime, Lionel wondered if, in attempting to abandon his sisters to exile in Crawley without him, he might assuage his conscience by promoting Hetty's scheme to marry off Miss DeWitt and their father. It was probably useless, but she must give him credit for the attempt. But how on earth would he go about such a thing? He could hardly burst out with, "I say, Papa, why don't you marry Miss DeWitt?" But he had been the one to suggest that he strategically praise Miss DeWitt to the skies, after all. He must lay out in earnest, he supposed. But how to introduce the topic? And which of her qualities should he blazon forth first?

To the very great relief of both father and son, their unpromising *tête-à-tête* was here interrupted by the library door opening for a second time, revealing Betsy. "Your pardon, Mr. Hapgood, Master Lionel," she apologized, curtsying. "Miss DeWitt is here."

Lionel found himself on his feet at once, his chair scraping back and nearly pitching over. Miss DeWitt here? Surely this was an example of what Mr. Benfield called a *deus ex machina*! Or, at the least, it was a sign.

"Oh!" Rosemary pulled up short before entering, nearly colliding with the retreating servant. She had removed her bonnet to fan herself, but she hastily clapped it back onto her head. Mr. Hapgood here? She had not prepared herself for this! "Forgive me. I did not mean to intrude."

"It is no intrusion," answered Hugh (over his son's more enthusiastic "halloa, there, Miss DeWitt!"). "Although we did not expect—that is, Betsy did say you and the Benfields were at the church preparing for the school recital."

"We were—*are*—indeed," she replied, collecting herself. "I have only returned to fetch a book Mr. Benfield required for one of the older pupils." She could not carry out her mission right away, however, as Hugh stood squarely in front of the bookcases. She didn't like to ask him to move, and she most certainly was not going to try to move him herself!

Lionel, in the meanwhile, had begun making goggly significant eyes at her behind his father's back. To his credit, he had forgotten for the moment the promise exacted from her and was only thinking wildly that he must somehow, somehow throw his father and Miss DeWitt together. Having no notion what was going through his mind, however, she responded only by widening her own eyes. *No, of course I have not forgotten my promise to speak to your father! But I hoped it would be at a time of my own choosing.*

The boy then began gulping noisily, and, grabbing two fistfuls of his own hair, he tugged on them.

These signs of distress attracted his father's attention, and Hugh turned. "Lionel, are you all right?"

"Yes. That is—no—that is, I mean to say I think I—I—I—I think I have to relieve myself! Desperately! At—at once!" cried Lionel, bounding up from his seat and letting Horace tumble to the floor. Before his father or Miss DeWitt could react, he fled the room, slamming the door behind him and pressing himself against it. It was no pirate kidnapping, but it must serve. Did he dare lock them in? He must have lost his mind! And what would he do if they called for Betsy?

"In for a penny, in for a pound," he muttered, turning the bolt. He would find Betsy and drag her from the house on some pretense. What the consequences of this rash act would be he hated to think, but it was done now, and at least he could tell Hetty he'd done his share and not waited around for some stupid dinner party to be arranged.

Back in the library, Hugh blinked in bemusement for some moments before uttering, "My dear Miss DeWitt, I cannot think how to excuse such an astonishing display of bad manners on Lionel's part."

Rosemary turned away, torn between laughter and annoyance. That wretched child! Laughter was winning, however, and she could not answer until she had her face under control. "Please, Mr. Hapgood, do not apologize. This is not my first encounter with Lionel." Her mouth twitched again, and she hid it by stooping to retrieve Horace.

Hugh found himself thinking that Miss DeWitt's tawny eyes not only lit her countenance when she was angry but also when she was amused. And she *was* amused, he realized. The thought warmed him, for some reason. Everyone loved Lionel and made allowances for him, of course, but most gentlewomen of his acquaintance would have been affronted by the boy making such an indecorous remark. Lavinia certainly. And the boy's own mother. He felt his mouth curving in a most unfamiliar grin, and, if his brother-in-law Wellington Sidney had been present, he would have marveled to glimpse the old mischievous Hugh Hapgood of their university days.

As she straightened, Rosemary caught the fleeting expression, and something funny happened to her insides that brought heat flooding to her cheeks. She had already, to her embarrassment, found him a compelling man, but seeing his habitually somber features thus transformed made her breath stop. Why—it was better that the man only smiled rarely. Because, when he did do so, she supposed all the world would come to a tumbling halt as she had, transfixed. Spellbound by his dash. His...charm.

*Ah,* she said to herself. *So Lionel does not get his winning ways only from his mother.* This thought was followed by, *whatever you do, do not reach out and touch the man again!*

Hugh broke the spell. The momentary lightness vanished, and he stepped back from the shelves of books, gesturing toward them. "You said you came to retrieve something? Do not let me delay you."

"No, to be sure." Shaking herself inwardly, she marched over and ran her eye along the volumes until she discovered Mr. Benfield's copy of Cary's *The New and Correct English Atlas.* Too large a book to stand upright, it lay atop an entire row of theological works, and Mr. Hapgood further embarrassed her by reaching to take down the unwieldy thing.

"Perhaps I might help you carry it, Miss DeWitt?"

"So kind of you, but that will not be necessary. The church is fairly near at hand, and the book is not heavy, despite its proportions." When the words left her mouth she realized that, much as she would like to flee with the atlas and escape his disturbing presence, there was still her promise to Lionel, and she could not pass up the opportunity the boy had gone to such lengths to provide.

*Very well. Get it over with, Rosemary Palmworth DeWitt. It's a fool's errand in any case.*

Carefully she lay the volume on the study table and pressed her palms to it for courage. "Mr. Hapgood, if you have a minute—as I was saying, this was not my first encounter with Lionel…"

Unable to guess the reason for her lingering but perfectly willing to spend longer in her company, he gave her a look meant to encourage. "Do not tell me I have other things I must apologize for, on my son's behalf."

"Not at all." She cleared her throat. "As I told you at Bramleigh the other day, Lionel has flourished with the Benfields—no, please, let me speak. I do not intend to badger you about leaving him again, I assure you."

What, then? Hugh waited to hear what this rather interfering, rather *arresting* woman would say next. And again he felt that long-unfamiliar curl of his lip.

Rosemary's eyes grew large to see that devilish grin threatening to reappear, and she quickly turned her gaze to the cover of the atlas, running her finger along the binding. "I mean only to say that I have been in Lionel's company some few times over the past couple months, and he—he has asked me, as one also involved in the education of children, to share my own recommendations with you, in selecting a tutor for him." Such an absurd, pompous speech! But how else could she put it? She could not say, *Your son does not trust you to have his best interests at heart and therefore asks me, nearly a perfect stranger, to advocate for him. It's none of my business, but there it is.*

"Pardon me, Miss DeWitt." His rusty voice seemed even more of a growl than usual. "You are saying my son *asked* you to interpose yourself in this process?"

She could manage only a nod.

Hugh grimaced, unseen by Rosemary's averted eyes. How had this woman, this plain, commonsensical schoolmistress, managed to gain his son's trust and confidence in so short a space? How came it to be that Lionel would call upon this person to speak to his own father? Did he not think his own father would hear him out? At that thought, another twinge took him: had that not been his intention, when all was said and done? To tell Lionel what must be, however the boy felt about it?

"Mr. Hapgood, please do not take this amiss," Rosemary heard herself plead. "I am certain no words of mine are necessary—" (If they were not necessary, why then was she speaking them?) "—but given how well Lionel has flourished under Mr. Benfield's tutelage, I only wish to...suggest...that whomever you choose would be in the same vein."

"And what vein would that be?"

She threw up her hands helplessly. If Lionel had his way, he would want Rosemary to recommend an athletic, active man of Squire Hapgood's ilk, one also capable of parsing Greek and proving mathematical theorems, and who knew whether such a tutor were anywhere to be found in all the United Kingdoms! "I—I suppose a man of energy as well as education. One who would...remember well what it was like to be a lively young boy."

"Have you a particular person in mind, Miss DeWitt?"

"I? No."

"No candidate to put forth?" he pressed. "You give your advice with singular specificity. But perhaps it is your 'involvement in the education of children' that makes you so confident of both who should suit my son and whether such a gentleman even be in existence."

It was certainly a jab at her, and she could not even think his resentment unjust. Well, she had done her duty and kept her word to Lionel, and that must be all the satisfaction she could garner from being forced to stick her oar in again. If Mr. Hapgood were to engage a dried-up, moldering scholar to tutor his son, it would not be for lack of warning. She washed her hands of the matter and only wished she might also wash her hands of desiring the man's approbation.

"I am only acquainted with your son's disposition, Mr. Hapgood," Rosemary said weakly. She swung the atlas off the table and held it to her body like a shield, wishing she might hide behind it entirely. "And I wish you all success in securing teachers for both Lionel and your girls. If you will excuse me now, I will bring this to Mr. Benfield."

"While you are dispensing counsel, do you not also want to suggest the ideal candidate for governess?" Hugh asked dryly.

She had accepted his first provocation as only her due, but at this second baiting she felt a flare of anger. If Hugh Hapgood thought Rosemary too apt to interfere where she was not wanted, he would find his own daughter Hetty needed no instruction there! But Rosemary managed to keep her lips pressed together and only a scorching glare betrayed her thoughts.

Bestowing a queenly nod upon him, she made to sweep from the room, but when she took hold of the brass door latch, Rosemary found that it did not give. Startled, she tugged on it again, with the same result.

"I do believe the door is bolted."

Hugh had caught himself admiring Miss DeWitt's anger again, and it took him some moments to respond. "How odd. I will ring for Betsy," he said obligingly, glancing about.

But in a manse so small as the vicarage there were only bell ropes abovestairs in the bed chambers.

"Betsy!" called Rosemary, rattling the latch again and then rapping gently on the door, "Betsy! Lionel?"

"Lionel," repeated Hugh. "He did this. That boy is the mischief." He was by her side now, giving the latch a rattle of his own and the door a good solid hammering.

"Stay—wait, Mr. Hapgood," urged Rosemary, holding up her free hand. "I have just remembered we must not kick up a row, lest we wake old Mrs. Benfield."

He raised an eyebrow at her, and Rosemary *swore* she saw the corners of his mouth lifting again. Three times in the space of an hour? Could it really be? It was three times too many for her peace of mind. "I—perhaps I might be able to squeeze out of the window," she stammered, keeping the atlas between them and slipping past.

Now his grin took hold, and he gave a short laugh as he followed her. "Lionel was leaning out there earlier, disposing of a spider, he claims, and you would have to climb out, Miss DeWitt, and avoid the shrubbery below."

The indignity of the idea alarmed her, but equally alarming was the thought of being locked in a room with this man who set her so a-flutter and who most likely thought of her (if he ever thought of her) as a busybody old maid. "Never mind, I will manage." She tried to inject her voice with confidence. "If you would be so kind as to hand me the book when I am safely on the ground again outside..."

"Miss DeWitt!" he cried, as Rosemary climbed upon the chair. It rocked, and he reached to steady her.

"Oh!" Rosemary turned all-over scarlet as she fought the urge to tear her arm from his warm grasp. Well, they were even now, she supposed, at one touch apiece. Though she supposed his could be excused because it served an actual purpose.

The man was now grinning at her like a pirate. "Miss DeWitt, I insist. My rogue of a son was the one who locked the door, so you must allow me to be the one who wriggles out the casement, falls in the hedge among the spiders, tears his clothing, curses, and comes around to unlock the door."

Now she did yank her arm away, afraid he would feel her racing pulse. "Nonsense, Mr. Hapgood. The casement is far too narrow for one of your—your frame."

"And far too high for one of *yours*." Deliberately his eye traveled down her outstretched length to her ankles, which, she suddenly realized, were immodestly now exposed to his view.

With a smothered gasp, she lowered her arms, that her gown would no longer ride up, and wondered if it were possible to blush so hard one actually combusted. "Perhaps—perhaps if you were to give me a boost, I would not have to reach so far."

"Miss DeWitt—"

"No, we cannot waste more time arguing," she said decisively, not meeting his gaze. "Mr. Benfield must be wondering what on earth has detained me."

Hugh opened his mouth as if to speak again, but then he shrugged, laced his hands together and held them out for her to place her slippered foot in.

*Pretend he is Faddles*, she counseled herself, picturing one of Marchmont's grooms. *This is precisely how Faddles assists you when there is no mounting block handy. There is no call for these ridiculous blushes!*

And yet, when she placed an unexpectedly dainty foot into his hands and felt him lift her with ease, she could not help but think Mr. Hugh Hapgood was nothing at all like Faddles, and Faddles' assistance had never thrown her into such a state, half pleasure, half panic.

This would never do. She must escape his presence and recover her calm as quickly as possible.

Rosemary reached to grasp the head of the casement, that she might balance upon the sill, but, with a shredding crunch, the piece of wood came away in her hand, and she slid ignominiously right back into the room, landing upon Hugh. In the surprise of it, he threw up his arms, more from instinct than an attempt to catch her, and the force of her landing caused him to stumble backward, tangling his boots in the legs of the chair and sending them both tumbling to the floor: Hugh flat on the Axminster carpet, Rosemary flat atop him and the chair tipped atop her, while her bonnet slipped forward to cover their faces.

At the very same instant the latch of the library door swung down and the door flew open, admitting the Benfields, Lionel, Betsy, and Roscoe DeWitt.

# Chapter Eleven

**Now seest thou not, how many good ends
this contrivance answers?
—Samuel Richardson, *Clarissa* (1748)**

"What is the meaning of this?" bellowed Roscoe DeWitt, as his sister attempted to untangle herself from Hugh Hapgood's arms and clamber to her feet. "Rosemary—has he injured you?"

His challenging words were nearly drowned in the simultaneous gasps and cries from the vicar, his sister, and the servant, but both Rosemary and Hugh caught them clearly. Would the disconcerting events of this day never end?

Rosemary's bonnet had rolled away, her gown was rumpled, and half her hair had come loose of its pins, so she didn't expect it to calm Roscoe much when she answered breathlessly, "I am perfectly fine.

No one has injured me. Mr. Hapgood only tried to catch me when I fell from the window."

"Fell from the window!" her brother all but roared, launching himself to her side and tucking her behind him, as if to defend her from further assaults. "What need had you to be climbing out the casement, unless you felt yourself in danger?"

Eyeing Roscoe's menacing posture warily, Hugh Hapgood regained his own footing. He gave his frock coat a jerk to straighten it and made their audience a small bow. Rosemary marveled that his face had not flushed scarlet as her own, but perhaps it was because he truly was innocent of any inappropriate thoughts. More so than she, in any event. Taking advantage of the partial cover her brother provided, she tried to smooth her tumbled locks, but, as she could hardly scrabble along the floor for her lost hairpins, she reluctantly removed the remaining ones so at least her black tresses would hang uniformly.

"Sirrah," blustered Roscoe, advancing a step, "I demand an explanation."

"To be sure, Mr. DeWitt. Mr. Benfield. Miss Benfield." Hugh nodded at each in turn. "Miss DeWitt has spoken the truth. I have not harmed her and had no intent to harm her. I called earlier to speak with Mr. Benfield and found him from home, and Betsy admitted me to see Lionel in the meantime."

"That's so," agreed Betsy.

"Miss DeWitt arrived, having come to claim an atlas the vicar required," he continued, gesturing at the volume, "but when she made to leave, she found the door locked. Lionel had earlier excused himself, and we could only imagine Lionel bolted us in."

All eyes turned on the boy, whose own gaze darted back and forth. Just when Rosemary thought he would break down and confess, his chin rose and he declared, "I might have—bolted the door. Did, in fact, bolt it. I—wanted to ensure no one interrupted Miss DeWitt because she had *special business* with my father."

"Lionel!" said more than one of his auditors, their voices striking notes from reproach to incredulity to outrage.

Roscoe whirled on his sister. "What 'special business,' Ros? What can be the meaning of this?"

"For pity's sake," cried Rosemary. She dearly wanted to tell both her protective brother and Mr. Hapgood's impish son that they only made matters worse with their dramatics. She was hardly a tender maiden whose virtue required vigorous defense! Even if she had been reckless enough to retort on them, however, the consciousness that her loose hair hung down her back like a schoolmiss held her in check.

"It is all quite simple and not nearly deserving of all this fuss," she began, folding her hands calmly in front of her. "It is precisely what Mr. Hapgood has already described. At Lionel's request I was going to speak with his father about what sort of tutor would best suit the son. That is the business he refers to. Finding Mr. Hapgood here, I did so, and then discovered I was locked in the room. Because Mr. Benfield expected me, I decided it would be most expedient to climb out the window. This proved a trickier maneuver than I imagined, however, and I slipped from the sill and knocked down

Mr. Hapgood, who had been trying to assist me. That is the entire matter." For the first time since everyone had burst in, she turned to look at Hugh. "Have I omitted anything, Mr. Hapgood?"

There was that quirk of his mouth again, and Rosemary hardened herself against it, even as she tried to interpret it. Was it amusement? Irony? Disdain?

"An admirable account," he said. "Complete, succinct, and reasonable."

"That's that, then," spoke up the practical Miss Benfield, as Rosemary swallowed against the warmth Mr. Hapgood's praise gave her. Not disdain, then—*admiration*. "I hope you both will understand our shock and dismay at appearances."

Roscoe alone appeared doubtful. "Rosemary, are you certain that is all that happened? Would you rather speak to me apart?"

"Yes, I'm certain," she retorted, with a flash of indignation. "And I do not need to speak to you apart. If it were not exactly as I have described it, I would not have said it."

Instead of looking chastened, Roscoe gave the merest shrug. Then he unbent enough to make Hugh a stiff bow. "Please excuse my vehemence, sir."

The bow was returned, and Hugh said, "It did you credit, Mr. DeWitt. I hope my own son may be found so staunch in defending a sister's reputation."

Miss Benfield here gave Lionel's ear a tweak. "You're no gallant knight yet, my young sir. We will have a talk shortly. Locking doors and 'special business,' my eye!"

The boy had been watching the scene unfold expectantly, but when he saw everyone so determined to interpret things in such a pacific light, he looked inexplicably cast down and barely registered Miss Benfield's threat. Rosemary could not think what made him so sorry. Had he wanted to see Roscoe and his father come to blows?

Miss Benfield excused herself to check on her aged mother, but first she retrieved Rosemary's bonnet and gave her hand a squeeze when she returned it. "I will recover your hairpins later and return them, for we also must have a talk, my dear," she whispered in passing, and Rosemary hoped her dismay went unnoticed. The sharp-eyed vicar's sister most likely wanted Rosemary to give her a private accounting, one that explained the blushes and breathlessness, and Rosemary would have to come up with a brace of lies. *That* account might be succinct, if she could help it, but she could not vouch for it being 'complete' or 'reasonable.'

"Pardon me," interjected the vicar, when Miss Benfield had been followed out by Betsy, "but one thing I still do not understand. My dear Miss DeWitt, how came you to be discussing a tutor for Lionel?"

"Oh!" In all the to-do, Rosemary had completely forgotten that Mr. Benfield knew nothing of Mr. Hapgood's plans to remove Lionel from the vicarage. She threw Hugh a helpless glance, and he struck in with, "Just so, Mr. Benfield. I was hoping to speak with you at some point about how Lionel was progressing and our own family's plans, but it can wait until the morrow. You have your recital to tend to, and I—"

"We have done for the day, sir," said the vicar mildly.

"But the atlas, Mr. Benfield!" Rosemary protested.

"Never mind, my dear. With some prompting little Timmy was able to recall many of the geographical features on his own." Mr. Benfield patted her shoulder absently. "If you please, I am at liberty, Mr. Hapgood."

"I thank you, but beg that we may postpone our discussion," Hugh persisted. "I have much to meditate upon."

"By all means, by all means," said the amiable clergyman. "Perhaps you and the DeWitts would like to stay and share our humble luncheon?"

To this invitation both parties declined, and, after a brief leavetaking, soon found themselves outside. In the next instant, Mr. Hapgood was excusing himself, and, with one last glance at Rosemary, stalking off in the direction of Bramleigh.

She wanted to watch him go, but she ruthlessly turned away, pulling on her bonnet over her flowing hair and tying the ribbons as if they'd done her an injury. "However did you come to be at the vicarage, Roscoe?" Rosemary asked.

"I wasn't *at* the vicarage," he replied. "I was leaving my gig at Weston's for some repairs to the paint and met the Benfields saying they didn't know where you'd got to. Naturally, I accompanied them to make sure you had not gone missing." Taking hold of her hand, he placed it on his arm, and they began their walk back to Marchmont. The day had grown warmer, but with that tentative heat that began to hint at the coming of autumn.

"I say, Ros," said her brother after some minutes, when they had left Patterton behind them, "you look rather fetching with your hair all loose like that."

She gazed at him in wonder, both for the rarity of the compliment and the fact that it came from Roscoe. Not that her brother Norman would ever say such a thing either, but that was more because Norman was not wont to say much at all on any topic. "Thank you," she murmured.

Roscoe had more on his mind than her looks, she suspected. With the crop in his free hand, he was absently slicing the heads off weedy flowers they passed. She waited him out and was rewarded after they slipped through the hedgerow to cut across the fields. "You know, don't you," he went on then, "that what passed at the vicarage might have been turned to account?"

"Turned to account?"

"Yes. What do you think? We all burst in to find you and Hapgood flat on the floor, with your frock and hair and bonnet all awry and his arms around you—"

"They weren't *around* me!" objected Rosemary, pulling her arm from her brother's so she could clap her hands to her heating face. She remembered other details of the moment even more vividly—the firmness of the man's body, the buttons of his waistcoat digging into her belly, their breaths mingling beneath the brim of her bonnet. "I told you: I fell and he made to catch me—it was self-protection as much as anything, as you might have done, if some person were to land on you from above."

"Yes, yes, you explained that, Ros." He waved away her embarrassment and pique. "But *I* am saying that, were you not always so hopelessly honest and matter-of-fact, you might have turned such an episode to account."

Her brown eyes sparked, and she stopped dead to face him, hands curled in fists. "What in heaven's name do you mean, Roscoe? Do you mean to say, because the situation appeared compromising, I should have let myself be compromised?"

He shrugged, incorrigible. "Would it have been so bad? Don't you ever want to get married, Ros?"

"Not that way, certainly no!"

"Come now."

"No, you come! I do not see that having an unmarried sister will affect your own life in any great way. If I am a burden, it will be on our father, and when he is gone, you may have to suffer my presence at Marchmont, but I will have fortune enough of my own that I will be no drain on the estate."

"Rosemary..." Roscoe placed a placating hand on her arm, which she flung off childishly. "Rosemary, there's no need to fly into the boughs. I can't see what ails you! Don't you want to be married? I thought all women did."

Not trusting her voice to be steady enough to answer, Rosemary flounced off, but her angry strides were no match for her brother's longer legs, and he caught her easily. "I know you're not the romantic sort," he persisted. "You're happy enough to teach school and help our mother with the housekeeping, but do you never want a home of your own?"

"Does this mean you are finally going to ask that flighty Miss Porterworth to make up her mind?" demanded his sister nastily. "Otherwise, whence this sudden urge to arrange my life and send me packing?"

This time it was Roscoe who halted, and, when she drew up and looked back, already regretting her show of temper, she found him turning his beaver hat in his hands, his color high. "I'm not trying to send you packing. But—you have guessed it. I am going to ask her, Ros. I've decided. Tomorrow. When the gig is repaired and I can put my best foot forward."

"Oh—oh, Roscoe, forgive me. How out of sorts I am today." He was a provoking brother, but, in fairness to him, she recognized his remarks would not so fire her if they did not concern Mr. Hugh Hapgood and if there were not some nugget of truth in them.

She walked back to him and took both his hands in hers, penitently. "Miss Porterworth, then. You have...cared for her a long time."

"You are not wrong to call her flighty. She *is* flighty," he admitted, "but I always hoped it was because she simply wanted to be married, and, in her eagerness, she threw her net wide. I think—I hope—she'll have me."

His sister's smile was rueful. She suspected Miss Porterworth would, indeed. If not for love of Roscoe, at least for appreciation of his eligibility. He was young, wealthy enough, attractive. And was this not what Roscoe meant, when he accosted Rosemary thus? He wanted to know why she lacked that predictability shared by women of her class, that, given an opportunity, she did not leap at the chance for an establishment of her own, if the man were unobjectionable enough.

She gave his hands a squeeze meant both to apologize again and to encourage. "And if you are so fortunate with Miss Porterworth? What then?"

"Then we will rent a house in Patterton. Or Taunton, if it would please her more." He made a wry face. "I was not in town only regarding the gig. I peered in the windows at that vacant place—the one that belonged to old Simpson and his daughter before he died and she went to live with some aunt."

"You would not want to remain at Marchmont, then? There is certainly room enough, and what work you have is all in following our father and Mr. Otway around to manage it."

He grinned at her, pleased that she would assume his suit's success. Tucking her arm in his again, he set them once more in motion. "That would be the difference between you and me, Ros. You might be content to live the rest of your days under our parents' watchful eyes, but I would like to have a measure of space to myself and have my own castle to be king of, even if I could throw a stone from my castle to Marchmont."

"I did not say I would not ever like my own space," she returned. "But for a woman it is different. I will never be king of any castle; therefore, if I must be a vassal, I should wish to serve the king who rules his subjects with the lightest and wisest hand."

"Ah, here we will never agree, since I have told you time out of mind that Father indulges you far more than Norman or me.

But that is neither here nor there. Do you mean to say you think Hapgood would be a despot?"

"I fail to see what Mr. Hapgood has to do with the matter," Rosemary prickled.

"Don't be thick, Ros. You could have had Hapgood in the bag today, but you didn't want him, for some reason. Too old? Too many children? Too far away, Sussex? You might start in Sussex, but you would end back in Somerset, whenever the squire shuffles off this mortal coil."

"Oh, Roscoe. I have already said: I would not want a husband I had to catch in a trap. One who had to take me because he had no alternative."

"You might come to be fond of each other. They say Miss Alice Hapgood and that naturalist she trapped are happy enough now."

"Yes, and Alice Hapgood was a lovely young creature whom Mr. Joseph Tierney might have chosen on his own, eventually. Whereas..."

"Now, you're well enough," her brother said stalwartly. "And Hapgood's no spring chicken."

"Roscoe, I beg you—stop speaking of Mr. Hapgood."

"—And who says you two might not come to be fond of each other as well?" he ignored her. "I only say you must give these things a chance."

"Oh, honestly! I do not see where you come by your expertise. Miss Porterworth has not accepted you yet."

But he was not to be put off. "If the man came to realize the benefits of the match and offered for you on his own, would you send him off with a flea in his ear?"

She stared at him. First little Hetty Hapgood, and now her own brother! Was all the world turned matchmaker?

"It matters not," she answered unwillingly. "The only suitors I have attracted thus far were drawn by my portion. Someone like Mr. Hapgood has no need of that."

"No need for your money, true enough. But any man encumbered with three young children and having the means to remedy the situation would be a fool not to remarry." He spoke with the dismissive note of a free young man who could not imagine how some people made such a muck of things. "Are you saying you wouldn't have him on any terms, Ros?"

He addressed his question to the brim of her bonnet, as his sister had dropped her gaze to the grass below their feet. "I...I did not say that." The confession came dragging from her. But it was only, she feared, the truth.

She might not be willing to entrap Hugh Hapgood, but if he came to her by his own volition—even if he sought only a helpmate and a schoolmistress to his children—she did not think she would have the strength to refuse him. No, not even if it meant little Hetty crowing with triumph over her.

"I would be satisfied to accept him," she said, so low that he had to lean to catch it, "if I felt I at least had his respect."

Roscoe gave her arm a swing, his mind returning to the buxom Miss Porterworth, who might soon be his very own Miss Porterworth. Ah, then he would be the happiest man in the world, and all the rest might fight over the scraps! In this generous mood he declared, "Well, the more fool he, if he don't. But you only have yourself to blame for his escape today, then, Ros, since you wouldn't let me duel any sense into him."

# Chapter Twelve

**In me thou seest the glowing of such fire
That on the ashes of his youth doth lie,
As the deathbed whereon it must expire,
Consum'd with that which it was nourish'd by.
—Shakespeare, *Sonnet 73* (1609)**

It would have confused Rosemary further, had she been able to observe the disturbing Mr. Hapgood after he left them, for he walked not a quarter mile in the direction of Bramleigh before he stopped and leant against a stile. Then, growing too warm after some minutes, he retreated some ways to a small copse, where he might rest on a stump in the shade.

He ought to have been pondering the Lionel situation: when and how he would inform the Benfields of the boy's withdrawal; what sort of tutor he might engage, and how one went about finding a suitable candidate; how to balance the desires of his son for, effectively, a playmate, with someone more qualified to prepare him for university—but it was none of these things troubling him, try as he might to focus on them.

No, Hugh found his wandering attention stubbornly fixing instead on Miss Rosemary DeWitt. Her vivid eyes. The length and weight of her body pressed against his when they fell to the floor. How she scrambled up, her color coming and going, a wave of lustrous dark hair loosed from its pins and streaming nearly to her waist. And then when she peered around her belligerent brother and Hugh saw all her hair unconfined. It was astonishing. As if the plain, unexceptional woman he had classed in his mind had been transformed, transfigured, in an instant into an alluring mermaid.

Something must be desperately wrong with him. He had been too long without female company. Was he not done with the foolish parts of life? He had thought himself past the age when heat in the blood drove a man's actions, and yet here he sat, working to regain ownership of his thoughts and feelings. As if all his experience had taught him nothing.

It was nonsense, of course. Merely the shock of physical contact, paired with the suspicions and insinuations of that brother of hers, putting ideas in his head. And the fact that Hugh was still in a muddle about it was all the more embarrassing when he considered how calmly Miss DeWitt had addressed them all. Though their spill might have upset her when it occurred, she recovered speedily enough. Recovered and wasted no time in quashing any notions of compromised virtue or Steps That Must Be Taken.

If she had not done so—if she had not so effectively stamped out the danger like a smoldering ember—would he have taken up the cause to prove his innocence?

Surely he would have. Nothing *had* happened, after all, and Miss DeWitt was no lissome miss of sixteen. The thought of compromising situations, when the parties involved were so advanced in years as they—why, it was material for a stage farce!

But he no sooner called Miss DeWitt "advanced in years" than his uncooperative thoughts presented him once more with her dark hair, her bosom pressed to his chest, those eyes flaring with anger or amusement. Very well, very well—she was not quite as old as he, he amended. And apparently *he* was not quite as old as all that, either.

Nevertheless.

Perhaps he should call on her the following day, to ensure she harbored no ill will about the affair. It would be the well-mannered thing to do.

But Hugh was not a man to deceive himself for long. If he were to call, he knew it would be to test whether his madness outlasted the passing of the day. If he were to call and find the mermaid vanished, leaving only prim, plain, reasonable, and kindly Miss DeWitt, he would be cured. He would shake his head in disbelief over the short-lived fit and take up the reins of responsibility again.

Yes, that would be the best plan. He would call, be disillusioned, and continue with his life, a wiser man, all in the space of twenty minutes. He must! There was work to be done and decisions to be made, decisions not clouded by fantasies of a second youth.

Having made up his mind, Hugh resumed his walk back to Bramleigh and the company of his family, but whether he was equally successful in banishing Miss DeWitt from his thoughts the remainder of the day is known only to him.

Hetty heard the pebbles ping against the glass. Throwing one wary glance at her cousin Edith's bed to make sure she slept on, she climbed quietly from her own and stole over to the window.

It was Lionel, of course. She didn't think he could see more than the white of her nightgown, but she waved and nodded and pointed at herself and then at the ground. *Wait for me. I'm coming*.

The door opening from the kitchen onto the garden gave a fearful creak, and Lionel was on her in an instant, fingers to his lips as if *she* had made the ruckus, but Hetty swallowed her indignation in her eagerness for news. "What happened on Papa's visit? He spoke not a word about it to anyone when he returned, and I did not dare to ask. When will he take us away?"

"Shhh! You pipe like a piccolo, Het. I don't know when we're going. Papa didn't even speak to Mr. Benfield alone because the vicar wasn't home when Papa called."

"Then what are you come over to tell me?" she said more quietly. "I was nearly asleep."

"Well, sleep, then, if you don't want to hush up and listen," retorted her brother maddeningly. To his satisfaction he saw Hetty heave a deep breath and press her lips together, determined to be silent, and then Lionel heaved his own sigh. After all, his news was not good.

"I tried that silly plan of yours, Het. The one about locking Papa and Miss DeWitt somewhere together and hoping he would compromise her—hush! Hush! Be quiet and I'll tell you all."

"Start at the very beginning, Lionel!" she commanded, and he did. How their father and Miss DeWitt chanced to be at the vicarage together; how Lionel managed to flee the library and bolt them in; how he lured Betsy outside to the henhouse with tales of a fox; and how, after the Benfields and Mr. DeWitt came upon them outside, they all returned to find Miss DeWitt and their father in the most compromising position imaginable. When he came to describe said position, Hetty's eyes grew enormous in the moonlight.

"Then is it done, Lionel? Papa has been forced to offer for her?"

"No."

"No? You mean to say he would not come up to scratch, even with a vicar looking on?"

"I don't know what he might have, Het, because Miss DeWitt would not give him the opportunity. My father tried to explain what had happened, but, of course, in a situation like that, one can't just take the man's word for it, you know," he added knowledgeably. "So Miss DeWitt took over, and she was so...calm and reasonable about it and said nothing at all had happened, and so it ended by Papa doing nothing and nothing coming of it. It's like I told you, Het—I don't think Miss DeWitt is at all anxious to marry, much as it might suit us, and we had better resign ourselves."

"How easily you give up!" flamed Hetty. But, truth be told, she was more angry at herself than him. If only she had not cornered Miss DeWitt at Bramleigh and put her on her guard! It was all very well for Lionel to speak of resigning himself—he still hoped to be allowed to remain in Somerset.

Faced with the failure of their first plan, she must somehow think of a new strategy, one that would lull Miss DeWitt into complacency.

Lionel gave a noisy, drawn-out yawn. "Well, I have told my bad news. Maybe a new idea will come to us in the morning, and you are shivering. Night, Het."

She didn't know if she would be able to fall asleep when she stole back to bed, but at least she would be warmer. Without answering him, Hetty turned on her heel and stole back inside.

After passing a restless night, Hugh awoke at last to find the sun high and the Hapgoods of Bramleigh well into their day. So much for a morning call upon Miss DeWitt—the afternoon must do, and, rubbing the dreams from his eyes, he rather felt as if he had spent the last few hours with the woman.

Breakfast had long passed, and Hugh had been visitor at Bramleigh long enough to know that any request for food at this hour would arouse the cook's ire, but no sooner had he dismissed his man and ventured down than he found Hetty waiting for him. She looked rather pale and fatigued, but her hair and dress were neat.

The former constraint had come upon them again in recent days, but she stood up from her seat on the stairs and patted his forearm. "Good morning, Papa. Look—I have saved you some buttered bread."

"Thank you." Briefly he rested an awkward hand on her bright head before taking the napkin bundle she offered. "Where is everyone this morning?"

"The squire has gone for a ride, Margaret and Edith are seeing to the chickens, and their mother is in her chamber, as she always seems to be." Hetty followed him into the empty breakfast room. "Should you like some tea or cocoa? We can ring for Dorcas."

And send Dorcas to her doom, to face Button the cook, he supposed. He shook his head. "The bread will serve."

"Papa…" Timidly Hetty drew out the chair beside his to keep him company. "Did you see Lionel yesterday?"

"I did."

"And must we return to Sussex now?"

His brows drew together. "I had thought you were glad to return with Rosie—that you preferred that to the school in Worthing. And that you would be glad to have Lionel with you."

"I—I had thought so, too," admitted his daughter. "Only I find I rather like it here with our cousins in Somerset."

Hugh remained silent, chewing his bread. So she, like Lionel, preferred Bramleigh to their house in Crawley, and her Hapgood cousins to the Sidneys. What, then? If he were to exercise his rights as their father, remove all his children to Crawley, hire a rambunctious tutor for Lionel and as plain a governess as could be found in England for the girls, would he only be racking his brain six months hence for another solution to their unhappiness?

"I must work," he said only, "and my work is in Sussex. Nor can we stay indefinitely with the Richard Hapgoods. Are you saying you would rather I find a school in Somerset for you and Rosalie?"

"N-no," she faltered. Her hand crept out and touched his sleeve again. "But might we not all...take lodgings? And stay a little longer? Rosie would get strong in the country air." This had been the only plan that occurred to her after hearing the failure of their first. They must have more time, and perhaps her father's and Miss DeWitt's eyes would open of their own accord.

"Lodgings?" repeated Hugh.

"You might have Aunt Lavinia send your banking books—or you could fetch them when you fetch Rosie," Hetty hurried onward. "They have managed without you while we have been here. And you only visited Cuckfield and East Grinstead and Ryegate from time to time, Papa, and you might still do that, and the post is so very good and fast now." When he only continued to stare at her, Hetty felt her insides shrink, but she was too far gone to stop now. "And—and Lionel could continue at the Benfields if he liked, only, he might live with us in the lodgings if you preferred, and—and—and perhaps Rosie and I could be day pupils at a school here, or share a governess with our cousin Edith."

"Your cousin Edith has no governess," said her father, with the air of one shipwrecked in deep waters, floundering for any spar to save himself.

"Only because the squire cannot pay for one at present," Hetty answered baldly. "I asked Edith. And she said she would dearly like to continue her education, and that though Margaret might know nearly as much as Miss Hapgood and Cousin Alice did, which she doubted, nevertheless Margaret has no patience to teach. So, you see, it would be an act of charity to stay in Somerset and help our cousin and it would certainly help the squire, who isn't entirely well, you know."

"You seem to have given this all some thought."

"Yes." She swallowed and shut her eyes for one moment before her final plunge. "You know how Mr. Benfield and Miss DeWitt plan a recital for their pupils—"

"Miss DeWitt has said she only teaches the poorer girls of the parish," he blurted, jarred to hear her name. "Ladies of her class do not go out for governessing."

"I know, Papa," replied Hetty patiently, though she actually had not known this before. "But I thought she and the vicar might help us both with finding lodgings and finding a governess. I don't think the squire would know much of either because our Hapgood relations keep much to themselves."

The girl was observant, quick. Hugh regarded her thoughtfully, and Hetty did her best to look wheedling and innocent. She must have succeeded because he said at last, "I will consider what you have said, my dear. You must trust me to choose what is best for our family."

"Yes, Papa."

He gave her a gentle push. "Why do you not find your cousins? I have business today."

Business! What business could it be? Had he listened at all to what she had said?

Turning to hide her face, her small features screwed up in a prayer: *Only let him consider what I've said and let us stay here, and I promise I will never ask for anything again!*

# Chapter Thirteen

**Ten thousand happinesses wait on you.**
—Thomas Otway, *Friendship in Fashion* (1678)

Marchmont being twice the distance from Bramleigh as the Benfields' vicarage, Hugh borrowed one of the squire's horses and set off. He passed through Patterton, his mind full of Hetty's preposterous suggestions (they *were* preposterous, were they not?), but when he found himself in open country again his thoughts turned once more to Miss DeWitt.

He hoped he would find her plain and humdrum again today. Dull and colorless and in no way interesting. Though—had he ever thought her so? Even the first time he met her? He had thought her plain in appearance, yes, but not unpleasant. And never dull or colorless in her personality.

Why Hugh himself had taken extra care with his appearance he could not say. He was not a man overly concerned with his attire, but he had rejected Bundish's first two attempts at tying his cravat, after the man had to wait hours while Hugh slept uncharacteristically on and on.

Marchmont was a classical edifice, three modest wings surrounding a court, all faced in smooth golden stone and occupying the lowest part of a hollow, like a jewel in the palm of a hand. It was neither so stately as Viscount Marlton's Pattergees, nor so rambling and ancient as Bramleigh, but it was a property any man raised to the knighthood as Sir Cosmo was must be proud of, and which even kindly neighbors could not help but think was more elegant than he deserved.

The various servants who relieved Hugh of his horse, who greeted him at the entrance, and who ushered him into the drawing room seemed all to be suppressing excitement of some kind, but Hugh had too much on his mind to wonder at it. The butler announced him with a ringing, "Mr. Hugh Hapgood!" and Hugh saw Sir Cosmo and Lady DeWitt flanking their daughter Miss DeWitt, the three of them bathed in warm light from the open casement and clutching each other's hands.

"Pardon me," said Hugh. "Am I interrupting?"

"Mr. Hapgood, Mr. Hapgood, you are very welcome to Marchmont," cried Sir Cosmo, releasing his daughter's clasp and coming forward with a hasty bow. "Far from being an interruption, you have come at a most auspicious time."

Hugh raised questioning eyebrows, even as he made his own bow and threw one lightning glance at Miss DeWitt, who seemed to hang back. Something was different about her this morning, but he could not gaze long enough to discover what it was.

"You must congratulate us, Mr. Hapgood," Sir Cosmo continued, rubbing his hands together. "We have received this day the very best sort of news."

"The very best," murmured Lady DeWitt.

Hugh felt his breath catch, even as Sir Cosmo could no longer restrain himself and proclaimed, "A wedding! At long last, the first among our children."

Something invisible seized Hugh around his middle, rendering him unable to move or respond for some interminable space, but, with an effort, he beat it back and heard himself saying, "I do congratulate you, Sir Cosmo, Lady DeWitt. What joy. Miss—Miss DeWitt, I wish you all happiness."

"Me?" breathed Rosemary, suddenly scarlet. "Sir—you mistake us. It is not I who am engaged."

"It's Roscoe, my older son," beamed Sir Cosmos, grabbing Hugh's hand and giving it a shake. "He's about here somewhere—went to find his brother Norman, to tell him. Roscoe engaged to Miss Porterworth, don't you know?"

"Ah," said Hugh. The painful constriction released him as suddenly as it had come on, and he added, "Pardon me. Yes, your son Roscoe. I wish *him* all happiness." For the first time he gazed directly at Miss DeWitt and his grin flashed. "Not that I wish you *un*happiness, Miss DeWitt, as a result of my misunderstanding."

Still embarrassed, she managed a smile of her own, and he realized what looked different about her: she had styled her hair in a new manner. It was higher atop her head but pulled back more loosely, and her maid had been more lavish with the iron in curling it. Whoever's decision it had been, it had been an inspired one. The softer swoops of her hair filled out her face's narrower angles, and the higher lines drew one's gaze upward to her best feature, those golden-brown eyes. She looked decidedly *un*plain. *Un*dull. *Un*colorless.

"We plan a ball," Lady DeWitt was saying, after her husband finally released Hugh's hand.

"And you must carry word back to Bramleigh that we hope the squire and his lady (and you, sir) will grace us with your attendance. I suppose the squire's two younger daughters could not be prevailed upon...?"

"Dear sir," protested his wife, "they are not yet of age for balls."

"Just so, just so. Well, then, let it be the squire and his wife and you, Mr. Hapgood."

With difficulty Hugh recalled his thoughts and made an appropriate reply. He doubted his cousin's wife could be prevailed upon to leave her chamber for a ball, but it would be for them to make their own excuses. He had other matters to attend to now, such as speaking aside with Miss DeWitt.

This purpose was thwarted anew by the entrance of Roscoe and Norman DeWitt, and the whole engagement had to be discussed again—its origins, history and fulfillment—and congratulations given again and received, and the plans for the ball ventilated at excruciating length. Roscoe throughout was swelled with pride and could not hear enough on his good fortune to have secured such a prize, though Hugh privately thought the chattering and flirtatious Miss Porterworth would drive quieter men like himself to drink.

"I will be the happiest man in England," declared Roscoe for what felt like the twelfth time. "Constance is all that I could desire." Then followed a rehearsal of his determination to take lodgings in Patterton until the couple could find a fitting home of their own, a plan countered by Sir Cosmo and Lady DeWitt, who urged them to make their home at Marchmont.

"You might have the east wing all to yourselves," suggested Lady DeWitt, "and you and Miss Porterworth might make them over however you wish. And then she need not take housekeeping upon herself all at once."

"We would not trouble you a jot," Sir Cosmo put in. "Once a man has married, he requires his own space, and your mother and I would respect that."

"Never mind my presence in the east wing," murmured Norman DeWitt dryly, in his sole contribution to the argument. "I'm sure I will clear out."

"Sometimes a man wants his own castle," their older son said, not even acknowledging his brother's jest, but Hugh could tell from his musing tone that Roscoe had not ruled out being won over.

"Lodgings in Patterton are hardly a castle," Sir Cosmo pointed out. "Are they Rosemary? My dear, help convince your brother."

"It is not I he must listen to now, but rather Miss Porterworth," said Rosemary. "In any event, I am sure we have tried Mr. Hapgood's goodwill long enough. We need not subject him to every detail of the deliberations."

Hugh hoped his impatience had not been so obvious, but he gladly availed himself of the opportunity to address her. "One can never hear too much of happiness, I imagine."

She met this with a skeptical expression (which almost drew a laugh from him), while her family made the expected apologies for their preoccupation before launching directly back into the subject. At the least, everyone having paid lip service to what politeness demanded, Hugh could now make his way across the drawing room to address the object of his call in a lowered voice. "I hope you are recovered from the excitement of yesterday's tumble, Miss DeWitt."

"I was recovered within five minutes of it having occurred," was her answer. This sounded dismissive, even to her own ears, and she added with an effort, "You as well, I trust?"

"Yes." That is, he had suffered no physical harm. His mental equilibrium was another matter entirely.

Reaching for an embroidery hoop, she seated herself on the light blue Windsor chair nearest her and, after a beat, he settled on the matching sofa. What had he meant to say, on this call? Roscoe DeWitt's engagement and Miss DeWitt's hair had driven it from his mind. Ah—right. The purpose of the call was to prove to himself that she was not a particularly attractive woman, but he did not seem to be making progress toward that goal. His eye traveled from that bewitching hair to her equally dark, downcast lashes.

"You have known Miss Porterworth for some time, it seems?" he asked, after casting about for a way to make her speak.

"All her life, since I am some ten years her senior." No sooner did the words escape her than she twitched. What earthly reason did she have, to remind this man she was an on-the-shelf spinster?

Not that Hugh noticed her discomfiture, being too busy upbraiding himself. He had not intended to imply he thought her old. He realized she was not so young as Miss Porterworth, but he didn't mind that, being nearer forty than thirty himself. What would he and a Miss Porterworth ever find to talk about?

"All her life? How fortunate for Miss Porterworth, then, to have so admirable an example set," Hugh managed. *Lord*. This was even worse! It sounded like flattery. Possibly even flirtation. What was he about? He had better leave, if such words were going to tumble from him, unbidden.

Rosemary shifted in her seat, pulling her needle of scarlet yarn through the material stretched across the hoop. If Mr. Hapgood were her brother Roscoe, she might interpret this comment sarcastically, but surely that was not the case here—he hardly knew her well enough to tease. Could he be sincere? But, if he were, would that be any better? Frivolous, coquettish Constance Porterworth taking solemn, plain, dull Miss DeWitt as an example?

She kept her gaze on the pattern of her work.

With something like desperation, he plunged in again. "I was sorry yesterday to delay or interrupt the preparations for your pupils' recital."

Finally, the tawny eyes flashed up to meet his, and she even smiled. "There was no harm done, Mr. Hapgood. My girls had already spoken their pieces and learned from Mr. and Miss Benfield their order and to sit quietly in the pews awaiting their turn."

"How many pupils have you in your school?"

"There are nearly a dozen altogether. Mr. Benfield takes seven of the village boys, and I have four girls in my charge. Sometimes one more, sometimes one less, depending on the season and the requirements of their families."

"And when does the recital take place?"

"This Sunday after service. The villagers have too much work during this time of year to take another morning or afternoon for such an activity. In fact, it has been something of a battle to hold a recital in the summer at all. Mr. Benfield waited through the barley and wheat harvests, but he wore them down, and they agreed the oats were too much to ask."

There it was again: the urge to smile. Whatever it was about Miss DeWitt, she made him feel more light-hearted than he had in years. "Are all the pupils farmers' children, then?"

"Not all, but here in the country we all of us bow to the agricultural calendar. Perhaps it is different in…Crawley?"

"It is, though we too have our wheat, barley and oats. Crawley is a busy town, a market town, perhaps five times the size of Patterton. We have many coaches between London and Brighton along the turnpike, and travelers frequently pass the night."

"Our corner of Somerset must seem very quiet to you."

"It does, but that does not mean it is not pleasing." He frowned here and rubbed his fingers back and forth on his knees. "In fact, I would say my children prefer Somerset."

Rosemary's needle paused. She knew Lionel preferred to stay where he was—he had made himself quite clear. Did Hetty as well, or was her supposed preference part and parcel of her matchmaking efforts? Mr. Hapgood's frown must mean he found his children's opinions inconvenient—of course they were—and her own interference in his affairs threw her firmly in the nuisance camp.

She was spared answering by Mr. Hapgood beginning again: "I have not yet spoken with Lionel about removing him from the Benfields'...but you and he have broached the matter already."

"Mr. Hapgood, Lionel did ask me to speak to you, as I told you yesterday. Perhaps he felt it would give his opinions increased weight. Otherwise I would never have dreamt of meddling again, especially after I accosted you at Bramleigh."

"Yes, you mentioned Lionel calling upon your educational experience," nodded Hugh. "But was there no other reason he wanted you particularly to speak to me?"

Rosemary wrestled with this a minute. How could she tell this man she hardly knew that his son found him forbidding and distant? "I suppose that, in our few conversations, Lionel and I have managed to forge a connection of sorts. Perhaps it is easier to speak of one's troubles to strangers who have no stake in the matter. I have kept my word to your son, in any event, so you need not fear I will bother you with any more recommendations."

A silence fell and Hugh was surprised to discover the rest of the DeWitts were no longer in the drawing room. He had been so intent on his conversation with Miss DeWitt he had not noticed them leave. They were alone.

A dozen thoughts chased each other through his head. What would she think, if he were to ask, *Why do you think my son does not confide in me?* Or, *My daughter Hetty recommends we take lodgings in Patterton and I supply a governess for my girls and my cousin's daughter—what would* you *counsel*?

And why, precisely, did Hugh crave her opinion? Did he, like his son, find Miss DeWitt so appealing a confidante?

He did. Or, at least, he found her alarmingly appealing, and he wanted to confide in her. He rose abruptly, running a finger between his neckcloth and his throat. "I have stayed too long. Please give Sir Cosmo and Lady DeWitt my regards again."

Rosemary laid her embroidery hoop aside and stood as well. "I will."

She curtsied, but he made no move to go, instead blurting, "Are there many lodgings in Patterton?"

"I—I don't know. My brother spoke of one, which used formerly to belong to a Mr. Simpson. Perhaps there are others."

He bowed in acknowledgement, and she bobbed again. Still he made no move to go.

"This recital—are visitors welcome to attend?"

Rosemary stared. A few of the parish benefactors would be present, of course, and her girls were braced for this brush with greatness, but she could not imagine anyone *not* compelled by duty would want to see a collection of modestly literate village children speak pieces.

Interpreting her expression rightly, Hugh hastened to add, "My daughters Hetty and Rosalie were not particularly happy at the school where I placed them in Worthing, even before the scarlet fever hit. I should be sorry if their last impression of schooling were an unpleasant one. Only Hetty is with me, but Rosie tends to follow her lead in all things. If Hetty were to say education and school were not so bad, I believe it would not take long for Rosie to be convinced."

Rosemary could not say she was anxious to see the girl again, after Hetty had accosted her at Bramleigh and made so bold as to try to arrange Rosemary's life. Especially if the girl's keen wits comprehended Rosemary's growing willingness to cooperate. But, like so many things, this could not be uttered aloud, and at last she only murmured, "Mr. Hapgood, as the recital will be held in the church, I suppose anyone at all who wanders by will be welcome to enter."

"Our presence would be tolerated, you say, but perhaps you and Mr. Benfield have objections to our appearance?"

She shook her head. "No, Mr. Hapgood. No objections."

"Very well. We will see you Sunday, then."

"Sunday."

With one last bow, he took his leave.

# Chapter Fourteen

**...Prithee, how can money be better employed than in the service of fine women?**
**—Fanny Burney, *Evelina* (1778)**

"If Papa does not come soon, his tea will be cold," complained Miss Margaret Hapgood, "and we dare not ask Button to warm it."

"Never mind your father," fluttered Mrs. Hapgood faintly from her seat by the fire. "The day is so lovely I'm certain he could not bear to be indoors. Bring me a cup, Edith. Margaret will surely spill it."

"Papa was blustering and bellowing in quite his usual manner again," said Edith, taking the cup from an offended Margaret and carrying it to her mother. "You are right, Mama. I am certain he is out with Caractacus."

"He isn't with Crack," Margaret declared, "because I heard him muttering about how it was a 'demmed shame' family obligations interfered with care for one's hounds."

"Don't curse, dear."

"I'm not, Mama. I'm *quoting*. He said *that*, and later I saw him walk off with Cousin Hugh in the direction of Patterton."

"Patterton?" murmured Edith. "I suppose they went to see about Lionel."

"Mr. Hugh Hapgood has no need for Papa to accompany him, if he is only going to see about Lionel," her sister pointed out in a scathing tone.

"Hetty, Hetty," moaned Mrs. Hapgood, "do not kick your feet so. It is giving me the headache and scuffing the furniture. I cannot think why your father did not take you as well, child. I am sure he has forgotten all about you."

Hetty blanched at the reproof. She had been on her very best behavior ever since she and her father returned from Sussex, but she knew Mrs. Hapgood still thought of her as "that very naughty girl" because of the mischief she caused when the eldest Miss Hapgood was still at home.

"Tea?" Edith asked her sympathetically. "Biscuit?"

Hetty accepted the offerings, but she drew further rebukes from the highly-strung Mrs. Hapgood because it was so difficult to remain still. She fidgeted and paced and dropped crumbs. She tried confining herself to the window seat, that she might look out for her father, but as the windows opened on the rear of Bramleigh, she knew she would not see him returning from the direction of Patterton. When

Dorcas was summoned to build up the fire for her ever-cold mistress, Hetty bounced over to the open door to peep out and listen.

"Sit down, child!" Mrs. Hapgood said again, waving distraught hands before her face, as if the wind caused by Hetty's restlessness blew her about.

"They have returned," the girl announced, flying back to the window seat.

"—It will do, it will do," the squire was saying dismissively as the men entered. With a curt nod at his family, he strode over to take the cup of tea Margaret was pouring for their cousin Hugh. "Well, Edie, we have had a day's business, to be sure," he boomed. "What do you say to having a governess?"

Edith's eyes were wide, and it was left for Margaret to burst in with, "We can't afford a governess, Papa. Don't you remember? After Alice's marriage portion and Uncle Alec's difficulty with the woman he—"

"Don't speak of her!" shrieked Mrs. Hapgood. "That dreadful woman my brother Alec had to lay out money for—"

"*Papa* laid out the money," Margaret reminded her. "And now there is Elfrida's marriage portion, although Mr. Frederick Tierney has not yet asked for it to be handed over."

The squire grumbled at this. "I am not certain elopers may demand marriage portions."

"I hope Mr. Frederick Tierney does not depend on Elfie's money, since it could amount to no more than ten pounds until next Quarter Day," said Edith, "and I thought you were pleased they eloped,

Papa, because then there was no need for a trousseau or wedding breakfast."

"Mr. Frederick Tierney has no need of Elfie's ten pounds, Edith," Margaret switched tacks with a roll of her eyes. "He's rich as Crocuses."

"Don't you mean Crowsies?" asked Edith.

"Croesus, I think" interposed Hugh with a cough. "Rich as Croesus."

"Creases Who?" demanded the squire. "Never heard of him."

"He was an old king of somewhere, Papa," explained Margaret. "A rich one. Are we sure he wasn't Crocuses?"

"This is what I mean!" cried the squire, thwacking the back of the sofa with the palm of his hand to regain the floor. "See how your education is wanting? Not that I set any store by kings of no-account countries. But it's time we mended matters."

"But how *will* we afford a governess?" Margaret pressed, with a sidewise glance at Cousin Hugh. If Elfie were still at home, she would be pressing her younger sisters' toes and giving them stern looks that meant *You must not discuss such matters before our cousins, especially since Cousin Hugh is the heir to Bramleigh!*

"Funds, funds," said the squire airily. "It has all been arranged. In any event, it seems our cousins, the Hugh Hapgoods, will be remaining in Somerset for the near future—" (here a squeal of joy escaped Hetty, who began to hop up and down with excitement, while a squeal of dismay escaped Mrs. Hapgood, who fumbled for her hartshorn bottle) "—and since the girls will require a governess, and we have a perfectly good schoolroom at Bramleigh, you will all study together."

Both Margaret and Edith tried to express their surprise and approbation for this plan, but they were hampered by having to flank their mother and fan her back to full consciousness.

"Oh, oh!" gasped Mrs. Hapgood, the back of her hand to her forehead as she squeezed her eyes tight shut. "How hard it is to be left in peace! Are the vultures still circling?"

"What vultures, ma'am?" asked Edith, earning herself a sharp dig from one of Margaret's elbows.

Their mother tried to struggle up again, caught sight of Hugh Hapgood with his frightful daughter still clinging to him, and decided to feign a relapse.

Hugh could see where he was not wanted and tactfully announced that he and Hetty were going for a walk. They had barely stepped through the casement to the lawn before the swell of voices erupted behind them, above which he caught his cousin's wife, sounding now not at all feeble: "Richard! Are they to stay until we are cold and in our graves? What deal have you struck with the devil?"

Hetty regarded her father with questioning eyes. "Papa, is it my fault that your cousin's wife wishes us gone?"

"No, my dear. You have caused some consternation here in recent months, but I suspect she objects more to the fact that I am the heir to the estate. She would oppose any person in my situation. I am just a placeholder."

"But, Papa, we have money of our own. We do not covet theirs."

He gave her a half-smile. "Did you not only yesterday beg that we might stay in Somerset longer? You may not covet their money, but you seem to covet Bramleigh."

Trotting by his side (though he tried to shorten his strides), she considered this. *Did* she covet Bramleigh? She loved Somerset, yes, and her cousins, and being near Lionel, but Bramleigh itself was rather dilapidated and drafty and the grounds bedraggled, and the cook Button was a termagant. The main reason to draw out their time here was so that Papa and Miss DeWitt could fall in love, but, even if things wound to that sought-after conclusion, would she still not rather live here than in Crawley? It did not take her long to realize she would.

"I think you are right, Papa," Hetty confessed slowly. "And your cousin's wife is right as well, then, to call me a vulture. Though I do believe I would be happy anywhere in Somerset. It need not be Bramleigh. I told you it could be lodgings."

He stopped, his smile spreading now. "Funny you should mention lodgings again. It so happens that the squire and I visited a house in Patterton that was to-let, and, with the squire vouching for my character, I have signed a lease. It is a cozy place, but it will fit you and me and Rosie, my man Bundish, and a servant named Olcott. And the cook from the Swan will provide our board."

By the time he finished his speech, Hetty was clapping her hands and hopping about again. "Oh! Oh! I am so glad! But you haven't forgotten the governess, have you, Papa? Will our lodgings fit the governess as well?"

"They will not."

"But you said—"

"I said you would have a governess and share her with Edith. Here is the bargain my cousin and I have struck: he will house and feed the governess and provide the schoolroom at Bramleigh, and I will pay her wages." He did not think it worthwhile to mention that he had also promised the squire an additional sum that would offset the governess' room and board, so that, what with getting rid of the Hugh Hapgoods and *their* room and board, as well as his married daughters' room and board, the squire would be better off than he had been in years.

"Oh, it is too wonderful, Papa!" Hetty cried, hugging herself and then him again. "Thank you, thank you, thank you. And now Lionel may stay with the Benfields and Rosie may get strong and healthy." And her father and Miss DeWitt would have months and months to realize they might do better married than apart! And she, Hetty, would have more time to make Miss DeWitt forget all about their scene at Bramleigh, so that Miss DeWitt might get over her aversion to Hetty and decide, after all, that marrying a rich man was not so bad, even if he did come with three motherless children.

"When will we remove there, to our lodgings?" she asked finally, when her racing thoughts had slowed enough.

"In a fortnight or so. I must visit Crawley again to settle matters, and I must fetch Rosie, of course. And somehow, I must then find and hire this governess," he added with a frown. "Perhaps by the end of September you will begin lessons."

"How will you find our governess, Papa?"

"I—I suppose I will advertise. I believe that is the usual method. I will copy another advertisement." She suspected he was thinking aloud and deciding as he went along.

"Might you not...consult Mr. Benfield and...Miss DeWitt?" she suggested, almost choking on Miss DeWitt's name. "Because they are teachers themselves?"

He began walking again and was looking off into the distance. "Yes. That would be wise, would it not?"

Hetty didn't answer, not wanting to interrupt his thoughts if they chanced to alight on Miss DeWitt, and her silence paid off when he continued after some minutes, "Tomorrow they are having a recital of their parish school pupils after their church service. Should you like to attend with me? I will address them afterwards."

She weighed this. She would very much like to see Miss DeWitt again, but would Miss DeWitt like to see her? Had she not just determined that Miss DeWitt must forget all about Hetty's interference? Only see how Miss DeWitt had wriggled out of Lionel's attempt to compromise her with Papa! Hetty could not be absolutely certain that it was not her own actions which had put Miss DeWitt on her guard and made her resistant. But, if she stayed away, how could she observe for herself whether Miss DeWitt liked Papa any better now, or he her?

She would go to the recital, she decided. Go and be an angel and pretend she had never been otherwise, and maybe that would allay Miss DeWitt's fears.

Hetty's hand stole into her father's. "Yes, Papa. Please. Take me with you. I should very much like to attend."

# Chapter Fifteen

**Th'am'rous Heathen comes to Church to view His female Goddess dizen'd in her Pew.**
**—Edward Ward, *Nuptial Dialogues and Debates* (1710)**

So preoccupied was Hugh with the momentous undertakings in his own life that he forgot to announce Roscoe DeWitt's betrothal, and the Hapgoods of Bramleigh were left to learn of it via their maid-of-all-work Dorcas, sister to Tabitha, a maid at Pattergees, home of the Honorable Miss Birdlow...

"There's to be an engagement ball, Miss," Dorcas marveled, absently brushing Margaret's hair into her eyes. "And Tabby says Miss Birdlow's maid Fiers says Miss Birdlow is fair beside herself that Miss Porterworth will take precedence over her, and her a viscount's daughter."

Margaret parted her hair and peered through it. "A ball! I don't suppose we'll be invited."

"Whole county will be invited, Tabby says." Dorcas screwed Margaret's hair into a not-inexpert knot atop her head, but then she dropped Margaret's ribbon and had to let all Margaret's hair spill down her head again.

"Yes," sighed Margaret, "but not girls who aren't *out*. And without Elfie or Alice to go, I will never know what it was like because Mama will surely refuse and Papa could hardly go alone."

"We'll find out, for certain," insisted Dorcas, holding up the ribbon like a prize. "Miss Birdlow will attend, and her maid will tell Tabby about it, and Tabby will tell me, and I will tell you."

"Yes," Margaret sighed again, "but that is not exactly the same as attending oneself."

Edith banged into the room. "Papa says to hurry or we will be late for church."

Margaret turned crossly on her stool. "Is Hetty even awake yet? I'm never the last one ready."

"Hetty and Cousin Hugh have already left because they're going to Mr. Benfield's church in Patterton today."

"Mr. Benfield's church! Was it because they wanted to hear the banns read for Mr. DeWitt?"

"What banns?"

Then there was the whole business to go through again, with frequent interruptions from Dorcas, so that, by the time the girls scrambled downstairs, their father was in a fever of impatience, and Margaret and Edith had almost to chase him to Bramleigh Downs.

Hugh and Hetty, on the other hand, arrived at Mr. Benfield's church at the time they would have chosen, when most of the congregation was seated and would take no notice of any strangers. In the penultimate pew Hetty sat upon her knees, that she might see over the heads and hats. That must be them—in the very front pew, on the right-hand side—the family from Marchmont. She had never seen Sir Cosmo or Lady DeWitt or Miss DeWitt's second brother Mr. Norman DeWitt, but there was the right number of them, and she *thought* she recognized Mr. Roscoe and Miss DeWitt.

Not paying the least scrap of attention to Mr. Benfield or the service, Hetty watched them steadily, only glancing away from time to time to the pew facing, where Lionel fidgeted and slouched beside Miss Benfield, and she would pinch his ear to bring him around. But when Mr. Benfield read the banns, all doubt was laid to rest, as every head in the congregation, including Lionel's and Miss Benfield's, turned toward the DeWitts.

Hetty held her breath because Mr. Benfield sounded so solemn when he said, "If any of you know cause or just impediment why these two persons should not be joined together in Holy Matrimony, ye are to declare it." But no voice rang out. She did not know what one would do if someone objected—it would be too awful if she and Lionel managed to bring Papa and Miss DeWitt together, only to have some mischief-maker declare an impediment! Suppose Miss Carstairs and her mother sprung up and cried, "They must not marry! We saw him first!" Or if Aunt Lavinia were to declare, "He must not marry! He must preserve the memory of my late sister!" But the Carstairs' and Aunt Lavinia were counties away in Sussex. Surely

Hetty need not waste worry over that. After all, nobody wanted to marry Miss DeWitt (possibly they could not even convince Hetty's Papa to do so), and no one in Somerset showed any sign of wanting to marry Papa (except possibly, one hoped, Miss DeWitt). They were safe.

In this fever of thinking, Hetty didn't notice the service ending and people filing out to greet Mr. Benfield and to congratulate the DeWitts until Hugh laid a hand on her skinny shoulder and shook it gently.

"Are we not staying for the recital, Papa?"

"We are. I imagine we have some minutes before it begins." He bowed as Miss Benfield approached, trailed by Lionel, and he and Hetty followed them out. While their father made polite conversation with the vicar's sister, Hetty yanked Lionel's arm and led him aside.

"Lionel, we are staying in Somerset! Papa has taken lodgings in Patterton, and Cousin Edith is to share a governess with Rosie and me!"

Her brother whistled in appreciation. "That's a packet of news, Het! And just what you hoped." He gave a little caper as the further ramifications sunk in. "And it means I'll get to stay with the Benfields, and I won't have any dreadful dry stick of a tutor! For how long did he take the lodgings?"

"I don't know. I told Papa Rosie needs to recover her health, so I imagine we have at least a couple months, but I hope longer. What use would it be to engage a governess for only a couple months? Surely one must do six months or a year, don't you think?"

"I don't know a thing about it."

"But I think in any case it will be long enough for Papa and Miss DeWitt to get to know each other and like each other," she continued. "I don't think they need love each other. Plenty of married people don't."

"Aunt Lavinia and Uncle Wellington certainly don't," agreed Lionel. "And they're as married as may be."

"Yes. They just need to like each other enough that Miss DeWitt can be lured from her spinsterhood."

"But, hey—what if Papa falls for this governess, or the governess tries to entrap him?" Lionel asked. "He does have money, you know, and he is an heir."

Hetty's eyes widened. Here was a new danger! "Well...it shan't happen. I won't let it. Besides, the governess is to live at Bramleigh with the Richard Hapgoods. That is the agreement the squire and Papa have come to. Surely he cannot fall in love with her if he rarely sees her."

Lionel considered this. "Or you may come to prefer the governess to Miss DeWitt, and then you needn't mind if the governess entraps Papa. Though," he mused, "if she's young, she'll probably pack you and Rosie off to school. Back to Worthing for the both of you."

His sister's brow grew thunderous. "Isn't that just like you? As long as you're happy and you get to stay in Somerset with our cousins, you don't care what happens to Rosie and me!"

"Oh, stop hissing at me," said her maddening sibling. "You look like a red goose, and—look out—here comes Miss DeWitt."

Hetty thought he might be fibbing, but she didn't dare risk it. Swallowing her resentment, she smoothed her frock and stared at her boots until she could school her expression. But her hard-won calm evaporated when she saw Miss DeWitt approaching, followed by four pupils neat as pins. Some twig or other natural debris had fallen among the flowers on Miss DeWitt's bonnet, and she was bareheaded as she worked the item from its entanglement.

"Lionel!" she hissed again, in quite a different tone. "Look at her hair!"

Groaning at the silly things girls said, he took his time in complying but then said in surprise, "Why, it looks different today. *She* looks different. Not so old or something. She looks...better, I think."

"Yes, better. Much better. And look at Papa—he thinks so too."

Sure enough, Lionel perceived his reserved father observing Miss DeWitt closely, and there was even some color in his cheeks. The boy whistled again, low. "Say, Het, I think progress has been made."

She had no time to reply because Miss DeWitt and her pupils were upon them, leading the way back into the church, followed respectfully by half the people who had just emerged.

"...We are all hopeful they will find a new curate for Holliton," Miss Benfield was saying to Hugh. "The wages are quite modest, and the bishop takes little interest because he has already installed his favorites in better livings but at least the parsonage is available, as Mr. Deed the incumbent spends all his time in town. He had the cheek to ask Arthur to fill in, as if my brother had not duties of his own! But Arthur is too soft and agreed to interview candidates, as he and Mr. Deed are old friends from their university days."

"I wish Mr. Benfield all speed and convenience with the task," murmured Hugh, not actually paying close attention and having never passed through the neighboring Holliton. His eye was drawn again to the straight back of Miss DeWitt, as she led her little charges, and perhaps Miss Benfield noticed because she ceased to speak and an inquisitive little sparkle appeared in her own eye.

It was a small enough gathering for the recital: the Benfields, Miss DeWitt and her father Sir Cosmo, the Hugh Hapgoods, the collection of pupils, and the pupils' parents. The children performed stiffly, eyes wide with strain, but they mustered through. Halfway through Nolly's recitation from the Gospel of Saint Luke, the boys got up to mischief, ending with the smallest one falling off the end of the pew and being marched out of the church by Miss Benfield in disgrace, but otherwise it was considered by all a success. Seeing the rows of proud parents and the equally proud instructors, Lionel pictured himself declaiming from Horace while his father and an admiring Edith looked on. They would all remark on his powerful gifts, and then he would go to university and win a fellowship and—and—here his imagination stalled because, of course, if he were to win a fellowship, he could not keep it if he wished to marry. But, seeing as he *did* wish to marry, it would just have to be given up. Perhaps his cousin Edith would not mind. The glory would have been won in any case, but, as a country squire, he would have no use for academic laurels.

Not forty minutes later the recital was behind them and they were filing from the church again. Betsy had brought a basket of shortbread biscuits to be shared among the children, who all looked proud and relieved to be done and who made quick work of thanking their instructors.

Miss DeWitt stood beside the Benfields, and when the crowd of parents expressing their thanks had dispersed, Hugh approached, Hetty in his lee.

"Mr. Benfield, Miss DeWitt," he rumbled, "a most satisfactory display. I congratulate you."

The vicar puffed up as delightedly as any of the pupils and bestowed a beneficent smile upon them all. "Ah, Mr. Hapgood, we in turn are thankful that God has put such industry in the population of Somerset. The children have worked hard, have they not, Rosemary?"

"They have," she agreed.

"Yes," rejoined Hugh, "but you have taken this group of unlettered, humble children and given them a foundation of learning."

"Yes, you have," Miss Benfield echoed, swelling in her turn to hear her brother praised, though, in truth, Mr. Hapgood's remarks might have been addressed ever so slightly more to Miss DeWitt.

"Once one learns to read," Hugh went on, "one can never unlearn it."

A regretful expression crossed Rosemary's face, and she glanced at the vicar as if to apologize for returning to a too-long-discussed subject. "If only they might learn more! To read a gospel or recite a memory piece is an achievement, yes, but...but I am sorry that, after we crack the door open to the life of the mind, they do no more than peer through."

Before Mr. Benfield could call upon his usual responses, Hugh said, "It is a praiseworthy hope for their teacher to have for them. You never know, Miss DeWitt—perhaps some of them—not all, but a few—will choose to push the door further open throughout their lives, even if they must do so in moments stolen from their work. How far we each go, with the advantages we are given, only each individual can answer for."

His encouragement brought a trembling smile in answer, and, for one alarming moment, Rosemary thought her eyes might fill. But she managed to swallow down the lump his words caused, and she only nodded her thanks. She remembered the first time she met him, when they seemed to share a fleeting understanding. Here it was again. He recognized her frustration with the limits life placed on her pupils, and, perhaps, even on herself.

No sooner did she think this than doubts assailed her. Perhaps these instances of accord were merely her own fancy; she must not imagine they imported more than an intelligent man speaking his mind, a mind that sometimes ran parallel to her own. It was not Mr. Hapgood's fault that she met such characters rarely.

"Mr. Hapgood," came Sir Cosmo's cheerful voice as he joined them, "what is this I hear about you taking lodgings in Patterton?"

Rosemary raised wondering eyes, but then she caught Hetty's alert gaze on her and was forced to wipe her countenance of eagerness.

"Yes, sir. Before I signed the lease with the agent, I insisted he send to Marchmont. I knew from my call that your son Roscoe had expressed interest in the Simpsons' house."

"It all worked for the best," answered Sir Cosmo, beaming upon them all. "As water wears away the stone, I convinced Roscoe to make renovations to our east wing, that he and his future bride may remain under our roof."

"I am glad to hear it," Hugh bowed. "I know that was your wish. Once I was assured I would not be inconveniencing your family, the squire and I agreed that Simpsons' would exactly suit my purposes."

"You mean to stay among us in Somerset for some time, then?" questioned Miss Benfield.

"I do." His eyes skated past Miss DeWitt (not that she was looking at him any longer) and rested on the Benfields. "Like the parish pupils in their way, Lionel too has flourished under your aegis, Mr. Benfield. But my girls did not enjoy the best health at school, and we have decided to be united as a family for the near term. If Lionel remains here, so too do we, and the country air will be good for my Rosalie's complete recovery."

"Splendid!" declared the vicar, having seemingly forgotten there had been any danger of Lionel's removal. Rosemary could see Miss Benfield calculating all that had been unknown till now in her head, however, and saw the good woman's lips tighten. As Rosemary had suspected, Charlotte Benfield would have taken offense for her brother's prize pupil to be withdrawn so summarily.

"Will your girls attend the school in Taunton?" asked Sir Cosmo.

"I believe not. I intend to advertise for a governess, who will teach my Harriet and Rosalie at Bramleigh, along with my cousin's daughter Miss Edith."

"Splendid!" cried Mr. Benfield once more. "We welcome new faces, do we not, Charlotte? There will be this governess and there will be the new curate at Holliton, with whatever family belongs to him."

"It had better be a very small family," said the practical Miss Benfield, "with the pittance Mr. Deed affords from the living."

"When will this governess come among us, Hapgood?" Sir Cosmo pressed.

"As soon as may be, though I will be absent from Somerset for perhaps a fortnight, in order to tidy my business affairs and fetch Rosalie. Perhaps I should not even advertise yet because I could not possibly handle the matter until after my return, and it would prove frustrating for any applicant to await a response until then."

"Ah, but if you do not advertise until after your return, it might be a month or more before the girls have a governess," Mr. Benfield pointed out. "Why do you not advertise before you depart, and, if a suitable applicant presents herself in your absence, why, Charlotte and I may inquire after her references and, if possible, meet with her. That way no time need be lost. Perhaps you might assist us as well, Miss DeWitt?"

"Sir, I could not burden you with—" Hugh began.

"Burden?" laughed Mr. Benfield. "I do not think you will be inundated with replies, Mr. Hapgood. Impoverished gentlewomen may be thick on the ground in Sussex and nearer town, but they cannot all be easily lured to this corner of the kingdom."

"The last time your cousin the squire advertised for a governess, some years past, I do believe it was a six months' process," Miss Benfield warned.

Hugh suspected this might have more to do with the exceedingly small wages the squire could promise, and he hoped for better results with what he was prepared to pay. "In any event, while I appreciate your willingness, I could not ask—"

"Oh, nonsense," interrupted Miss Benfield. "If you are to be our neighbor and parishioner now, Mr. Hapgood, you must expect us to involve ourselves in your affairs and pray you will do the same in ours." She smiled, that he would realize she spoke partly in jest, but only partly. "How better will Rosemary and I stay atop Patterton gossip, if we do not have a hand in choosing this person?"

One corner of Hugh's mouth went up wryly, and he managed to catch Rosemary's gaze when it fluttered up to his and away. "If I am to understand you aright, Miss Benfield, you call interference in the affairs of others the best proof of neighborliness?"

"I do indeed," she said firmly.

His grin spread. "Then I do not dare risk being thought ill-natured. By all means, if you Benfields would be willing to review any responses to my advertisement that come in my absence, to weed out the unworthy and praise the proper, I will be grateful for your assistance." He regarded Miss DeWitt briefly again, adding, "And, your expert opinions in the matter of education would be more than welcome."

"That's settled then," said Sir Cosmo. "Now you must make a second promise before you go, Hapgood. You must absolutely promise to be back in Somerset before the music strikes up at our ball."

# Chapter Sixteen

**Beauty shall not bribe me on your side...
I am Beauty-proof.**
—Samuel Richardson, *Sir Charles Grandison* (1753)

Mr. Hugh Hapgood had not been absent from Somerset a week before the astounding word spread from Holliton to Patterton and beyond that Mr. Deed was sending a young, unmarried curate to assume his duties, and this new curate came with an also-unmarried sister who had answered Mr. Hapgood's advertisement for a governess!

"It will be most awkward if she be found unsuitable," Charlotte Benfield told Rosemary over tea. Lionel had been cast out of the vicarage, that she might speak freely, but she still spoke in a hushed voice that Rosemary leaned to catch.

"But Charlotte, surely we cannot compel Mr. Hapgood to employ Miss Parvill simply to make things easy for the rest of us."

"Of course not. I only mean to say that it would be *most* convenient for all if this…Elinor Parvill were an educated gentlewoman."

"She will be a gentlewoman at least," said Rosemary. "The sister of a curate cannot be otherwise."

Miss Benfield heaved a sigh. "Portionless sister of an impoverished curate from somewhere north—Northamptonshire? Nottinghamshire? Surely not Northumberland. In any case, if she makes her home with her brother, they must certainly be orphans."

"Or they might have an ailing parent, as you and Mr. Benfield do," suggested Rosemary.

"Dear me! I hope not. Another mouth to feed, and who should have time to care for the parent, if both the son and daughter must work for their bread?" Miss Benfield demanded. "Surely they would have mentioned such an encumbrance to Mr. Deed."

"Does Mr. Deed say he knows them personally?"

"He writes to Arthur that he does not, but this Mr. Henry Parvill is reputed to be brilliant—a fellow of Queens' College, Cambridge, no less."

Rosemary murmured appreciatively. "If he be a fellow, that means he will receive a fellowship, will he not?"

"He will, but he will also have the sister. Between the curacy and his fellowship, the Parvills will just manage to keep out of the poorhouse, but the wages Mr. Hapgood offers would go far to make them comfortable. Oh, Rosemary! Suppose she is *not* suitable? Then we will have the Parvills among us at Holliton, and we will never be able to look them in the eye, knowing it was in our power to relieve their poverty, and we refused."

Wincing at the idea, Rosemary shook her head. "But Charlotte, if she is unsuitable, imagine the alternative! Suppose we urge her upon Mr. Hapgood, and we thus jeopardize the education of his daughters and Miss Edith, not to mention we embroil him in a situation from which there is no easy escape."

Miss Benfield allowed herself to grumble. "If it were so bad as all that, I suppose he could make his excuses and uproot the family back to Sussex."

Rosemary sat back as she considered this. "You are right. He could flee to Sussex. And take Lionel with him."

"And take Lionel with him." Miss Benfield sighed again as she picked up her needlework. She was quite fond of Lionel. "And then this Miss Parvill would take up residence with her brother again, but they could not reproach us in that instance. We would have done our utmost."

Silence fell for a minute, with each woman deep in thought. Then Rosemary said, "There would be another possible escape for Mr. Hapgood from a bad situation."

"What would that be?"

Straightening, Rosemary said boldly, "He might marry her, and then she would be excused from her teaching duties, if he chose."

Her friend eyed her sharply, but Rosemary was prepared for it and kept her chin up.

"He might," Miss Benfield replied cautiously. "Men do such things."

"After all," Rosemary persevered, "did he not come into Somerset with precisely that intention? He was to marry Miss Hapgood and find wife, mother, and educator in one, if possible. At the very least she would play two of the three roles. Only, she would not have him."

"What you say is true, but, to be fair, I cannot think that Mr. Hapgood was unduly disappointed to have his attempt foiled."

"Perhaps because she already loved another. I don't suppose anybody would be pleased to marry someone who preferred someone else."

Miss Benfield completed half a row of precise, tiny stitches to the cuff of one of her brother's shirts. Then she ventured, "Do you suppose Mr. Hapgood prefers anyone?"

"No!" cried Rosemary, too loudly. She turned pink and added, "That is—I know nothing of the man, much less his preferences. I—I suppose he is as heart-whole as any man who lost his wife some months earlier."

Miss Benfield had formed her own suspicions from the moment she saw her friend lying atop Mr. Hapgood in the vicarage library. Having further detected Rosemary's discomfiture around the man, and how Mr. Hapgood observed her friend both in church and around the recital, the suspicions burgeoned into the beginnings of hope. A wish for her friend's well-deserved happiness. Why should only the beautiful girls have all the eligible gentlemen? And Miss DeWitt, with her respectable family and respectable fortune, deserved better than she had met with thus far. If Mr. Hugh Hapgood were to choose Rosemary out of all the world, Miss Benfield, for one, would admire his discernment. And surely a man who was well on his way to appreciating Rosemary DeWitt properly would not then be caught in the net of some penniless curate's sister, however young or pretty or designing she might turn out to be?

"In any event," Miss Benfield rejoined, "we have promised to respond to any applications. We must send for this Miss Parvill's references and arrange to meet her when they arrive in Holliton. After that, it is in the Lord's hands."

It was Miss Constance Porterworth who caught the first glimpse of the Parvills. Not only was she the cynosure of most eyes at this time because of her betrothal, but to be the first with news of the new residents seemed an especial dispensation of favor from Providence. Winding up her visit to the draper's in Holliton, she sped first to Pattergees to enlighten her bosom friend Miss Birdlow and then to Marchmont to edify her beloved.

"I spent as long as I could in the window of the draper's, which you know, Roscoe, is directly across from the parsonage in Holliton," she began breathlessly, straightening her bonnet, which had gone askew in her haste.

"That I do *not* know, love," her intended answered, but Rosemary, who was also present, gave an encouraging nod, and Miss Porterworth needed little more to rush onward.

"They arrived on foot—they must have got down from the stage at the Crown and Stars and were followed by a wagon of furnishings and such. They were arm in arm. He is a tall young gentleman—on the slender side—they are both slender. She comes but to his shoulder, and she wore a beautiful but rather faded Paisley shawl. I saw, when she turned to look at him, that she had hair as black as his, and they are both monstrously attractive! I could not decide which most drew my eyes! They both have black hair, as I said—"

"And we know your liking for black hair, don't we?" interjected the black-haired Roscoe, torn between annoyance and teasing.

With a cooing giggle she fluttered her lashes at him, but she was not to be long distracted from her tale. "—And Mr. Parvill, Mr. Henry Parvill, has a nice straight nose, rather long, and a firm jaw, and I liked how he was clearly a good, protective brother of Miss Parvill because he put his arm about her and shielded her from the rumpus of the removers and the horses stepping and such. Quite manly of him! I suppose the absent Mr. Deed will be amazed at the attendance in Holliton, now that Mr. Parvill is come. I intend on asking Papa if we may go hear him on Sunday, though I suppose it will be a sad crush, and perhaps we should wait a fortnight, when everyone in the county has had a chance to satisfy their curiosity. Do you intend to go, Rosemary?"

Thus addressed, Rosemary started. She had been following her own dismayed thoughts, to hear that this Miss Parvill was so beautiful. She and the Benfields would have learned it soon enough, as they were to meet with her on the morrow, but it was certainly a blow. "Er—I have not considered it," she murmured.

"Oh!" Miss Porterworth looked disappointed to find her soon-to-be sister so unsatisfying an auditor, but she soon recovered. "Well, in any event, *I* will. Or at least I will get Papa to call on them, that we might be introduced. Will you go too, Roscoe?"

"Not I."

"But I want them to come to our engagement ball!"

"What should a destitute curate and his governessing sister be doing at a Marchmont ball?" he complained.

"Governessing?" echoed Miss Porterworth, round-eyed. "Is she then a governess?"

"She has written in answer to Mr. Hugh Hapgood's advertisement," explained Rosemary quietly. She wondered that Miss Porterworth could be the only person in the county who seemed not to know this. "But no decision has been made yet on the position." Never mind that Miss Parvill was the sole applicant and that her references had turned out to be sterling.

Roscoe dismissed this with a wave. "It matters little whether Hapgood take her or not. If he don't want her, the woman will still have to seek elsewhere."

"Oh, what a shame, for then she could not keep house for her brother, and they appear so fond of each other! I hope Mr. Hapgood likes her, then. He is such an imposing, forbidding man, however. I am sure he is very hard to please."

"He might seem stern," Rosemary could not help speaking up, "and grave, but remember he has recently been bereaved, and he has much on his mind with his three children. I have found him…to be a kind person."

"Hmmm," was Miss Porterworth's dubious response. But old, severe Mr. Hugh Hapgood could not capture her interest long when there were other fish to fry. With another giggle, she gave Roscoe a mischievous nudge. "Only guess what I told Agnes! It made her so angry!"

"I cannot conceive."

His sweetheart gave a bounce on her seat. "I told her she should set her cap for Mr. Parvill! I told her that, though he has not a farthing, he is so *extremely* handsome. And, being a viscount's daughter, Agnes has portion enough to make them easy for life. And she could get him the Pattergees living when Mr. Chomley is gone. I told her Mr. Parvill is as handsome, in his black-haired way, as Mr. Frederick Tierney was in his blond-haired way, and I, for one, if I had to choose between marrying that cousin of hers Geoffrey Winstanley, or Mr. Parvill, I would choose Mr. Parvill, oh, at once!"

"Then perhaps you had better do so!" cried Roscoe crossly, springing rudely to his feet. "I've had just about enough of these Parvills, and I haven't even met them."

Miss Porterworth, having excited her lover to this jealous display, then spent several delighted minutes in soothing and reassuring him, an exercise Rosemary had no desire to witness and from which she quickly excused herself. But, while she could flee the room, it was another matter altogether to flee the anxieties taking root. Was this Miss Parvill so very beautiful, in addition to being so very qualified? Well, and what if she was?

"You are ridiculous, Rosemary DeWitt," she scolded herself when she reached the privacy of her chamber. "And you will make yourself even more ridiculous, if you continue to harbor these feelings toward Mr. Hapgood." It did seem unjust of the universe that, after the incomparably beautiful Elfrida Hapgood refused him, he should next be presented with the incomparably beautiful Elinor Parvill. Did all men have to run such a gauntlet of beauties? Well, unjust or not, Rosemary was forced to administer the same medicine she had given herself in the case of Miss Hapgood. She must acknowledge the too-obvious possibility. "Is it not plain what will happen? He will love this Miss Parvill, and she will be glad of his attentions, whether she loves him or not, because she is so poor. They will marry and return to Sussex, taking the children with them, and you will never see the lot of them again." And, to her mortification, she discovered that one-and-thirty, besides being an age not beyond blushing, was equally an age not beyond crying into one's pillow.

The following afternoon found Rosemary in Mr. Benfield's library again, being introduced to Miss Elinor Parvill. If she had any hopes that reports of Miss Parvill's beauty were exaggerated, those were laid immediately to rest.

The would-be governess was of middling height, with blue-black raven hair, which made the blueness of her eyes the more vivid. Her shape and complexion were flawless, and somehow the plain, twice-turned gown she wore only threw her fineness into greater relief.

Both the Benfields and Rosemary absorbed this vision in stunned silence, but the vicar was the first to recover, gesturing to a chair for his guest. "Please. We are delighted to make your acquaintance and to welcome you and your brother to Somerset."

Miss Parvill nodded once and settled gracefully on the edge of the seat.

"Ahem. Yes. Well. How are you finding the parsonage thus far? Mr. Deed wrote me that there were some items in need of repair but that the general condition was satisfactory."

"It will be a charming home. My—brother and I are confident we will be satisfied there." She spoke in a clear, modulated voice, which an idle portion of Rosemary's mind noted would sound well in teaching and reciting. "We have already been welcomed by some members of our parish with gifts of food."

"Yes," smiled Mr. Benfield. "We are a hospitable bunch. I am glad to hear of it. The former curate Mr. Douglas was quite elderly and did not get about among the flock as often as he did in earlier years, but he was well loved, and I am sure Mr. Parvill will also be."

To this she nodded once more.

"You and your brother hail from Northamptonshire, I believe?" persisted Mr. Benfield.

Faint color rose to her cheeks. "We do. From a small village near Stamford, though we no longer have living family there. Or indeed anywhere, really."

The vicar was the last man to press a painful sore, so he hurried away from the topic of family and antecedents. "Of course. Quite tragic. Our sympathies. In any case—er—Northamptonshire. Not very familiar with the place myself, but I hope you will come to love Somerset and feel at home here."

Having, apparently, nothing to add to the matter, Miss Parvill turned the subject. "I see, from Mr. Hugh Hapgood's advertisement that the governess he seeks would live at a place called Bramleigh, which is, I believe, very near Holliton?"

"Very near," spoke up Rosemary. "Perhaps a walk of twenty minutes from your brother's parsonage. Bramleigh lies a little nearer Patterton, but only a little."

"I wonder, perhaps, if Bramleigh is so near to Holliton, if Mr. Hapgood would consider a governess who lived out? I would never be late. I am very punctual. I only ask because it would help my brother Henry so very much if I could keep house for him. He might be able to manage without a servant then."

Rosemary had a brief picture of Squire Hapgood capering with delight when he found he would not even have to house this governess that she suspected his cousin was already paying for, and much the same must have occurred to Mr. Benfield because he smiled and said, "I am certain that would be no obstacle, Miss Parvill."

"Your reference from the headmistress of your school was excellent," Miss Benfield then addressed her. "She wrote that you have much experience with young ladies of various ages."

"Yes." The young woman bit her lip, and it took her a moment to go on. "From the time I was fourteen, I was given charge of younger pupils. I have, over the years at Highcross, taught French, history, literature, mathematics, geography, art, and music."

"My, my," breathed Miss Benfield, her glance meeting Rosemary's. There was no question of Miss Parvill's qualifications, unfortunately.

"May I ask the age and number of girls the governess would be responsible for?" was this paragon's next question.

Rosemary could see Mr. Benfield puzzling, and she was not sure Miss Benfield even knew, so she replied, "There is Mr. Hapgood's elder daughter Harriet—Hetty—who is ten, his younger daughter Rosalie, who is six, and their cousin Edith, who is eleven, I believe.

Hetty and Rosie will live in Patterton with their father, and Miss Edith is at Bramleigh, which has a schoolroom that can be used for lessons."

"I see." Miss Parvill's gloved hands were folded neatly in her lap, but Rosemary saw them clench a moment, and then the too-lovely candidate added, "I should be very glad of the position, if you will see fit to recommend me to Mr. Hapgood. Both Henry and I should be very glad of it. May I—may I ask if the applicants have been many?"

Before the ingenuous Mr. Benfield could blurt out that not a single other person had applied, Miss Benfield cleared her throat with a bark. "Not so very many. And you are the first we have spoken with." She rose, drawing the rest to their feet as well. "This has been a great pleasure, and, whatever comes, we will be glad of you and your brother in the community."

"Will Mr. Hapgood return to Somerset soon, to make his choice?" Miss Parvill pressed.

Here both Benfields looked to Rosemary, and she felt telltale heat rise in her face. Why should she, especially, speak to his whereabouts? Widening her eyes slightly at Miss Benfield, she said, "Why, Charlotte, did he not say to us all at the recital that he might be absent a fortnight altogether? Which means he will be back any day now."

"Thank you," said Miss Parvill simply. Her blue gaze rested an instant longer on Rosemary than the others. Then she made her curtsy, and Mr. Benfield saw her out. When he came back, he was rubbing his hands together with glee. "What a blessing! I believe we may in all conscience recommend her highly to Mr. Hapgood."

"There is certainly no fault to be found with her references or her abilities," his sister agreed slowly. "And she is a gentlewoman, to be sure."

"Then why do you sound doubtful, Charlotte? Miss DeWitt, did you not also find her ideal? She is, perhaps, a trifle reserved, but chattiness is not desirable in a governess, I do not think."

"She might just be shy," said Rosemary, avoiding his question.

"I do not believe shyness to be the cause of her reserve," Miss Benfield considered, with knit brow. "You saw she was direct enough in her questions. It was only about her family and Northamptonshire where she seemed incommunicative."

"We cannot censure her for that, my dear," protested her brother. "It must be painful to be orphans and so poor that they must leave the only home they have known to settle among strangers. And what a pity that Parvill's curacy and his fellowship do not together pay enough to keep them, but she must also go out to work."

"You are right, Arthur."

Pleased, he beamed upon them. "Then we are agreed? I will write to Hapgood immediately to give her our hearty endorsement. Barring any unforeseen circumstances, he will have a governess for the children, Lionel will remain with us, and Mr. and Miss Parvill will be made much more comfortable in their new life! Ideal, ideal. We could not have contrived a better solution if we had worked at it till Doomsday."

Rosemary's answering smile was not very steady, and she could not help feeling that, it seemed, Doomsday was already upon her.

# Chapter Seventeen

> **The inefficacy of advice is usually
> the fault of the counsellor.**
> —Samuel Johnson, *Rambler No. 87* (1751)

"I cannot imagine how this has all come to pass," Lavinia Morrow Sidney sighed. She shook her head slowly and mournfully, as if she were witnessing her brother-in-law condemned to execution. "Why you should choose to uproot your life, your work, your children—and for what? You must not let the children dictate matters, brother. They are too young to know what is best for them."

Hugh straightened the stack of accounts he had gathered and tied the ribbon about them before placing them in the chest. "I do not remain in Somerset only to please the children, Lavinia," he said, not for the first time. His stay in Sussex had been as brief as he could make it, but his wife's family—that is, Lavinia—made the most of their limited opportunity. "We should all of us prefer to be together at present. I am contented with Lionel's situation. Rosie needs to recover her health, and country air suits us."

"You cannot tell me the squire's wife is pleased to have you hovering about, waiting for her declining husband to expire altogether!"

"No, in truth, I cannot," he admitted. "Therefore, we are removing to lodgings. But I believe the squire himself bears no resentment. In fact, I daresay he welcomes our stay."

"As a purse-pinched man does, when he finds someone to pay his expenses!" cried Lavinia. "Brother, I hope you have not been fooled."

"I have not been fooled," snapped Hugh, losing his patience and dropping the Ryegate ledger into the chest with a mighty *thump*. "His youngest needs a governess; my two daughters need a governess; they will all three enjoy learning more if they do it together. He will provide the schoolroom at Bramleigh. Why should I not do my share? One day—not too soon, God willing—I will be head of the family, and I am certain I will not regret providing for my cousin's daughter's education."

"Well, you are not head of the Hapgoods now," she tossed back, "and it is up to the squire to provide for his own children. You did more than could be expected of you, when you offered for that disgraced, eloping, scandalous Miss Hapgood! That family! I marvel that you would have your girls more closely allied with them, such goings-on as they have had, this past summer. Suppose Hetty were to take up dressing as a boy, like her cousin Alice, or Rosie were to run off with some rakehell, as Miss Hapgood did?"

"How did you hear of Alice's mishaps?" he asked, rolling up some blank sheets of foolscap.

"Hetty wrote Caroline about it," Lavinia said shortly. "Do not dodge me, brother."

Hugh shut his eyes and indulged in a brief daydream about being alone on an icy cliff somewhere in the Alps, far, far from this officious woman; perched there, he would grin as her shrewish harangues died away in the distance, muffled by wind and snow.

Alas, that reality would intrude. Miss Rosemary DeWitt might call herself a meddler (and he might even have thought of her as one, at one time), but her gentle efforts could not hold a candle to Lavinia's assaults. Hugh's lone regret in leaving Sussex for the near future came from guilt—guilt in abandoning his brother-in-law Wellington Sidney to shoulder the burden of Lavinia alone.

That same Wellington was throwing him sympathetic glances from behind his newspaper, but Hugh knew this was the alpha and omega of aid he would receive from that quarter.

Seeing her brother-in-law would offer no satisfactory answer to her question, Lavinia huffed her indignation and stalked to the door, barking, "Mr. Sidney!" Her husband scrambled up to join her, springing aside when she whipped back around, crossing her arms over her middle. "I suppose, a month hence, I will receive a letter from you, brother, saying you are to marry the governess!"

"What utter nonsense you speak, Lavinia! I believe I may safely promise you I will never marry the governess, whosoever she might turn out to be."

"How can you be so certain?" she demanded, tossing her head and coming some way back into the room. "It happens every day. You have never met the creature, so you had better not pass your word. What did that vicar say in his letter to you? 'A most qualified and well-mannered young gentlewoman, and most attached to her brother the curate'?"

Hugh ground his teeth and just managed not to slam the lid of the chest shut. "There must be several *thousand* young women in the kingdom who can be thus described, and, it seems, I have managed to resist every one of them."

Rapidly changing her point of attack, she retorted, "I cannot see how you can speak to resisting this *particular* young woman, when you know very well you have never seen her and yet have hired her! On the word of others! Perhaps you ought also to ask your new, dear friends in Somerset if they think her as *marriageable* as she is capable."

"I trust my 'new, dear friends,' as you call them, to dispense the best advice possible in the matter of educating the children. Mr. Benfield has done excellently with Lionel, and Miss—" he just caught himself— "*Miss* Benfield also knows well what she is about." He met his sister-in-law's gaze directly then, and she took a step back to see the unwonted fire in his eyes. "But hear me, Lavinia: when it comes to choosing a wife for myself, if ever I again choose a wife for myself, I will trust no one's counsel but my own."

Indignant and embarrassed, she rounded on her husband. "Well—*well,* Mr. Sidney! I see our advice is despised here. I suppose you have nothing to say, husband, when he speaks thus to me?"

"Now, Lavinia…" muttered Wellington, turning red.

"Don't you 'now, Lavinia' me!"

Gripping the edges of his desk to steady himself, Hugh took a deep breath and released it slowly. This would never do. He could not draw closer to one side of his children's family at the cost of alienating the other. Nor could he see his brother-in-law crushed without some attempt to rescue him.

"See here, Lavinia," he tried again. "I am sorry you cannot approve my decisions, but I hope you will join me in wishing they turn out for the best. It may be some time before I am here again. Perhaps not until the partners of the Ryegate bank hold their quarterly meeting. But I will bring the children with me then, if it can be managed."

"The Ryegate bank? What about the Cuckfield bank? East Grinstead? Do they not hold meetings as well?"

"They do, but I have resigned from both the Cuckfield bank and East Grinstead. It will be enough for me to manage Ryegate from afar." Not to mention he wanted more time with his children, to know them better and—perhaps—win them.

She looked as if she would like to comment on these professional decisions as well, but instead she nodded and shut her mouth so rigidly her lips disappeared. As her late sister had always delighted in making known, the Hugh Hapgoods were amply provided for, and Hugh might never work another day in his life, if he so chose. The same was largely true of the Sidneys, but Lavinia nevertheless urged her husband to work as much as possible because she hated to see him lounging about.

"I will miss the children," she said. "As will little Caroline, while they are in Somerset gamboling with their Hapgood cousins."

Another wave of irritation lapped at him. "My cousin Richard's remaining girls are past the age of gamboling, even were they so inclined. Come, Lavinia. Let us part on good terms. I will write to you and Wellington and keep you apprised of things, and I hope you will do the same."

She nodded wordlessly, and his heart softened, to see her chin tremble. The woman was vexing, to be sure, but she meant well. It would be easier to love her, however, from the distance of some 150 miles.

"I wish you safe travels, brother. And I want you to know that, while you make this new beginning, I too continue to grow and change. I was once most opposed to your remarriage, but that is no longer the case."

Considering her jabs about the governess, Hugh had his doubts, but he held his peace and heard her out.

"Yes," she went on. "Several months have passed, and I see caring for my sister's children weighs heavily on your mind. Therefore, I would like to say that, if it would bring you all back to Crawley again, Mr. Sidney and I would not now be opposed to you forming an attachment to Miss Carstairs."

Lest he burst out anew in thundering curses, Hugh only bowed. Good Lord! He should marry the next woman he chanced upon, if it meant he might never hear Miss Carstairs' name again. He had

had but one glimpse of the proposed bride and her mother on this visit—they had nodded politely in passing—but he could vouch that, each time he passed in or out his door, the window coverings across the street twitched.

At last the Sidneys took their leave. With the door finally shut behind them, Hugh pulled out the desk chair and sank into it. He had not expected his plans to be well received, and they had not been. So be it. But there was at least one area in which he deemed himself satisfied: for all her provocations, his sister-in-law had not succeeded in discovering or drawing one word from him about the only woman in the kingdom he was lately given to thinking about.

With a steady hand, he wrote the directions of his Patterton lodgings on the label of the chest. He would go next from Crawley to Worthing to retrieve Rosie, and then, in perhaps two more days, he would again be in Somerset.

Somerset.

Where Rosemary lived.

While Hugh's sufferings might all be traced to his sister-in-law's scoldings, the unhappy fortnight Rosemary passed in his absence had myriad causes. First there was the alarming revelation of Miss Parvill's beauty. Then there was her fitness for the role of governess, even if she had not been the only applicant. Then there was Mr. Hapgood's response to Mr. Benfield's letter, agreeing to Miss Parvill's request to live out and authorizing the vicar to engage her services.

It was done then. And she did not need prophetic vision to see how this story would play out. Having no one to confide in, her fears preyed upon her. Rosemary's family was too preoccupied with the impending ball and Roscoe's nuptials to notice her depression of spirits (and she made every effort that they should not notice), and Miss Benfield, the only one who might have comforted her and held out hope, did not speak of the matter because she did not want her friend to be disappointed. But Rosemary was already disappointed.

"If only Mr. Hapgood were as sorely pressed for money as the squire," she thought as she sat at the pianoforte one evening, playing her father's favorite songs by rote. "Then he would perhaps choose me—five thousand pounds are not nothing. That would make him a fortune hunter, I suppose, but he would not be like those others who offered for me. They saw nothing in me to like except my portion. He at least seems content to speak to me and welcomes my opinion in certain things. I think. I rather think he almost...likes me, as a person." And, however much she might admonish herself for presuming to feel heartbroken now, she could not help but believe that Mr. Hapgood *did* like her. Not enough to marry her, of course. Not when there would be a younger and far more beautiful woman at hand who could serve his purposes equally, where his children were concerned. But he might still like her as someone sensible and kind and dependable. If she had been a boy, they might have been friends.

Her fingers stumbled as she remembered his pirate grin when they were locked in the Benfields' library. He did not grin at her as if she were a sensible and kind and dependable *boy*. He grinned at her as if she were a maiden he had kidnapped, and not entirely against her will.

Feeling suddenly too warm, Rosemary let her playing fade mid-verse.

"Don't stop, Ros!" urged her brother Roscoe, seizing his mother's hands and pulling her to her feet as she protested laughingly. "Play us a dance, why don't you?"

Glad of the distraction and that her mood passed unnoticed, she obediently launched into "All in a Garden Green" and even found herself laughing with them as Roscoe whirled Lady DeWitt about the carpet and they bowed to and wove among invisible fellow dancers.

"Another!" cried Roscoe when the song ended, but his mother shooed him away and pushed Rosemary from the pianoforte stool.

"I am too old to keep up with Sir High Spirits. You must partner him now, my dear."

Then it was Rosemary's turn to spin and step with Roscoe while Lady DeWitt played The Spinning Wheel with more loudness and speed than accuracy. "I wish you might get engaged every day," Rosemary gasped, her upturned face pink with the exercise and her hair coming loose. "It improves your temper marvelously."

"And I wish you might dance every day," countered her brother, "for if other people saw you thus, you might be engaged yourself."

She scowled at him in mock anger, but after the evening closed and she mounted the stairs with her candle, she had much to ponder. She did not credit Roscoe, of course. His gallant words stemmed from his joy at having everything his own way. She had been to balls before and danced before, and nothing had ever come of it, but she had never been to a ball before where it mattered to her whether another person were present or not.

A fortnight had come and gone. Mr. Hapgood would surely return soon, and surely he would attend the ball at Marchmont. He would attend, and his destiny, Miss Parvill the governess, would not. For that one night and perhaps no other, Rosemary might watch him and speak with him and stand near him and dream that her life could turn out otherwise. The day after the ball would be soon enough to stand to the side and let matters take their course.

*They may not*, whispered a rebellious voice in her head as she brushed and braided her hair before her looking glass. *You thought he would surely marry Miss Hapgood, and he did not. And Miss Parvill, for all her beauty, is no more beautiful than Miss Hapgood.*

"If he was willing to marry Miss Hapgood for the sake of his family," she told her reflection sternly, "why should he be less willing to marry Miss Parvill?"

*Marrying Miss Hapgood would have helped the entire family he will one day head,* argued the devil's advocate. *How will marrying Miss Parvill do the same? He might marry anyone now and please himself.*

"That is just it." Rosemary jabbed an admonishing hairbrush at the mirror. "If he marries now, it will be to please himself. And what man, not in need of funds, would not choose a lovely young woman, if he might?"

*Perhaps a man who chooses to be loved.*

Her lips parted in surprise. Rosemary, having few confidants in life, often resorted to confiding in herself, but she did not often argue so as to change her own mind.

Would a man choose to be loved, rather than to love? Would he choose the woman who loved him over a woman with whom he was himself in love?

It would be a simple matter if it were put to Rosemary. Without hesitation she would choose to marry the man she loved, rather than someone who loved her, would she not? If Mr. Hapgood were to offer for her tomorrow—and were he only to offer her friendship and partnership in raising his three children—she would say Yes. She would not plead for time to consider. She would say Yes.

But would a man do the same? Would *this* man do the same?

*You'll never know*, pointed out the practical voice. *Because how will he ever know you love him?*

"I can hardly tell him," she murmured. "Gentlewomen don't just come out and say such things." She blew out her candle, as one who has just had the last word in an argument.

But, as she lay in her bed in the darkness, her inner debate opponent had one final retort.

*If you say so. But, I imagine, if Miss Parvill decides a husband is a better bargain than penury and servitude, she will find a way to let him know.*

# Chapter Eighteen

**A little Learning is a dang'rous Thing.**
—Pope, *Essay on Criticism* (1711)

Their new lodgings in Patterton were clean and cozy. Hetty and Rosie, who shared the front bedroom, awoke to the sounds of the mail coach arriving at the Swan, and the girls rushed barefoot in delight to the casement to peer out.

"The guard is checking his watch," breathed Rosie. "He frowns. Do you suppose they are late? No—they are right on time because there are the church clock chimes."

"You there! Stop dawdling and unload the parcels or I'll behead you with my cutlass," cried Hetty, pretending to speak for the guard as he unlocked the coach-box and pointed his commands.

"And look!" Rosie jabbed a little finger at the glass. "There is Olcott crossing the street. Do you suppose she is getting our breakfast?"

"Of course she is." Hetty took hold of her younger sister and spun her back toward the wardrobe. "We had better get dressed because Papa says he will walk us to Bramleigh this morning, in order that he may meet our governess, and you must have enough time to eat a *lot*. You are still far too thin and pale."

Rosie was too young and had missed her family far too much to protest the maternal tone Hetty adopted, and she stood still to let her sister brush out her hair and tie her ribbons.

"Did you like traveling with Papa?" Hetty questioned.

"I was glad to think I would see you and Lionel again," said Rosie. "But Papa is a little scary, even though he pats me on the head now. He does not talk much and his mind seemed elsewhere. I wanted to ask him if he had chosen us a new mama yet, but I didn't dare."

Hetty rounded on her and held up a warning finger. "And *don't* you dare! Remember what I told you yesterday when you came: you leave this to me. Lionel and I have someone picked out, but it will all go awry if we are not careful."

"I know, I remember," Rosie whispered. "You said you have chosen Miss DeWitt. When will I meet her?"

"I don't know. Perhaps you will see her on Sunday. Now that we have come to Patterton to live, I suppose we will go to Mr. Benfield's church, and she goes there as well." Hetty bit her lip. For her father and Miss DeWitt to see each other but once a week, and that in church, did not seem very promising. And what if this governess was artful and began work on Papa today?

Rosie gave a shiver of anticipation for entirely different reasons. "I hope Miss Parvill will be a nicer teacher than Mrs. F. If you don't like her, will you plague her, like you did Elfie?"

"No," answered Hetty solemnly. "I went about things all wrong with Cousin Elfie, and I know better now. If I drive Miss Parvill away, that only means Papa will decide this new plan does not work, and we will have to begin all over again, with being sent away to school." Seeing Rosie's worried eyes, she did not tell her that, if Miss Parvill were to ingratiate herself with their father, the girls might end up being sent away to school in any case.

She took her sister's hand to lead her downstairs. "Come on. Papa will be waiting for us."

The walk to Bramleigh seemed to take no time at all. They crossed the fields populated only by sheep, cut through the edge of the wood that used to be Alice Hapgood's especial haunt, and descended the long gentle slope to the house. Hugh and the girls did not say much, but it made his heart lift to see them darting about, laughing and chattering and picking flowers.

"I will come by when your lessons have finished this afternoon," he told them, thinking that Rosie might not yet be strong enough for the uphill return.

"Yes, Papa," said Hetty, with a ripple of panic. Suppose he were to make a habit of accompanying them, and Miss Parvill were to take advantage of this habit? She would see him twice a day, five days a week, and Miss DeWitt would only get that little glimpse on

Sundays! "Thank you, Papa. But you will not need to walk us every day. Lionel says he can run from the vicarage to Bramleigh in seven minutes—though I think he exaggerates."

Her father frowned. "Well, I will certainly come in the afternoons for the time being."

Before they reached the house they could hear Button the cook hollering at Hal in the kitchen garden, and Dorcas flung the door wide for them, looking flurried and red in the face. "Schoolroom's ready," she panted.

"Is *she* here yet?" Hetty asked.

Dorcas nodded and pointed back over her shoulder. "Drawing room with the squire and the young ladies," she whispered loudly behind her hand. "She got here *early*, and I can tell the squire don't like that because he said he's got no time in the morning to be entertaining governesses."

"Very well, thank you, Dorcas," said Hugh. "We will announce ourselves."

To be frank, Hugh had not given much thought to the new governess, apart from being relieved that one had been found and grateful to his new friends for their assistance in selecting her. The vicar had not deemed it fit to mention her appearance in his letter, nor had the Hapgoods of Bramleigh made her acquaintance before this appointed first day of lessons.

Therefore, when Hugh and his girls entered the drawing room, it was to find the squire and his daughters still paralyzed with wonder. Hugh himself caught sight of Miss Parvill, who had just removed her bonnet and held it in her hands, and he halted with such suddenness that Hetty and Rosie ran into him.

Miss Parvill had some experience with the initial effect she had on people, and she stood quietly, her eyes cast down, until they should recover.

It was Miss Margaret who spoke first because she was always speaking first. "Why, you're very beautiful. Quite as beautiful as Elfie, is she not, Papa?"

The squire only managed a strangled cough. Little Edith agreed silently with her sister and found her fingers itching for pencil and paper with which to capture this vision.

For his part, Hugh Hapgood was struggling to mask his dismay, while Hetty's mouth hung open in sheer horror. Only Rosie, from where she peeped out behind her father, gave a timid smile at the newcomer.

"However," Margaret went on, flustered, "my eldest sister, now Mrs. Frederick Tierney, has golden hair, which is far more fashionable than black."

Were either of Margaret's elder sisters still home and unmarried, there would have been an epidemic of eye-rolling at this (and perhaps a smothered "Ma-a-a-argaret!"), but Miss Parvill did not seem to take it amiss. "It is indeed," she replied. "More fashionable."

With an effort, Hugh gathered himself, as one who faces an unpleasant duty, and cast up a hasty prayer that Lavinia should never *ever* lay eyes on Miss Parvill, lest he never know peace again. Then he strode the rest of the way into the room. With a glance at the squire, who was still too agog to make the introductions, he said, "You must be Miss Parvill. I am Hugh Hapgood, and these are two of your new pupils, my daughters Harriet and Rosalie. I see you have already met my cousin Richard Hapgood, Miss Margaret Hapgood, and your third pupil Miss Edith Hapgood."

Belated bows and curtsies followed, after which Hugh politely asked how Miss Parvill found her walk that morning, and she as politely answered. When the squire still said nothing and merely looked longingly at the window as if he would like to escape, Margaret leaped into the fray again. "You'll want to see the schoolroom, I suppose. It isn't much, but at least Dorcas cleaned it, which she wouldn't have, if I hadn't hounded her. And if any lesson books you're wanting seem to be missing, ask Dorcas to search Elfie and Alice's old room because it's almost certain Alice was using them to press weeds and flowers."

"I see," said Miss Parvill, though this must have been a somewhat mystifying speech to her. "Yes, please. If you would show us the schoolroom, we can get started. Unless the squire or Mr. Hugh Hapgood have any questions for me...?"

"None," croaked the squire as he edged toward the door. "Day. Hounds. Pardon." And he was gone.

Hugh repressed a sigh. His cousin was never one for the niceties, but Hugh would have appreciated a bit more effort in this situation, not to mention how much it would have helped if someone had forced Augusta Hapgood to rise from her couch of infirmity for just one morning.

"Let us see the schoolroom, Margaret," he said, gesturing for her to lead the way.

"How are you finding Holliton, Miss Parvill?" he asked, as they followed the parade of girls up the staircase and through the corridor. Only Hetty hung back with them, sticking close to her father and staring steadily at the new governess.

"We are but recently arrived," Miss Parvill replied, "and my brother has preached only the one sermon as yet, but everyone has been most welcoming. We hope to like it here very much."

"Yes. Mr. Benfield was delighted that we could find both curate and governess at one fell swoop, as it were."

"We count ourselves fortunate as well, that the opportunity presented itself."

Hetty was a little relieved to find that Miss Parvill neither tittered nor fluttered her lashes nor gave coy smiles when she spoke to her employer, but perhaps modesty was her preferred method of fascination. Glancing up at her father to measure his response, Hetty thought he appeared the same as ever—sober, grave, polite.

"Mr. Benfield says your brother was made a Fellow of Queens' College, Cambridge," ventured Hugh. "You must be proud of him."

At this Miss Parvill lifted her head and color flooded her lovely face. "I am very proud of him. Henry is clever and perceptive. He was unmatched at school. If His Majesty ennobled men for their intellect, my Henry would be a duke! And a wealthy one."

Hugh blinked at this fervor and was thankful for the bustle of arriving at the schoolroom. He muttered only, "Your pride does you both credit." He supposed all unmarried sisters of clergymen felt strongly about their brothers because their stars rose and fell together. Miss Benfield, for instance, certainly viewed her own brother with a protective and proud eye, even if she did not claim dukedoms for him.

Alarmed by how Miss Parvill's high color rendered her even more striking and by her father's resulting confusion, Hetty gave him a little push. "You had better be going, Papa. We have much to learn, and Miss Parvill cannot be expected to teach with everyone hovering about."

"To be sure," he answered. He paused again in the doorway, however. "Miss Parvill, will this be an acceptable time to begin lessons each day? I understand the walk from Holliton is slightly longer than from Patterton."

"This time will work well," she replied. "And a walk is an invigorating way to begin the day."

Hetty widened her eyes at her father to express, *Thank you very much, now* do *go, Papa!* But, to her consternation, he failed to take note and said, "I found it so myself, in this fine weather, but perhaps when the weather turns it might be necessary for me or for Hal—the hired boy at Bramleigh—to ferry you and my girls back and forth."

"Please do not trouble yourselves," Miss Parvill said, her color coming again. "I walk in all weathers, and—and my brother Henry will accompany me as often as he can."

"That is kind of him, but I do not suppose his duties will always grant him the liberty."

"I prefer to walk with Henry," she insisted, a strained note entering her voice.

Immediately Hugh held up his hands in surrender. "Very well. Only do let me know if it becomes difficult." He wondered if the woman thought he was trying to bully her into giving up time with her precious brother or—worse—if somehow she mistook his question for a sign of overfond solicitude. He grimaced. She was beautiful, but she was not *that* beautiful. *Have no fear*, he told her silently. *I have no designs on your person or any ambition to challenge the place your brother holds in your affections.*

"Good-bye, Papa," shrilled Hetty.

This time he did not frustrate her. He bowed his farewell.

"I'll go too," cried Margaret, at his heels. "Miss Parvill, just ask Edith if you need to know anything. Button—that's our cook—she'll have some food laid out around noon or so."

"Then I will return for you at two, girls," Hugh informed them. He didn't know what to make of the ferocious scowl Hetty gave him when he said this—he only hoped it didn't presage a day of naughtiness on her part. But how could it, when the girl had got everything she asked for?

He need not have worried. The moment he was gone, Hetty heaved a sigh of relief, and her face was pleasant enough as she hurried Rosie to a seat at the table and chose another for herself. She would have preferred Papa not mentioning when he could next be operated on by Miss Parvill's wiles, but she would work very hard to convince him that he need not walk them back and forth each day. For this to happen, the lessons must go *flawlessly*, and she dearly hoped Miss Parvill were as skilled in teaching as she was in stunning people with her looks.

She was not.

It was not that Miss Parvill was a bad teacher, Hetty thought several hours later, when they were partaking of Button's dry sandwiches, fruit confit and tea. It was that her heart did not seem to be in it. The morning was spent in measuring how far along each of her charges was. They were each made to read aloud, to figure, to repeat facts from history and names of kings, to find places on maps, to conjugate French verbs (or, in Rosie's case, to learn the verb *chanter*). When it was not their turn to be tested, Miss Parvill told them to choose a passage to read in the Bible that she could question them about later. Hetty quickly turned to the Christmas story in the Gospel of Luke because then she needn't bother reading it, and she could spend that time observing. And what she saw was that Miss Parvill seemed to do a lot of daydreaming.

When Edith was reciting her multiplication tables, Hetty saw Miss Parvill's gaze wander to the window. Nor did their teacher correct her when Edith could not recall eleven multiplied by twelve and she guessed 134.

When little Rosie stumbled and mangled her way through her reading passage, even saying "Stuffier little children" instead of "Suffer the little children," Miss Parvill just said, "Very nice, my dear."

The only time Miss Parvill perked up was when she told them they were going to memorize speeches from *Romeo and Juliet* and perhaps even play a scene. "Have you seen or read Shakespeare before, girls?"

"I have seen *The Comedy of Errors* and *All's Well That Ends Well* at the Taunton fair," volunteered Edith, as her cousins Hetty and Rosie shook their heads.

"Well, you will like *Romeo and Juliet* far better," declared Miss Parvill. "It is about a pair of star-crossed lovers who fall violently in love, but whose families are bitter enemies. Therefore, they must marry in secret."

Her listeners gasped appreciatively.

"Is it a comedy or a tragedy?" asked Edith.

"A most heartbreaking tragedy."

Rosie looked worried. "I think it will be hard for me to read, Miss Parvill."

"I will help you. And it was written nearly the same time as the Authorized Version of the Bible, so the language is much alike, and you did splendidly in reading your passage. Tomorrow I will bring you my copy of a new book called *Tales from Shakespeare*, by a brother and sister Charles and Mary Lamb. If you read the story first, it is easier to understand the play."

"By a brother and sister!" cried Rosie. "How clever they must be. Like you and your brother, Miss Parvill."

A shadow flitted across Miss Parvill's glorious countenance, but it vanished before Hetty could even be sure she had seen aright, and there was no more talk of Shakespeare that day.

Matters improved somewhat after their luncheon because Miss Parvill said it was time for music and drawing. None of the girls could play, so they learned their first notes and chords on the Hapgoods' old spinet and how to read the treble music staff. Then Miss Parvill thrust them aside and pounded out a marvelous concerto that brought Margaret and Dorcas and Button and Hal to peek around the open door. A burst of applause greeted its conclusion, and, for an instant, Hetty thought the governess might cry.

"What is it, Miss Parvill?" asked Rosie, drawing near to her and touching the faded material of her sleeve.

"It is nothing," was the stony reply. She turned her head sharply, her glare scattering the audience of Margaret and the servants, and then stood up and clapped her hands. "Time for drawing. Did you bring the paper and pencils, Harriet?"

Hetty held them out but thought it fair to warn her, "Miss Parvill, I don't know if anyone has told you, but my cousin Edith is marvelous gifted with pencils and chalks and charcoal and paints."

"Are you?" Miss Parvill smiled upon the young artist. "You must show me some of your work."

So great was Edith's desire to capture the beauteous governess that she blurted, "Might I not draw you now, Miss Parvill? A sketch, and then you can judge."

"Very well. But what will your cousins do in the meantime?"

"Watch Edith!" piped Rosie, and Hetty nodded in hearty agreement. Watching Edith work was sheer magic.

This was how Mr. Henry Parvill came upon them, some time later. Miss Parvill was seated beside the open casement, her hair gleaming blue-black in the light and her face seen in profile as she gazed out. Opposite, on the sofa, gathered the clutch of pupils, heads bent to watch the likeness emerge.

The young curate had been admitted by Dorcas after rapping on the door for some time and being on the point of abandoning the venture and going around the house. Just as Miss Porterworth had told the DeWitts, Mr. Parvill was every bit the equal of his sister in beauty, and Dorcas had been so awestruck to behold this young god and hear him say, "I have come to fetch the governess, my sister Miss Parvill," that she could only gawp at him. Belatedly, she stabbed a finger in the direction of the drawing room and let him pass, drawing back as if her rumpled skirts might besmirch him.

He paused as he entered the room, taking in the tableau, and a smile came to his face. "Good afternoon, ladies, Elinor. Elinor, it seems I have come too soon?"

"Henry!" She sprang up and crossed to take his arm and pull him toward the others. "This was meant to be a drawing lesson, but they tell me Miss Edith already knows more than I could ever teach." Her eyes glowing with more spirit than she had shown all day, she performed the introductions, and, in wide-eyed silence, each girl received her bow from the head-turning young man.

"May I see?" He held out a long-fingered, elegant hand for Edith's drawing.

"'Tis only a sketch," gulped Edith.

Perhaps, but even Edith's most slapdash creations had a charm and life of their own, and this of her teacher was no exception. Mr. Parvill stared at it for a full minute, his face still and unreadable.

"Is—is it not good?" Edith ventured.

He was looking at his sister, and some wordless communication passed between them. Then he turned back to Edith. "It is *very* good, though your subject looks rather pensive, as if her mind and wishes were elsewhere." He held up the paper. "May I keep this? That your teacher may study it tonight and discover how best she might teach such a prodigy."

Edith went scarlet with pleasure and embarrassment, and she nodded. She hoped to have many more opportunities to capture Miss Parvill, but if only she had the courage to ask *Mr.* Parvill to sit! Perhaps she might ask Margaret to do it? Though Margaret was sure to do so in a way that made everyone uncomfortable.

Shortly thereafter, Mr. Parvill whisked his sister away, and all Hetty's earlier fears were for naught. If Miss Parvill hoped to work further on enchanting Hugh Hapgood, it would have to wait for the morrow.

# Chapter Nineteen

**Abroad as I was walking,**
**Down by some greenwood side,**
**I heard a young girl singing,**
**"I wish I were a bride."**
—Folk Song, "Abroad as I Was Walking" (18th c.)

Five days had passed since Hugh Hapgood's return from Sussex with Rosie. Five days in which they had removed from Bramleigh to the Simpsons' place in Patterton, and his girls had begun lessons with their new governess. Five days in which the swell of gossip surrounding the Parvills only grew, as more and more people saw them or became acquainted.

"I don't believe I can recall one word of his sermon," Constance Porterworth reported to her soon-to-be sister-in-law. "I could not even tell you the text! And you cannot imagine the crush inside,

Rosemary. I thought Papa and I might have to stand, but we managed to squeeze into the very last pew. Of course, Holliton Church is no Exeter Cathedral, thank heavens. To be in the very last *cathedral* pew would render Mr. Parvill no bigger than a speck, and it would not be worth the trouble to go to see a *speck*, even if you knew it was a very handsome speck."

"From the very last pew of Holliton Church, was Mr. Parvill more the size of a homunculus, then?" asked Rosemary innocently, choosing a new color of thread from her workbasket.

Miss Porterworth gave her arm a playful shove. "Oh, how funny you are. I have no idea what size a homunculus would be, though perhaps it is nearly the same size as a monkey? It sounds the same, at any rate. Well, he has a very nice voice, and you might have heard a pin drop while he spoke. And then the crowd gathered round him and his beautiful sister after the service! I told Agnes it could not take longer to be presented to Their Majesties at St. James than it took to be introduced to the Parvills. Oh, Rosemary, I do not know how you can bear your curiosity and not go to see them. I tried to get Papa to take me again to the evening service, but he was so stubborn and said he would not be put to such trouble again! You, at least, are known to Miss Parvill and might call on them at their parsonage, if you pleased. I asked Roscoe again if we mightn't invite them to our ball, but he absolutely refuses and says, for all their good looks, they haven't a penny and nobody knows their family. I want to go to Holliton again this Sunday, but I dread asking Papa. Why did you not go, Rosemary? Might *you* come with me?"

Rosemary did not go to Holliton Church the Sunday prior because she attended Mr. Benfield's church, as always. And if her heart beat faster in hopes of seeing Mr. Hugh Hapgood, she was disappointed. In fact, the Hapgoods had not removed to Patterton until the Monday and had spent the Sunday at Bramleigh and attended Bramleigh Downs.

It had now been nearly three weeks since she had seen Hugh Hapgood, and, were it not for the engagement ball approaching on the Friday, she began to think she would never see him again. Why had he not called? Were they not friends now? She knew from Miss Benfield that he had called at the vicarage twice already, since his return. She knew, from the same source, that he walked his girls home to Patterton from Bramleigh each afternoon, following their lessons. Had he already fallen under Miss Parvill's spell? Would he, like half the county, crowd Holliton church on Sundays, the one day of the week Rosemary hoped she could glimpse him?

"He expressed his thanks to us for our assistance in securing Miss Parvill," Miss Benfield reported to Rosemary. "And he told me pointedly that I should pass those thanks on to you, since he had not had the good fortune to meet with you."

*'Good fortune'? Did it require 'good fortune'?* Rosemary demanded of the universe. Did it not simply require him to take the trouble to walk to Marchmont? But he could not be bothered, she supposed. He had already forgotten her, and those moments of rapport she had attached significance to were no more than inventions of an overactive fancy.

She would have been much comforted, no doubt, to know that Hugh was as troubled as she. After he had overseen his family's removal and got the girls settled into their new routine, he sat down to his ledgers and attempted to work, only to find himself restless. He had set up his study at the front of the house, that he might have a view of the street, and too often, when a carriage passed or he heard voices or saw movement, he would raise his eyes expectantly, only to be disappointed. Where was she? Did she never walk into the village anymore? He tried to think of an excuse to call at Marchmont, but after he had already called twice at the vicarage, bringing the girls to see Lionel, and asked the Benfields to be sure to thank Miss DeWitt for her help as well, it would seem oddly insistent to appear at Marchmont just to say the same. He sighed and took to mending his pen. He would see her at the ball, at least. She could not fail to appear at her own brother's engagement ball.

Another day passed, and then, on the Thursday before the ball, Lady DeWitt greeted her daughter at breakfast with a kiss and a request. "My love, what would you think of gathering some autumn crocuses and lady's-tresses? I thought to fill the two bronze vases for the ball. You have been much at home and doing nothing but teaching your school and walking our grounds. And why don't you stop at Mr. Weeks' and tell him to send up an extra two dozen spermaceti candles?"

"Very well," agreed Rosemary, painfully glad to have a reason to venture into Patterton again.

If she was going to be traipsing the fields she would need her boots and a gown that could stand some dust and wet, but if anyone might see her (she did not even in her mind specify a particular person), she wanted to look as neat as she might. She chose a plain, reddish-brown frock, woven with a dark-gold ribbon in the neckline that matched the ribbon of her chip bonnet. Selecting a capacious basket to carry her findings, she set out, determining that she would allow herself to walk the main street of Patterton *twice,* once up and once down, but she would not allow herself to hesitate before the Simpsons' place, much less glance over.

Hugh finished checking the tally of August's deposits, congratulating himself that he was at last settling to work, when he happened to look up and saw Miss DeWitt passing. He could not say for certain how he knew it was Miss DeWitt—he had not seen a dress of that color on her before, and the woman's face was hidden by her bonnet, but he could determine that her hair was dark, and, having spent a disgraceful amount of time thinking about her person, he would be willing to swear it was she.

In his haste to rise and don his frock coat, the receipts cascaded to the floor, but he paid no heed to this. Precious minutes were lost in dashing hither and yon with no success until he called to the servants, "Olcott! Bundish, have you seen my hat?"

A tall, lean, colorless woman appeared presently, frowning over the disarray she saw behind him, but he only snatched his looked-for hat from her hands, saying, "Leave them—I will sort them when I return," before rushing from the house.

"Thank you, Mr. Weeks," Rosemary was saying to the chandler. "I told my mother we had candles enough, but I suspect she wants to set Marchmont ablaze."

"And why shouldn't she?" returned Mr. Weeks, openly grinning at the large order placed. "It's not every day you hold a ball to celebrate an upcoming wedding. First of you children getting married. This calls for every branch and chandelier in the place to shine forth. You tell Lady DeWitt they will be there before she can say Jack Robinson."

"If that is the case," Rosemary smiled, "they will be there before I am there to say such a thing." She held up her empty basket. "I have a second task to attend to."

"Why, Miss DeWitt," came a rumbling voice she knew too well behind her. "What brings you to Patterton today?"

Mr. Weeks touched his hat to them both and backed away, and Rosemary barely had the presence of mind to nod her thanks to him before she turned. "Mr. Hapgood." She was relieved her voice was steady. "My mother gave me a few tasks in preparation for the ball tomorrow. I see you have returned to Somerset. Your family are all well?"

"Yes, thank you. And yours?"

"Well. All well. How—how do you find the Simpsons' place? I hope it is comfortable."

"It is no palace, but it suits our purposes admirably." He gestured at her basket. "I would offer to carry that for you, but I see you have not yet filled it."

Her face blossomed into a smile. "And when it is full, it will hardly be heavier than when empty. You see, my mother has asked me to gather some autumn crocuses and lady's-tresses. She wishes to arrange them in vases for the ball. I decided I had better order the candles first because I might not be presentable after I have trailed through the fields and woods."

"I was just starting out on a walk myself," said Hugh. "Might I join you?"

Her heart leaping, she could only nod, and they set off in the direction of Bramleigh because that way lay the little wood and the confluence of streams. The September day was fine. The morning chill had passed, promising mild warmth and blue sky. Rosemary hoped they would not fill the basket too quickly, and yet it would be awkward to draw the task out, for then he might have to excuse himself. He did not appear to be pressed for time, however, merely sauntering beside her as if he too meant to enjoy the day.

"I hope," he began after some minutes, "that the Benfields delivered my message of thanks to you, for your assistance in employing Miss Parvill."

"Oh, yes," she assured him, her throat constricting at the introduction of that woman's name. "I hope she is proving satisfactory? The girls have begun lessons, have they not?"

"They have. My Rosie, whom you have not yet met, seems already quite happy. I find her writing on anything she can find and reading words to herself. And it is not only the schooling. It seems each day she has more color in her face and can manage the walk home more easily. There is an incline from Bramleigh back to the village, you are probably aware, Miss DeWitt."

"Yes. That could be a steep slope for little legs. But I am glad to hear it, Mr. Hapgood. Glad to hear of her love for learning and her improving health. I know you were concerned for her." She stooped to tug gently on several stems of lady's-tresses, only to have the first few tear in half. "Oh, dear. They're rather fragile."

"I have a knife," he offered, crouching down to slice them at the base and hand them to her.

"Thank you. They're rather spindly and hard to spy out, are they not? This may take some time, Mr. Hapgood, and I fear you did not understand the difficulty of the task you volunteered for."

His eyes gleamed at her. "But the knowledge has come to me too late. We've already seen that you rip them in your vehemence. Unless you wish to hand your mother a basket of green shreds for her vases, I must keep my shoulder to the wheel."

Rosemary laughed. "Very well, very well. My mother and I both thank you for your willingness and your skill with your knife."

They wandered the field in perfect amity, speaking of the changing season and the many preparations for the ball. Rosemary would stop and point when she discovered the frail, furry stalks with their miniature white blossoms, and Hugh would bend to cut them.

"How do you suppose these came to be called lady's-tresses?" he wondered. "No lady of my acquaintance has green and white hair."

"Perhaps they reminded some early botanist of a mermaid," Rosemary suggested. "Do not mermaids have green hair?"

To her surprise, Hugh flushed, his dark eyes looking at her sharply before he turned away. "The only mermaid I have seen had black hair," he said under his breath.

"You have seen a mermaid?" she faltered. There could be no mistaking his meaning—if Hugh Hapgood claimed to have seen a siren with black hair, it could only be the alluring Miss Parvill. A little pain pierced her, and she felt as if the sun disappeared behind clouds. She had been reveling in his company and thought him contented as well to be with her, but his mind—his heart—was elsewhere.

That he might not guess her unhappiness, she stalked a few steps apart, her eyes now sweeping the grasses blindly for the wretched plants.

Hugh watched her with chagrin. She could only have walked away because she suspected something underlay the intensity of his look and his remark, and she did not want to know what that something was. And yet she had let him accompany her on this walk…! It could only mean that she liked him well enough, but she did not want him to suppose she welcomed anything more from him than this pleasant fellowship.

And why should he himself want more?

He could not say, but he did.

He wanted more. More of her. Her entirely, truth be told.

Rosemary, having ruthlessly taken herself in hand again, raised her voice a little and called over, "You did not say what Hetty thought of her new governess."

Hugh's mouth twisted, wishing the new governess at the devil. He did not wish to talk about the new governess at present; rather, he wanted to jerk Miss DeWitt's bonnet from her head and make her nightwing lady's tresses tumble about her shoulders to her waist as they had in the library. Had he known then how that vision, that moment, would haunt him, he would never have let her wriggle her way out of the consequences so easily.

"Hetty doesn't say much of her," he answered roughly.

"Oh." His tone took her aback. She wondered if the girl still clung to her notion of Rosemary marrying her father and was therefore uncooperative with her new teacher. Giving an uneasy laugh, Rosemary said, "Ah, then let us hope it is as the Italians say: Nulla nuova, buona nuova. No news is good news. Hetty does not strike me as one who would hold back, if she had a complaint."

"Just so."

They carried on harvesting lady's tresses in silence, Rosemary abashed and Hugh struggling to overcome his mood. When she went to dampen her handkerchief in the stream, that she might keep the plants fresh, he came upon a clutch of autumn crocuses at the edge of the wood. Digging under the soft purple blooms gently with his knife, they came free. He turned and presented them to her, his eyes narrow and inscrutable.

"Thank you! What beautiful ones—a few more bunches like these and our work will be done."

"Will you dance with me at the ball, Miss DeWitt?"

Rosemary could do no more than blink at him for a long moment, her heart racing with anticipation and joy at this unexpected request. She had not imagined he would dance. He still wore mourning for his wife, after all. In her most extravagant fancies, she had only pictured him at a card table or at supper, perhaps saying a few kind words in passing. But he would dance—and he wished to dance with her!

"I would be honored," she murmured. "I am so glad you will come. My father will be glad of it too."

His countenance brightened and a corner of his mouth lifted. "I must have some reward for my labor. I am certain you walked up and down the street in Patterton until you could find a willing victim."

"No, I declare," she laughed, blushing at how near the truth he struck.

"It has been very long since I danced," he went on, "so I will have my revenge upon you, when you see what a punishment it can be to stand up with me."

When he jested with her in that manner, the pirate grin making a fleeting appearance, Rosemary thought she would be happy to stand stock-still and stare at him the livelong day, but she strove to answer lightly, "Then I will wear my sturdiest boots and you may do your worst."

His worst?

Hugh's grin faded. Miss DeWitt could have no notion of what he seemed capable of, at his worst. Hugh had had no idea himself. But the woman certainly did seem to inspire the most unruly thoughts in him. He was standing near enough now that he might have reached and touched her. He might have grasped her by the waist and pulled her against him. She would lift those tawny eyes, and he would thrust his hands into her lustrous hair—

"Oh! Do look, Mr. Hapgood," Rosemary gasped, tearing her gaze from his and pointing beyond him. "There are enough there to satisfy a thousand bronze vases."

"So there are." He pulled out his handkerchief and dabbed at his brow, though the day was hardly hot. Good Lord, what was coming over him? If he were not to compromise Miss DeWitt in a closed library, with her lying full across him, it seemed he wanted to try his luck on the edge of this quiet wood, in plain view from nearly all directions. How might she explain it away then?

She kept her distance from him after that, perhaps sensing danger, like a mouse eyed too greedily by a cat. The flowers were cut; the basket was filled. They spoke calmly of safe subjects: her brother's engagement, her own pupils, Lionel's progress, Hugh's work.

"And how will you like being partner of just one bank, instead of three?" she asked, when they were nearly back to his lodgings.

"That remains to be seen. But I have liked having more time to see my children and to attend to other, more important aspects of life."

She guessed they had circled completely around, and he once more hinted at taking a second wife. It was a depressing end to a delightful and, at moments, thrilling morning, but Rosemary rallied herself. Thinking of Lionel, she said, "I am sure your children welcome more time with you. Having—lost—their mother, their remaining parent can only hold increasing space in their hearts."

"I hope so," he agreed in a quiet voice. "I have discovered, in recent months, how dearly I value them. It brings me joy to have them all near at hand and to learn more of their characters and habits. I only hope it may continue long."

"Mm," was Rosemary's response.

He feared, then, that marrying Miss Parvill might result in the family being broken up again? Surely a governess would not want to send the girls away. But perhaps her duties and attentions would be so centered on her new husband and any children that might result from this second union, that she would have no strength for the three which had been left over from the first. Miss Parvill appeared very capable, but she was also very young.

A little wry pity mixed with Rosemary's feelings toward the governess: if Hetty suspected her new mama wanted to ship her away to school again, she would not go without first taking her pound of flesh.

They parted before the Simpsons' place, after Rosemary thanked him and assured him again that she could carry the basket perfectly well back to Marchmont. They were both a little dejected, she still lingering over Miss Parvill's blessed good fortune, and he supposing the serious talk of his children had only reminded Miss DeWitt how much she preferred her carefree life.

But, despite this, each could not help but look forward to seeing the other at the ball. Hugh planned to shut his study door and the drapes, that he might practice his dancing steps beforehand and not have to concentrate overmuch at Marchmont when he would rather be enjoying her company. And Rosemary could not keep from thinking that, though Miss Parvill might have captured his heart, there would be no Miss Parvill at the ball.

At the ball, Rosemary would have him all to herself.

# Chapter Twenty

**A thousand Loves around her forehead fly;**
**A thousand Loves sit melting in her eye.**
—Coleridge, *Lines on an Autumnal Evening* **(1790s)**

"Papa, how dashing you look," cried Rosie, staring at him in his evening dress. He had abandoned his black breeches for buff ones, and his waistcoat was pearl gray. His man Bundish rejoiced at the chance to lay aside the sober mourning clothes and display his skills once more.

"Thank you, my dear."

Behind Rosie stood Hetty, hands clasped, a-tremble with eagerness. He *did* look dashing! Surely even Miss DeWitt might think so?

Hetty had jealously watched her governess's interactions with her father every afternoon that week, and she began to think her Papa might be safe from the dangers of Miss Parvill. For one thing, after the initial encounter, he no longer seemed overwhelmed by her beauty, and he was no more than polite. As for Miss Parvill herself, Hetty suspected she would much prefer a younger man, like a Romeo or a County Paris or her adored brother Mr. Parvill, who faithfully walked her from Bramleigh to Holliton every afternoon. When Miss Parvill spoke of *Romeo and Juliet* and read them the story out of *Tales from Shakespeare*, it was the young lovers she sympathized with. "Only see what a terrible dilemma Juliet faces! She is not naturally undutiful. She wishes to please her father, but he cares only to make a good match for her, and he cannot see beyond his prejudices." Nor did Miss Parvill seem ever to think a man of Lord Capulet's or Lord Montague's age could be a suitable match for Juliet, even if Romeo were not around. Indeed, if the Parvills were not so hideously poor, Hetty might have told Lionel the whole idea of Miss Parvill marrying their father was laughable, and they need not waste more worry on it.

But the Parvills *were* poor. And Romeos and Counties Paris were not plentiful in Somerset or anywhere other than Verona, it appeared. Be that as it may, if Miss Parvill had not yet lighted on Hetty's father as a solution to her money woes, Hetty would be the last to inform her.

"Tomorrow you must tell us all about the ball, Papa," she said. "What people wore, and who danced with whom."

He grinned at her. "Does that interest you? I will, then."

"Will you dance, Papa?" asked Rosie.

He got a musing look in his eyes. "I hope to." Then he grabbed a hand of each of his daughters and spun them around, laughing.

"You must practice with me, before the Benfields' carriage comes, lest I embarrass myself at Marchmont."

Then they were all three laughing and dancing in the cramped parlor, and Hetty almost cried because she could not remember her Papa ever doing so with them before or seeming so light-hearted. When the carriage came, he gave them each a kiss on the forehead. "Good night, my dears. Be good for Olcott."

"Good night!" They scurried to wave at him and the Benfields from the study window, Hetty swallowing what she really wanted to say, which was: *Try, if you can, Papa, to love Miss DeWitt!*

The DeWitts was gathered at the entrance of Marchmont to greet their guests, and, as Lady DeWitt intended, the house was ablaze with candles. It was not so very big a ball, but to a man who had not attended one in some thirteen years it was enough. Hugh recognized the Porterworths, the viscount's family from Pattergees, and his own party, but the rest were strangers to him. As he had guessed, the Richard Hapgoods were not in attendance, his cousin pleading his wife Augusta's ill health.

"How fine Rosemary looks," Miss Benfield remarked. This was addressed to her brother, it seemed, because she did not look at Hugh, and the vicar replied, "Very fine, indeed. Lovely."

Silently, Hugh agreed. Miss DeWitt wore a gown of rose mull with an overlay of sheerest silk organza, and the fabric set off her fine complexion, complementing the paler rose of her cheeks. Her rich hair was dressed in her new fashion and wound with pink rosebuds and ribbon, and into his mind came the verses he heard his girls reading aloud the past week: "Oh, she doth teach the torches to burn bright!" What came after that? Ah, yes. *It seems she hangs upon the cheek of night like a rich jewel in an Ethiope's ear, beauty too rich for use, for earth too dear.*

"Welcome, Mr. Benfield, Miss Benfield. Mr. Hapgood," Sir Cosmo greeted them when they reached him.

Hugh scarcely noticed the man. Or his wife or two sons, though he made his bows correctly. His eyes sought Miss DeWitt's, and he found hers on him. She blushed rosier and made an attempt to smile, and neither one could muster any speech before the line moved on and Hugh's party found itself in the ballroom.

While the musicians tuned, Mr. Benfield performed various introductions. The Wynstanleys, the Penders, the Reverend So-and-So, the Venerable Something-or-Others. The Something-or-Others included two tittering daughters, and Hugh was pumped and probed by their mother. He could see he must ask the daughters to dance at some point because the only way to avoid it would be to declare he did not intend to dance, but that would mean giving up Miss DeWitt, and Hugh would rather suffer a dozen quadrilles with a dozen interchangeable Miss Something-or-Others than lose that chance. He wished he had been more specific with Miss DeWitt when they walked together. He should have asked her particularly for the first dance and for the supper dance, and it was perhaps a sign of how far gone he was that he worried she would already be claimed.

The guests received, Sir Cosmo gave a signal to the musicians, and Roscoe DeWitt and his betrothed strode radiantly to the head of the room to take their place for the opening set. The Honorable Miss

Birdlow followed, partnered by her cousin Geoffrey Wynstanley, and, as Hugh looked this way and that for Miss DeWitt, he saw her take her place with her brother Norman.

"Would you do me the honor?" he demanded suddenly of the nearest Miss Something-or-Other, and when she shrieked and giggled behind her fan and gave him an arch look and her sister a triumphant one—in brief, once she got through the whole process—he led her up the rows until they could squeeze in beside Rosemary and Norman. Miss Porterworth called for The Indian Queen, and the dance began.

The figures afforded Hugh and Rosemary but one opportunity to speak, as they joined hands and went in circle twice before the pairs moved in opposite directions up and down the room.

"I see you have found your first victim," teased Rosemary, while Hugh accosted her with, "May I have the honor of the next dance?" He grinned at her joke, and she nodded at his question, and the figures separated them.

Twenty minutes later, he returned Miss Something-or-Other to her mother's protection, taking care that his gaze did not meet that of the younger Miss Something-or-Other, and went to claim Rosemary, who stood beside Norman and Lady DeWitt.

"Did Miss Cumberstock's feet escape harm?" Rosemary rallied him, as he held her gloved fingers and led her to the floor.

"Whose?"

"Mr. Hapgood! The young lady you just danced with," she laughed.

Hugh had the grace to look abashed. "Was that her name? Mr. Benfield introduced me to so many people they became an undistinguished mass, I'm afraid. She happened to be nearest at hand when the set was forming."

They each had to take their place in their line, and, as many more couples formed sets for this next dance, both Hugh and Rosemary inwardly rejoiced that it might take a half-hour or more for them all to work through the figures.

"How did your mother's vases turn out?" he blurted, the first time they clasped hands.

"Charmingly," she replied when they armed right and left. "You will see them on the center supper tables."

He waited until they were leading down the set to say, "I might need your assistance to locate them—perhaps you would honor me as well with the supper dance?"

In response she smiled with shining eyes, and Hugh felt his high spirits buoyed still higher.

There is no place for serious conversation on a dance floor, but Hugh and Rosemary contrived to talk as much as they could, and, while neither could be accused of anything so frivolous as flirting, they spoke in a more playful manner than usual. Roscoe and Norman DeWitt knew this side of their sister, since the DeWitt family enjoyed a good frolic, but it was doubtful any of Hugh Hapgood's acquaintances would have recognized him at first. Perhaps only his brother-in-law Wellington Sidney, who had those long-gone Oxford memories for comparison, but Mr. Sidney was counties away in

Sussex. Or Harriet Morrow Hapgood might recall this light-hearted man from their earliest encounters, but she lay in her grave.

"Mr. Hapgood, I do believe you have not been a truthful man. You dance very well."

"A skilled partner, perhaps."

"Nonsense. You have not stepped once on my feet or my gown, and you have never hesitated or gone the wrong direction."

"I will tell you a secret: I have been practicing."

"And did you have a partner for this practicing?"

"Not until this evening, when I enlisted Hetty and Rosie to partner me."

"Oh, delightful! I should have liked to see that." Then it occurred to Rosemary that the peerless Miss Parvill might also play the role of dancing mistress for the girls. Another link in the chain: Miss Parvill danced with Hetty and Rosie, and Hetty and Rosie danced with their father, and governess and employer looked forward to the day they might join hands with none between. But Rosemary pushed the thought away. Not tonight. Tomorrow would be soon enough to think such things.

"With whom do you practice, Miss DeWitt, to make you so nimble?"

"With my family, to be sure," she answered. "We all love to dance. Even my brother Norman, who does not love anything else about a ball, will dance and dance. Though he prefers the livelier pieces, where little conversation is possible with one's partner." Rosemary was grateful that, between Roscoe and Norman, at every ball or assembly she always had several dances claimed as a matter of course.

In her modesty she thought it was only her brothers' example or her father's standing which induced other gentlemen to ask her, and perhaps that accounted for some of her partners, but it was certainly the case that she was not obligated to sit out even once dance on this occasion.

If Hugh's sister-in-law Lavinia Sidney had been present, his next venture would have alarmed her, for it sounded very much like flattery. "The rosebuds in your hair are charming, though perhaps I might prefer the autumn crocuses."

"Even were I brave enough to filch crocuses from my mother's vases, sir, they are not so sturdy as rosebuds," Rosemary returned. "And a ball is hard work."

"Not in your company."

For the first time, Rosemary's eyelids fluttered at him. It was not coquetry; it was surprise—incredulity. She was glad the dance called for her to cast outward, that she might have a moment to recover. What could it mean? Why should he say such things to her, if he meant only to be her friend? Could he intend more? But what, then, of the black-haired mermaid? He could not—he could not possibly have meant her...?

Seeing the confusion he caused her, Hugh had his own doubts. He was grown rusty. He no longer knew how to win a woman, yet that was what he wanted to do. Years ago, when he courted Harriet, she had more than met him halfway. She would have received a compliment like that with a smile, an arch look, a low laugh. She would have challenged it, purring, "How you flatter me, Mr. Hapgood, or do you say such things to every young woman?" Then he would have to insist, that she might be doubly gratified. But Miss DeWitt—with Miss DeWitt he could not read if she were more pleased or dismayed.

Their dance ended, and, before Hugh could take her hand to return her to Lady DeWitt, Roscoe was upon them. "Come on, Ros! Norman has Constance—let's make our square for Hole in the Wall."

Rosemary threw Hugh an apologetic look, which he responded to with a smile and a bow, and she was hastened away.

Now that he must wait for the supper dance, Hugh retreated to rejoin the Benfields. The second Miss Cumberstock must be asked to tread a measure at some point, but she was partnered by Wynstanley for this set, and Hugh could watch Miss DeWitt unhindered.

"What a crush there was in Holliton, I hear," the Reverend So-and-So was saying to Mr. Benfield. "All to see this new curate, this Parvill?"

"He is reputed to be a clever young man," answered Mr. Benfield, "a fellow of Queens' College, Cambridge, no less."

"It was not his intellect that drew so many on Sunday, we hear," his sister put in dryly, "but rather his beauty."

"Indeed!" cried the reverend. "And what say you—is the man so beauteous?"

"We have not yet seen him," admitted Mr. Benfield.

"But we have seen the sister," Miss Benfield said, "and if Mr. Parvill be half as attractive, I would not be astonished if Holliton were to experience a 'revival' such as the Methodists claimed in New England."

"Charlotte," chided her brother, even while he chuckled.

Miss Benfield turned to demand Hugh's opinion on their additions to the neighborhood, but she saw he had not been attending. He was watching her friend Miss DeWitt, a half-smile curving his lips as she and her brother worked their way down the room. The vicar's sister could not resist wanting to see how the land lay.

"Mr. Hapgood, I was pleased to see you left off your mourning tonight and that you are willing to partner our young ladies. It does me good to see the young people dance."

He only bowed his response.

"Miss Cumberstock is charming, is she not?"

"She seems an amiable girl."

"Yes. There's a lass who will make a fine wife and who longs to be one," continued Miss Benfield. "I fear she has not the resources for contentment in unmarried life, such as I have, or Miss DeWitt."

She had his attention then. "Is—is Miss DeWitt content to remain unmarried?"

"It seems. She has had offers, of course, though she has never been thought a beauty."

"She is well enough," was his short reply.

They watched the dancers in silence for some minutes, but then Hugh said, "Perhaps her heart was not engaged in the previous instances."

Miss Benfield hid a smile to see the fish was indeed on the hook. "I am sure you are right, Mr. Hapgood. Her heart was not engaged. When I said Rosemary had the resources to be content in unmarried life, that did not mean I thought that should be her fate. She is too clever and sensible and loving a creature. I would hate for her to be what Mr. Grey calls a 'flower born to blush unseen.'"

He said nothing, joining with her in the general applause when the dance ended, but Charlotte considered a good day's work put in and was not sorry when the younger Miss Cumberstock hovered so close that Mr. Hapgood was forced to ask her for the next. Dear Rosemary could only benefit by comparison with the Cumberstocks. Whether she would also benefit by comparison to Elinor Parvill was another matter, Charlotte worried, but Elinor Parvill was not here.

When the supper dance was upon them, Rosemary found Mr. Hapgood at her elbow, and she was both delighted and sorry when Auretti's Dutch Skipper was called for. Delighted, because it was one of her favorite dances, and sorry, because it was so lively that they would not have opportunity for conversation.

But if they could not converse, they could look and smile. And there was the thrill each time their hands came together, a thrill Rosemary could feel through her gloved fingertips all the way up her arms.

When the music ended and the lines broke up to go to supper, he was beside her again. "Pardon me," he said, reaching to touch her hair. "One of your rosebuds is askew."

Rosemary's own hand flew up, but then she withdrew it, afraid it would brush his and remind him of her forwardness at Bramleigh, when she had laid her hand on his sleeve. She stood and waited while he arranged the wayward ornament, aware of his nearness and the warmth between them after their recent exercise. Each strand of hair his fingers grazed seemed to light up with sensation, and she shivered. When he finally lowered his arm, she glanced up, expecting to find him still scrutinizing his handiwork, but his eyes were on hers. For one long moment, neither seemed to breathe. They only looked.

Somehow they were at the supper table, and Mr. Hapgood was pulling out a chair for her, but Rosemary had no memory how she got there. She was still breathless and dazed and almost fearful for the strength of her reaction to him. What would happen, after the ball and her fantasy were ended?

For the engagement of their son, Sir Cosmo and Lady DeWitt were not content to offer a mere sideboard collation. They must have a well-served meal with soup and roasted meats, cheese and fruits, cakes and jellies, wine and punch. After so much dancing, Rosemary was grateful for it.

"How are you enjoying the ball, Miss DeWitt?" asked the gentleman to her left. She vaguely recalled him being one of her father's former business partners, now also wealthy and retired.

"Vastly. I wish it might go on forever."

He chuckled and waved a knowing finger at her. "I know another, more likely solution. If you were to marry yourself, I do not doubt Sir Cosmo and Lady DeWitt would rejoice to give you a ball of your own. You would not take my William, but perhaps someone else might do, eh?"

Embarrassed, she was relieved to have a footman appear at her elbow offering venison. She nodded and was served, but the subject was not dropped. Now it was Mr. Hapgood on her right who said in his low voice, "*Are* you opposed to marriage, Miss DeWitt, or did the problem lie with this unfortunate William?"

"I—I am not opposed," she answered, ruffled. "In principle." Nervously she found herself tearing the piece of bread on her plate into fragments. With an effort, she flexed her fingers, put down the bread, and tried for levity. "But the possibility of a ball does not seem sufficient inducement to enter the married state. I am not certain 'a ball is worth a marriage.'"

"Nor would Henri IV have converted to the Romish religion if they had not dangled Paris before him," he followed her easily. "A ball might be worth a marriage, if the person one married were tempting enough."

"Perhaps you are right," she agreed, that she might direct the conversation elsewhere. No more talk of herself—she was afraid she would give too much away. "You—you say it has been very long since you were at a ball, and yet you dance well. You must not be very fond of the occasions yourself."

"I suppose one gets out of the habit," he said. "Mrs. Hapgood and I were married for thirteen years, and soon enough we had children."

"Yes, of course."

Rosemary pictured evenings spent by the fireside in domestic bliss: Mr. and Mrs. Hapgood sitting close together on a sofa, watching Lionel and Hetty play while infant Rosie nestled in her mother's arms. She almost sighed. No, she would not have wanted to go anywhere or do anything else either.

Certain that the memory must pain him, she choked, "I...am so sorry. How you must miss her and your life together."

Hugh stared at the bronze vase before him, glad Miss DeWitt's own gaze was fixed on her plate. The urge to blurt, "Miss her? Miss *Harriet*?" was repressed, but it was a near thing. He thought of the years spent treading upon eggs, trying to keep her happy, to raise her spirits, to hear out her endless complaints, to find common interests. And then, when he had given up these struggles, still more years spent living in unspoken truce, polite and distant. No, he confessed to himself now. He did not miss Harriet. Neither Harriet nor their life together. If he regretted anything, mourned anything, it was that, in keeping his distance from her, he also shut himself away from the children.

When he thought he had mastered himself sufficiently, he thanked Rosemary for her sympathy. Then he sought to steer them from danger, away from himself and his past. "You must have a very happy home life yourself, Miss DeWitt."

"I consider myself fortunate. But, really, apart from the years I spent at school in Taunton, I have never spent significant time away from home." She gave him a rueful smile. "I was terribly homesick there—though it was within easy reach of Marchmont!"

"Were you there long?"

"Several years. But I was home every holiday and had letters weekly, and once a month my parents would visit. Still, I was glad when my mother decided the school was inadequate. She let me return to Marchmont and have a governess."

He nodded slowly. "My girls seem to prefer that arrangement as well. Although," he added, his brow furrowing in puzzlement, "their home to this point has been Sussex, and they do not seem to miss Crawley at all."

Rosemary made a little noise in her throat. "Perhaps because they have discovered their home is wherever *you* are."

Her candid gaze met his, and Hugh felt his own throat constrict.

They both turned back to their food then, she deciding she had spoken too intimately, and he deep in thought.

Could it be true? Did Hetty and Rosie feel their home was in whatever place he might be found? It was not impossible. He had made the same discovery himself in recent months: he wanted to have them near. Not just Hetty and Rosie, but also Lionel, though the boy did not appear to share his sisters' growing attachment to their father. If Hugh represented home to his children, they had also come to represent home to him.

And there was one other piece, he knew now. He could not say precisely how or when, but somewhere in the time since they had first come to Somerset, Miss DeWitt became a part of this new life he was building. He wanted a home; he wanted his family; he wanted Miss DeWitt for his wife. Whether she wanted him for a husband was another matter, but he would not let that remain a mystery much longer. If he were to suffer the fate of the rejected William, it would not be for lack of trying.

But before he asked her, he would raise the idea with his children. Life had forced many changes on them of late, but this was one he wanted them to share and to welcome, if possible. He would offer for Miss DeWitt in any event, but to do so with his children's blessing, Hugh decided, would crown all.

# Chapter Twenty-One

**As in some wether-glass my Love I hold;**
**Which falls or rises with the heat or cold.**
—Dryden, *The Conquest of Granada by the Spaniards*
(1672)

Hugh held his peace and made his plans. On the Sunday following the ball, he and the girls attended Mr. Benfield's church again, and Hetty's were not the only Hapgood eyes drawn to the DeWitt pew. But, aside from greeting that family afterward, thanking Sir Cosmo for his hospitality and telling Miss DeWitt he hoped she was recovered from the festivities, Hugh had not much more to say to them, and both Rosemary and Hetty went home disappointed.

Hetty's spirits were still low at her lessons on Monday, but, as she was always muted around Miss Parvill, and as Miss Parvill was always abstracted, the lessons proceeded as usual. The end of the school day brought welcome diversions, however. For once, Hugh appeared before Miss Parvill's brother, and he came in a cart, no less, driven by Lionel!

Miss Parvill and her pupils were out of doors that afternoon, Edith and the girls set to sketch the ragged flowerbeds while their governess stared at nothing, so Lionel arrived to an appreciative audience and much fanfare.

"Lionel! Lionel!" shrieked Hetty and Rosie, crowding to greet him. Edith hung back, smiling, and Lionel took care to bring the horses to a smooth halt before handing the reins casually to Hal.

"Lionel, what are you doing here?" asked Rosie.

"Papa and I are doing some driving," he declared airily, "and then I will have dinner with you all to discuss Family Matters."

"Miss Parvill, allow me to introduce my son Lionel," said Hugh. He rather expected the boy to fall out of the cart open-mouthed when he saw the governess for the first time, but perhaps Lionel was too young to be overwhelmed, because he only made the most cursory bow and then leapt down, asking to see the girls' drawings.

"Hetty, yours is rubbish," he pronounced, "and Rosie's little better. Cousin Edith, let me see your masterwork."

Amused, Hugh turned back to Miss Parvill. "You see I have investigated and found this cart to rent from the Swan. It's too small to use in harvest, so the landlord has allowed me to reserve it for the afternoons, to drive you and the girls home."

"I thank you, Mr. Hapgood, but, as I mentioned, my brother Henry comes to fetch me."

"I remember, Miss Parvill, but I persist in thinking it worthwhile that we have an alternative plan, in the event of inclement weather or your brother's work preventing him from coming." Hugh felt a flare of impatience. Honestly, if it were not an impolite thing to do, he would just pick up his girls and leave the governess to fend for herself. It was not his fault she chose to live out, when a home had been offered her. The woman need not eye him as if he had anything more in mind. Though, to be fair, if one looked like Miss Parvill, perhaps other men always did have something more in mind.

Assistance came from an unexpected quarter, with the arrival of Miss Parvill's brother. The curate came on foot, as ever, and Miss Parvill's face lit up, as ever, when she caught sight of him. "Henry!"

Little Rosie had told her father of the surpassing beauty of Miss Parvill's brother (and how their cousin Edith was working on a secret sketch of him the few minutes each day he was among them), but the doubled impact of the two Parvills did take some getting used to, the first time one saw them together.

This being his fourth encounter with them, however, meant Hugh's awe was that much diminished, and it diverted him to see that Miss Parvill's excitement in seeing her brother was not so different from Hetty's and Rosie's at seeing Lionel. By Mr. Parvill's age, though, the brother was grown enough to respond with affection and courtesy, rather than with scorn. This godling took his sister by the waist and planted a kiss in her hair before returning Hugh's bow. "Mr. Hapgood. This might be the last fine day for a drive, I suspect—the glass is falling. I fear we are in for a spell of stormy weather."

"So I hear," answered Hugh. "I hoped to convince your sister that, on days of dirty weather, when I come to drive my girls back to Patterton, she would first accept a lift from me back to Holliton. Then you need not come to fetch her."

"What say you, Elinor?" Henry prompted. "I've been meaning to make the walk out to the Trull cottages, but I have put it off because it will take most of the afternoon."

"But you would not go if it was storming, Henry," she protested. "Think of your health."

He grinned. "I'm strong as an ox. It's the Gillings' whose health needs looking after, which is why I must go out there."

She submitted with poor grace. "Very well. Mr. Hapgood, if the weather is bad tomorrow, I will accept your offer of a lift to Holliton. Otherwise, I will walk, as I do in the mornings."

Hugh bowed his acknowledgement.

In the meanwhile, Lionel and the girls had taken to batting around a ball Hugh suspected was made of the girls' crumpled drawings. Or, rather, Lionel was batting it around, out of Hetty's and Rosie's reach. Laughing at their squeals and protests, their brother clasped his hands together to make a cricket bat of his outstretched arms, and he clubbed the ball high above their heads. It arced over them, all eyes upon it, and came down neatly into Mr. Parvill's open hand.

"Ah ha," he said, his hand closing. "Not a bad hit, considering this is far too light and irregular for a cricket ball."

"My brother was a celebrated bowler at Queens' College," boasted Miss Parvill, and Hugh hid a smile.

"And now, I am a not-very-celebrated curate of Holliton Parish," he teased, poking her playfully in the side.

"That will come," she said stubbornly.

"Did you really play for your college, sir?" asked Lionel, regarding the brother with far greater interest than he had shown in Miss Parvill.

"I did."

"And do you play no longer?"

"I have my work now," he told the boy. "But I still have a worn-out ball or two in my possession and a bat, should the need for them arise."

Lionel's eyes glowed in response, and Hugh wondered suddenly if Mr. Parvill were the mythical tutor-athlete neither he nor Miss DeWitt had truly believed in. Heavens! If that were the case, and Lionel clamored to study with the new curate, how would Hugh then make excuses to Mr. Benfield? His mouth curled ruefully. Miss DeWitt would have to help him navigate that particular situation, and thank God for that.

It was a cheerful crew that piled into the cart for the drive home, Lionel being allowed the reins again, and it was not until they were sitting down a few hours later for the dinner that Olcott carried over from the inn that Hetty asked, "Is this a special occasion, Papa?"

"Certainly. It is our first meal in months with only us."

"But is that all?" she pressed. "It is no one's birthday, unless it is yours."

He smiled. "Nor is it my birthday. What's this? I thought you told me how dearly you wanted us all to be together. Is that not why we have taken these lodgings and employed Miss Parvill?"

"It is. And that Lionel should be able to continue with Mr. Benfield." Hetty and Lionel exchanged a glance, in token of the other motive which could not be mentioned.

Hugh paused as Olcott finished serving them all and, when he nodded at her, withdrew. Then he set his soup spoon down and gathered his courage. "My dear children—" he felt a stab of sadness when he saw their reactions to being thus addressed (Lionel startled outright) "—for you are dear to me—each one of you—Hetty is right in guessing I have more to say to you tonight."

Three other soup spoons came down with a clatter as they watched and waited.

Hugh cleared his throat. "We have had an eventful few months, have we not? The loss of your mother, our visit to Bramleigh, Lionel going to live with the Benfields and you girls being sent to school, the scarlet fever, our second removal to Somerset, the new governess…"

When he trailed off, the children said nothing. Hetty felt all the blood draining from her extremities. Why should he linger so long over the new governess? Was the something he had to tell them to do with her? Papa and Miss Parvill had not appeared to behave any differently with each other today, but what did Hetty know of how a serious man like her father would conduct his affairs? Perhaps he had proposed to her while Hetty and Rosie were wrangling with Lionel.

"It has been eventful," croaked Lionel at last. Hetty felt him nudge her ankle under the table, and she knew his thoughts had followed the same downward spiral.

"Yes. I am certain we all hope for greater stability in the future," Hugh forged onward. "Here in Somerset we have now a home, we have each other near, we have arranged for your education, and I am settling to my work again. I would…perhaps…propose just one more change, and I hope it will be equally tending toward our happiness."

The moment was upon them. Hetty felt sick. She reached for her glass, but her hand was trembling, so she did not dare pick it up.

"Is it that you want to marry again?" asked Rosie innocently, for which she was rewarded with swift kicks from each of her siblings. Her face screwed into a pout, but the rest of her family were too preoccupied to pity her.

Hugh released a slow breath in relief. Having it put into words for them all by the youngest among them made it seem less astonishing.

"That is it precisely, Rosie. Would you children welcome another mother?"

Rosie glanced at Hetty and then nodded vigorously. "Oh, we would, Papa! Wouldn't we, Hetty, if it meant we wouldn't be sent to school again?"

"It depends on the mama," Hetty said through clenched teeth, glaring at her soup bowl.

Hugh's eyebrows rose at the hostility in her voice, and he remembered with a sinking feeling the old Hetty who had made things so unpleasant for all when he had offered for Miss Hapgood. Would she attempt to sabotage this match as well?

"Have you someone in mind, Papa?" asked Lionel quietly. He saw Hetty would be no help in the matter, and, since he had the least to lose by it, he supposed the sooner his sister could be made to submit, the better off everyone would be.

"I...do."

"Is she pretty?" Rosie bounced in her seat. Hetty hissed at her, and the younger girl quailed and sank back with another pout.

"I find her so," Hugh replied. "But, far more importantly for us, she is kind and understanding and knows something of children." He waited, but neither Lionel nor Hetty asked for her name, and Rosie was too abashed now to do so. Checking his sigh, he made the final push. "I do not know what she will say—it is a lot to ask of a woman, that she be mother to three children not her own. I have not yet asked her. I wanted to give you all a chance to get used to the idea, first."

"A chance to get used to the idea," repeated Hetty, still scowling straight ahead, "but not a chance to oppose it?"

Lionel sucked in a sharp breath and Rosie stared.

Hugh's eyes gleamed as he watched his middle child. Ah, he was right. The old Hetty had been in abeyance, but she was there still. When he spoke again, his voice was low and calm, but it had the cut of a lash. "I am afraid, Harriet, the only person I will grant the right or the power to veto this plan is the lady herself. If she...accepts me—accepts *us*—I hope you will come eventually to agree that we will be very, very fortunate."

Hetty only chewed her lip and squinted her eyes against the tears that threatened.

"Who is she, Papa?" Lionel ventured again, hoping Hetty would keep her potato trap shut this time.

By this point the soup was probably cold, but Hugh knew none of them would have any appetite until all had been revealed, and possibly not even after that. His gaze swept across the three of them, taking in Lionel's determination to be manly, Hetty's tear-choked rebellion, and Rosie's alarm. He thought he was getting to know and understand each of them and grieved that this might create another hurdle in their relationship, but he truly believed it was for the best. And, God help him, even if it weren't, he suspected he already loved Miss DeWitt too well to give her up, cost what she might. But nothing prepared him for his children's response when he finally pressed his palms flat on the table and declared, "I intend to ask for the hand of Miss DeWitt."

Lionel hurrahed and threw his napkin in the air. Hetty screeched, bolting from her chair to come and fling her arms around his neck, pressing kisses to his temple. Rosie hopped up and down in her seat, clapping and laughing to see her siblings' joy, though she rather liked Miss Parvill and wouldn't have minded her either.

"What is this?" laughed Hugh, giving way to his own joy and relief. "I know Miss DeWitt is a prize, but I hardly expected *this*."

"Oh, Papa, I was afraid you might marry Miss Parvill!" Hetty cried, kissing him again.

"Miss Parvill? Whyever would I marry Miss Parvill?"

"Because she is beautiful," explained Rosie.

"And not so old as Miss DeWitt," put in Hetty.

"Even the ancient Miss DeWitt is some years younger than I am," Hugh said dryly. He eyed them a moment longer. "So you would welcome Miss DeWitt simply because she is *not* Miss Parvill, who, I might add, seems a nice enough young lady?"

"No, Father," spoke up Lionel. "I like Miss DeWitt tremendously, for her own self. She's first-rate! She's sensible and can talk to boys, maybe because she has brothers, and everyone I know loves her."

"She likes children, too," Hetty said. "I don't know how much she likes me, because I am more difficult to like, but I know she would try."

Hugh shook his head, reaching up to pet his daughter's bright hair. "I am sure she would not only try, my darling, but she would succeed in liking you." Hetty only buried her head against his shoulder, afraid she might cry and Lionel would plague her.

"When will you ask her, Papa?" asked Rosie next, when they had all settled down and begun on their meal, still beaming at each other.

"They are quite caught up in Miss DeWitt's brother's wedding at present," he answered, "but perhaps I will ask her after Mr. DeWitt and Miss Porterworth are married this Sunday."

"Papa," began Hetty worriedly, "suppose Miss DeWitt refuses you. What would you do then?"

He swallowed. "I suppose I would wait a while and try again, after I try to make her like me better."

"You wouldn't ask Miss Parvill, then, would you?" Hetty pressed.

"Good heavens!" he cried. "For the last time, I have no interest in marrying Miss Parvill, but it concerns me that you seem to dislike her. Is she not a good teacher?"

"She's a good teacher," said Rosie.

Hetty sighed with relief. As long as her father would not fall back upon Miss Parvill if his other plans failed, Hetty was free to speak approvingly of her. "She is just fine as a teacher. And she makes Shakespeare such fun. I am not certain she loves teaching best in the world, but she certainly knows a lot."

"She's very fond of her brother," Rosie added.

"Yes," agreed Hugh, aware of his own flood of relief, that he would not have to sack the governess and cause county-wide upheaval. "Yes, I have gathered that. In fact, if it storms tomorrow and I must drive Miss Parvill to Holliton, I think a few thoughtful questions about her brother will generate conversation to fill the entire journey."

The evening spent by Hugh and his children was not so different from what Rosemary imagined them enjoying while his wife Harriet was alive. They sat by the fire, drinking cider and playing games and hearing the children declaim the passages they were learning, until it was time for Hetty and Rosie to go to bed and for Hugh to walk Lionel back to the vicarage.

Each went to sleep with a smile upon his lips, and not one guessed that, unfortunately, county-wide upheaval indeed lay in store for them.

# Chapter Twenty-Two

**He that has and a little tiny wit—**
**With heigh-ho, the wind and the rain—**
**Must make content with his fortunes fit,**
**For the rain it raineth every day.**
—Shakespeare, *King Lear* (1606)

The renovations of the former steward's lodge being nearly complete, the Honorable Mister Frank Birdlow and his wife of one year Mary had decamped from Pattergees to their new home at the beginning of September, that they might live entirely under their own roof. But, sadly, it was precisely this roof which had Mr. Birdlow standing in his dressing room, fists on hips, gazing upward in disgust. For there, spreading across the newly-painted ceiling, was unmistakably a water stain, and Frank supposed it would not be long before actual dripping began.

Ringing the bell accomplished nothing, so great was the wind and rain battering the house, pressing and rapping insistently at the new glass windows. And Frank supposed, at Hilbert's age, the old servant wouldn't hear the house itself collapse over his head, so he crossly stamped down the back stairs in search of the man.

To his surprise, he met with a completely empty kitchen, but he followed the sound of voices to the side entrance, where not only Hilbert, but also Fruthers the housekeeper and two of the servant-maids were gathered in a semicircle before the open door, Hilbert's upheld candle illuminating a draggled, mud-splashed couple, the man tall and lean and dark, with his sleeve half torn from his greatcoat, and the woman red-eyed and weeping, clutching the material of her cloak closely about her.

"Dear me!" cried Mr. Birdlow. "What is happening here?"

"I heard a knocking, sir," quavered the second maid Judith, "and I opened up and look what we have here."

"Vagabonds!" muttered Hilbert.

"I think not, Hilbert," said Mr. Birdlow, approaching nearer. Despite the damage to their attire, even in the semi-darkness he could see the pitiful pair were dressed too well to be vagabonds.

"We have met with an accident," rumbled the man, "and have been wandering, lost, for some hours in the darkness and rain."

"Is that—can that be Mr. Hugh Hapgood?" wondered Mr. Birdlow, all amazement.

He saw the man's shoulders sag, though his sigh was carried away with the wind. "It is. May we please come in?"

Fruthers pursed censorious lips at the master, and he knew they were not only for the sodden mess Mr. Hapgood and the woman would make on floor and furniture. No, clearly good Fruthers' face was also meant to express, *Mr. Birdlow, I have served Lord Marlton's family for seven-and-thirty years, and I have* never *let a woman of ill repute cross the threshold!*

Frank Birdlow tried to assume an authoritative stance, such as his father the viscount might use, and he said loudly, "Come in, Mr. Hapgood. You and...your companion—er—this is Marlton Lodge you have stumbled upon. I do not know if you remember me—we were introduced at the Marchmont Ball. I am Mr. Frank Birdlow, son of Lord Marlton of Pattergees."

"Best to have them in the kitchen, sir," Fruthers suggested sullenly as the servants backed up to allow them entrance. "Save the carpets and such."

"Very well," said Mr. Birdlow. "And if someone would make them a hot cup of tea. Hilbert, Judith, Tomkins, if you might fetch blankets, that they might be out of their wet clothing."

No sooner were they herded into the warm kitchen and dripping upon the flagstones, than Mr. Hapgood said, "Mr. Birdlow—I beg of you. If I might borrow a horse. I must let Miss Parvill's brother know that she is safe, and I must let my family know the same of me."

Mr. Birdlow had naturally heard the name of Parvill, and his brows shot up his forehead. Now, with the light of the kitchen fire flickering over her, he could see the woman's much-talked-of beauty, despite the bluish tinge of her skin and her red-rimmed eyes, in which tears still welled. "Miss Parvill the governess, I believe," he said. "Sister of the new curate at Holliton."

She did not reply, only cast her eyes downward and clutched her cloak more tightly about her.

Mr. Birdlow chewed the inside of his cheek, inwardly bemoaning that he should be faced with such a deucedly disagreeable situation. His father was a magistrate, after all, and what if something should have happened to the young lady? If he were to say he had allowed Mr. Hapgood the use of his horse, that the man might flee!

"It—it is wretched out there, as you well know," Mr. Birdlow fumbled. "Er—you—you had better stay here, Mr. Hapgood, and let me send servants to Holliton and Bramleigh."

Like a defeated man, Hugh sank wearily, heavily, on the settle, heedless of the water still dribbling from him or the fact that Miss Parvill remained standing.

The servant maids returned with a heap of blankets, and Judith led the automaton-like Miss Parvill aside. "Let me take your cloak, miss. You'll be warmer without it." But no sooner had she tugged on it, than Miss Parvill gave a whimper and resisted. Her numb fingers were no match for Judith's sturdy ones, and the cloak came away. "Oh, Lor'!" breathed Judith, taking in the sight of Miss Parvill's muddied and torn gown. "I'm sorry, miss. Best to come into the butler's pantry, then."

Fruthers slammed the kettle on the table, followed by two clattering cups and saucers. Plainly she thought things were going from bad to worse, and disapproval ran off her as water did from the intruders.

"Thank you, Fruthers," said Mr. Birdlow, affecting not to notice. "If you and Hilbert would choose two servants to deliver the message that Mr. Hapgood and Miss Parvill are safe…"

"Have to go up to the Great House for that," she said tersely.

The Great House. Yes. Mr. Birdlow's spirits sank further. "Very well. And…send word to my father that, if he would please to step over…?"

She gave a mighty sniff, that he might know she thought it outrageous that his lordship must leave the comforts of his fireside and expose himself to the elements simply because neighborhood riff-raff chose such a night for disreputable goings-on.

When the room had cleared, Mr. Birdlow pulled out the settle opposite Hugh and took a seat. "Mr. Hapgood, I'm afraid you'd better tell me again what has happened."

Hugh raised his head slowly, and Mr. Birdlow was alarmed to see the dead expression of his dark eyes. "I have said," he answered flatly. "Though, of course, the woman always has the final word." Hugh shut his eyes for a moment, his unwilling thoughts recalling that day in the Benfields' library when, faced with a similar threat of scandal and consequences, Rosemary had dismissed it all briskly with her steady good sense. Miss Parvill, on the other hand, only wept on and on, making damning circumstances appear all the blacker.

"Miss Parvill, as you know, is governess to my daughters and Miss Edith Hapgood. She teaches them at Bramleigh, but, because the weather was so wretched this afternoon, I offered to give her a lift back to Holliton before taking my girls home." He paused here, letting his cloak fall wetly to the settle and wrapping a blanket about himself. "Unfortunately, we are both newcomers to these parts. I have never been to Holliton, and Miss Parvill has only ever walked, cutting across the fields to take the shortest route to Bramleigh. Therefore, when we drove, we rather easily lost the way. The rain worsened. The light was poor and fading. We met with no one, from whom we could ask proper directions. The road became so muddy we feared the cart would soon be stuck, but instead the horse lost its footing, and we were overturned. I had to cut the traces, and the horse bolted. If it has reappeared at the Swan in Patterton without the cart and without *me*, I'm sure quite the alarm has been raised."

Mr. Birdlow nodded, beginning to be lulled by Hugh's matter-of-factness. "What then, Mr. Hapgood? Why did you not keep along the road?"

Hugh's mouth contorted. But he may as well be hung for a sheep as a lamb. "Miss Parvill spoke of a wood between Bramleigh and Holliton, through which she passed every day. She suggested we abandon the road and take to what she assumed would be a more familiar path. That way, also, the trees would provide some shelter from the wet." He watched Mr. Birdlow consider this, shaking his head, and Hugh heaved a sigh. "Yes, you need not tell me. It was not the best-laid plan. We should have clung to the road, whether it deposited us at last in Land's End or London. At least a passing mail coach could then have set us right." And yet, he thought, would it have made any difference in the end? Would he not still be in the identical predicament, even if a mail coach had picked them up?

It had not taken long—perhaps a half-hour—stumbling over roots and being whipped by branches, trying in vain to determine where in the sky the afternoon sun might be, if the sun were anywhere to be seen, before Hugh began to feel the heavy, inexorable weight of his doom settling upon him. There were the hours passing. There was the lack of witnesses. There was their torn clothing, which spoke of struggle and even violence. There was Miss Parvill's distraught state, alternately weeping and moaning her brother's name.

He could not say he even felt relief when they at last spied the dim glow of lights in several windows of Marlton Lodge. He did not know where they were; he only knew that safety came with a reckoning, and that reckoning must now be paid.

He had turned to her, before they approached to pound on the door. "Miss Parvill, this has been a fateful turn of events for us."

She did not reply or raise her streaming head (her bonnet lay somewhere in the wood, hooked off her head by an unseen tree limb), and he had to fight a constriction of his throat. He thought of Rosemary, his black-haired mermaid who could now never be told what she was to him. He thought of his children's joy and his own when he shared with them whom he had chosen. He thought of his painstaking arrangements for his family's future, now again in pieces at his feet.

All lost.

"Miss Parvill," Hugh said again. "You need not fear for your reputation. I will do what will be required. We must make the best of things."

"Henry," she murmured.

He lifted his voice over the wind, surprised he could still feel something so trivial as annoyance. "There will be some talk, naturally, and he will likely face some awkward conversations, but it is you and I who will bear the greater burden, the greater opprobrium." Lifting his fist to beat on the door, he added, as much to himself as to her, "It shall pass."

As Fruthers foretold, Viscount Marlton was not best pleased to be called out into the muck and wet, in order to investigate yet another outrage traceable to a Hapgood. First there was Miss Alice's scandalous impersonation of a boy, that she might entrap his lordship's guest, the naturalist Mr. Joseph Tierney. Then there was the shameful brawl between Miss Alice's uncle and Mr. Tierney at Pattergees' Midsummer Ball. Then Miss Alice's older sister Miss Hapgood preyed upon the viscount's next houseguest, Mr. Frederick Tierney, causing him so to forget himself as to elope with her. And now—now had even the heir to Bramleigh, this Hugh Hapgood, brought about the ruin of the new curate's sister? It was not to be borne! Lord Marlton considered himself a good neighbor: well-meaning, at peace with all and sundry, a fair magistrate, and dismissive of the little gossips and froths and bubbles and molehills which people ordinarily transformed into mountains, to the unhappiness of all. But, within the space of a few months, these Hapgoods had managed to set the county repeatedly on its ear, and this could not be allowed to continue. He was sure news of this latest escapade was already penetrating distant corners of Somerset, the presence of so many servants and witnesses adding fuel to the fire.

Therefore, the viscount was rather stern in his questioning of Hugh, going multiple times over the details of the story. He found the perpetrator oddly calm. Resigned. Rueful, but not defensive.

"You may confirm all this with Miss Parvill herself," Hugh wound up, "if you can get anything out of her besides tears."

"Mr. Hapgood, I hear no remorse in your voice."

"Lord Marlton, as I have explained, I have done nothing to be ashamed of," Hugh returned, his chin lifting with his first show of spirit. "But, having been made a plaything of circumstance, I will do the honorable thing. You need have no fear on that count."

"Very well, very well," said the viscount, sharing a glance with his son. In spite of themselves, they found the man convincing and even imposing. "Call in the young lady."

By this point, Miss Parvill had changed from her wet clothing to a dry frock Judith had found for her, and her streaming hair had been dried and was neatly braided and pinned up. She looked rather like a Quaker maid, his lordship thought, and she would have been a remarkably beautiful Quaker maid, were her face and eyes not puffed and reddened with weeping.

Judith led her in and Mr. Birdlow sprang from his settle that Miss Parvill might occupy it.

"Miss Parvill, I believe? I am Viscount Marlton, and you have seen my son, of course, the Honorable Mr. Frank Birdlow. You have found your way to Pattergees, my estate, after your mishap, which Mr. Hapgood has been telling us about. Suppose you share your memory of it."

But this was too much for the governess and brought on a renewed flow of tears. She shook her head, her head bowed.

His lordship waited some minutes, but as the flow did not seem to be ebbing, he said, "Well, then—let me recount Mr. Hapgood's story, and perhaps you can interject if you have any corrections or additional details you would like to provide. Will that serve, my dear?"

She nodded and listened in silence as the viscount repeated Hugh's statement. She made no sound at all, except to stifle a sob when Lord Marlton came to the bit about her suggestion to enter the wood, but the end of the tale, like the beginning, drew nothing from her.

"That's the long and short of it," he concluded, "according to Mr. Hapgood. Have you anything you would like to say?"

She shook her head.

The viscount frowned at her reticence. He would be remiss if he did not enquire further. "Miss Parvill—I believe we will ask Mr. Hapgood to leave the room. And we will call Fruthers back in to sit with you and hold your hand. Sometimes it is easier to discuss such matters individually."

This finally drew a response from her. Her head whipped up and her blue eyes flashed. "There is no need for that. Everything he has said is precisely true. He has not...harmed me in the least." Then her courage waned, and she covered her face with her hands. "My poor Henry," she groaned. "What have I done to him?"

"Come now," urged the magistrate, palpably relieved to hear her defend Mr. Hapgood's honesty. "It has been a wretched, shocking day for you, I am sure, but I daresay things will look brighter soon." Pulling out his pocket watch, he consulted it. "Your brother the curate—and your family at Bramleigh, Mr. Hapgood—will know by now that both of you are alive and physically unharmed. And if your reputation has been placed in jeopardy, Miss Parvill, it will soon recover when it is announced that you and Mr. Hapgood are to be married. I am sure your brother will feel this is the best outcome, and, in time, you may even come to view it as providential."

It would have restored Hetty Hapgood's peace of mind entirely, were she able to see how little this prospect cheered Miss Parvill. Even Hugh, who had no wish at all to marry the woman, couldn't help feeling rather insulted. Was he truly so repugnant? He might be much older and have three children, but he *was* wealthy and (until this cursed day) respected, and Miss DeWitt did not seem to find him repulsive. *Don't think about Miss DeWitt.*

"I can...agree to nothing until I have seen Henry—seen my brother," she said.

The viscount and his son exchanged another glance. If the young lady could only hear what was likely being said of her within a ten-mile radius, she would not require her brother's advice to snatch at the rescue being offered her!

"Very well," answered his lordship.

They had not long to wait. Outside, the rains and wind were diminishing, and presently the clouds shredded and dissipated enough to reveal a faint, lingering sunset glow. From another room, a clock chimed seven. Within a few more minutes, a thundering of hooves was heard, followed by the crunch of gravel and a pounding at the front door. At a nod from the viscount, Hilbert went to admit the visitor, and, when he reappeared, he was hastily pushed aside, that Henry Parvill could sweep in.

"Elinor!"

"Henry!" She flew into his arms, bursting into tears once more and burying her face in his chest.

The handsome curate turned wild eyes on the onlookers, even while he crushed his sister to him. "Are you hurt, Elinor? Look at me."

"I am unhurt," she choked.

"Thank God! I could not believe you still had not come home when I returned from the Trill cottages. I walked straight on to Bramleigh, to see if you decided to stay there, but they were panicked as well and said you had driven off with Mr. Hapgood, and they could not imagine why he was so long in returning." He pressed a fierce kiss in her hair and rocked and hushed her, while the others present made shift to give them some privacy.

Presently, as Miss Parvill gradually became calmer, the viscount cleared his throat and began again with introductions and the tale of the day's adventures. This was only the fourth time Hugh had to go over the account, but it already felt like the four-hundredth, and he suspected he should hear it four thousand times more before this was all over.

Eventually the tale was told, and Lord Marlton ended by saying, "There will be some notoriety, unfortunately. Some gossip, some tittle-tattle. But in the end it will come right. Mr. Hapgood has expressed most honorably his willingness to offer for your sister, but she has not yet agreed to this solution. She prefers to consult you first."

"Elinor," said Mr. Parvill softly. He loosed his hold and stepped back, waiting for her to raise her head and look at him. Still trembling, she took a few gasping breaths, but then she met his gaze.

"Elinor," he said again, a sad smile playing about his lips, "we must not have notoriety."

"But, Henry—!"

"We must not."

She darted a sharp look at the others and then took hold of his arm. "Henry—" she began again. His hand covered hers and pressed it, and, with difficulty, she swallowed whatever she had been on the point of saying. He continued to wait, watching her. At last she murmured in a broken tone, "I have done nothing, and yet I have brought ruin upon us."

"Ruin? Stuff and nonsense!" declared the viscount roundly, glad to see the pacifying effect the curate had on his sister. Nothing was ever accomplished by blubbering and feminine unreason. "Have I not made myself clear? Ruin is precisely what you will escape, my dear, by accepting Mr. Hapgood's offer." Pulling his watch from his pocket again, he thought longingly of a warm fire and his feet up, Lady Marlton and Agnes sewing beside him.

"Lord Marlton is right, Elinor," Mr. Parvill said in that same soft voice. "If you leave here as Mr. Hapgood's intended bride, the scandal will be but a nine-days' wonder, forgotten the first time I read the banns in church. And, three weeks later, who will have anything to say? You will have time—a month!—to accustom yourself to this change in your condition before it takes place. Many things might happen in a month."

She was docile now, reminding Hugh of a cornered animal, numb with fear. Taking a deep breath, she addressed the flagstones: "Mr. Hapgood, I accept your offer. Lord Marlton, Mr. Birdlow, I thank you for your assistance in helping me understand the matter. May we go home now, Henry?"

"I have already had the coachmen bring the carriages," Lord Marlton said. "One for Bramleigh and one for Holliton. No—please—I am happy we have resolved this, and I supposed you had each of you more than enough walking and wandering for one day."

Once out of doors, Mr. Parvill leaned and whispered something in his sister's ear, and she nodded. Making her curtsy to Hugh, she said, "Harriet and Rosalie will be awake late tonight. Should we begin their lessons later tomorrow?"

Hugh passed a weary hand over his face. His daughters would not be the only ones suffering sleeplessness. But he answered, "Let us say no lessons tomorrow, Miss Parvill. Thursday will be soon enough."

She curtsied again, and they climbed into their respective coaches. The sky had cleared and stars winked. If not for the condition of the roads and his uncomfortable damp clothing, one might have thought the afternoon's tempest a passing nightmare.

But it was real enough, and its consequences might haunt him the rest of his days.

# Chapter Twenty-Three

**He in his wedding-trim so gay, I in my winding-sheet!**
**—Thomas Tickell, *Colin and Lucy* (1729)**

If for no other reason, Rosemary DeWitt was grateful for her brother's wedding because it provided a distraction from the complete overthrow of her life.

There was the removal of Norman from the east wing to the central wing of Marchmont. There was the flurry of renovations and the accompanying painters, plasterers, paper-hangers. There were furnishings to be distributed elsewhere in the house and furnishings to be ordered and delivered. There was the menu for the wedding breakfast to be planned and prepared. There were the endless discussions with Roscoe of his happiness, the wedding journey, the perfections of his beloved. There were the daily visits from Miss Porterworth—Constance, Rosemary supposed she should call her now—keen to oversee the preparations for her new home.

It was Constance, naturally, who brought the scandalous news. She whirled in, accompanied by Miss Birdlow, kissed Rosemary on both cheeks, and cried, "Have you heard?"

Rosemary returned her new sister's embrace and greeted Miss Birdlow before answering. "Heard what, dear? Shall I call Roscoe? I believe he is with Papa and Papa's steward Otway."

"Never mind Roscoe. Only come sit down, Rosemary. Indeed, you had better sit."

"Gracious!" Rosemary looked from one to the other. "What is it?"

"It is yet another Hapgood impropriety, I'm afraid," Miss Birdlow gave a little sigh of regret.

"'Impropriety!'" echoed Constance. "'Impropriety' does not begin to describe it."

"You had better just tell me," said Rosemary, her heart beginning to beat irregularly.

"Very well—only, take my hands, Rosemary. Why, you're shaking already! I am sorry to tell you, but that new governess you and the Benfields sifted and recommended that Mr. Hugh Hapgood employ—it turns out this Miss Parvill is no better than she should be, sister of a curate though she may be!"

"What can you mean, Constance? I could shake you."

"I mean she eloped with Mr. Hapgood himself! Mr. Hugh Hapgood I mean, of course—not the squire. Under cover of the storm yesterevening. Only the carriage or cart or what-you-will overturned in their haste. Then they tried to continue on foot, only they were come upon by Agnes' brother, Mr. Frank Birdlow, were they not, Agnes?"

"They were," Miss Birdlow concurred.

"And such was the state of Miss Parvill's gown that Mr. Frank held them until the magistrate could come—"

"—My father, Lord Marlton," put in Miss Birdlow.

"—And make a thorough investigation! That Mr. Hapgood claimed nothing at all—er—*untoward* had happened, apart from getting lost in the storm as he was driving Miss Parvill home from Bramleigh, but we know that must be utter nonsense because they were absent over four hours!"

The gossipmongers delighted in Rosemary's pale face, Constance in particular because she could not help but feel her sister-in-law regarded her as a mere child. To have the power to shock her, to disturb her calm demeanor, was a treat indeed.

When she could trust her voice not to tremble, Rosemary fixed her gaze on Miss Birdlow and asked, "Did Lord Marlton call Mr. Hapgood's explanation utter nonsense?"

The viscount's daughter gave the merest shrug. "Papa recognized that, plausible or not, the consequences of such a misadventure must be met."

"Then he did find the story plausible, you mean to say?" Rosemary pressed.

Miss Birdlow's finely arched brows rose a fraction of an inch, and her nostrils flared. She was not used to being pressed and her father's judgment questioned. Sir Cosmo DeWitt was a mere knight of recent creation, while Miss Birdlow's father was a viscount with a half-column to his name in Debrett's *Peerage*, after all.

Constance intervened. "You know Mr. Hapgood is so very grim and serious that he must have been quite convincing, no matter his story—but Miss Parvill would only weep and weep, so what was everyone to think? It might have ended very badly—imagine if Mr. Parvill were required to defend his sister's honor and call out Mr. Hapgood? She has no one else in the world to protect her good name! Or—rather—her name that used to be good. But Mr. Hapgood agreed to marry Miss Parvill, so everyone must be content and not kill anybody."

"I see." Rosemary's voice was barely audible. She took a steadying breath and said more loudly, "I see."

"Is—is it not shocking?" ventured Constance. Truly, if she did not love Roscoe to distraction, she would be most dissatisfied with such a block-like sister! A little paleness was all the reaction she received, for such delicious news? Where was the fun in telling shocking stories, if Rosemary would not join them in the excitement?

"It is," said Rosemary. "Shocking. But I fail to see why Mr. Hapgood would need to elope with Miss Parvill in the first place, when he might have courted and married her in the usual fashion without the least objection or scandal on anyone's part."

"Oh, Rosemary!" groaned Constance, "That is exactly what you said when you thought Mr. Hapgood ran away with Elfrida Hapgood. And see how wrong you were there."

Rosemary stared at her. "I was wrong in that instance because I mistook which parties were involved, but the reasoning still holds. There is no cause for a perfectly eligible gentlemen to...resort to such an extreme and reprehensible course of action when not a single person would object if he went about it in the usual manner."

"Perhaps Miss Parvill objected," interposed Miss Birdlow. "Hence all her weeping."

"Who speaks nonsense now?" Rosemary flashed.

"Rosemary!" breathed Constance, wide-eyed. *Nobody* addressed Miss Birdlow in that challenging fashion.

Rising to her feet, Rosemary marched across the room to the pianoforte, that she might put some distance between herself and the visitors. She gathered the sheet music in a tidy pile, which she then slapped back down on the closed lid. "Mr. Hapgood would have no cause to...*force* Miss Parvill to anything. If he asked her, and she refused, he would accept it. He would not...abduct her against her will!"

"She is very beautiful," squeaked Constance, goggling at this Rosemary she had not seen before. She simply could not resist the urge to poke her again.

"As was Miss Hapgood," snapped Rosemary, "yet Mr. Hapgood saw no need to—to—pirate her away!"

"You speak with authority on the man's character," observed Miss Birdlow. "And yet I believe you found it surprising, though not impossible, to imagine him eloping with Miss Hapgood when you thought we brought that news."

"I did not know him then," declared Rosemary, more calmly now, Miss Birdlow's cool voice recalling Rosemary to herself. "I have since become better acquainted with Mr. Hapgood and would never make a similar mistake in judgment now."

"Well, well, the man has found a champion."

She felt her cheeks redden, but Rosemary's chin lifted. "He has. I consider Mr. Hapgood a friend, and I will not believe this ill of him. If he says he was simply giving her a lift and the carriage overturned and they wandered in the storm for several hours, then—then that is what I believe happened."

Constance looked from one to the other, but, when neither re-entered the lists, she gave a little sigh. "In any event, men hardly need women to defend them. It is rather the other way around. And Miss Parvill, whether she wanted to marry him at the outset or not, will be glad to hide behind her promised marriage in the coming days."

Rosemary said nothing, and, after a minute, Miss Birdlow rose lightly from her seat and paced the room, making a slow study of the knickknacks and a middling painting by Sir Cosmo's father of the sea at Minehead.

"Miss DeWitt, do you not think it necessary that Miss Parvill marry Mr. Hapgood?"

Rosemary had seated herself at the pianoforte by this point, and she brushed her fingers over the keys, pondering. "I did not say that. Only see the conversation we have had this morning, and imagine it played out in every household in Somerset. By our behavior, we leave them no alternative. Either they must be married, or Miss Parvill must be ruined, and her brother must lose his employment."

The somber manner in which she pronounced this made Constance feel a little stab of guilt—she couldn't say why. But she wasn't sorry when Rosemary rose again, saying, "Constance, Miss Birdlow—you must forgive me. There is much to do before my brother's wedding, and my mother and I have set aside this morning to make a count of the linens." Then, rather rudely, without inviting Constance to participate, and with only the barest curtsy to Miss Birdlow, Rosemary was gone.

The remainder of the week passed in a blur. Rosemary worked herself to exhaustion, that she might fall into bed at the end of each day and have no time for more than a tear or two slipping down her cheek before she fell into oblivion. But the tasks she undertook during waking hours still left much of her mind unoccupied, and she found herself going over and over the catastrophe.

But, really, had she not foretold this? Had she not a thousand times feared and imagined Mr. Hapgood marrying Miss Parvill, after having seen Miss Parvill with her own eyes and witnessing the way her beauty transfixed others? Yes, she had. Why then was she so upset? Was it the suddenness? The unexpected way it unfolded? Would this have been easier for Rosemary, if she had seen Mr. Hapgood and Miss Parvill fall gradually in love? Would it have been easier to suffer a death by inches than to be felled thus, in one blow?

"It would," Rosemary whispered, as she aired and ironed and folded. As she advised her mother on the arrangement of furniture.

As she sewed and tasted and wrote letters. "It would have been easier than seeing him marry where he does not love."

Of course, she realized, she had never seen Mr. Hapgood and Miss Parvill together. Perhaps, in the short week of knowing each other, Mr. Hapgood tumbled headlong into just such love with the young lady. Rosemary still thought he would never have abducted her or forced her to elope with him, even if his head had run away with him, though she supposed he might have…pressed his suit as he drove the governess to Holliton. She did not doubt, remembering his dark looks, his intent gaze and curling grin, that so young a woman as Miss Parvill might have found an unlooked-for advance alarming in itself. And though Mr. Hapgood (and Rosemary, taking his part) would know Miss Parvill was never in any danger from him, Miss Parvill might have panicked nonetheless.

Rosemary supposed she would never know what really happened. She wished she might see him again, without him seeing her, just to determine for herself how far he loved and how far his love was returned. It would be painful to witness, of course, but she was already in pain. Certainty and resignation could only help.

She did not venture into Patterton. Miss Benfield came once to call but was too kind a friend to make more than the slightest mention of the subject most on people's lips. When she took her leave, she grasped Rosemary's hand and gave it a squeeze, her eyes apologetic. But in that little gesture, Rosemary understand something of the hopes her friend had had for her.

If not for Roscoe's wedding, which would take place at the end of the morning service, Rosemary might even have begged off church.

She could not stop her ears when Mr. Benfield read the first calling of the banns for Mr. Hapgood and Miss Parvill, but she could keep her eyes lowered and not look round at him. Once the service and the wedding were over, however, she discovered she need not have feared.

As she stood with her family and the newlyweds to receive congratulations, Rosemary overheard one parishioner saying to Mr. Benfield, "I suspected that Mr. Hapgood wouldn't have the brass to show his face in church today."

"Now, now," replied the vicar. "Mr. Hapgood is our neighbor and fellow congregant, and he and the young lady will be respectably married soon enough. If he is not here this morning, it is because Mr. Parvill, the curate of Holliton Church, will have also been reading the banns there as well, this morning. Most likely Mr. Hapgood attended Holliton Church, to be with his intended."

His listener snorted. "He might do better to remove to Holliton altogether, vicar, if the whole of Somerset be not too hot for him now."

Rosemary's bosom swelled in wrath, but fortunately Miss Benfield stepped in.

"Thank you, Mr. Plinders," she said coolly. "I and my brother consider Mr. Hapgood a friend and would be sorry to see him refused the hand of Christian grace, especially as we are certain there is more to the story—or, rather, *less* to the story—than gossip would have."

Her eyes met Rosemary's, and Rosemary heard her own voice add, "Yes, indeed."

"Ma'am, ma'am," returned the chastened Mr. Plinders, touching the brim of his hat to each of them. But when he was going away, Rosemary was not the only one to hear him mutter, "No smoke without some fire, I always say."

Twenty years onward, as Mrs. Constance DeWitt helped her daughter dress for her wedding day, she would grumble that her own triumphant wedding was completely overshadowed by the Hapgood-Parvill uproar. "As if I were not marrying the most eligible bachelor in the county! Your father—so terribly handsome that day, though he is still quite distinguished," she complained to Marianne. "But all anyone wanted to talk about was the latest misbehavior of the Hapgoods and the outrages of the Parvills." But this grudge the bride held for decades was partly a trick of memory. As the years passed, Constance collapsed in her mind the to-do of the overturned carriage and hastily-announced betrothal with what came afterward, until the events that unfolded over multiple weeks grew into a single outrageous jumble.

To Rosemary, on the other hand, the misery stretched, and each successive blow left its own distinct mark. On this particular morning, however, she celebrated with her family; she threw wheat and flowers at the happy couple; she smiled and assisted at the wedding breakfast; and she waved and blew kisses when Roscoe and Constance set out. Then, just before she fell asleep in her bed that night, she thought, "And now these is nothing more but the rest of my life. I will teach. I will work. I will care for my parents and any children my brothers may have. I will help the Benfields." In short, she would continue on as she had already. She had been largely content with her lot in the past—largely. And, if she experienced twinges of despair and restlessness, well, who did not? Why should Rosemary DeWitt be spared the general fate of all mankind?

It was a good lecture, as such self-inflicted lectures went. But, like most sermons, whether preached by oneself or by another, putting it into practice would be another matter entirely.

# Chapter Twenty-Four

**I was taught early not to tell Tales out of School.**
—**Samuel Richardson,** *Pamela* **(1741)**

However unhappy a week Rosemary passed, there was not one particle more joy to be found among the Hugh Hapgoods. The night after the accident, Hugh sent Olcott to the Benfields to fetch Lionel again, and another family supper was held, this one as sober as the first was joyous.

"But Papa, why are you going to marry Miss Parvill, when you said you wanted to marry Miss DeWitt?" asked Rosie, while Lionel and Hetty stared at their plates.

He had prepared for this, rehearsing his speech as he lay awake much of the night before. "My dear, when you are older, you will understand that it is not seemly for an unmarried gentleman and unmarried gentlewoman to be alone for extended periods of time, with no one else about. Because of the cart overturning, and the darkness from the rain, and the fact that neither Miss Parvill nor I knew up from down or Holliton from Hampstead Heath in those conditions, we were alone for a very long time. Apart from getting very wet and uncomfortable and worried, there was no danger to either one of us. But, once it was over, there was a very great danger to Miss Parvill's reputation because people will talk. They would say she was ruined."

"Ruined?"

"That she had been with a man as if he were her husband, when he was not."

"But she was with you, Papa," said the mystified Rosie, "and you are not her husband yet, so does not that make her ruined?"

"That is what I mean to say. Miss Parvill would be ruined, if I did not marry her and become her husband in truth."

"Why can she not just swear up and down that no harm was done?" muttered Hetty, glowering now.

"She could," he answered, "but there might always be those who did not or would not believe her, and the damage would be done."

"When—when I locked you and Miss DeWitt in the vicarage library," Lionel croaked, "*she* said no harm was done, and everyone believed her."

A wave passed over his father's face, which no one but Rosie saw, and she wasn't sure of it afterward.

Hugh pushed his plate away and folded his hands on the table. "Miss DeWitt is well-known and respected here, and, on that occasion, those who came upon us loved her well and could be trusted not to gossip. This is not the case with Miss Parvill, who, along with her brother, is very new to Somerset, and has no family or family history to stand behind her or defend her. Because I was responsible for her being in that situation, it is my duty to bear the consequences and make things right."

"Perhaps if—if you told Miss Parvill that you preferred Miss DeWitt, she might excuse you," Hetty persisted.

"That wouldn't solve anything!" Lionel snapped, taking his frustration out on his sister. "Except to make Miss Parvill feel guilty and more unhappy, and it would embarrass Miss DeWitt, if she ever heard."

"Well, *I* wouldn't want to marry someone who preferred somebody else, even if it would make people stow it and mind their own business!" she declared. "I would tell the gentleman to take himself off, and I would keep my head down and—and never mind them until everyone had something else to talk about."

"I wish this might never happen to you, my dear," said Hugh, "but, if it did, I hope the gentleman in question would do what honor required to restore your good name." His voice sounded wooden, even to him. He pressed onward. "On one thing we must be clear: no one must be told of my...former preference for Miss DeWitt. Not Miss Parvill, not Miss DeWitt, not anyone. It must be buried and forgotten. Our course lies before us, and the sooner we can accept it, the sooner we will make the best of it."

A long silence met this speech. Hugh pulled his plate back toward him and began to eat, mechanically, hardly aware of what he put in his mouth, and, after another minute, his children followed his example. It was only after they had finished and Olcott cleared away the meal that Lionel again spoke.

"Father, will Miss Parvill remove to Patterton after you are married?"

"That has not been decided yet."

"Papa, will Miss Parvill continue to teach us?" was Hetty's question.

"Yes. You must walk to Bramleigh tomorrow."

"But what about after you are married?"

"That has not been decided yet."

"She would be sorry to leave her brother," observed Hetty.

"Maybe you all should move into the vicarage in Holliton," suggested Lionel.

"Who says you will not have to come too?" His sister was scowling again. "And we have never seen the vicarage. Perhaps it is too small."

"We will not live at the vicarage," said Hugh. He could not be certain of much, but he knew he must have his own roof.

"You could live very nearby, then," said Lionel. "Like in Crawley, when we lived near Aunt Lavinia and Uncle Wellington."

Hugh had utterly forgotten his sister-in-law, so preoccupied had he been with watching all his hopes and wishes destroyed. Yes, he supposed Lavinia must be sent the news at some point, and he could already imagine her response, half gloating and half sour with doom. It hardly mattered. He was so numb with misery that he didn't give a fig for Lavinia.

Another silence fell. Both Lionel and Hetty felt they had a thousand things to ask or say, but finding their parent metamorphosed once again into a reserved, aloof figure cowed them. He might call them "my dear," but all the warmth and the joy that had conjured answering delight in them seemed vanished.

There was no lingering by the fireside this night. Hugh walked Lionel back to the Benfields', though not before Hetty hissed in her brother's ear that she must speak to him—alone—and he had better sneak back later.

Lionel affected annoyance, but she knew he wanted to talk about this as much as she did. "It'll be late, Het. Patterton is not Bramleigh. I can't just stand in the street and escape notice."

"After Olcott is abed, I'll come down and unbolt the front door and wait for you in Papa's study."

She kept her promise, wrapping up in a blanket and sitting at her father's desk until she fell asleep, only to be awakened by a merciless shaking of her shoulder.

"When you all are living in Holliton, these midnight meetings won't be so easy," he said, a jaw-cracking yawn almost swallowing the end of his sentence.

"We aren't going to live in Holliton," Hetty replied fiercely, or as fiercely as one can when woken from a dead sleep.

"Oh, aren't you? How do you propose to prevent it?"

"Papa cannot marry Miss Parvill," Hetty insisted. "You see how unhappy he is!"

"I don't see what happiness has got to do with it," Lionel said, pulling a stack of registers off the other chair in the room, that he might throw himself in it. "Don't you remember when we were plotting to get Papa and Miss DeWitt together? We wanted to lock them in a closet until it was too late. But we know how that turned out, and now Papa has gone and locked himself in an even greater closet. No, Hetty, he's good and caught now."

"Aren't you the least bit sorry for him?" she demanded.

"Of course I am. And sorry for Miss DeWitt, too, because who will ever marry her if Papa doesn't? But we can't do anything about it all. Like Papa said, the sooner we accept it, the sooner we can make the best of it. I think you'd be better off spending your time getting her to like you, so she doesn't ship you off to school."

Hetty was on her feet, flapping the blanket as she spoke in her vehemence. "You are positively the least helpful brother in the world! You don't care if Papa is unhappy; you don't care if Rosie and I are unhappy—as long as you have everything you want, the deuce take the rest of us!"

Lionel leaped up, clapping a hand over her mouth. "Lower your voice, you mischief! And you better never let Papa hear you swearing like that, or he'll be the one sending you away. Look: I told you I was sorry about it. What do you propose we do, if you're so clever?"

Here she astonished him by bursting into tears—Hetty, who never cried. "I don't know! I don't know what we should do. Maybe we should ask Miss DeWitt."

Her brother's eyes grew round as half-guineas. "You blockhead! That is precisely what Papa told us we may not do. You will have to think of another plan because I'll have no part in defying him outright."

"Oh, oh," groaned Hetty, pressing her palms to her eyes. "I don't know, then. If we cannot speak to Miss DeWitt about it, and we cannot speak to Miss Parvill about it, what will we do?"

"But Hetty, don't you see? Even if we did manage to prevent Papa from marrying Miss Parvill, he would still be unhappy because Miss Parvill would be ruined, and he would feel responsible." Lionel felt a contrary swell of pride. "Papa is a man of honor, you know."

"I know." Hetty supposed she ought to be proud of her father as well, for being an honorable gentleman rather than a scoundrel, but she could not help but wish that, when satisfying the demands of honor did not also satisfy the desires of one's heart, the former were required to give way.

She chewed her lower lip. "We have a little time, at any rate. Mr. Benfield must read the banns three Sundays in a row."

He considered this. "Yes, at least three weeks. And, since Miss Parvill attends her brother's church, I suppose Mr. Parvill will read them in Holliton as well."

"Oh, I did not think of that. Two places. I wonder—who do you suppose will marry them? Mr. Benfield or Mr. Parvill?"

"How should I know?"

"I think it will be Mr. Parvill," decided Hetty. "Miss Parvill adores him and would not want to be married by anybody else, I am certain. In fact, I would not be surprised if Papa makes us attend Holliton church from now on."

"Why would he do that?"

Hetty shook her head, not bothering to answer this. "Which means I will be at Holliton with him, and you will be in Mr. Benfield's church as always. Lionel—suppose, when Mr. Benfield read the banns, you were to object? And, in Holliton, when Mr. Parvill read them, *I* would object? Then they would have to investigate, and that would give us more time to think of a better solution to this problem."

"That wouldn't work at all!" Lionel protested. "It would take either of them a half-minute to realize there was nothing at all in our objections but naughtiness, and we would be back at the beginning again, only this time Papa would be furious and Miss Parvill would hate us—and *you* in particular."

"What a chicken heart you are," she frowned, ignoring his indignant sputters to try further schemes in her head. "I could wait until the third time they read the banns, and I could say I had documents or—or witnesses—or I could say Papa was already engaged to—to Miss Carstairs! Therefore, if he married Miss Parvill, Miss Carstairs could sue him for breach of promise."

Lionel groaned. "Yes, and Papa would *behead* you for telling such falsehoods."

"Yes, but Mr. Parvill would be obligated at least to write to Crawley, to determine if there was any truth in the matter, and that would take several days."

"And then what? And then, several days later, they would all know it was a lie, and—again—Papa would be furious and Miss Parvill would hate you. Give it up, Het. That plan won't fly."

"I will think of something presently," she said obstinately. "And, if my plan works, everyone should be glad I delayed the wedding."

"Lord," was Lionel's only response, as another yawn threatened to dislocate his jaw. "If you succeed, I will be the first to applaud you."

"You can do more than that. You must do some investigating for us, Lionel."

"What are you talking about?"

"I mean, you must find out how Miss DeWitt is doing—whether she seems happy or sad about Papa getting married."

"How am I to do that?" he howled.

"When she comes to call again, or in church, or tag at Miss Benfield's heels if she goes to Marchmont. There is no use in me saving Papa from marrying Miss Parvill if Miss DeWitt won't have him in the end. We must know once for all."

"Lord," repeated Lionel. "What else would you like me to do? Overthrow the monarchy? Sail to the West Indies? You had better give me the entire list."

"Hmm," Hetty mused. "I suspect you should go take a look at the vicarage in Holliton and see how many people it will fit and how many servants they have and whether anyone knows of any family connections they have. Perhaps Miss Parvill might be shipped off to an aunt or a cousin until the fuss blows over."

"And why can't you do this?"

"Because I am in the schoolroom with Miss Parvill most every day, and this must be done when she is not at home to mind. So you must think of an excuse to get out of your own lessons and go over to Holliton."

"Suppose Mr. Parvill is sitting at home while I am poking about his business?"

"You'll think of something," urged Hetty. "Talk to him about cricket some more. Ask about university."

Her brother's eyes glowed. "Cricket! Yes, yes, I will. All right, Het. I'll go nosing about and see what I can discover."

She almost hugged him, but he dodged her. "Thank you, Lionel. But remember—you're not just there to talk cricket. Find out about family. And remember there's the other task, too—"

He was escaping, but before he squeezed out the door he turned and said, "I know, I know—Miss DeWitt. No promises on that one, though. Night, Het."

# Chapter Twenty-Five

**But when we with caution a secret Disclose,**
**We cry Be it spoken (Sir) under the Rose.**
—*The British Apollo* (1709)

As duty was now to be his stern taskmistress, Hugh sent a note to the Holliton vicarage the very day after the carriage accident, asking if he might call on the Parvills. After rather a long delay, he received one line in response, asking if he would please wait to call until the following Sunday, after the banns had been read for the first time.

With the guilty feeling that he had been reprieved from the gallows for a few days, Hugh gladly stayed home, ostensibly "working," but in truth doing little but pace and fret. A thousand times he thought he would call on the Benfields. A thousand and one times he thought he would walk to Marchmont. He saw the Benfields a few times from his study window. Miss Benfield nodded and Mr. Benfield raised a hand, and Hugh returned these salutes, but he did not emerge from the house.

He did not see Miss DeWitt.

He supposed (correctly) the whole DeWitt family was occupied with wedding preparations, but he could not help his disappointment that these preparations did not bring Miss DeWitt into Patterton again. (They would have, several times, but Rosemary's courage failed her, and she sent servants in her stead.) In his few months of knowing her, she had become someone he trusted. Someone who would provide rational yet compassionate counsel. Who better to lay this hard case before, in which he found himself? And yet she was the very last person he could confide in, because how could he tell her anything at all, without confessing that it was his love for her that made the course he now charted so unnavigable?

Hugh told himself he must rearrange the furniture in his study so that he no longer gazed directly upon the street, but he put off this task from day to day. *I only want to see her*, he told himself. *As I have the Benfields. I would not go out or attempt to speak with her.* He would not bolt for his hat and coat as he had that one afternoon; he would not make that pretense again of being just starting off on a walk; he would not allow his mind and eyes to range so freely over her face and hair and person.

But he did not see her.

Lionel was altogether more favored in his endeavors. On the Friday after the carriage accident, Mr. Benfield announced that Pasty the Swineherd had caused some upset among the neighboring cottagers, and the vicar himself must try to restore peace among his flock. He assigned Lionel a translation before departing, and Lionel worked on it until he heard Miss Benfield go upstairs when her mother rang. Then he slammed the book shut, looked this way and that to make sure he eluded Betsy, slipped out quietly as a thief, and took off running in the direction of Bramleigh. He hadn't the least idea where Holliton lay and thought it a prize opportunity to see his cousin Edith and ask her. Of course, she would be with her governess, and he could hardly ask Edith how to get to Holliton without having to explain to Miss Parvill what he wanted there in the first place, but he would cross that bridge when he came to it.

It was not Edith but the squire he came upon instead. Or, rather, the squire came upon him, having just taken a low hedge on his horse and landing in the very path Lionel was following. "What—hey—watch out!" Richard Hapgood bellowed. "Oh, it's you, boy. What are you doing, lurking in the hedgerows?"

"Good morning, sir," Lionel replied eagerly, bending down to rub the ears of the hound Caractacus who followed the squire faithfully. "I am headed into Holliton, but I've never been before, so I was going to ask the way at Bramleigh."

"Humph. I should say trying to find Holliton has caused enough problems for your family, has it not? You'd better climb up behind, and I will take you there myself."

For an instant, Lionel weighed wanting to see Edith against wanting to ride pillion with the squire, but he was twelve, after all, and riding won out. He was hoisted up, and then they were off in the squire's usual neck-or-nothing fashion, Crack lolloping behind.

At first there was only the joy of the sun and wind and fresh air and the imperative to hold on tight to the squire, and Lionel quite forgot his whole purpose in being out that day. But eventually they came to a crossing of paths and a signpost for Holliton, and the squire slowed to a sedate walk. "Now, boy, tell me what you're about, going to Holliton by yourself."

Lionel was glad to be sitting behind the squire, that he need not look him in the face. As it was, it was a trial to answer the bluff frankness he loved with anything less so.

"Well, sir, you know my father is to marry the governess Miss Parvill?"

"Yes. Got himself in a pickle. At least she's a beauty because she has nothing else to contribute: no family, no property, not a penny unless he himself gives it to her." If he spoke grimly, it was because life had taught Richard Hapgood some harsh life lessons, he having also chosen a beauty without much more to recommend her.

"I suppose she's accomplished." Lionel felt called upon to defend Miss Parvill, if only to make his father's predicament less shameful. If he had been a wilier debater, or a malicious one, he might have added that, at least Miss Parvill had her health and did not come with two spendthrift brothers who must also be supported, as the squire's Miss Arbuthnot had.

The squire made a noncommittal sound in his throat. "Anyway, what has your father's state of affairs to do with you?"

Lionel watched the hound Crack, who had run to sniff something out under the hedge and was only now catching up. The boy was doing some hard thinking: his father had only said they must not speak of the matter to Miss Parvill or Miss DeWitt. (This was not exactly the case, but Lionel's memory was conveniently fuzzy here.) Surely, then, he would not mind if Lionel consulted the head of the family? Not that Lionel was willing for his father to learn he had done so.

Taking a deep breath, he plunged in. "Well, between you and me, sir, my sisters and I hoped he might make a better marriage. We knew he would *have* to remarry. We're too much trouble to raise ourselves, and our Aunt Lavinia living so nearby in Crawley—she's very interested in everyone's business, sir, especially Papa's—I suspect she would make it too hot for him to stay there. But we all like Somerset and your side of the family. So Het—Harriet—and I hoped our father might find a wife in Somerset, and we could live here together for always."

Another humph from the squire. "Then what's your complaint, boy? This Miss Parvill will do all that for you. Her brother's here—she won't want to leave the neighborhood. And, if she's poor, your father has more than enough." He managed to say this last without any bitterness.

Lionel shut his eyes briefly and then passed the point of no return. "She'd do, I suppose, except for two things: Hetty fears Miss Parvill will send her and Rosie off to school after they're married, just to get shut of them, because she doesn't seem to love teaching, and—"

"And?" his listener prompted, sending up a prayer of thanks that he wasn't paying the governess's wages, if the woman were so mediocre. As for shipping Hetty and Rosie off, there was no denying that Hetty was a nuisance, and Miss Parvill had the usual survival instincts of the species, he imagined. Couldn't blame her for that.

"And—and our father—we suspect he prefers someone else."

Here the squire drew rein and swiveled as far around in the saddle as he was able, to pin Lionel with his stare. "Someone else? Who are you talking about, boy?"

Lionel swallowed loudly. "Miss—Miss DeWitt, sir."

The horse they sat upon sidled and stepped as its master absorbed this information. The dog took advantage of this halt to flop onto his side and chew a burr from his forepaw.

"That wouldn't be a bad match at all," the squire admitted. "For either party."

"Yes!" Lionel was delighted to meet with such good sense. "We—think—we *hope*, rather, that Miss DeWitt is growing fonder of him, and he is certainly fond of her, whereas Miss Parvill seems completely indifferent to Papa—at least Hetty says so—if not even the littlest bit *repelled* by him, because he is so old and severe and has the three of us, I mean. Though, really, I thought Papa was severe all this time, and it turns out he has only been unhappy, I think, because, before the carriage overturned and everything horrid happened, Papa was a completely different man for a short space! He even smiled and called us 'dear' and confided his plans in us—to ask Miss DeWitt to marry him—and Hetty says, before he went to the Marchmont ball, he took hands with her and Rosie and *danced*!"

The squire, who had faced front again to spare twisting his neck and back, here risked them once more to gape at Lionel. "Hugh confided in you children that he was going to offer for Miss DeWitt before this happened?"

"Yes," said the boy, simply.

Giving a wordless grunt, followed by a slow whistle, the squire nudged his horse into motion again, a bare walk, to give him further time to think. They were approaching a crossroads, and Lionel could see a wagon loaded with cider apples creaking up the opposite path.

"What do you propose to do in Holliton?" the squire asked, when he had nodded at the wagon driver.

"Investigative work, sir. I am to discover whether these Parvills have any other family at all. Hetty and I thought that, if they did, Miss P could be fobbed off on them until the scandal passed."

"That won't work a bit, son. Everyone will just say Hugh got her with child, and she had to go away until it was born and could be passed off or buried somewhere."

It was Lionel's turn to gape. "We didn't think of that, sir."

"Of course you didn't. No, I'm sorry to say, the case is hopeless. Your father will just have to feel the weight of his bad luck. Unless you can get this governess to marry someone else in half a jiffy."

"I—I don't see how that could be." Lionel felt as if he'd been struck a blow.

"She's a pretty enough baggage," the squire rejoined. "It needn't be a completely wasted effort today. I say, pump the brother and the servants and see if you can get anyone to say if she's had a wooer about, before she came into these parts. If anyone can put a stop to the match, it must be Miss Parvill herself. Who knows but she'll be fool enough to throw away wealth and reputation because she still dreams of some Northamptonshire blockhead."

"Yes, sir," Lionel agreed weakly.

There was not much more to say about this doomed mission (for Lionel could not help but feel it was doomed now), and he climbed down in Holliton and watched the squire ride off, Caractacus at his heels.

But Fortune continued to favor the boy. He knocked at the parsonage, noting its modest size. Papa and the girls could not well squeeze in here, so at least Papa might have the wish for a separate establishment granted.

To his surprise, the door was not opened by a servant but by Henry Parvill himself. The very handsome young man wore spectacles and had inky fingertips and looked most surprised to see the boy. "Goodness! It's...Lionel Hapgood, is it not?"

"Yes, sir. May I come in?"

"Er—I don't see why not, I suppose. What brings you this way?"

"Oh, well, just seeing more of the countryside," he answered vaguely.

Mr. Parvill opened the door wider and gestured for Lionel to enter, but then rushed ahead of him to lead him to a small parlor, closing another door as he passed it. The parlor was dim and obviously had not been used that day. The window draperies were shut and some teacups and saucers cluttered a side table. The curate whisked about, snapping the draperies open and gathering the china with a clatter and disappearing with it.

When he returned, Lionel said, "I am sorry to disturb you, sir. Have you no servant to turn people away when you are working?" He pointed at Mr. Parvill's spectacles, which the man then whipped off.

"No, no servant." He tucked the spectacles in his pocket. "Please—sit. My sister Elinor keeps house for me, you know. Or, she has until now."

Lionel thought of the dirty teacups and felt some doubt about Miss Parvill's housekeeping skills, but truly those were the least of their worries. He had better get on with it. While the squire recommended looking for evidence of Miss Parvill having a past lover, Lionel supposed there was no harm in ferreting out the relatives as well, for Hetty's sake.

"Had you and Miss Parvill no ancient aunt or cousin who might have lived with you and kept your house?" he asked innocently.

The curate's eyes narrowed, but then he smiled. "Sadly, no. Elinor and I have no one else in the world but each other. And little enough money for servants. But we have been happy and considered our situation here more than we could have asked for."

No relatives then.

"Did neither of you never want to marry?" Lionel blurted, stumbling over his grammar.

"What a curious young fellow you are," mused Mr. Parvill. "But...as we are shortly to be one big happy family, I suppose there is no harm in satisfying your curiosity. Elinor and I are extremely close. Were it not for this...*contretemps* involving your father and my sister, I imagine we would have continued for years and years—perhaps forever—as we have been. To be honest, I might never have the fortune to support a wife, and Elinor would never have had the portion to win a husband."

"You both look well enough, though," pointed out Lionel. "Everyone says so."

The curate grinned. "Why, thank you."

"My cousin Miss Hapgood—you don't know her—she's married and lives in Buckinghamshire now, she was accounted a great beauty, and she got a gentleman to marry her, even though her portion came to only about ten pounds in a good harvest."

Mr. Parvill gave a silent chuckle. "You are a forthright one, aren't you, Lionel?"

"I mean to say, sir, have no gentlemen ever had a go at Miss Parvill, even though she was portionless? On account of her good looks, you know?"

"If there were any such gentlemen," he answered dryly, "there were none that she cared for enough to accept, it appears."

Dead end after dead end, Lionel thought ruefully. No faraway cousin to take in Miss Parvill, and no secret sweetheart to tempt her to reject this offer. Hetty better think hard and fast if she was going to prevent the inevitable!

His disappointment might have added an edge to his next suggestion. "So," said Lionel, "If that's the case, what you call a 'contratomps' must not be all bad, to your minds. Now your sister will have money enough."

The grin vanished. "Elinor is a woman of honor. She would not have chosen this means of getting married for all the gold in Christendom."

"All right, all right." Lionel managed not to roll his eyes. He'd have to let Hetty know Miss Parvill wasn't the only one touchy and defensive about her sibling. These two were cut from the same cloth, it seemed.

Watching his visitor's face closely, the curate managed to regain control of his own temper. "This was all so unexpected, what is happening between your family and mine," Mr. Parvill began again in a conciliatory tone. "It will take adjustment on both sides, and we do not know each other well yet. I thank you for calling and…trying to understand the matter better. What do you say, if we make a recess from this uphill labor and go bat a cricket ball around? If you would excuse me, I can dash up to the attic and dig in various chests for my ball and bat."

His visitor's face lit up. "That would be first rate, sir! If it wouldn't be too much trouble."

"Give me five minutes, at the utmost." And the young man dashed from the room, pounding up the parsonage stairs as if he were but twelve himself.

Lionel wasted the first minute in his seat, observing the faded furniture and faded paper while Mr. Parvill thumped around above. Then it occurred to him that, if he were going to bring Hetty the bad news of Miss Parvill having neither an accommodating relative, nor a former lover, he had better be able to claim he was exhaustive in his investigation.

Hopping to his feet, he tiptoed back down the hall to the door Mr. Parvill had closed, pausing to listen and make sure the man was still busy in the attic. As Lionel guessed, the door led to the curate's study, but, on cracking it open, he saw Mr. Parvill's study looked nothing like Mr. Benfield's or Lionel's father's.

Mr. Parvill's study resembled the aftermath of a shipwreck. The curtains were drawn in this room as well, casting it in semi-darkness. The bookshelves were empty, all their contents to be found in the open chests lying about on the floor. An unfinished letter lay on the ink-spattered desk, beside bottles of ink, quills, and a pen knife, while balls of crumpled and discarded drafts littered the floor. For a poor man, the curate certainly was not stinting in his use of paper!

Darting over to squint at Mr. Parvill's tiny, precise script, Lionel had just time enough to decipher:

*Sir, though we have displeased you, we pray that, now the deed is done—*

Then, over the pounding of his own heart, Lionel discerned the pounding of Mr. Parvill, descending the stairs. The boy scrabbled at some of the balls of rejected paper, thrusting them up his sleeve, and sprang as far from the desk as he could in one bound, just as the door swung further open.

"Why, there you are," said the curate. In his hands he held a bat and a weathered ball. In the gloom, his eyes glinted, flicking from Lionel to the desk and back. "How came you to be in here?"

"I—I am a budding scholar myself, you know, and might one day be a clergyman," Lionel lied manfully. "I wanted to see what a clergyman's study looked like."

"Aren't you boarded and under the tutelage of a clergyman?" Mr. Parvill asked. "Does Mr. Benfield forbid you his own study?"

"I meant a *young* clergyman," said Lionel, feeling perspiration break out under his arms. He hoped his sleeve wasn't bulging. "A *young* clergyman's study. Mr. Benfield is quite old and—er—set in his ways and thoughts."

Mr. Parvill set the bat on his untidy desk, directly over the unfinished letter, and placed the ball carefully beside it. "And what have you discovered, then, about *young* clergymen?"

"Ahem. Well, I cannot generalize, since I have only seen your study, sir, but you do seem—er—rather at odds and ends. Would it not be easier to have your books on the shelves?"

"My sister and I are but recently arrived in Holliton. As you know, we have no servants, and I have not yet had the time to unpack."

"Oh." Lionel thought of the nearly three weeks that had passed since the Parvills arrived in Holliton. But, as he was no marvel of cleanliness and organization himself, he shrugged this off. He only hoped, for the sake of his sisters and Edith, that Miss Parvill was a better governess than she was a housekeeper. First the dirty crockery and now the utter shambles of a study!

"Any other questions, Lionel?" asked Mr. Parvill, his lip beginning to curl again.

"Nah."

"I do have one of my own, then."

Lionel gulped. "You do?" He wanted to swing his arms casually, to appear relaxed, but he was afraid the purloined letters would fall out. The man couldn't possibly have noticed two crumpled balls missing from the floor, could he? He might. Who knew what a distinguished Fellow of Queens' College was capable of?

"One question: Lionel, does Mr. Benfield know you are here?"

The boy grinned in relief, but he tried to make it appear sheepish. "He does not, as a matter of fact. I'm playing a little truant today, and I hope you won't mention it to him or to my father, please! Surely you must sympathize with a schoolboy who needs a reprieve...?"

Mr. Parvill nodded, matching Lionel's grin. "I do. Sympathize. Therefore, I will be mum about this visit of yours. Shall we do some bowling and batting, then?"

"Oh, yes! Yes, sir!"

The curate took up the equipment again, while Lionel furtively adjusted his sleeve so it would neither crunch nor leak damaging evidence, and they left the darkened, disorderly confines of the parsonage for the charms of a late September morning out of doors.

# Chapter Twenty-Six

**Some most irreligiously have plotted
to obtain their purpose.
—William Covell, *Polimanteia* (1595)**

"What can they mean?" wondered Hetty.

She and Lionel were holed in the girls' bedchamber, the two letters Lionel had pilfered from the Parvills uncrumpled and spread upon the counterpane.

They were nearly identical, both bearing Mr. Parvill's minute script. The first read:

> *Sir, fully aware you have no cause to love me, I nevertheless take up pen to write, in hopes you will read this for Elinor's sake*

And the second:

*Sir, I have not Elinor's permission to address you, but for her sake I risk your anger and take up my pen to beg*

The word "beg" was crossed out several times, with even a puncture in the paper, as if the writer could not contain his vehemence. The second sheet bore also great blots where Mr. Parvill dribbled ink and, scrawled upon the reverse, "R. K. – Stamford."

"And tell me again what the letter on the desk said," Hetty urged. "The one he was working on when you interrupted."

"'Sir, though we have displeased you, we pray now that the deed is done…'" quoted Lionel.

Hetty muttered this under her breath, tapping her chin with her finger. It was Sunday afternoon. The banns had been read in Holliton and in Patterton, and their father had gone to pay his call on the Parvills. Lionel made quick work sharing the discoveries and disappointments of his call (though he left out the bit about playing cricket for an hour), letting Hetty grow increasingly despondent as she listened, only to surprise her the more when he produced the stolen papers. Both she and Rosie rewarded his efforts with shrieks and admiration of his daring.

"These may be our only remaining hope," Hetty declared. "We just have to decide how to make use of them."

"Who could he be writing to, if they have no family?" her brother asked for the third time. "And do you suppose it's this 'R.K.' person?"

"Whoever it is, and we may as well call him 'R.K.,' Mr. Parvill expects this person to be angry with him or with them both."

"Maybe it's someone he knew from Queens' College? His tutor or the college president?"

"Why should such a person be angry with him? Or with *both* of them?" Hetty objected. "Even if it were a person from the college, he could have no reason to be angry with Mr. Parvill's sister, of all people. No, Lionel, I can only think that Mr. Parvill has not told you the whole truth."

"About what? You think he lied to me, and him a clergyman?"

"Aunt Lavinia says that telling untruths is a sin," Rosie spoke up, wanting to participate in her siblings' conference.

"Exactly," said Lionel. He reached over to squeeze her foot, where she sat on the bed.

"I don't know about 'lied,'" Hetty worried, "but I think maybe he did not tell you all. Don't you think, if the recipient of these letters has reason to be angry with both of them, they must both have wronged him?"

"That makes sense, but how?"

Hetty was biting her lower lip. She smoothed the second sheet, running her finger under the script. "I think it has to be what the squire suggested: that there was some young man who fell violently in love with Miss Parvill, but she refused him, for whatever reason, and so he is angry with her."

"But then you have the opposite problem, Het. Why then would R.K. be angry with *Mr.* Parvill?"

"Perhaps...perhaps Miss Parvill was torn," his sister suggested. "Perhaps she thought briefly of accepting this young man—maybe even gave him her promise. But then Mr. Parvill told her it wouldn't do, and hadn't she promised to keep house for him, her brother? And Miss Parvill, who does dearly love her brother, could not bear to break that earlier promise to him, so she went back to R.K. and told him it was impossible, and they must be parted forever."

"Oh-h-h-h..." breathed Rosie.

Lionel considered this, nodding. "I see...I see...yes! That does make sense. Only, it doesn't answer the question of why Mr. Parvill would now be writing him and wanting to make some request."

It did not, and the Hapgood children sat some minutes in frustrated silence, Rosie glancing back and forth between them impatiently.

"Miss Parvill might have told her brother that, if she must marry somebody after all, she would rather it be R.K. than Papa," Hetty said at last. "Although, I don't know why she wouldn't just write to him herself, in that case, and say, *Come save me, R.K.!*"

"It's like Mr. Parvill said," Lionel rejoined eagerly, drawing himself up haughtily and frowning in imitation of the curate. "'My sister is a woman of honor.' He knew Miss Parvill would never approve of him writing R.K., so he is doing it behind her back!"

"That's right," agreed Hetty, catching his enthusiasm. "Without telling Miss P, he's writing R.K., begging him to rescue her from having to marry our poor papa. So...do you think we need only sit back, and this R.K. will come swooping to her rescue?"

Lionel huffed out a long breath. "I hope so. Though, if you could have seen the heap of refuse—all the rejected versions—littering his study, you would know Mr. Parvill is finding it a rough go to put his request into words. Supposing his nerve should fail altogether?"

Round eyes met his. "Oh, dear. Or suppose he decides to wait and see how this meeting with Papa goes, before he writes? Papa might be his stern self and cow them both."

"That he might," frowned Lionel in agreement. "Papa is a hard man to cross. He might say to Miss P, as he said to us, that the sooner she accepts it, the sooner she will make the best of it."

Hetty clenched her fists and jammed them on her hips. "We cannot leave it to chance, Lionel. We must help Mr. Parvill stand firm in his resolution."

"What on earth are you proposing? That we tell him he must send this letter that we are not even supposed to know about? He would know I had been prying! And, supposing we convinced him to overlook that, why should the man listen to us?"

"No, no—that is not what I mean at all," she assured him. "I mean that we should write to R.K. In case Mr. Parvill doesn't."

"Write to R.K?" echoed Lionel, aghast. "Us? Why should R.K. care what we write to him?"

"We won't write as *us*, Lionel. We will write as Mr. Parvill."

"But what if Mr. Parvill *does* send his letter? Wouldn't R.K. wonder why the man's handwriting changes from moment to moment?"

Pacing now, Hetty puzzled this out. "You're right. We cannot write as Mr. Parvill. Then—then—we must write as *Miss* Parvill. We will say—she will say—that she is in a frightful pickle, and, if he loves her and still wishes to make her his wife, he must come immediately for her. And that her brother will make no difficulty this time and all will be smooth. Even if R.K. receives both letters, one from Mr. Parvill and one from us, posing as Miss Parvill, he will assume they each act without the other knowing."

Lionel threw himself back on the bed, the letters crunching beneath him, and folded his arms behind his head to regard the ceiling. His sisters watched him anxiously. If their older brother quashed this plan, who knew what would happen?

"Very well," he said at last. "We'll do it. But suppose R.K. does come, Het, but Miss P still refuses to marry him?"

"Then I don't know!" Hetty wailed. "But it is the only course open to us. If it fails, at least we know we made every effort. Let us quickly get paper and pen from Papa's desk and compose it before he returns. And then you must post it tomorrow, Lionel. Oh—I only pray Miss Parvill isn't even this very moment beginning to think that Papa will serve quite well, after all!"

They need not have worried. Neither their father nor the Parvills appeared to be warming to the approaching nuptials.

Hugh found himself in the same faded parlor where Mr. Parvill had led Lionel, seated on the same chair with threadbare and rocky upholstery. Miss Parvill sat opposite, on a sofa which had a positive *rip* in it, and her brother leaned against the mantelpiece, staring into the empty hearth.

"Miss Parvill, I hope you are fully recovered from the effects of the storm and the carriage accident," Hugh said politely.

The woman was pale as marble and would scarcely meet his eyes. "Certainly. I have been teaching the children, as you know."

Of course he knew that, but he could hardly see her for the first time since the calamity and *not* ask if she were recovered. Her response gave him pause, however, because he could not interpret it—was she resentful that she must continue to teach?

"About the teaching, Miss Parvill," Hugh rumbled. "If we are to be wed within these three weeks, perhaps you would prefer to leave that off?"

That brought her round. "Who says we are to be wed in three weeks?"

Her brother glanced over at her challenging tone, and Miss Parvill swallowed and spoke again, more quietly this time. "Why must we be wed so soon?"

"Your brother has just read the banns for the first time. Over the next two Sundays, he will read them for the second and third time. And then people will expect us to marry."

"Reading the banns and announcing our engagement will be enough to stem the tide of gossip, I suppose," she persisted. "We need not rush into...the rest."

Hugh smothered a sigh. If complete honesty were allowed in conversations, this one would go differently. He would say, *See here, woman. The fates have backed us into a corner. I don't love you and you don't love me, but that doesn't change things. I am trying to behave honorably and sacrifice my own wishes to preserve your character, and you aren't helping one little bit. I'm not expecting enthusiasm, but I did hope to talk sense.*

Out loud he said, "I suppose there is no clerical law that requires us to be married immediately or even soon after the third reading...? Perhaps you would like to suggest—that is, when would you prefer to be wed?"

Miss Parvill looked to her brother, but he was staring into the fireplace again. "I need more time," she declared at last. "What would you say to two months from now?"

Two months? To sit under this sword of Damocles for *two months*?

"Very well," he conceded. "In two months." Nevertheless, he heard himself saying what he had told the children: "While these circumstances are not ones of our choosing, Miss Parvill, I believe the sooner we accept them, the sooner we will make the best of it. We already respect each other, I hope, and perhaps in future will grow to be—er—fond of each other, if we are willing. I do already appreciate that you are an educated, accomplished young woman who has experience with children." He managed to say all this without outwardly wincing, but his mouth twisted when she made no verbal response. Fortunately, this went unseen because her gaze was fixed on the carpet.

Hugh felt his own resentment rise. Why must she treat him as if he had forced this upon her? As if he had been hanging about, plotting to ensnare her? She was not the only one to lose by this, and there would certainly be many who would consider that she, a penniless girl of no family, had struck the greater bargain.

With difficulty he forced his anger down enough to speak. "Which brings us back to the subject of teaching. Would you prefer to continue, or will you need the time to make arrangements and preparations?"

"I will continue," she said. She unfolded her clenched hands, only to grip the sofa on either side of her. "Even as I make my arrangements and preparations."

Her mouth worked in silence after she said this, and he waited. He was clearly not the only one in the grip of unpleasant emotions. When her eyes rose to his, he drew back at their intensity. "Mr. Hapgood—you know I am a portionless woman—I wonder if—if you might advance me my wages, that I might buy my trousseau."

As soon as she made her request, she flushed scarlet, as did her brother, who passed a hand over his eyes, and Hugh felt his own face redden, to witness their defeated pride. He had been too hard on her. With the shame of this request hanging over her, it was small wonder she was unfriendly.

"Certainly. Of course. Absolutely," he stumbled over the words. "I will send it to you this very afternoon. Although—if we are to be married and one family—perhaps you might need a greater amount?"

"No!" both brother and sister rejected this proposal in unison, glaring at him, before Miss Parvill shook herself and added, "Thank you. You are generous. That will not be necessary. I would prefer to spend only what I have earned."

Hugh's eyebrow rose. The banker in him could not help but calculate that, if he paid the woman thirty pounds per annum for, say, fifty weeks of teaching, and if she taught only ten of these fifty weeks before their marriage, he would owe her a mere six pounds.

Not much of a trousseau to be had for six pounds. But rather than fire off the Parvill pride again, he nodded. "Very well. Just your wages, then."

That matter settled, the next to grapple with must be where they would live.

Seeing the work was to continue all uphill and that he must bear the brunt of it, Hugh made a beginning. "Ahem. Now, as to where we will live when we are married." (He pretended not to see her flinch.) "I have only very recently taken my lodgings with my daughters in Patterton, but I suspect you would like to live somewhat nearer to your brother and to attend his church. Therefore, I thought to seek a home in Holliton—"

"No, no," fluttered Miss Parvill. "Patterton will do. Please do not sign an additional lease. Once we are married, I am content to remove to Patterton."

Trying to disguise his surprise, Hugh said, "But Mr. Parvill's church...?"

Her hands flew up to smooth her black hair, which needed no smoothing, for it was pulled back into a very tight knot. Tighter than Miss DeWitt had ever worn hers, before she adopted her present style, with its looser waves and curls—*For the love of God and your own sanity, do* not *think about Miss DeWitt!*

"Henry must manage without me." Miss Parvill gave a short, mirthless laugh. "Keep your lodgings, sir."

Hugh hardly knew what to think. So much for her irrational adoration of her brother! He had thought detaching her from Mr.

Parvill's side would be nearly impossible. He had thought, indeed, that she would insist on them all sharing the man's parsonage.

Perhaps they had argued. Perhaps Mr. Parvill blamed his sister for what had occurred, and she wanted to punish him in return. In any event, they were such a reticent pair that Hugh knew he would never know what they truly were thinking unless they had a mind to tell him.

"I see," he said, not seeing at all. "Well. Patterton it is. If you feel differently later, we can revisit the question another time. I would like to keep Lionel under Mr. Benfield's tutelage, but if the girls and I remove to Holliton or remain in Patterton, either will serve to keep us near him." For his own part, Hugh would rather remove to Holliton. To continue to live as Miss DeWitt's neighbor and fellow parishioner for the foreseeable future sounded equal parts pain and pleasure, and he could not in good faith try to make his new marriage a success if he were always looking out the window for his lost love.

Later. They could revisit the question later.

He waited to see if Mr. or Miss Parvill would introduce any concern of their own, but they did not. A glance at the mantel clock showed a mere quarter-hour had passed, but it felt like one of the longer ones of his life.

"Ah...Miss Parvill," ventured Hugh, "I did want to ask if there was anyone besides your brother who would need to consent to our marriage?"

"Whom can you mean?" she cried. "You know Henry and I have no family yet living. Whom can you possibly refer to?"

Hugh held up his palms in amazement. "Forgive me. I fear I have pressed on a painful subject."

"Elinor," murmured Mr. Parvill. He strode away from the mantel to stand behind the sofa and put two fingers lightly on his sister's shoulder. She shut her eyes a moment and then said, "You must pardon me in return, Mr. Hapgood. Our—our orphaned state is indeed a painful subject for us."

Hugh made a sound of acknowledgement in his throat. He was hard put to think of a subject that was not painful to his betrothed today and had a sinking feeling that marriage to her would involve as much trepidation and unpredictability as marriage to Harriet Morrow had. It was not an encouraging prospect. With another glance at the clock, he decided he would settle one last matter, if he could, and then allow himself to flee.

"Well, then. One more concern I hope we might discuss: my girls' education," he said. "Miss Parvill, both Hetty and Rosie have indicated to me that they would prefer not to be sent away to school again. I understand you will likely not want to continue teaching when we are married, but I hope you would be willing to let them remain with us."

Panic flitted across her lovely face, and Hugh saw Mr. Parvill's fingers tighten on her shoulder. "Please—Mr. Hapgood. Please do not make any changes on my behalf. Of course they need not go away to school."

Pleased, Hugh smiled for the first time that afternoon. "Thank you. I will, perhaps, advertise for a new governess in the meantime? I assume you will want to relinquish your duties?"

"Yes. No. I don't know. Mr. Hapgood, please. May we leave things as they are for now? Precisely as they are? Or—or perhaps you might advertise in a few weeks. I don't know. Please don't press me anymore today."

He held up his hands again. Enough was enough for one afternoon. "Just as you wish. I will take my leave now, unless either of you have any questions you would like me to answer?" Questions, perhaps, about his own family? His income? His favorite color?

Of course they did not. And, when they saw him out, he could not mistake their relief in watching him go.

In daylight and fine weather like this afternoon, when a walker might leave the road and cross the sheep-dotted meadows, the distance between the Holliton parsonage and the Simpson lodgings was no more than a couple miles, but it was long enough for Hugh's thoughts to wander further afield.

He had told the children they must accept what could not be changed. Thus had he counseled Miss Parvill as well; and so did he counsel himself.

Miss Elinor Parvill was to be his wife. She was beautiful and accomplished. She was willing to let the girls stay home and have a new governess. Clearly, where she did love, she did so fiercely and loyally.

But would she ever love him? Would he ever love her? Would he ever even *like* her?

He banished that frightening thought as quickly as he could. He must learn to like her. The alternative was too grim.

His first marriage—his marriage to Harriet—had begun in infatuation and metamorphosed into mutual disappointment and dislike. He could not bear for a repeat of that—this time without even the infatuated beginnings. Whether or not Miss Parvill could ever learn to love him, for his own sake he must make the attempt to love her.

His eye fell then on a patch of autumn crocuses, and his steps faltered.

In another world—a world no longer open to him—he would gather every autumn crocus in Somerset and present them all, all...to the other one. The one who spoke easily and listened. The one whose eyes sparked with anger or lit with amusement. The one who danced lightly beside him but who could also challenge him, allure him, make him smile.

Mr. Roscoe DeWitt and Miss Porterworth would be married by now and the wedding breakfast past. Now what would Miss DeWitt do? Would he see her in the village again, calling on the Benfields?

And, if he did, how precisely would he take everything he felt for her and bury it so deeply she would never know?

# Chapter Twenty-Seven

**Anye impietie may lawfully be committed in loue, which is lawlesse.**
—John Lyly, *Euphues: the anatomie of wyt* (1578)

In later years, Hugh blamed Lavinia and the servant Olcott for what happened next. Lavinia for her letter and Olcott for catching a nasty cold.

Hugh had been as matter-of-fact as possible, informing his sister-in-law of his impending marriage. Shortly before his interview with the Parvills, he sent Lavinia a letter worthy of his cousin the squire or of Miss DeWitt's taciturn brother Norman—the barest paragraph:

*Lavinia and Wells, I write to announce that I will be married again within three more weeks. My bride will be Miss Elinor Parvill, an educated young woman of Northamptonshire, who is indeed the girls' governess at present. Her brother Mr. Henry Parvill is a curate in the neighboring village. You may continue to direct your letters to Patterton. –Hugh Hapgood*

Lavinia, in response, sent a full sheet of paper, crossed, of which the first few lines were enough to make him wad it up and hurl it across his study:

*Mr. Hapgood, your letter was a terrible shock, especially after your having specifically assured us that you would <u>never</u> marry the governess under any circumstances. I can only surmise that she has indeed been too artful for you to withstand. Of course we wish you what happiness we can, but forgive us if we worry that this young woman's wiles have operated on you at a most vulnerable time—*

He startled himself by giving a bark of a laugh. Miss Parvill's 'wiles'? The woman wanted nothing to do with him, nor he with her! Lavinia assumed the governess's youth and beauty had vanquished him. A humiliating conclusion at his age. Passing a hand over his eyes, Hugh wondered how old Miss Parvill was. Not much older, he supposed, than his other would-be bride Miss Hapgood had been.

There was no help for it. Lavinia would think what Lavinia would think. The world would think what the world would think, say what he might. His only resort was to settle down quietly with Miss Parvill and lead a life so uneventful and dull that everyone would turn elsewhere for amusement and forget to marvel at them. Not an enchanting mental picture, but he could not see an alternative at this point.

Hugh had a sudden urge to escape the house. It was eleven o'clock in the morning. The girls were at their lessons at Bramleigh, and the servant Olcott lay abed with a stuffy head and streaming eyes. For ten days now, he had avoided going out, apart from church in Holliton and his awkward call at the Parvills'. Not only had he wanted to be forgotten by his neighbors while the scandal raged, but he wanted to avoid temptation. Temptation in the form of Miss DeWitt and any friends or family of hers that might mention her.

But this morning, fueled by Lavinia's letter and knowing Olcott to be bedridden, he determined that he should step across to the Swan to order his luncheon delivered. And then he might venture one brisk turn about the high street before returning to his self-imposed seclusion.

He told himself he was not seeking Miss DeWitt out, for why should she be in Patterton that morning, in any event? He had not seen her even once since the day after the ball. And yet, when his turn up and down the high street yielded no glimpse of her, he found himself dawdling, despite the curious stares and whispers of the villagers. He stepped in at the grocer's and purchased tea. Then he visited the chandler and selected some beeswax tapers. What Olcott would make of this shopping expedition when she rose from her bed, he didn't know. All Hugh knew was that he didn't encounter Miss DeWitt in either place, although she taught daughters of those shopkeepers, and he did not remember what her other pupils' fathers did.

As he hesitated outside the chandler's, he heard his name hailed and turned to find Miss Benfield striding toward him. "Why, Mr. Hapgood. I began to think we might never see you again, though we could throw a stone from the vicarage to Simpsons'. Or, at least, Lionel probably could," she smiled.

While his heart warmed at her friendly overture, his voice was guarded. "I thought it best to lie by 'in silence and obscurity' until the nine days' wonder had passed."

Her chin rose indignantly. "For one, more than nine days have passed. And, for another, perhaps I might agree with that course of action if you were friendless in the world, Mr. Hapgood, but you most certainly are not!"

"Then I thank you and Mr. Benfield for your trust and good opinion."

"It is not only our trust and good opinion you may rely on," she said boldly. "There is Miss DeWitt's as well."

"There is?" In his surprise, he could not prevent the hope that lit his countenance. "Has she said as much?"

Seeing his response, Miss Benfield gave a rueful smile. She had guessed correctly, then. He did have feelings for her friend, and, had circumstances been otherwise, Miss DeWitt would have been rewarded with the happy fate she deserved. That Rosemary returned his feelings and would have accepted him Miss Benfield did not doubt, especially considering how she had been avoiding Patterton as much as Mr. Hapgood in the days since the carriage accident.

Not far below Charlotte Benfield's commonsensical surface could be found a thick layer of sentiment, and this layer must have been responsible for her feeling that life could be so very unjust! Why should her young friend be deprived even of learning that someone had loved her, even if that discovery could never be acted upon?

She should not.

She would not, if her friend could help it.

"She has not needed to put it into so many words," she answered him. Giving herself an inward nod of encouragement, she went on to say, "You must cling to your friends in these times, Mr. Hapgood, and not let their loyalty to you go unacknowledged. Come. I am just now walking up to call at Marchmont, and you must accompany me."

"I?" he blanched.

"You. You have not congratulated Sir Cosmo and Lady DeWitt on Mr. DeWitt's marriage, have you? And you were not present at the ceremony, of course. They will be expecting it, and I suppose Rosemary wonders what has become of you, that you would not even inform her of your betrothal, that she might wish you well."

If Hugh and Miss Benfield conversed as they walked to Marchmont, he had no memory of it afterward. It seemed the very next moment they were being ushered into the sitting room, where the remaining DeWitts all stood to welcome them. Unable to bring himself to look at Rosemary, Hugh did not remark how stunned she was to see him, how her color came and went, how her hands flew up to smooth her hair and frock. Miss Benfield saw enough, however, and it made her all the more determined these two should have a chance to speak apart.

It was no trouble to get rid of Norman DeWitt. His discomfort with small talk ensured he disappeared from the room as soon as humanly possible, but Sir Cosmo and Lady DeWitt were another matter. They wanted to talk about the wedding and the first letter their new daughter Constance had sent from Weymouth (Roscoe having immediately delegated all family letter-writing duties to his new wife). Then portions of the letter must be read aloud and talked over, as if the DeWitts had not already done so among themselves.

"Constance reports that Roscoe made her tour the ruins of Sandsfoot Castle in the rain, poor thing," Lady DeWitt reported, "but the next day it cleared, and they were brave enough to venture into the water in the bathing machines."

"Shall they pass the rest of their journey in Weymouth?" asked Miss Benfield, masking her impatience. They were all seated now, and Mr. Hapgood was holding his hat and rotating it round and round in his fingers. Rosemary had taken up her sewing again, though Miss Benfield would vouch for those being some pretty thoughtless stitches being put in.

"Oh, they are gone on by now," said Sir Cosmo. "I expect they will be in Poole."

"Will they go as far as Brighton?"

"Dear me, no," said Lady DeWitt. "Constance is very anxious to see London. So, after more bathing at Poole, they will go up to town."

This went on for another five minutes or so, but then Miss Benfield could bear it no longer, and she blurted, "Sir Cosmo, Lady DeWitt, might I beg you to walk with me through your lovely grounds? My brother plans a botany unit for Mr. Hapgood's son Lionel, and I thought I might note some likely specimens for him."

Lady DeWitt's brow knit in puzzlement. "The grounds? I think it had better be Rosemary to—"

"No need for Rosemary," interrupted the vicar's sister decisively. She stood, forcing the gentlemen to their feet as well. "I will merely point, and you both can tell me if we may pluck some or only come later and sketch. Not a moment more of sunlight is to be lost! Off we go."

After only another minute of discussion and bustling about for Lady DeWitt's shawl, the two older DeWitts and Miss Benfield quit the room, leaving Hugh and Rosemary alone.

Rosemary's heart was pounding, and she accidentally stabbed her finger with the needle as she pulled it through the cloth. Hugh was not faring much better. His hat slipped from his fingers and rolled away, and when he rose to retrieve it, he accidentally booted it even further across the room.

If she weren't so unnerved herself, Rosemary might have giggled at the sight, but instead she took advantage of his distraction to pop her injured fingertip in her mouth, just managing to whip it back out when he turned to face her.

"Rose—Miss DeWitt, rather—I would like to express my thanks. I am tardy with them, but I hope you will accept them all the same."

"Your...thanks?"

"Yes." He placed his hat gingerly on the ormolu table where it would not trouble him, but then he did not know what to do with his hands, so he picked it up again. "Miss Benfield tells me that she and her brother the vicar and—and *you* have...not thought ill of me for what happened nearly a fortnight ago. I mean to say, the carriage accident with Miss Parvill, that led to my engagement to her—the Benfields and you did not believe the rumors that I had...harmed her in any way—"

"Of course not." Outrage glowed in Rosemary's eyes at the suggestion. "Of course we did not. *Do* not. You may depend upon it, sir. Mr. Hapgood. No true friends of yours would ever doubt your—honorable nature." She choked on the last words and fell silent abruptly, afraid she might do something wild, like burst out weeping, if she continued.

Hugh felt wild enough himself. He sank back down on the sofa across from her and dragged a hand through his dark hair. Then he could resist no longer—it had been too long. He let himself stare at her. He indulged in the sheer luxury of gazing at her: her lustrous hair, her flushed face, dark lashes casting shadows on her cheekbones, the curve from her bare neck to her shoulder. He got no farther because she raised her eyes to return his look, and he saw the gleam of tears in them.

"Rosemary—"

The sound of her name drew a hiccupping gasp from her, and she turned in her seat to hide her face. When she heard him rise again, however, she was on her feet, hurrying to the window. "It is both honorable of you and kind," she said hastily, her eyes cast downward, "to protect Miss Parvill's good name. And—and you will find, I trust and pray, that heaven rewards you for your deed. She is a beautiful young woman whom you will easily come to love, that is, if you do not already—"

"Rosemary." He lingered over the syllables this time, his low voice coming from directly behind her.

She felt his hands close on her upper arms, and her head snapped up. Rosemary's alarm mingled with a thrill that—ah—this contact between them was entirely his doing, and she could not say if the alarm or the thrill was greater, though she suspected the latter. As for Hugh, now that he had a hold of her, he could not have released her to save his life. He had no right to touch her, no right at all—what was he *doing*?—but the impulse was too sweet. His hands ran down the length of her upper arms before returning, tighter, to grip her shoulders, and the next instant he whirled her around and pulled her against him, full-length, bending to kiss her. It was not a gentle kiss. If anything, it was rough—desperate. But Rosemary made no objection because, over the astonishment she felt, something answered in her, and she threw her own arms around his neck to return his embrace. For how long they might have gone on neither could say, if the clear voice of Miss Benfield hadn't then floated in the casement from the grounds below.

"These asters are an unusual shade—darker than I have seen before."

Rosemary pushed Hugh from her, stumbling a little as she stepped back and putting her fingers to her swollen mouth. "Oh, dear."

She was amazed to see his face utterly transformed. The gravity and burdens of his life, which set it in its usual grim lines, were vanished. In their place were joy and—and desire for her. He looked ten years younger. More.

"Rosemary." He took hold of her arms again. "My darling. Forgive me. I have no excuse for my behavior except to say what I have no right to say: that I love you. *I love you!*" He shook his head, laughing silently. "And I have even less right to ask you, but—do you love me? Can you return my feelings?"

Gulping, she managed a nod. Her insides were doing revolutions, as her own joy struggled with guilt. And then he had a hold of her again, his mouth claiming his ownership of her, one hand pressed against the small of her back and the other stealing up to thread fingers through her hair.

"Mr. Hapgood," she gasped against his lips.

"Call me Hugh."

But she could not call him anything, for all the kissing, and only when they were both breathless and she felt her hair coming unpinned and tumbling down her back did she manage to push him away once more. This time she put the sofa between them. "Mr. Hapgood, this will never do," she panted.

His heavy-lidded eyes regarded her as he followed her to close the distance, and his mouth curved wickedly in its pirate grin. "My black-haired mermaid."

She paused in her attempts to re-pin her streaming locks and she felt herself sway. "Did—did you mean me, that day?"

"Of course, you."

"I had thought you referred to Miss Parvill."

"You." He was beside her again. "Only you. Ever you."

"Oh." She seemed in danger of giving way to him entirely as he reached to run a light finger along the side of her jaw and down the center of her neck, but *someone* had to think in this instance, and clearly he was in no mood to do it himself.

"Mr. Hapgood—"

"Hugh. My name is Hugh."

"Mr. Hapgood," Rosemary insisted, taking another step back to escape his touch. "You must not forget—we must not do this—you are engaged to be married."

"I don't love her."

"Yes, well, that hardly matters in this instance."

"Nor does she love me."

Rosemary didn't know what to say to this. If Elinor Parvill was a fool, she was a fool.

"She doesn't want to marry me," Hugh continued, his voice low and purring.

"Not—not even to save herself and her brother from ruin?" she asked faintly.

Hugh had a hold of Rosemary's hand now, and, with the other, he reached up to tug a lone curl from the severe knot she had twisted it in, stroking the length of it and winding the tip around his fingers. "She agrees to marry me for just those reasons," he murmured, "but neither one of us wants it."

She took a slow breath. She could not keep moving away and away from him, but neither could she run at him like she wanted to. "The more credit to the both of you, then, for choosing duty over—over desire."

His eyes gleamed. "I did choose it, unwillingly. But I did not know then that it was not my desire alone I denied."

"What do you mean?" she asked, not wanting to hear the answer.

"I did not know you loved me in return."

Shaking her head vehemently, she said, "I should not have confessed it. Or kissed you. Or let you kiss me. We—"

"It's too late for these regrets, my love. You have let the cat out of the bag."

"I rather think the cat was dragged out of the bag tail-first."

The pirate grin widened. "However it came to pass, it is out, Rosemary, so we must come up with another plan than me marrying Miss Parvill."

"Hugh! Mr. Hapgood, rather—I will not be responsible for the ruin of that young lady or her curate brother. Nor will I be responsible for your abandonment of duty and honor. And I will think the less of you if you do abandon them."

"I love the way your eyes flash when you are furious."

"You must stop this." This time she fled him in earnest, putting the length of the room between them. "I should not be a party to this."

"Rosemary, wait." Still exultant, he dragged his hand through his hair again, shaking his head to clear it. "You have carried me somewhat beyond myself, I admit, but I can still hear and speak reason. Please. Come back. Sit." He indicated her chair. "And I will sit a safe distance away and keep my hands and lips from you, if possible, though I now firmly intend to make your person mine—no, no—sit down, please. I will behave like a gentleman now." With an effort, and by dint of pressing his hands to his face, he managed to wipe away the piratical look that so unsettled her. "Listen, my darling. As I said, Miss Parvill agreed with great reluctance to marry me, to save her reputation and the career of her brother, but only with difficulty did I get her to name a date. She declared that, rather than marry me after the third reading of the banns, she would do so after two months altogether passed. But no one knows that date save me and her brother, and now you. I believe I could easily persuade them to postpone the happy occasion still further, if necessary. As long as the engagement stood, they would be safe from gossip and scandal."

"I do not understand, sir, how postponement will change anything." She felt her heart sinking. It was not that she wanted him to betray his honor—she could not ultimately be happy if that were so—but an endless engagement...? To occupy this limbo for any length of time would be torturous. She would have to go away, she decided suddenly. Visit an aunt. An old schoolmate. She could not wait here in Somerset, knowing that any day might bring a visit from Mr. Hapgood and all the temptations that would entail.

Hugh's brow was furrowed with thought, and any witnesses to the scheming of his children would have recognized the family resemblance. "Postponement will give me a chance to find Mr. Parvill another position, away from here," he explained.

"Have you any connections in the church?" Rosemary wondered.

"I have not," he conceded, his frown deepening. "But Mr. Parvill is a scholar, as well, is he not? Perhaps he might also find another position as a tutor."

She was already shaking her head. "But how could you help him find employment as a tutor, either? And, if he were hired as a tutor in a household, he could not bring his sister, so she would need another position as a governess. And, if that were so, would she not prefer rather to be married than to uproot them both? I fear it is all too complicated."

He could sense her withdrawing from him, and his fist clenched on his knee. "It can be done! It just may take time and persuasion. I may not have the connections to smooth the way, but I have the will and I have the money. Mr. and Miss Parvill are deeply attached to each other. I think they could be convinced to move to new situations, as long as they might do so together. And—and I could supply Miss Parvill with a marriage portion, or even the both of them with a measure of independence. If she were not penniless, she has looks enough. She would find another husband, and most likely one who appeals to her more."

"Oh, Hugh," sighed Rosemary.

"It will work!" he insisted. He tried not to think of how the Parvills, in their pride, had refused even his offer of trousseau money outright. "You must give me time. And, when she is married, you and I will be free to marry."

Her only answer was silence.

He could no longer sit still but was on his feet again, pacing, throwing her looks from time to time as he watched her resolve harden.

"Rosemary, please."

"Hugh." A tear slipped down her cheek, but when he moved toward her, she held up her hands in warning. "No."

"I only ask that you wait for me, Rosemary," he pleaded. "That you give this a chance. A year, perhaps? I cannot ask for your promise, of course, that you will never marry someone else."

"Marry someone else?" she gave a humorless laugh. "I am in no danger of marrying someone else, sir. But I cannot agree to any understanding between us. It would not be right. For as long as your engagement to Miss Parvill stands, it must stand. It would not be right for me to be kept on the reserve. We could not have...scenes like these going on for an indeterminate amount of time."

"Very well. I cannot exact any promise from you. I can only say that, on my side, I will hold myself only to you. I will marry you, or I will marry no one."

"You cannot promise even that," she protested, with the beginnings of anger. "If Miss Parvill undergoes a change of heart, you cannot then refuse to marry her."

He stiffened at this suggestion. Of course, Rosemary had not been present at the Pattergees Lodge or when he called on the Parvills. She had not seen with her own eyes how stricken Miss Parvill was at the thought of submitting to marriage with him. But Miss Parvill seemed to be alone in the world in holding this opinion. Lavinia thought him a prize worth catching, worth exercising "wiles" to capture. Many others, he knew, thought Miss Parvill could not have done better for herself if she tried. She, a pretty and penniless governess, had caught the wealthy and familied heir to Bramleigh. Was it possible she might come to see the match in a prudential light? That she might, indeed, insist on him fulfilling his obligation?

Hugh gritted his teeth.

No. No, no, no. It could not happen.

He would not let it.

Not now, when he knew Rosemary loved him and would be his if he were free. He would use any fair means to extricate himself. He would offer the Parvills money, despite their blasted pride. He would seek a new and more comfortable situation for the brother. He would keep his distance from the sister. These maneuverings could all be done through correspondence, and, with two months before him, he need not even mention it to them yet. He had no more wish to see them than they him.

Resolved, he took up his hat from the table. "Rosemary, I will go now. You know my feelings and intentions. May I—may I call again soon?"

She gave him a lost look. "I think not. I think you had better not."

"But I love you and you love me. Tell me it again."

"Shhh. We had better not speak of that, either. Please, Mr. Hapgood, for my sake. I was surprised and weak today. It will not do. We had better be acquaintances now, if we meet at all."

He stared a minute longer at her bowed head. Acquaintances, be damned. But he knew better than to try to kiss her again in this fierce mood.

It would wait.

He would wait.

She heard the door open and shut and he was gone.

# Chapter Twenty-Eight

> **Abimelech called Isaac, and said, "Behold, of a surety she is thy wife; and how saidst thou, 'She is my sister'? And Isaac said unto him, "Because I said, Lest I die for her."**
> **—Genesis 26:9, *The Authorized Version* (1611)**

On Sunday, the Hugh Hapgoods suffered through the second reading of the banns, this time in their home church of Patterton. Heads turned. Whispering and clucking and even some pointing ensued, and then the moment passed. The greetings between the Hapgoods and the DeWitts were public but in no way marked.

Hetty, in turn, suffered through her lessons and the abstraction of both her father and her governess. She could not read or understand either of them. Papa was busy, thoughtful. Always off in his study writing letters. He seemed neither happy nor unhappy—only busy. Miss Parvill was present in body but absent in spirit. She grew paler and left her charges to longer periods of reading and drawing. She showed no especial or growing interest in the girls who would shortly become her daughters. Papa had said, when asked, that Miss Parvill agreed they need not be sent off to school again, but how could Hetty find comfort in that, when the woman was so indifferent to them? He had also said, again when asked, that Miss Parvill would live in Patterton after the marriage, for which Hetty was glad, because she wanted to remain near Lionel, and sad, because in her childish way she had imagined Miss Parvill could somehow go on living with her brother forever. As for Hetty's erstwhile hopes of Miss DeWitt, the woman had entirely disappeared from their lives. If not for church, she would never see her.

"Lionel," she cornered him after that second Sunday, "did you send our letter?"

"Of course I sent our letter, you ninny. I said I would."

"But do you suppose R.K. received it? Has he responded?"

"How am I to know that?" he asked crossly, because he had wondered the same thing. "We didn't sign it 'Lionel and Harriet,' now, did we? And if he responds, his letter will go to Holliton. I would say you have a better chance of finding out what you want to know. Why don't you ask your governess if she's got any interesting letters lately?"

"I couldn't possibly," protested Hetty, thinking of how Miss Parvill ignored her as much as a governess could.

"I don't see why not," he groused. "But if you won't, you won't."

"Lionel, suppose R.K. isn't in love with her anymore, and he doesn't bother writing? The banns have already been read twice now. We're running out of time!"

"Well, I don't like it either, Het, but we've done all we can do, short of murdering Miss Parvill, and there I draw the line."

Which was how it came to pass that, the following Sunday, when Mr. Benfield read the banns for the third and final time, intoning, "If any of you know just cause, or just impediment, why these two should not be joined together in holy Matrimony, ye are to declare it," Hetty found herself on her feet, her heart in her throat. And just as she gathered breath to call out (what, precisely, she was going to call out she couldn't say), she heard a voice from the back of the church cry, "I declare an impediment!"

Well, as Lionel was to say later, *that* woke everyone up.

In one rustling motion, accompanied by the creaking and cracking of the wooden pews, the congregation turned as a body to view the interloper. Hetty was glad she was already standing so that she could see over the people and the ladies' hats. There stood a dark-haired man in the last pew. He was perhaps Hugh Hapgood's age or a little beyond, tall and straight and handsome and stern. A complete stranger to all present.

Hetty glanced from the stranger to her father (who thankfully had not noticed that Hetty rose before the man called out) and saw that he had no more idea of the man's identity than anyone else in the church. Then she clapped a hand to her mouth and turned to catch Lionel's eye. *Could it be R.K.? It must be R.K.!*

Her brother nodded vigorously, though what R.K. was doing in Patterton, when he ought surely to do his objecting in Holliton, was a puzzle.

From the pulpit, Mr. Benfield seemed dumbfounded. In all his years of ministry, this had never once occurred, and it was his sister who finally hissed at him from her pew, "Arthur, you must ask him the nature of his objection."

"Er—good sir," Mr. Benfield called obediently, "what is the impediment you declare to the marriage of Mr. Hugh Hapgood and Miss Elinor Parvill?"

"It is this," said the man evenly, "Elinor Parvill is already married."

His next words were swallowed by the wave of gasps that met this pronouncement, and Mr. Benfield, after waving his hands to get everyone to quiet down, was forced to ask him to repeat himself.

"I said, Elinor Parvill is already married."

"But, sir, how can this be? To whom?"

"She is married," the man said distinctly, "to Mr. Henry Parvill."

Well, if the stranger's first declaration woke everyone up, this one threatened to start a riot. Such a roar of gasps and discussions erupted in Patterton Church as likely had never been heard before or never would be heard henceforth. Hetty saw her father on his feet then and feared he might stride over and sock the man, and she leaned to grasp the tails of his coat.

"Sir! Sir!" Mr. Benfield was compelled to thump his Book of Common Prayer against the top of the pulpit to make himself heard above the din, and when they saw this, his flock hushed with startling speed because they did not want to miss a word. "Sir, you must retract your statement. You wrong Miss Parvill and Mr. Henry Parvill. They are brother and sister."

"And I tell you, they are not," returned the man. "They are man and wife. She is Mrs. Henry Parvill, but she was not born so. She was born Elinor Kimball, and she has no brother. I tell you this on the authority of her father, Reginald Kimball, because that is who I am."

Hetty's eyes caught Lionel's round ones again, and they both mouthed *R.K.!* "R.K." was no former suitor of Miss Parvill—he was her father! Those two were not utterly without family, as they had claimed over and over. Mr. and Miss Parvill, the supposed orphan brother and sister, were Mr. and Mrs. Parvill, the not-entirely-orphaned husband and wife!

All was uproar again for some minutes, and Hugh, being already on his feet, was torn between incredulity and an overpowering sensation of relief. Could it be possible? It could not be. It was too unnecessary, too absurd. Why would they lie about such a thing? And yet, he couldn't help himself—he found his own gaze seeking that of Miss DeWitt in her family pew. He saw her gloved hand clutching her brother Norman's shoulder, and he could see the flowers on her bonnet trembling, and he knew she was thinking the same thing. *Could it somehow be possible?*

Unable to restore order to the congregation, Mr. Benfield was forced to sweep down the aisle toward the stranger, with his sister hard on his heels and the irrepressible Lionel on hers, and then everyone was shushing each other again, while they also stood and craned to watch. As Mrs. Watters told Mrs. Cropper later, it was "better than any play," and she was certain missing that day's excitement was "a just punishment for those who stayed a-bed and didn't come to church."

"Mr. Kimball," began Mr. Benfield, "if you will forgive me, I must ask for some proof that you are who you say you are, before we address your statements."

"Proof?" demanded the man. "What proof would I have, in this place where no one knows me? Ask my daughter, and she will not deny me to my face."

"Well, sir, I might ask why you did not make this declaration in your—er—at Mr. Henry Parvill's church in Holliton, rather than here."

"Send, and I believe you will find there were no services in Holliton today."

"What *can* you mean?"

The man was searching the pockets of his greatcoat, and he held up a handful of letters. "Perhaps these might be proof enough for you. One is from my son-in-law Henry Parvill, and the other purports to be from my daughter Elinor, though the hand is not hers and the thoughts expressed are incomprehensible to me—"

Hetty nearly tumbled from the pew, and Lionel drew breath so sharply he choked and fell into a fit of coughing, but all eyes were on Mr. Kimball.

"Do you see what Parvill says? 'Sir, though we have displeased you, we pray now that the deed is done...'" read Mr. Kimball. "I received this over a week ago, and it was the first I heard from them since they eloped secretly some months prior. I'm not ashamed to say I was against Elinor marrying him. He was handsome enough, but he didn't have two farthings to rub together, and if he married her, he would lose the only income he had—that fellowship from his college. So they married in secret and took up this position where no one knew a thing about them. Took up two positions, from the sound of it. And I might never have learned of their whereabouts or any of it, if Elinor hadn't gone and got herself entangled with this Hapgood person. Well, then the fat was in the fire, to be sure. It was either make my girl a bigamist or beg her scorned Papa for rescue."

"Ahem. Ahem! They chose the latter course, I see," Mr. Benfield said, darting a glance at Hugh, who was already making his way out of the pew to join them.

"Sir." He bowed briefly. "Pardon me for intruding myself, but I am the 'Hapgood person' you refer to."

The bow was returned just as briefly. "Reginald Kimball. She can't marry you," the father said, as if he expected Hugh to insist on it. "I'm sorry if your heart is set on it and you've gone to great lengths to bring it about."

Seeing the fire kindle in her papa's eyes, Hetty regretted releasing her grip on his coattails, and she squirmed past Rosie to get closer to him.

But though Hugh was irked by the man's manner and assumptions, if what Reginald Kimball claimed was true, he might insinuate what he pleased! "I assure you, sir, I deeply regretted any part I had in placing—er—Miss Parvill in a precarious situation."

The man's eyes narrowed as he took Hugh's measure. "Well, and I say she's no longer in a precarious situation. I've money enough to fix them, until her penniless young man can support them both without having to resort to lies and desperation and deception, as he's practiced on all of you, I'm afraid. What's done is done, I say, and, if he's the son-in-law I must put up with, well, so be it. Sir, will you be willing to renounce and relinquish all claim on my daughter, under these circumstances—not that I see you have any alternative but to do so?"

Hugh nodded. "I am. I make no further claim on Miss Parvill—"

"Excuse me," interrupted Mr. Kimball. "You mean to say *Mrs.* Parvill."

"Yes," agreed Hugh. "I make no further claim on Mrs. Parvill. Mrs....Henry Parvill. And I release her from our engagement, if such an engagement had been possible in the first place, which it was not."

"Papa." Hetty tugged on his sleeve.

Lionel was not the only one present who expected him to shake her off with a "Not now, dear," but Hugh only favored her with a bemused smile. "Yes?"

"Will Mrs. Parvill still be our governess?"

"She will not, I expect," answered Mr. Kimball. "I mentioned earlier that there were no services in Holliton today—it is because Henry and Elinor have 'cleared out,' as the expression goes. I told them they would leave some loose ends, which I would take care of, if they would return to my roof in Northamptonshire, and they agreed to my proposal."

"Oh, my," muttered Mr. Benfield to his sister, "Mr. Deed will have to come down from London now, until Mr. Parvill can be replaced."

Mr. Kimball heard this and grunted. Replacing his letters in his greatcoat, he next retrieved his pocketbook. "Mr. Hapgood, I suppose you will have to advertise again for a governess, and you may have lost wages to my daughter."

Hugh was shaking his head. "Please. She had received only what she already earned. And I will further say, in their defense, the 'lies and desperation and deception' (as you call it) that they were forced to practice, made them ill at ease, I believe. The whole matter of the carriage accident perhaps accelerated their reconciliation with you, but I truly think it would have come at some point, sir."

Mr. Kimball's mouth set at this, and Hetty understood that, for all his brusque manner, he was moved and upset and did not like to see his daughter's reputation exposed thus to public airing. She crowded closer to her own father and felt his hand on her head.

"I thank you for your words, sir," Mr. Kimball said, replacing his hat and nodding at Hugh. "And for hearing my objection," he added, with another nod at Mr. Benfield. "I believe we are finished here, and I will be on my way." His eyes swept the congregation, and then he gave one final bow and departed.

Afterward, Hugh rather felt as if he were the victor in a prize fight. Hetty and Lionel and Rosie were bouncing around him and shouting; Mr. and Miss Benfield were clapping him on the shoulders and congratulating him; even those he knew only by sight or not at all were smiling and nodding at him, as if they had not all been talking about him and picking him to pieces over the past month. The Hapgoods had to flee to their lodgings to escape all the attention, but not before Hugh's eye caught Rosemary's and made her a promise which she met with an answering smile.

That evening, as their family lolled about contentedly before a cozy fire, Lionel poking at it, Rosie perched on Hugh's knee, and Hetty tucked up beside him, Rosie asked, "Papa, will you marry Miss DeWitt now?"

"I will," he replied, giving her a squeeze. "Unless it turns out she is already married to Mr. Norman DeWitt."

Lionel and Hetty burst out laughing, probably harder than his little joke deserved, but they were all so very, very happy. Lionel and Hetty were probably also very, very relieved their part in the letter-writing campaign remained their secret, and Rosie was just happy to see the rest of them happy.

"May we come too, Papa," she pressed. "When you ask her, may we come too?"

Lionel groaned. "You little goose! No one wants an audience for that sort of thing."

But Hugh was tapping thoughtful fingers on Hetty's ankle. "You know," he said, "it's not such a bad idea. If Miss DeWitt is to agree to this, she had better see all that marrying me would entail. Yes. Girls, since you are without a governess again, you will come with me tomorrow, and, Lionel, I will send a note to have Mr. Benfield excuse you from your studies for the morning. I must speak first with Sir Cosmo, and in the meanwhile you children may either charm or terrify Miss DeWitt, as you will."

"But Papa," protested Hetty, knowing that, if any one of them were to terrify Miss DeWitt, it would be her, "suppose Miss DeWitt does not like us children well enough, and then she refuses you? Won't you be very angry with us?"

Hugh knew as well as Hetty what was going through her mind, and he took her hand in his. "Hetty, my dear. I only ask that you be yourself because that is who Miss DeWitt must approve."

"We're doomed," Lionel complained.

"I hope not," said Hugh.

"Hetty, you must behave tomorrow," Rosie urged her solemnly.

"I will!" she choked. "For I want Miss DeWitt to marry Papa very much."

"Shhh…" her father soothed. "Just be Hetty, and we will take our chances. If she says No, we will just keep at it until she says Yes. All right?"

Sighing, Hetty said, "All right, Papa."

"Good. Now off to bed with you. Lionel, let me walk you back to the vicarage."

# Chapter Twenty-Nine

**If I the prize, if me you seek to wife,
Hear the conditions, and commence the strife.
—Pope, *The* Odyssey of Homer (1726 trans.)**

Rosemary was walking the grounds of Marchmont the next morning when she heard her name called and saw Lionel and his sisters spilling from the house to join her.

Her hand fluttered to her throat, where her shawl was pinned, and she glanced beyond them for another face.

"Papa has business with Sir Cosmo," Lionel announced artlessly, "but he brought us with him to call."

"Ah."

They had caught up to her and gazed at her with such earnestness that Rosemary could not help but be amused. "I am happy to entertain my fine callers." She bent down to smile at Rosie. "We have not been formally introduced, have we? I am Miss DeWitt, and you must be Rosie."

Rosie smiled shyly back at her. "But I am a Rosalie, and you are a Rosemary."

"So I am," agreed Rosemary. "And how I wish my own brothers had called me Rosie for a nickname, rather than 'Ros'! So very pretty." She swept them all with her gaze. "Will you walk with me? It's a little frosty this morning—perhaps you would rather go inside?"

"Here is better," said Lionel, "and we are warm from our walk up from Patterton."

"Do you know why Papa wants to see Sir Cosmo?" asked Rosie, only to be hushed violently by her siblings.

Rosemary hid a smile. "I have a guess."

"Oh!" Lionel grinned. "We needn't make a secret of it, then. Hetty, you can stop pinching Rosie now."

Little Rosie rubbed her arm and frowned at her older sister. "We hope you will marry our Papa, in spite of us."

"Why in spite of you?" murmured Rosemary. "Would you rather I not marry him?"

"We would rather you did, actually," Lionel said cheerfully. "But we understand you might be hard put to do it because taking on three children is a fearsome trial."

"But Papa is rich, which is nice," coaxed Rosie. "And he is much nicer and not as scary as he used to be."

"I have never found him scary, I am pleased to say."

"Well, he's rich, then, still," Rosie persisted. She nudged Hetty, feeling that her sister ought to do her share of the persuading, but Hetty maintained mulish silence.

"I am not poor myself, fortunately," said Rosemary, "but money never hurts, I suppose."

"Lack of money hurts," pointed out Lionel. "Look at the Parvills. Too bad they had to go. I rather liked that Mr. Parvill. He was good at cricket." Then he recalled that no one but Hetty knew of him calling on Mr. Parvill, and even Hetty didn't know about the hour spent bowling and batting. "Er—at least Miss Parvill said he was. Er—Mrs. Parvill, that is. I say, did you know, Miss DeWitt, that our father received a letter from Mr. Parvill yesterday?"

She turned amazed eyes on him. "I did not. I hope he will tell me about it. I should very much like to hear what they have to say for themselves."

"We should too," agreed Lionel. "Papa just read it a few times over and told us all was well that ended well and folded it and put it in his pocket."

"All that time we thought she was boasting about her brother," Hetty at last spoke up, "but she was in truth boasting about her *husband*!"

And *such* a husband! thought Rosemary. He was handsome, to be sure, and clever enough to win a fellowship, but to engage knowingly in defying his wife's father, and then to perpetrate such a deceit on his college, the church, his wife's employer, and the people of Somerset...!

But she turned her thoughts from the Parvills to regard Hetty, now that the girl had finally opened her mouth. "Hetty," she began timidly, drawing to a halt beside a small fountain of a cherub holding a fish that, in summer, spouted water. "I know some months ago you were eager for your father to remarry, that you and your sister might not be sent away to school. Are you disappointed that he cannot now marry Mrs. Parvill?"

Glaring, Hetty swished her cloak against the rim of the fountain. "I am not disappointed. Miss Parvill—Mrs. Parvill—did not particularly like me either."

Rosemary's eyebrows lifted. "'Either'?" she repeated.

"My cousin Elfrida didn't like me because I wouldn't let her, and I drove her away from Bramleigh with my naughtiness," grumbled Hetty to the ground at her feet, "because I thought then that I didn't want Papa to have a new wife. And I suppose *you* don't like me because, after I changed my mind about Papa marrying, I decided I wanted you to marry him, though you had scarcely met him, and I told you so that day they all went shooting—"

"That did alarm me when you took me by surprise like that," Rosemary confessed. She watched Lionel lifting Rosie up to touch the stone mouth of the fish. "But I think more because I found I already did like him, and I did not yet want anyone to know."

"Really?" Hetty breathed, looking up now.

"Really. Though perhaps I shouldn't say as much because, supposing, while you all are out here seeking my approval, your papa finds that, oh dear, he cannot approve of *my* family? Then he will march out here and call you all home, and I will be terribly embarrassed."

Hetty's nose wrinkled in a giggle. "That won't happen."

"I hope not." Rosemary smiled at her. "Hetty, I hope you will let me like you. Because, if I haven't your permission, I might just have to do it secretly, and look where secrets got the Parvills."

In answer, Hetty only swished her cloak against the fountain again, but then she came and leaned against Rosemary for the barest instant, and Rosemary understood that the permission was given.

By the time Hugh and Sir Cosmo emerged from the house, the children were chasing each other through the grounds, Lionel plucking the frost-bitten heads of flowers to chuck at his sisters.

"I see the botany lesson proceeds apace," said Sir Cosmo dryly. But he turned and touched Hugh's arm. "You have made me glad today, sir, and I hope you will make my daughter a happy woman. Lady DeWitt and I have long wished to see her a wife and mother."

When Hugh and Sir Cosmo reached Rosemary, the children clustered around for their father to introduce them, Lionel making a very proper bow and the girls respectable curtsies, but Sir Cosmo wanted none of this formality. "What has Rosemary shown you? Did she not take you to the gazebo? You must come with me and see the carvings. There is a prize for whoever first spies the pineapple." He bent to kiss his daughter on the forehead, adding, "Mr. Hapgood has shared a most interesting letter with me this morning, Rosemary, and you must give us your thoughts on the matter." This pretext fooled no one, and after Hetty dashed over to grin at her father and hug him around his middle, they were off.

The October sun still struggled to banish the night's frost, but for Hugh and Rosemary it felt like summer had returned. They watched their family members weave their way among the hedges and flower borders for a moment before turning to each other.

"Are you chilled?" he asked. "Shall we return inside before I produce the 'most interesting letter'?"

Rosemary smiled. She suspected, from the look in his eye, that if they withdrew to the privacy of the house, he would find other ways to claim her attention, leaving her curiosity unsatisfied. In answer, therefore, she merely held out her hand, palm up.

Sighing, Hugh reached in his pocket and withdrew the letter. "I am sorry you can be distracted by trivialities at such a time, my dear. But, by all means, let us dispense with preliminaries. As your father said, I received this most interesting letter yesterday from none other than Henry Parvill, my would-be rival."

She was already shaking her head as she unfolded the sheet. "How can he possibly explain their actions?"

"Judge for yourself whether he succeeds," replied Hugh.

The letter read:

> *Stamford – October.*
> *My dear sir,*
>
> *As one of the people wronged by our actions—if not the chief—I recognize a letter from my wife and me can hardly be welcome, but we beg your indulgence. We hope greater familiarity with our circumstances might*

*lead eventually to forgiveness on your part and on the part of the many we deceived.*

*My Elinor and I met when I was a student at Queens' College. She is niece to one of the provosts of Corpus Christi and had come on a visit to her uncle. We soon fell in love, and she promised to marry me, though I had no family to boast of and but little means of supporting a wife. Mr. Kimball her father refused to condone a match between us, but so desirous were we of being together that we made the reckless plan to elope. I had been awarded a fellowship by the College, which came with a little stipend (the only income I could claim), but this would have to be given up, of course, if I married. The honorable choice would have been to delay our marriage until I could secure sufficient income through saving my fellowship and seeking additional employment, but I was afraid so beautiful and dear a girl as Miss Kimball would not fail to win many offers more eligible than mine. I confess I let my fears persuade me to pursue a dishonest alternative: if we hid our marriage, we might keep both the fellowship* and *any income we won. I promised her that, by dint of secrecy and hard work and thrift, we would eventually throw off the deceit and re-establish ourselves as husband and wife.*

*When we came upon the unlikely double opportunity—a curacy for me and a governess position for her—it seemed as if heaven itself smiled upon our plan. What harm could our small, white lies do anyone? I could pose as a still-single gentleman and Elinor as my unmarried sister. To aid her in securing her post, I composed a reference that might plausibly have been written, had she indeed gone on from being a prize pupil at her school to being a teacher.*

*Wiser people than we, however, could probably have predicted how difficult it would be to live with the guilt incurred by constant imposition on honest folk, and, believe me, sir, we were sorry to deal falsely with Mr. Deed, the Benfields, you, the Hapgoods—and, moreover, the whole of my Holliton flock. Each day, each falsehood, seemed to weigh more heavily than the one before, until our happiness in being together was nearly overmatched. When, at last, Elinor found herself entangled with you, through no fault of yours or her own, we found it the last straw. We must extricate ourselves from the moral quicksand into which we had sunk. But to do this would require time and secrecy—time to plan where we could go and what we could do, and utter secrecy, that we might leave behind these false versions of ourselves. Therefore, to quiet scandal, I counseled my wife to go through the motions of engaging her-*

*self to you, while I wrote letters like a man possessed, humbling myself to her father and seeking employment among any of my past connections.*

*You see how my father-in-law Mr. Kimball has forgiven us and offered us a home with him until we can establish ourselves honestly. It is more than we deserve. For all Elinor's pride in me, I have been a poor husband, a worse vicar, and not deserving of the name of gentleman. May the lives we live henceforward go some way to redeeming the mistakes of our past.*

*Mr. Hapgood, we thank you for your willingness to deal honorably with us, when we dealt only dishonorably with you. Again, we ask your forgiveness and hope your goodness will be rewarded in future by meeting with better people than your servants,*

*Henry and Elinor Parvill*

"Goodness," was Rosemary's first word, when she finished her perusal. "Only think: while Mr. Parvill was writing letters to every corner of the kingdom in search of employment, you were doing the very same thing, also begging someone to hire him!"

"Indeed," Hugh smiled. "Had we only known, we might have combined our efforts, or divided up the map to save time."

She gave him a playful nudge. "He gives you credit for dealing honorably with them, not knowing how hard you were working to unshackle yourself."

"Mr. Parvill would be the first to understand that everyone has his secrets," he answered. "Still more would he understand the desperate lengths one would go to...for love."

Rosemary could not sustain the intensity of his gaze, and she glanced away toward the distant figures of her father and the Hapgood children. "You forgive the Parvills, then?"

"Undoubtedly. I forgive them with my whole heart for leaving me entirely free to follow mine." He plucked the letter from her fingers, re-folded it, and replaced it in his pocket. "Now then, having dispensed with said preliminaries, we come to the main business I discussed with your father."

"Yes?" Her voice was nearly steady.

"Yes. I had a request to make of him," said Hugh. "And considering I was only yesterday engaged to a completely different young lady, your father viewed my petition quite charitably, I must say."

She beamed at him. "I rejoice to hear it, sir. But what petition was that?"

"My petition to foist my aging self and my three motherless children upon you," he returned. "Thus to quadruple your woes and quarter your joys for all your remaining days."

"My, that does sound dismal," said Rosemary. "I'm surprised he did not send you away with a flea in your ear, as Mr. Reginald Kimball did Mr. Parvill. And I do wonder what I would say to such a proposal."

"Let us find out for ourselves." He dropped with surprising grace to one knee and reached to take her hands in both of his. "My darling Rosemary, you know already that I love you, since I did not even wait for my freedom to tell you so. How much I love you I can hardly say. Enough that I have avoided you these past several weeks, lest I hurl myself at you and make improper suggestions as I did the other day. Enough that I have been writing those letters to 'every corner of the kingdom,' as you put it, in hopes that someone, somewhere might be begged or bribed or coerced to find a living, a position, a dry crust of bread for those confounded Parvills, that we might be released from each other. You see I am not very good at speeches such as these, but you are the only woman who will ever have to endure them from me. Rosemary, will you take me? Will you promise to become my wife?"

Her eyes sparkled at him, and she pulled him to his feet again to throw her arms around his neck. "Yes, my dearest Hugh. Absolutely yes."

"Even though I come with such drawbacks and encumbrances?" His own arms wound about her and held her still closer.

"What would those be?" she teased. "Little Rosie has already told me you are a rich man."

"Has she?" he laughed, ducking his head to kiss Rosemary's smile. "But has she also warned you that she has a sister named Hetty?"

At this she drew back from him and held up a cautionary finger. "None of that now. Hetty and I have come to an understanding this morning. She has given me permission to like her, and I plan not only on liking her, but also on growing to love her. I only hope she will grow to love me. Not just because she will not be sent away to school if you marry me, but love me for myself."

"Come back here," he growled, tugging her against him. "She will love you, if I have anything to say about it." Then he silenced her for several minutes with other activities, but when they drew breath she wriggled away once more.

"No, Hugh, I mean it," Rosemary protested. "You cannot insist that she love me. Hetty and I must find our own way. Please."

He gave her a rueful smile. "You have no idea of your power, my love. I can refuse you nothing."

"Good," she said unrepentantly, "if it means you will oblige me in this."

"What will you promise me in return, my mermaid?"

A woman like Constance Porterworth DeWitt would have played out such a moment, delighting in her power and wanting to torture her lover just a little bit, but that was not Rosemary. Rosemary bit her lip and struggled against a rising lump in her throat. "Oh, Hugh," she whispered. "I cannot believe this is happening. I cannot believe that you should love me and want me for your wife."

He traced a gentle finger down her cheek and lifted her chin. "I think I have loved you from the moment you sprang up from the sofa at Bramleigh. Your gown was stained with something and some of your beautiful hair had come loose, but you took me to task just as if you were mistress of the house."

"Oh, Hugh." She rested her forehead against his chest, laughing. "I feared you thought I was an awful busybody old maid."

She felt him chuckle. "Perhaps I did. A little. But I still thought about you. I didn't know it was love until the day in the vicarage library when you knocked me to the floor, literally and figuratively. From that moment, I could no longer call my thoughts or my person my own."

"I will take very good care of them," she vowed. "And I hope we will be as happy as you were with your first wife."

Hugh could not repress a shudder at this allusion to Harriet, but he said only, "My dear Rosemary, one day I will explain to you how much you, and you alone, have taught me of love. You have nothing to fear of me yearning for the past. But for now—I see your father returning with the children." Turning his body to hide her from their eyes, he pressed another kiss on her. "Tell me before they reach us, darling—will you marry me by special license? I do not think I can bear another three weeks of the banns being read and my name being called out, along with that of my bride *du jour.*"

"As long as I am your bride for always, I care not how it happens."

"That's my girl." He bent to steal just one last kiss, briefer but more urgent, groaning in his throat before he released her. "I warn you. I cannot wait long. Had you refused me, I would have waited forever, but, having accepted me, I cannot vouch for lasting the week. I should have quizzed the Parvills before they absconded and asked where one might elope most conveniently. Ah, well, perhaps my cousin Elfrida can tell me."

Which was why, when the others reached them, they found Hugh grinning and Rosemary blushing and laughing. And when Rosemary came forward to accept each child's congratulations and to seize them in a joy-filled hug, both Lionel and Hetty found themselves wondering how they had ever, ever thought her plain.

The adventures of the Hapgood family continue with Margaret's story in *Matchless Margaret*.

## THE HAPGOODS OF BRAMLEIGH

*The Naturalist*
*A Very Plain Young Man*
*School for Love*
*Matchless Margaret*
*The Purloined Portrait*
*A Fickle Fortune*

## THE ELLSWORTH ASSORTMENT

*Tempted by Folly*
*The Belle of Winchester*
*Minta in Spite of Herself*
*A Scholarly Pursuit*
*Miranda at Heart*
*A Capital Arrangement*

## PRIDE AND PRESTON LIN

# www.christinadudley.com

Milton Keynes UK
Ingram Content Group UK Ltd.
UKHW020232210824
447185UK00004B/235